M000082856

With Kennedy in the Land of the Dead

A Novel of the 1960s

With Kennedy in the Land of the Dead

A Novel of the 1960s

William Siegel

A Peace Corps Writers Book

WITH KENNEDY IN THE LAND OF THE DEAD
A NOVEL OF THE 1960s

A Peace Corps Writers Book — an imprint of Peace Corps Worldwide

Copyright © 2019 William Siegel

All rights reserved.

Printed in the United States of America

by Peace Corps Writers of Oakland, California.

No part of this book may be used or reproduced in any manner
whatsoever without written permission except in the case of
brief quotations contained in critical articles or reviews.

Stanzas from song "I-Feel-Like-I'm-Fixin'-To-Die Rag"
words and music by Joe McDonald (c) 1965
renewed 1993 Alkatraz Corner Music Co

Excerpt of lines from "RETURNING NORTH OF VORTEX"
FROM COLLECTED POEMS 1947-1960 by ALLEN GINSBERG.
Copyright (c) 1986 by Allen Ginsberg. Reprinted by permission of
HarperCollins Publishers.

Lyrics to the "Bells of Rhymney," by Idris Davies, Pete Seeger (c) TRO

Some characters and events in this book are fictitious.
Any similarity to real persons, living or dead, is
coincidental and not intended by the author.

Front cover image by 99designs/Reynaldo Licayan
Book design by Marian Haley Beil

For more information, contact peacecorpsworldwide@gmail.com.

Peace Corps Writers and the Peace Corps Writers colophon
are trademarks of PeaceCorpsWorldwide.org

ISBN-978-1-935925-98-9 (Paperback Edition)

Library of Congress Control Number: 2018965340

First Peace Corps Writers Edition, January, 2019

To Mary Ann

Light of My Life

IN RECOGNITION

WRITERS AND PUBLISHERS
Who maintain the vision and spirit of the Peace Corps

John Coyne — writer, friend, visionary, knowing soul

Marian Haley Beil — fond friend, skilled and caring editor, steadfast volunteer

WITH GRATITUDE

Donald Newlove, writer, critic, mentor, friend, editor

WITH AWE AND REGARD

For the many men and women, friend and foe, who suffered death or bear life-long physical injury and mental trauma from the 1960s generation of war in South East Asia.

When Lilacs Last in the Dooryard Bloom'd

When lilacs last in the dooryard bloom'd,
And the great star early droop'd in the western sky in the night,
I mourn'd and yet shall mourn with ever-returning spring.

Ever-returning spring, trinity sure to me you bring,
Lilac blooming perennial and drooping star in the west,
And thought of him I love.

O powerful western fallen star!
O shades of night – O moody, tearful night!
O great star disappear'd – O the black murk that hides the star!
O cruel hands that hold me powerless – O helpless soul of me!
O harsh surrounding cloud that will not free my soul.

– Walt Whitman

With Kennedy in the Land of the Dead

A Novel of the 1960s

Part I

✦

The Dream

♦

A KNOCK WAKES ME with a start. My heart races as I wipe sweat from the back of my neck. Pulling on pants I look out the window to see if the *amora* [vulture] escaped my dream before I sweep the door open to find several boys from the school in their rough khaki uniforms. They stare from behind large dark glasses, heads cocked sideways, ears forward. The government exiled these children who once begged in the streets of Addis Ababa. They have been hidden away in the small village of Sabeta, where I am the lone Peace Corps Volunteer teacher at the not yet finished Haile Selassie I School for the Blind.

"Excuse from disturbing, sir." A senior student, Desta, steps forward. Tall and thin, partially sighted, he bows in the formal Ethiopian way. "We have news of troubles in your country, sir. Many of your countrymen are died."

Tesfaye, a small thin boy clears his throat. "The radio says there is revolution in your country, sir."

"There *is* revolution," Kebeda, a short, dark-skinned younger boy affirms.

3

"Come in."

Fully awake I hold the door open while the boys file in, knocking against each other. Uncomfortable in their stiff jackets, they are bunched together in the single room where I sleep, eat, decipher their scraps of thoughts and some nights go crazy from loneliness and fear of the future.

"There are only two chairs," I tell them. "The rest will have to stand."

"We will stand, sir," Desta declares. "The radio is bringing sad news."

"Many are dead," Tesfye, the youngest, announces.

"You heard this on the BBC?"

"No, sir. Radio *Etiopia*," another boy gasps, his throat catching.

"The President Kennedy is dead from a coup d'état," Desta declares.

These are the same students who ask if their skin will turn white if they go to America though they know white only as a word, and venture to think that such a trip might even restore their sight.

"We have elections in my country," I say with an edge. I feel a roaring in my ears. A great wave breaks. I bend forward, narrow my look to detect the lie, but their shaded eyes have no opinions. The clarity of their voices brings a flush to my face.

"There was revolution in your country before," Mikhal, our historian, objects. "You have told us yourself."

"That was hundreds of years ago," I reply without breath.

"We too will have revolution," Tesfye says in triumph.

"You must travel to Addis to find the truth," Desta concludes. "Even Radio *Etiopia* would not make up such a story."

I make a further try, an unseen smile in my voice. "Are you boys joking me? I have lessons to prepare and tests to score."

I had counted on this Saturday to go off alone.

SOMETIMES IN THIS YEAR of isolation and listless longing, when confusion surfaces over why I find myself in this exotic land and where I would go next, I hike through a series of muddy culverts and sparse eucalyptus forests to a waterfall a few miles from the village. I lie in the grass next to a small stream that rushes over the rocks even three months after the rainy season, entranced by the enameled blue Ethiopian sky. The water falls no more than four or five feet, striking glistening rocks with the ring of a soothing bath. My own Niagara. When the wind is right a mild spray cools my face. I rest lazy among the ferns and eucalyptus, my mind loose and my gaze fastened on the impenetrable sky until the confusion fades and my heart returns.

When I'm feeling homesick, I dream of the ancient Ark of the Covenant, containing the original Ten Commandments carved into solid stone tablets — words so sacred that no man could look upon them without bringing death from the hand of God Himself, the holy writ, the engraved laws of the universe.

This biblical relic is said to be housed here in this ancient country, perhaps not far away. Given by King Solomon to Ethiopians to safeguard after the destruction of the first temple, the Ark was secreted away to an Ethiopian church in Axum.

Thinking of the legend I smile to myself as I feel close to that biblical moment.

Near my private waterfall I imagine my triumphant return home with this adventure under my belt. I imagine telling exotic stories to amazed friends of how I traveled more than halfway around the world to hike mountain forests and live in foreign villages. I would drench them in these grand thoughts by the falling water; stories so tasty they would be sorry not to have come along.

Other times sadness trips across the surface of the sparkling stream; I feel the heartache and regret at being here at all, hopeless that I am not making a difference in this ancient ragged country, and despair even, projecting distress in the faces of my students, burdened with the gigantic tasks of overcoming the daily toil of poverty.

At times, to distract these thoughts I slip back to the childhood star of my own movie, the cameras following me, catching my every move such as when I returned from a Saturday morning in the shabby movie theater where I watched serial westerns. Once my wallet slipped from my back pocket down to the floor littered with popcorn, broken Necco wafers and caramel wrappers. I left the theater and didn't discover the wallet missing until the bus ride home. I felt how the camera focused in on my wallet lying still and lifeless on the floor desolate among the debris, and then, as movies did in those days, followed me as I walked unknowing out of the theater. Often I would imagine cameras recording my every mistake, my every unconscious move as I trod on, blind and uncomprehending to the next stop in my life.

On these days when too much of my own feelings rebound from the deep sky, I fall asleep in the tall grass next to the stream, finding myself miserable again in dreams.

DESTA BREAKS IN, "We do not make a joke, Sir. You must go to Addis."

No BBC news until noon, the only phone in the village is locked in the principal's office. There is just time to shave before the morning bus departs for the two hour ride to the capitol. The boys follow my footsteps to the bathroom. What a fool to travel all the way to Addis on these rumors, walk into the embassy and ask for news of revolution.

I splash water across my face, tentative about the trip. A dark movement outside the window catches my eye. A slate-black amora settles in among the branches of an acacia tree at the edge of the compound. I am struck by a creature that I had never known in life, and still, it was part of my dream. The bird hunches under restless wings, head jerking on its bony neck, gloating out of blood-red eyes. Flashes of the night's troubling dream slip into my brain and spin away as I grab for some mystical clue that will steady my tumbling mind.

THESE BLIND BOYS, you know, they have me going. Empathy like a river is near to drowning me. This country with its magicians and holy men. The loneliness and begging pride. These exotic dark peoples, slender and tall with the bearing of ancient settled tribes, living in *tukuls* — round, thatched-roof huts — and wattle houses, farming on the backs of the raucous green mountains. The mysteries presented to my darting, starved, young mind, bent to discover a world different from my own.

The slim Ethiops walk so confidently, they strike me as ghosts from some dim time I can almost remember, so different from the strong imprint of American Negroes I grew up with. The surprise, the intrigue, the unbelievable stretch is that these people are just like me, dreams, emotions, questions, laughter, impatience, knowing looks, fears and desire. Just like me. Sometimes it takes my breath away, and I cannot abide the similarity. I am jumpy. I am waiting for things to change. Which one of us is real. These boys at the school are one long unanswered question, talking, talking, talking, impish, shy, eager to learn, wanting to know, thinking they could know. They never taught us this in training. These are real people here. They were supposed to be in need. But their only need is to be recognized. I might as well pack up and go home.

THEN THE DREAM breaks through, hung on a rafter of vague memory. I'm examining the tendrils of the thing as it spins on the light from the window, my winding sighs and exasperations flood the soundtrack as I watch children running away from me. The dream is real, but which children are real? I'm seeing my own hopes, vivid as pages of memory, burning in the flames of my own desires and I'm finding my own eyes, smoking sockets, fixed on what I want. I want to help, but they don't need me.

Memories of the dream wallop me. Out of breath, I escape the claws I've been outrunning for years. Sudden as the shock, I am relieved of the burden. Slipping into tall grass, I believe myself escaped through a look over my shoulder — my only defense. In this dream I struggle to free myself from the dream. I am safe and I do not know why. As the knower I run. There are no answers here, kicking at the twisted sheets. I bound forward. Leaping on the air, I drip. The searing sun tries to burn me black.

Chasing children through a meadow high in the Ethiopian plateau, shouting after them, "Get back! Stop!" A stream of them, silver and bronze leap over a cliff, arms outstretched in a game. I yell louder, exasperated, "Wait! Get back!" I watch helpless as they glide over the edge.

Shots ring out. The school principal, Mekonnen, appears with a small revolver. "We do not need you here," he says, his bald head glistening with sweat. "We aim to keep our ways."

A new brood of children appear.

"Don't be afraid," I shout, "Follow me."

"But we are playing, sir," these imps beam back. "We are jumping because we have always jumped. Don't be afraid, sir. Jump with us once, sir, so you can know our freedom. Alight with us in our homeland, sir, and live the life with us, just so you can know freedom, too. Freedom, sir."

Far below, small sheep and sly, thin dogs wander the village in search of food among the mud and wattle huts. Children and Mother Ruth circle each other laughing, racing to the river bank carrying armfuls of clothes. Stands of eucalyptus trees ring fields where narrow shouldered men plow the rich soil with wooden implements drawn by donkeys. Daylight gives way to evening cooking fires. A wailing hyena bounds across a moonlit field, disappears into forests where lions hunt. Dark amora glide out of the dawning sky on serrated wings, hesitate a moment in midair, flutter and settle into flat acacias.

My heart pounds as I jump from the cliff along with the children. Stretching my arms I'm pulled along the current of rushing air cooling the moisture on my brow, the wind puffs out my cheeks and riffles my hair. The children, clean and pure as new spring leaves, float beside me. Freedom rings in my ears. At the last moment before I scud to the ground, fear touches my soul. I struggle, battling for a hold in the waking world.

INSIDE THE CROWDED auto-bus I stand at the back. From the open windows a dense breeze rides my face warm and close as a razor.

"*Tenastelin* [hello]."

Some of the older men nod a greeting. Seldom does a *ferenji* [foreigner] ride the bus, and so they take notice.

I listen to the talk, trying to translate with my limited Amharic, but can make out nothing about disasters or calamities. My mind is calmed by the ordinariness of the ride. The passengers are country people, going to market on Saturday morning. Old women wrapped in embroidered shawls smell of butter and sharp spices; young women swaddle babies against their bosoms; men in rough twill suits covered by thin white shawls hold baskets of fruits and vegetables; children stare out of silent, aging faces.

Even before the final stop I push up the aisle. "*Sarraya, masarray* [excuse me]," I say trying a casual native tone in my eagerness to get off. I slide past men struggling with their bundles and step from the sagging, dust covered bus into the jostling chaos of the Merkato, the largest market in Africa, on the outskirts of Addis Ababa.

"Ferenji!" a boy shouts. He holds two squawking chickens trussed together. "You buy fat *doro*, ferenji!" The boy offers a perfect smile.

A wind raises a swirl of dust causing me to squint in the bright November sunshine before being swallowed in a sea of Ethiopian faces. Merchants and buyers take a moment to shower me with curious, wary glances. They follow my movements through the buzzing crowd, past dusty produce stalls offering round baskets of vegetables and beans. Patched pieces of canvas held up by eucalyptus poles shade fruits of every sort. Mangoes, kiwis, oranges, and small green and red apples are sheltered from the hot sun along with hanging cuts of stringy, raw meat. Windblown spices — the very hot Ethiopian *berbere*, chili peppers, cardamom, cloves and cumin — burn my nostrils. Clay pots and stoves, old tin cans, pieces of wire, pipes and wooden hammers overflow the utensil stalls. The market vibrates with shrill shouts and haggling; mongers of jewelry and black and white monkey-skin rugs press their wares.

Surrounded by the exotic cries of these peddlers, after more than a year among the Ethiopian people, I remain baffled with my foreignness. I'm jumpy and suspicious. Maybe my students are right about Kennedy.

I walk over to an Arab *bet* [shop] to buy a pack of Giselas. I tap it against the back of my hand before pulling out a single slender Ethiopian cigarette. The tobacco smells raw. After a snap of a match inside my cupped hands fire catches the cigarette in a movement not quite as smooth as I would like, awkward in fact. Although smoking is not a habit, there are times when the only way I can keep a stiff upper lip is to mouth a cigarette.

"Taxi ferenji? Taxi?" a voice calls from a blue and white Fiat *Cinquecento* [500]. The driver, dressed in a wrinkled, beige canvass jacket and pants, holds the door open. I bend deeply to fit myself into the back seat.

Immediately several squawking sellers surround the small car offering their wares. One holds out a set of steak knives, another a paper bag of oranges, and still another, an old man with a toothless grin, offers bottles of perfume and shaving lotion.

"*Magzat* [buy]," they shout through the window.

"*Kalakkala, kalakkala* " the driver says, shooing the hawkers away, turns to me, "*Weda* [going where]?"

"Americano Embassee," I say.

The driver maneuvers the car through the choreographed maze of people, horses and donkey carts.

"*'Taliano*?" The driver asks, peering over his shoulder. "*Parlare* Italiano."

"Americano." I answer.

"Oh, ho.*Tts, tts, tts*. America *morte*," the driver says. He shakes his head. Further up the dusty road toward the center of the city, he adds, "Morte. Morte."

"*Ware* [rumor]!" I snap.

"*Imbe, imbe.* [I don't agree.] Morte!" the driver persists, holding up a transistor radio playing reedy Ethiopian music.

In the stuffy back seat, smelling of roots and cayenne pepper, I hold back any thought of Kennedy — but images of the carved columns of the Lincoln Memorial haunt me.

The sun burns through the dusty window. The dirt road from the Merkato is lined with rows of whitewashed wattle houses. Donkeys and horse-drawn carts trudge out of the path of swaying lorries. The large trucks, streaked with dust and mud, are loaded high, ready to topple off the road with each turn. Old women with creased, stoic faces trudge from the market carrying bundles of firewood on their backs.

FIFTEEN MONTHS BEFORE, I caught sight of Ethiopia's extravagant evergreen mountains floating on a sea of desert. Groggy and weary after 18 hours in the air, the plane-load of Peace Corps Volunteers crowded the windows, leaning over each other to catch a first glimpse of blue Lake Tana, mother to the Nile. During our first week in Addis Ababa, Haile Selassie himself received our group in his Jubilee Palace. Waiters in red uniforms and wearing white gloves served champagne in crystal glasses.

In my early wildcat teaching, I left discipline to the side, feeding my student's hungry questions — any questions. In curious tones and random order they asked me to explain the world outside their isolated homeland. Raising their hands they strained to ask and be heard. Reared on hearsay and movies from the West, most longed to study in the States. The older boys, proud and confident, were eager to stride across continents and oceans to bring back riches.

Yes, my students were mostly boys, but there were a few shy girls in shawls — some recruited from small villages in the provinces — were also perched in eagerness to learn about the other world.

They all sensed this other world offered more than theirs. They sensed riches only the Coptic bible spoke of. They longed for freedom from dumb poverty. They longed to live clean among modern peoples. They were shamed by lack, not amused by the romance of hardship and adversity. They did not trust political solutions; they sought justice because it appeared just and obvious, and thus promised.

Me, still wet from college, the dreamer, their teacher, tried to explain the world so different from the one they knew.

With wily grins to cover their hearts they asked about the feel of snow? Why hadn't an Ethiopian invented the steam engine? Did

I have the answers to the university entrance exams? Better still, could I get them to America? They willed themselves aware, proud they spoke decent English, determined that education would make them prosperous. But they dreamed of justice. They were bright and matched my own eagerness, but they were impatient with the rudiments. They wanted the wireless before they understood the wire.

The principal warned me not to speak of politics. I learned to stick to lesson plans, diagramming sentences, writing paragraphs, working on pronunciation and vocabulary.

I ROLL DOWN THE TAXI WINDOW for relief from the heat of the sun, but the rush of air remains warm on my arms and face, blowing through my hair. In the Piazza I search among the modern shops and storefronts for some evidence of catastrophe. No suspicions in the outdoor Italian espresso bar where I sometimes sit with friends; the Greek Travel Bureau, Phaedra Express, both appear open. I look up Churchill Road past Giannopoulos Book Store. Business continues — a good sign. Foreigners stroll the Saturday afternoon streets. I want to stick my head out the window and shout like some demented sphinx — "Has some great calamity befallen the earth?"

At Arat Kilo the driver turns into the honking traffic of the roundabout between the Ministry of Education and Haile Selassie I University. In the center stands a statue of Menelik II astride a horse, Ethiopia's first modern emperor.

The driver points to the statue, "Ras Menelik. *Atse nigusa nigast* [emperor]." Then he gestures beyond the green misty mountains that ring the city. "Ah-mar-ica," he says, shaking his head.

Moving up the hill on Haile Selassie I Boulevard, over toward the Embassy, onto Algeria St deep inside this most exotic city, curving through donkeys and horse-drawn carts, dodging honking taxis and busses, and passing women with puzzled faces wearing white shawls and men wrapped in blankets hurrying somewhere with bundles, I remember my student's urgent faces to make sense of all the learning.

A dull knot of pain grabs at the center of my back. I try to focus on the eucalyptus and banana trees that grow along the avenues. We pass the French School, the Jesuit School, the Ministry of Culture and other government buildings. West of Sidist Kilo, along the crest of the highest hill in Addis, the little Fiat heaves into the wide gravel drive in front of the American Embassy. Stepping out of the taxi, I hand the driver two Ethiopian twenty-five cent pieces.

"Tts, tts." The driver shakes his head slowly. "Ah-mar-ica." A wrinkled question crosses his face.

The dazzling noonday sun reveals a naked landscape. Light pierces the eucalyptus leaves and sets them glowing. The stone buildings take on an opaque shine. The pavement shimmers in the heat. From here I gaze at Addis Ababa against the background of surrounding mountains. A thin cloud of smoke from cooking fires floats under the endless sky. The few tall buildings jutting from the area of the Piazza break the otherwise low and ragged skyline.

The embassy itself, set back in a grove of trees, is hidden inside a high-walled compound. Two concrete pillars support large wrought iron gates with the outline of an American eagle in the middle. I once attended a reception in the Ambassador's residence here.

A solemn group of fellow Volunteers are restless in their movements milling about near the entrance. Clued in, stunned, ruptured, I hurry toward this band near a dirt basketball court adjoining the embassy compound. I spot Ernie in faded sweatshirt and jeans. A few others stand with him. They greet me with various attitudes of despair, small hand waves and head nods.

"Kennedy's dead," Ernie says when I walk up to him. "Johnson and the Texas Governor may be, too."

"I don't believe it," I snap, breath snorting, as if to deliver a reprieve. A gasp, too, catches in my stomach. I'm trying to ward off the hot vapors rising inside. "What?" I ask. "Haah?" I cry to open my throat.

"Some crazy gunman in Dallas. We don't know anything else."

"When?" I push myself back, to catch a breath, to get a word out. A cloud of shock shrouds me, heavy and close as a *burnoose*. My stomach contracts. Nausea rips at my throat. I melt into a forsaken castaway, stranded on a rock in the high African plateau.

"How could they let it happen?" My words are chunks of stone. Torrents of unshed tears scratch at my eyes.

"The chargé came out a while ago and read the announcement."

"It's a hellava day for the Irish," Matt Noonan pipes up from where he sits on the ground. He scissors a basketball between his legs. "Let's have a game," he says. Noonan, a stocky fellow with reddish hair and a space between his front teeth, wears a crimson Harvard sweatshirt. He's a gargoyle of a fellow.

"I can't believe it," I speak to no one in particular. I cannot weep. I cannot find the emotional buttons. I reach out with an imaginary whip to crack the neck of the fool who pulled the trigger. I conjure science fiction machines that bring the dead to life, miracles performed for the good of mankind, stones rolled away from tombs. We must reverse time, I think; nab the culprit before the crime. I tasted real grief once for the loss of a dear aunt — felt pummeled by God himself, and scored for countless small infractions. Now I've been forsaken among these African mountains. My mind looses and tumbles to devise a way to bring him back. I am hungry for grief now, but cannot touch the shrieks straining my throat.

"It's true, Gil," Ernie says without flinching. His blue eyes warm and soft but not dripping, already in the moment.

Where are my dreams now? I choke on the thought. With the veil torn away, my wavering breath reveals a petty fantasy of glory. How can I return empty-handed? Chased by a swarm of bees. I asked not what my country could do for me. I staked my future on grappling with the solid earth of forgotten worlds, imagining myself something of a hero following a hero. Young, old, feeling creaky and unfit in this moment. Already I am the victim of history, drowning in arrogance and inexperience I fade into the fog of existence among shades. Death is such a poor father.

My brain, reduced to pulp, strains to find the Kennedy who inspired me.

TWICE I MET THE MAN IN PERSON. The first time, during the West Virginia primary in the chapel of my small college, shaded by leaded-glass windows and vaulted Gothic arches, the man brought a cast of religious fervor to my eye. I had no doubt Kennedy would win. The handsome, unassuming Brahmin awakened a fire. The candidate delivered his basic Appalachian speech about education, relief for black lung, and diversifying the state's economy. He dropped the names of local yokel politicians who choked on the word Catholic, and hard-scrabble towns run by the coal companies, spoke the names as if he'd known them all his life, though they'd been handed to him on scraps of paper only a few minutes before. He'd become a master of the usual whistle-stop stuff, taking a certain delight putting an extra syllable in "Wheeling," "Parkersberg" without the "r", visiting miners who lived in shacks down in the "halla," — the way he said it made the difference. He spoke about the Peace Corps, too, and caught me on an upward draft of idealism. Though there was already something wounded about that hero I could not put my finger on, something marked, almost careless in his charm, as if he'd already made the choice and knew this life was his to spend or throw away as he chose.

I remember how he leaned forward and yet appeared restrained sitting on the raised pulpit in the chapel — the same pulpit that served as throne of God or the stage for a Tennessee Williams play — waiting to be introduced. He crossed his legs and then uncrossed them, a bit nervous, impatient perhaps. The President of the college, a Campbellite Christian orator of some distinction, introduced the son of a famous Boston Catholic family, who had already had audiences with the Pope, and lived in the residence of the American ambassador to the Court of St. James. Kennedy stood at the close of the brief introduction with a mischievous smile barely visible, as if he'd taken an unauthorized day away from school, or returned a co-ed late, after midnight, in fact. The smile gave way to the confidence when he buttoned his jacket and stepped forward. He kept one hand in his suit pocket, afflicted perhaps, clenching his fist against some unbearable pain that he carried for us all. Then he leaned across the lectern. His upper-class Boston accent so foreign and hypnotic to those used to dry Midwestern-American or the dreaded West

Virginia r's' and ya's — the plaintive dropped syllable echoing the clacking of washboards.

After the talk he came down to the main floor not far from where I sat, and I hurried over. The Senator looked at me full of curiosity. Close up I could see the lines at the corners of his clear eyes. the ruddy Irish skin. He might have been a miner himself, had his great grandfather lit out for the Appalachians to find something, or escape something. He wore an expensive-looking dark suit with barely visible pinstripes. I had never dreamed a more luminous moment.

"I intend to go into your Peace Corps when I get out of here," I said. He put his hand forward.

"What's your name?" Kennedy asked. He held my hand, stopping the impatient line forming behind me.

"Gil," I answered. "Short for Gilbert." I stammered to meet some imagined Harvard formality in the future president.

"I like Gil," he said with a drawn laugh. "We need young people like you to teach where there are no teachers."

The soldier in me nodded a salute.

Kennedy continued to hold my hand. "If we win here," the politician said, "we have a good chance to go all the way. And if we do, I'd be pleased to have you in my Peace Corps."

I read that his right hand became bruised from thousands of handshakes through the primaries, but his hand felt warm and strong holding mine.

"I'll be ringing doorbells and passing out leaflets," I said.

Here stood the General I could die for. Never the thought that the immortal before me could be snatched from the face of the earth.

TWO YEARS LATER, on a muggy August day, motorcycle police — sirens wailing — escorted our Ethiopia-bound group of Peace Corps Volunteers in a motorcade of busses from Georgetown University to the White House. We filed into the Rose Garden and gathered on the lawn like newly picked cabbages.

Moments later the President emerged from a portico to greet us, flashing his confident smile. He stood in the steaming August light, a silhouette, a shade, a character from another universe. Confidence rose from him as he stepped forward, greeting us like new associates. He spoke of commitment; he said something about daring, something about idealism and freedom.

"Teach these new friends the best of our ways," he told us. Standing on the flagstone terrace, one hand in his suit pocket, just like the first time I met him. He spoke of our going and then coming home aware and ready to teach in the schools and serve in the government. He asked us to vanquish the image of the "ugly American," and build a new reputation for service. He said we would learn more than we could ever teach.

I believed him, every word.

NOONAN SLAPS THE BASKETBALL and looks up announcing, "Here's the outcast of Poker Flats, where the blind lead the blind. Now we can have us a game." He stands and bounces the ball, then quick passes it to me.

My hands are grateful to catch the ball, though my mind balks. I can't find the strength to resist Noonan, who possesses the knack of intimidating most everyone around.

In my first run-in with Noonan during Peace Corps training, he approached me after a spirited pickup game. "So, what college you from," he had asked. "You play like you come from Williams or some nice place like that?"

I mumbled the name of my small, obscure college. "It's in West Virginia," I explained, figuring he'd never heard of it.

"Oh," Noonan said. "A log-cabin college. Part of the Lincoln Brigade."

Walking off the court, burly Noonan put his arm around my shoulder. "You play pretty good for a softie," he told me. "The problem with you Lincoln Brigade sorts is that you think you can change the world. You don't believe this Peace Corps shit, do you?"

"Yeah, I believe." I had no comeback.

"The Peace Corps is gonna look good on my resume when I knock on the President's door," he continued. "Kennedy and my old man were in the same house at Harvard. Couple years of graduate school, first thing you know, I'm running the State Department, or maybe I'll head up one of those corporations that runs the State Department." Noonan squeezed my shoulder. "Now there's a Harvard education for you, Lincoln Brigade."

Walking away, he turned to my shrinking shell with a big laugh, projecting a practiced alter-boyish grin, "Hey, I'm only kidding, Brigade. We're all in this together. Brothers under the skin. You know, we got to have a few laughs."

I didn't like the guy. He was loud and embarrassing — though, in the next moment I had exhilarated in his bold presence. In spite of being tongue-tied, I felt awe. After that, the Harvard man would call me out across the campus. "Hey Lincoln Brigade," smirking with that gap-tooth grin showing through his round freckled face.

"THIS IS NO DAY for games," Ernie breaks into my thoughts.

"Begorra, it is." Noonan bounces the ball. "This is the best day for a game. Gilbert here is already wearing his low cuts."

I reach inside myself to claw at some sense of outrage at Noonan, but I'm bowled over by a sense of unreality – the sway of the trees turning up the white underside of eucalyptus leaves, the shimmering stones of the embassy compound wall, the luminescence of the cobalt sky. Here in the land of Africa, there must be some shaman magic capable of raising the dead — again. I'm coaxing a miracle, an awakening from the dream. I don't want to think about why we're loitering in front of the embassy, and I can't resist Noonan. The thought almost makes sense that athletic Jack would champion a game in his honor rather than a sulk. I shiver, unconvinced, but my body wants to move.

Tom, tall and slim, shakes his head, "You got no shame, Noonan."

"Will it bring him back if we don't play?" he insists.

"Show some respect," Ernie says.

"Tell that to the gunman."

I want to side with Ernie – keep to the edge of the court with my arms folded, knowing the distance between a right act and a wrong, but I can't overcome Noonan's carved iron face. I grit my teeth, rock on my heels, my stomach grinds.

"Come on, Lincoln Brigade, we'll show 'em how to play like Shakespeare." Noonan pulls me onto the court.

Intimidated, I stagger without looking, catch the ball and pass it back, incriminating myself. In that self-conscious moment I feel cameras focusing in on me, recording for all time this mistake, this embarrassment. Does my torment come from news of Kennedy's death, resentment of Noonan, or my own failings? Alone on the court, we shoot baskets and toss the ball back and forth. I hold my breath. Inside some ancient arena myself as a dreamer becomes a gladiator about to kill or be killed. After a time, Noonan cajoles Tom to join. He calls Howard out, too. One by one, Noonan wheedles fellow Volunteers into playing.

"Jack was a sports nut," he says with a casual turn of his short thick neck. "An absolute, compulsive, ready-to-play sports nut."

Only Ernie stands unmoved, his arms folded, eyes blinking in the sun. Marian and Phyllis, Barbara, Sally and Maggie, some wet-eyed, flash wary, sideways stares and silent talk. From a distance, the scene could be any Saturday afternoon, but it plays out on this Saturday.

"Tom and Gil and I against the rest of you pushovers," Noonan commands.

Not exactly talked into this wayward game, we fall into a swarm of turmoil pulling us forward, radiating with a devilish glow. We warm up, passing the ball back and forth, but I can't look anyone in the eye. Shouldn't we be solemn today, muster up a prayer? No, I shout to myself. Don't give in to this sentiment. Don't be afraid. Don't cry. Don't let this throw you. Retrieve the numbness.

Ringing gunfire stops the game cold.

We turn to see a ghost-parade of 30 or so Ethiopian soldiers dressed in black berets and Korean-War-vintage American uniforms. They march down the boulevard with guns raised, firing volley after volley into the bright sky. Behind this group, a cadre of Ethiopian women in dark veils and black mourning shawls raise their voices in the traditional high-pitched wail, "Uluuluuluuluuluuluu." Some women carry portraits of Kennedy on raised placards. I think of visits to Ethiopian homes, and there along with photos of Haile Selassie and Coptic saints are pictures of Kennedy cut from magazines. Gunfire rings off the mountains while the marchers pause in front of the embassy. They remain at attention for a few minutes and then continue down the boulevard, marching to rouse the city. Sometimes, too, I am the camera, recording, projecting, blinking through the moment.

I'm dizzy. How could this happen while I am stranded on a god-forsaken rock? Six thousand miles from anyone who would understand. What of the Peace Corps now? Would we be called back? I should have listened to my father. I recoil like a fired rifle, abandoned by a dead President amid the folly of climbing a mountain in ancient Abyssinia. The reality threatens to pull me to the bottom. I choke in the backwash of the news, flailing among the rocky waves.

"Everyone loves a parade," Noonan says. "But let's play ball."

Before we resume, a deep booming voice rings out from the far end of the court. "What is this?" Hamilton, the American chargè d'affaires, stands with his arms akimbo in suspenders and shirtsleeves. His eyes are red and filmed over, almost hidden by steam. After staring us players down, he walks in our direction. "What're you boys trying to prove?"

Noonan bounces the basketball in defiance.

The chargé and Noonan scowl.

"You gonna bring him back with indignation, Mr. Ambassador?" Noonan maintains his ground, while, with relief, we others turn and skulk off the court, a pack of wounded cats.

Hamilton directs his comment to Noonan's sweatshirt. "You boys have a knack for going too far. But this is far too far. Can it. Do you hear? Can it!" The chargé turns and walks back toward the embassy.

"Gil put us up to this," Noonan smirks to Ernie who is still standing on the edge of the court. "None of us civilized boys would vilify our dead President on such a God-forsaken day."

Even though Noonan's con is weak, I cannot hold back. My face burns. "Come on," I say, voice cracking.

Noonan turns with his smirking alter-boy look.

"Don't blame me, you arrogant bastard," I shout.

Noonan, a head shorter, stomps over to me and thumps one stubby hand on my chest.

I shove back.

"Hey, you guys." Ernie yells. "Cut it out."

"Where does this fool get off calling me arrogant? How do you think I feel?" Tears show up in Noonan's green eyes. He shoves me again and again.

I grab him by the shoulders, realizing my mistake too late as squat Noonan places his right leg in back of mine and shoves me to the ground. Fists clench. We tussle in the grass.

Tom and Ernie pull us apart hoisting and pulling us up panting.

"You two are crazy," Ernie says.

Ernie's angry voice stops me, but Noonan shoves me one more time before he picks up his basketball.

I catch myself in frustration at not having the last push. My breath sputters. I release my fists, flooded with sorrow for all of us abandoned on this mountain outpost, cut off from the grief of our countrymen. I'm ready to take the first plane back, give up this ghost and run as fast as I can to some cave.

"The grass doesn't stop growing 'cause some crazy bastard knocks off the president," Noonan spits. He takes the basketball in his right hand, whirls like a discus thrower and heaves the ball with all his might over the wall into the Embassy grounds. Without looking back he walks away in the direction of the faint echoing gunfire.

Over in the patchy grass near the Embassy driveway our small band of determined teachers and health care workers stand desolate; our vision of a better world fades into the dry mountain air. Memories of afternoons by the waterfall dim. The wretched news rips the future from my grasp. Looking toward the horizon I spy a single black vulture following its scavenger's route. Loneliness settles on me as I search the unbreakable Ethiopian sky for a way out.

African Nights

◆

A BASKETBALL RIDES the current of the bright San Francisco sun. I leap! Spear the ball out of the flash, flip it over the rim of the rope-less basket.

"All right," Franco says, running from the far end of the court. "You look ready to play a little one-on-one."

"Oh, I'm ready." I nod, chummy, daring a challenge.

Franco had showed up as the feathered friend I hadn't counted on. After we'd spent the morning moving into an apartment, I talked him into a friendly game of basketball. Twirling his spectacles in one hand, Franco humors me. "Sports eat your brain, man," he pronounces. He mocks the game by wearing a loosened tie, a dirty-white dress shirt with the tails flapping over red plaid Bermuda shorts, and black needle-nosed street shoes. I'm set out in a San Francisco State sweatshirt with blue basketball shorts; I'm embarrassed by Franco's getup.

"Those shorts blind me with color," I say.

"That's my whole strategy," Franco says, assaying my Converse low-cuts.

"One-on-one," he warns. He feints trance-like to the left, lobs the ball over my head, fakes right, goes left, catches the lob on the first bounce and the big galoot sinks a long jumper that clangs through the rim.

He takes the first game 22 to 10. We start another. Franco is panting. I think maybe I can get him on that, but he takes the second game, too — 22 to 15. Game . . . set . . . match. And all in that Bermuda-short getup.

I'm a little pissed that he beats me in the game which I feel entitled to win . . . and in Shakespeare class too, where he thrusts a witty sounding address to the teacher and gets the class to laugh as well. "The bare bodkin, sir, most scholars conclude, is used by Hamlet as a dire threat of suicide. But odds are that a bodkin, sir, according to the Oxford English Dictionary, could as well be used as a needle to mend his sock, sir. Thus rendering our hero no more than a tailor — and possibly throwing the entire 400 years of Shakespeare scholarship into disarray."

Though only a few inches taller, Franco towers over me in intellect and now I see, basketball, too. He maintains that I should have transferred directly from the Peace Corps into the Army. Every day we read of ferment in Southeast Asia on the blotchy back pages of the *Examiner*.

"Something's ha-happening here . . .," Franco sings — he stutters occasionally. He then says, "You have a chance anew to cast yourself as a hero, to chuck your textbooks and learn to use a rifle. Would you leave the grassy wa-walks and modern glass-and-brick buildings of slightly less than stately San Francisco State to persevere in a war zone where you might get killed, or worse, wounded and badly disabled. That sir, not the moldy, sentimental Peace Corps will prove the degree of your patriotism. Something that can be measured by the big stick. Shall I write to your draft board and tell them you're available? I know you want to follow your father who returned from the big one in Europe a psychological cripple. Yes, you still yearn to be some kind of he-hero. To let others know you have risen above your stature and mediocre goals. Eh?"

THE PEACE CORPS WAS part of my plan, but then Franco entered my life.

His mind, twisted and a little off — jagged sometimes in his ability to put me down — makes me feel dumb with his sharp diagnosis of the ins and outs of books, and claims to have read every classic I'd ever heard of — plus thousands more I never dreamed of. He is a fountain spewing quotes that make my brain peel, and is sure in his pronouncements about politics that staunch my bleeding heart. I have a hunch I can write a book, maybe a play, and maybe become a teacher. But Franco's keen, slashing wit and ability to shame and portray just about any behavior of mine as useless unless I board his bus, bends my will to support his latest pronouncements . . . and blows me up with anger and admiration. He spins my brain so that my thoughts tend toward self-destruction, intellectual horror stories and a fear of the future that has me walking on eggshells.

Where is the adventurer who went off to Africa in search of himself? I returned an idiot frightened of every shadow my mind conjured up, a piece of toast, burned at the edges, jumpy, unable to go after what I wanted — fearful of the future, fearful of the past, fearful of the moment that I had no idea how to make last.

I need some kind of hero, flaws and all, so what if he takes credit for my ideas. He spits them back at me more spiffy and informed more than any rhyme or reason I might have imagined. Franco sometimes makes me think that if he can be a genius, I can too, and so I try for a time. Have I conjured another Noonan for myself?

Franco reminds me of a cemetery, a field of rocks with inscriptions in random order, a book of sayings supported by dead men and women who carry no responsibility into the grave but the imprint of some bereaved relative pulled from a book of phrases. This often occurs to me when I hear Franco speak. But I can't object. I can't call him up short on a point. He will not let me, and I will not let myself lose touch with a hero to haul me to safety from the cold grasp of my own insecurity.

Oh, you don't believe this, do you? Franco — this corny guy from the Midwest, who thrives on chewing gum and RC cola, grew up with magazine racks full of girlie magazines and comic books, and learned to smoke at the local pool hall — all behind the backs of Jesuit priests. He likes to say Holden Caulfield and Jack Kerouac taught him how to bring sincerity to a boil, win an argument with the angle of his jaw, the grit of his gaze and the gulp of his Adam's apple. He says the word "Jesuit" like a neon sign. They didn't teach so much as cast a spell. I am jealous not of his education, but of his exposure. Showing how tough he mines your soul by never backing down, proving by words in the Bible what he could not prove living his everyday life. A crackerjack. Never a young man, always on the make. I can not hold my contempt and admiration in the same breath, can not dismiss his intellect and intelligence, and so he drives me a little crazy. I suppose that's why I agreed to room with him. I was already a little cracked from the Peace Corps and the assassination. I thought he was, too.

While I labored in the classroom among my Ethiopian students, Franco was spending several years as a merchant seaman after college. During the first year of our friendship he claimed many adventures. He'd jumped ship in India and spent time in an ashram near the cool glacial lakes of Kashmir; traveled to Nepal along the ancient silk road where he traded in hashish; and ended up in Washington, D.C. infiltrating the backrooms of power, hinting slyly he may even have worked for a certain secret government agency. From Franco's telling, he learned to navigate the oceans from the stars, haggle with drug traders on mountain roads, attained initiation into secret teachings of Buddhist traditions, escaped from a cult-like religious leader, had a play produced, and attended parties in the homes of Washington's power brokers.

Several years older than I am, he spins the air of someone destined to be the Rasputin of his time. Oh, and he has developed an occasional, devil-may-care, taste for heroin, he winks as an aside if the right person — a certain type of woman — is listening.

I do not believe all of these stories from this strange looking fellow. For all his travels, Franco appears bent by his worldly experiences into a premature stoop, his head drawn back to compensate, so that at certain angles, with a shaded face, he looks like an older man, an ancient shaman in a suit and tie, perhaps, a wounded spirit with a face pockmarked from recurring acne, and shiny with various medical concoctions to neutralize the acid pain.

"LET'S TAKE A BREAK," Franco says.

We sit on the grass to the side of the court. A breeze slides through the trees from the far Marina district, drying our sweaty shoulders, cooling the sun to a simmer.

"This San Francisco sun is thin as broth," Franco shrugs. "There's no warmth here because there's no co-consequences in make-believe places like California. People alternate positions, that's all, like a merry-go-round. California sun," he adds with a studied far off look of mystery, "barely strong enough to carry celestial particles from heaven to earth, like a baggage conveyor."

"Yeah?"

"Yeah," he says. "India, Tibet, Viet Nam, places like that . . . they have consequences — even Australia."

"Oh," I say, picking at blades of grass.

"No reality — no consequences — nothing really happens in this burg. That seems fairly obvious."

"Reality is a given, man." I smack my palm on the basketball, not really understanding or caring what I just said. This guy is so obtuse, I think to myself. A square and a trapezoid? What's the difference?

WHEN WE STARTED getting to know each other, Franco confided that he had secrets; that it was best people didn't know much about him — hinting that mysterious persons sought him for certain infractions; small crimes, perhaps slights toward people who didn't take slights lightly. Then, after playing hush-hush with me in private about his passage to India . . . his ports of call, he would mention these so-called secrets to a whole group. "Did I tell you about how I smuggled a whole shit-load of hash in a shipment of rugs, and then took the money and ran. No, I can't say that, then you'd be an accessory. Forget I said that. I jumped ship just to get ashore and was picked up by these Tibetan refugee fishermen, who took me to their temple. I didn't have papers and they kept me safe and taught me their secrets and smuggled me over the border into Nepal, where I learned the rug trade, or was it the drug trade." Then he'd make some owlish face of disbelief.

"YOU CAN'T GO to the store for bread and end up in the ocean. You understand, somewhere in the swampy sentiment that ate your brain, man, you understand. Don't ya'? You gotta have a map in your head. You gotta' picture something before you do it. Right? Picture it in the mind's eye ... there!" he says placing a finger to the middle of my forehead. "You understand. You got it? I'm sure you got it."

The rise in Franco's tone of voice heightens his ripping eyes. His ya's and gotta's, bouncing off my shorn ego, strike the bee sting of being caught stupid. Along with that, I sense Franco's disgust for having to explain — like I misplaced the smart molecule in my brain and Franco has to fish it out time after time; like I'm thinking, "I don't want to believe you have to picture something in your mind every time before you can do it, man. I'd never get anywhere, and would rather go headlong and find myself in the right spot — like magic, like it's supposed to be. No weary, trudging unwinding Jesuitical brain map for me."

Franco picks up the basketball. "Kennedy's murder, for instance." "The only event that brought the truth of the entire bloody half-century home to everyone. The constant bloodshed, the total lack of compassion endured by a world living under a cloud of Christian innocence. Kennedy's death delivered the word of reality home. Nothing matters any more. Life is a fantasy. There's no plan anymore. There are no consequences. Whatever happens, baby, happens. It doesn't matter."

"How about another game?" I ask, getting up and bouncing the ball to him.

He stands and wrinkles his nose, frames a set shot in his odd way, legs stiff, arms out, then sails the ball off the backboard, where it bounces several times before deciding to slip through the bare rim.

"Na," he says, "I'm done. Unless you admit you joined the Peace Corps to keep out of the Army. Then I'll play you one more, and beat you, too."

"Fuck you, man. My draft board's after me just the same." *I don't say "fuck" much. I wonder if I pulled it off.*

"Stay in school, Gi-Gilbert my boy," Franco says. "This war's just begun."

Now I'm thinking of that dream I had the night before I learned that Kennedy had been shot — the dream with the students jumping from the cliff. Only, I can't remember it all. I can't remember how it ended. I think I woke up. The shot, the school principal, the children in the tall grass. I can't remember. I want to remember just to get away from this accuser, this politically righteous fellow, whom I've invited to be my tormentor. I can't remember and I can't help myself.

DURING THE FIRST YEAR after my return from Ethiopia I began to lose the thread. I'd walk across the campus bewildered. The light brightened and faded. I floated in a fog. I couldn't navigate my whereabouts. Sparklers went off. I heard faint voices. I passed by classmates without seeing them. Reckless and abandoned, I felt a hunger to be carried away by the wind. The sunsets, bright strawberry clouds turning to blood red stretched across the Presidio, and set me to melancholy thoughts; I could find nothing that excited my mind or heart. I secretly yearned to end my life. I couldn't remember parts of my childhood. I'd break out weeping as I walked across campus, damning my shame for this safe life and remembering the people of Ethiopia poor and vulnerable. I felt guilty living in my home. I loathed the manicured sidewalks weaving in and out of lush trees, the carefree students, the idle chatter, and the full plates in the cafeteria. I didn't want to belong; my breathing became labored. My limbs felt disconnected and helpless, about to float away.

Sometimes I saw President Kennedy up ahead standing off in the trees, or in the doorway of the Arts Building. Fixing a shred of hope on a profile of a student or teacher, at times I felt an electric shock in the back of my head. It could have been him, I'd say to myself, just dropping in. Something crazy like that. Quick, a thunderstorm passed across my mind and the spell stopped, and I accepted privilege without a second thought, taking my carefree campus life for granted. Day to day, I'd weave this way and that.

"WHEN I GET TIRED of this, I'm going to ship out again and become a monk," Franco tells me as we leave the court. "Living on a ship — it's just like a monastery. I'm gonna watch the waves go by and let my mind wander to the far part of my head to see if there's some kind of answers back there. I already know there's something better than this. The Buddhists taught me that philosophy — not St. Francis."

I barely hear him as I gaze through the eucalyptus trees to our newly rented apartment on the top floor of an old Victorian. "I always dreamed of living on Steiner Street."

"Steiner Street?" Franco makes a face.

"From some corny TV show when I was a kid." I accent "corny" to cover myself from Franco's contempt.

"So, you've arrived," Franco says. "You've . . . you've achieved your life's ambition. Your dream's fulfilled. You can sit up there and . . . and crow." A smile lights up his face, stretching the creases at the corners of his eyes. "Come on, boy, we got to read us a little *Shake Spear*."

"Yeah," I say. I take a long look back at the court, debating whether to shoot solitary baskets for the rest of the afternoon. When we reach the row of narrow Victorian houses with sloping roofs, a friend of Franco's is lounging on the steps smoking a cigarette.

"Hey, Wayne!" Franco waves, crossing the street.

"Where you been? I come to help you guys move in," Wayne yells back.

We climb the steps to the concrete stoop, "You're about three hours too late."

"I heard you say afternoon," Wayne says with a straight face. "How could I miss helping you guys carry dozens of boxes up three flights?" His voice resonates with a slight Southern accent.

"Hey, Wayne meet Gilbert, my roommate, king of the basketball court." Franco turns to me, "Wayne is the best guitar picker you're likely hear."

"Man, I tell ya, I meant to help . . . believe me," Wayne carries on. He stubs out the cigarette on the step.

Wayne sports a big open smile and marble blue eyes. A light, wispy beard, almost invisible, comes to a point under his chin. His light hair hangs long over his ears and neck. He wears a denim jacket, pressed jeans and cowboy boots. Giving Franco's bermudas the once-over, Wayne whistles, "You must play in the rhubarb league, man."

"The turnip league," Franco says. He looks away. Lost in thought or lost in the ability to put on being lost in thought. I haven't been able to distinguish the difference yet.

Wayne rubs his beard before he shakes my hand, then glances all the way up to the peaked roof of the house. "Great location," he says.

"Come on upstairs." Franco motions toward the apartment.

"Can't now." Wayne walks down the steps. "I'll stop by later an' bring you fellows over to the house. "Float you some," he smiles.

As we climb the stairs, Franco assures me, "Wayne always has a great stash, and wait'll you meet his old-lady. We have a special thing goin' on, you know." Then he looks around, raises his eyebrows and tosses me a grin.

"Wha-da-ya mean?" I ask.

"Oh, they're cool, that's all." Franco gives a knowing look I can- not fathom.

"Oh," I say.

I'm afraid to ask any more questions, afraid ignorance of the lingo shows I'm completely naive, afraid my stint in the Peace Corps put me completely and forever out of touch with the heartbeat of young, hip, American life.

"Cool," I manage to say and nod my head to emphasize complete understanding. *I'm cool, man. I'm just so cool.*

A SMOKY-ORANGE SUNSET spreads across the evening sky thick as paint on a movie set as Wayne stands on the sidewalk outside our house dangling a brown paper grocery bag in one hand, holding the other on his heart and singing in a loud, twangy voice up to the third floor:

All of my love
All of my kissin'
You don't know what you've been missin'
Oh boy, when you're with me, oh boy!

"Come on boys," he shouts. "You got to come over and take advantage of your neighbor's generosity."

A few minutes later, Wayne, still humming, is ushering us up the street to another Victorian, this one with a turret. We walk into the driveway past a motorcycle and old panel truck hand-painted a splotchy orange. He leads us through a small door in a high wooden fence into the midst of an overgrown English garden full of bushy plants and tall sunflowers. He turns to the two of us and nods toward the house, and says "temptation," and smiles a bright but downward looking smile, a smile that could be read, had I chosen to do so.

A wind comes up, blowing the foliage to reach out to us. Feeling the chill, I follow Franco down an overgrown brick walk to an old, one-room carriage house at the back.

Wayne opens the door into a cozy room with a sleeping loft in the back. A table with a hotplate sits in the corner next to the bathroom. Printed paisley fabric billows from the ceiling, swaying slightly to rhythmic East Indian stringed music with moaning sounds.

Paying careful attention to the bag he had been carrying, Wayne places it next to the small refrigerator in the makeshift kitchen, turns on his heels, and looking very proud of himself, he produces a hand-rolled cigarette. As he croons a revised version of the song he sang earlier, "All of my love, all of my kissin', now we're gonna get high and listen, Oh boy," he proceeds to light the cigarette in one swift movement, takes a puff and hands it to Franco in a seeming prearranged ritual.

I'd heard about getting high. Here it is.

I receive the cigarette from Franco in an awkward pass, take the thin white, pasty, cigarette between my thumb and forefinger, not quite able to get it, negotiating with my other hand to keep it in position and then, in another awkward move, put it to my mouth to take a drag. As if I'd inhaled smoke from a wood fire, I cough. I push the homemade cig back to Wayne, not quite knowing how to pass it with any semblance of coolness. I'm already tired watching this ritual play out. I breathe in a wisp of pungent, acrid, breath-catching smoke, and await the consequences. My eyes bug out just watching Franco take a drag.

"Go ahead." He hands me the cigarette a second time. "It'll take you where you never been."

I cross the threshold of my first encounter with this stuff not knowing if I'm high. I wonder what "high" really is, and suspect I'm being put through some adolescent initiation.

"What's this?" I ask. "Really, what is it?" I force another puff, and cannot suppress my coughing.

"Call it smoke, 'cause it comes and goes and may not be there at all," Wayne says.

"Swa-swallow." Franco advises.

I hand the burning ember back to Wayne, who, with unbridled glee, accepts. "Thanks for the joint, man. It's a joint that's what it is. Not a cigarette. No tobacco, no cancer-addicting nicotine in this. Pure herb. God-given for us to ride the upward current of civilization from the monkeys to the grace of knowledge. This here's the Apple. Don't you know?" He gives a little bow toward me like, "Don't you get it? I'll show you. I'll help you get it."

WITH THE SMELL OF INCENSE in the room my thoughts return to Ethiopia — when night descended on the streets of Addis Ababa, and quieted the struggles of day in the section of Kasanchese where I lived for a time.

My narrow, unpaved street smelled of incense from the small Arab bet on the corner where a hooded merchant sat on the floor next to a round charcoal stove. The Arab would look up at each customer without a word, take a pack of cigarettes from the shelf, and exchange it for the soft murmur of coins passing from hand to hand.

I then would walk through the night along the lane without street lamps, under a billion beckoning stars.

I'm reminded of the softness of the darkening sky and the slight wind, as I made my way home from an evening stroll, floating through a calm spell from the day's challenges. I remember solitary evenings reading and grading papers — without even the thought of loneliness. I wonder that I can still remember the peace of those African nights.

FRANCO'S GAWKY BODY appears comfortable sitting cross-legged on a cushion, eyes closed, rocking back and forth in the wash of music and smoke. I study him, afraid to meet Wayne's eyes that may read the ignorance on my face.

I'm suddenly aware of these two who soon might forget my existence. They possess an off-hand sense of life in the moment, while I'm nervous and jagged. Then I imagine I'm Franco looking at me across the small room, sizing me up as some lost soul who continues to lug the entrails of ideals tied to impossible fantasies. A feather of fear paints me back into my own self, ready to defend my moral certitude. I am amazed by this transformation, this trading of bodies and viewpoints, but though I try, can't do it again.

Emptiness surrounds me. I shake my head to wake up my senses.

I accept a second . . . or is it a third round of the joint. I feel like a pro. I take another puff. "Who was that?" I ask, wondering as my breathless heartbeat catches, and I sense the shadow of a woman or a bird — some spirit that flares in the room.

No one answers. Instead, through the smoky wisps of pot and incense, a sensual wailing rises in the music, and the boards of the sleeping loft shudder with movement above my head. I'm struck dumb for a moment, bending my head over my folded legs. What is this? My brain trembles. Is it sex? My God. Is my mind playing tricks? I'd never been this close to these intimate sighs and whimpers. I'm embarrassed. I'm about to run from there. I want to scream. I want to laugh, but most of all, I want to be cool. "Don't scream, man," I whisper to my shadow, "be cool."

"Well, damn," Wayne says after a moment. "Little Claire's up in the loft ... I wonder who?" he sings, "I wonder who?"

Uneasy hearing Wayne over the silence, I stretch my cool to the limit. *Go ahead, man, pretend, Oh, yes, you're The Great Pretender* I snort to myself.

Wayne lights another joint. His eyebrows arch, pinching lines across his forehead. His hand trembles as he passes it. The sexual partners in the loft groan and squeal to a climax; the boards creak. I pretend to be absorbed in thought, but strain to listen to the sounds of the lovers until only the strands of music remain.

Maybe these funny cigarettes do make you cool.

When the record ends, Wayne goes over to the corner under the loft and picks up an acoustic guitar with a blond body and ebony fingerboard. I recognize that it's a Martin – THE VERY GUITAR I COVET.

Wayne cradles the instrument across his raised thigh. He drums his fingers on the fret board a few times, then picks out a line of melancholy notes in low tones, rising on a wing of loneliness. Then he hooks the pick inside the strings and sets the instrument down, like he's just sent a message.

Following Franco's lead, I nod to Wayne.

A ghost of recognition brings up the lost memory of music from my backwater childhood. I'm flooded with warmth.

"The Kentucky flash." Franco beams.

"You ever notice, Franco? When you get high, you stop stammering." Wayne says.

"I don't stutter, man. I hesitate, so you have time ... to ... understand ... what I'm saying."

"You oughtta stay high all the time," Wayne snickers.

I cannot keep my eyes from the sleeping loft. Soon, bare feminine legs carefully descend the ladder. A sliver of glossy panties appears, quickly covered by the hem of a green shirt. A small, slim girl turns and drops the final step to the floor. A glisten of sweat slips over her lip. A boarding-school girl, fifteen or sixteen. A trace of roughness on her cheeks, a glint of self-possession around her eyes suggests she might be a little older.

She turns to me. "I'm Claire, she says. "I live here with Wayne."

"I'm Gil," I reply, disarmed, . . . I room with Franco. Wayne brought us over to get . . .." My voice trails off. Claire widens the smile. Her light brown hair hangs in curls down to her shoulders.

After a moment of allowing herself to be admired, Claire sits on the cushion next to Wayne, who concentrates on lighting another joint.

A second pair of legs climb quickly down from the loft. He turns out to be a rough looking fellow in jeans, mustache, bare-chest, holding a shirt in one hand.

"That's Joe," Claire says for my benefit.

I nod to Joe, who shakes out his shirt.

She was a nice girl, a proper girl, and her hair hung down in ringlets, I sing to myself.

"Hey, Joe," Wayne says with a nod.

Joe, stocky and muscular, has ripples in his abdomen. A tattoo on his right bicep shows a dagger through a heart dripping blood. His long hair and shaggy brown mustache appear menacing. He takes his time putting on his short-sleeved shirt, carefully buttoning each button, tucking the tails into his jeans. Moving to the corner, he pulls on black motorcycle boots. He throws a look to Claire and makes a slight bow before sauntering out.

"Joe comes and goes . . . like smoke," Wayne adds, while putting on a Jimmy Rogers' record.

The strumming guitar and baleful voice carry me to lonely childhood Saturday nights, listening to country laments on the radio. I take a breath. A light shimmers around Wayne's blond hair in the shape of a ram's horn. The raw, bony set to his shoulders reminds me of a cow wrangler, though his face under the wisps of beard is a choirboy's — pink and full. *No, I'm not high. What's the fuss?* I feel like I'm in a cave ten thousand miles from this place, my thoughts bounce off ancient tattooed walls.

I suspect Franco and Wayne are putting me on. Claire wasn't really up in the loft screwing a guy named Joe. This is some kind of initiation to see how I react. They belong to a club and won't let me join until I'm cool.

Claire lay in Wayne's arms, a sleeping cat. Franco talks on about cosmic reality. Wayne has put on a cowboy hat, pulled the brim to a jaunty angle.

I want to make a speech. I want to tell them life is more than being cool, but I can't get the words out. Maybe they're right. I long to be cool, but I can't even get high. I'm flushed and hot. I can't breathe. My legs take hold, standing me up, pushing me toward the door. "This high stuff is all bogus," I mumble, pushing through the door.

In a moment I pass among the wild and fragrant gardens. Under the stars I walk toward Alamo Park feeling the air tingle on my skin, breathing the scent of eucalyptus. *Maybe I'm still in Ethiopia.* I wander up the hill into the park. I can see myself, solitary and thin, walking through the stand of trees to the basketball court. The asphalt catches in the moonlight. I sink into the nearby grass. Ghosts of Ethiopian evenings leap through my mind. The world ought to be different. The world ought to be better. I conjure the cool African highlands — the broad, bright moon and a billion stars casting shadows across the nightscape. I remember the pale brown bark peeling from the paper trees, savannah wood and the evergreen Prunus swaying in the breeze — the still, sharp night reflects the crackle of firewood and crickets. A light wind blows across acacia trees carrying the scented howl of hyenas. A thousand African faces loom through my brain.

I bring out the Kennedy half-dollar I'd been keeping in my pocket, turning the coin from one side to the other. The face of the man flashes before me. What had he said to us on the White House lawn before we left? I try to resurrect the excitement of that day, but my memories lay hidden under years of newsreels and magazine pictures. I cannot remember what the man said. All I recall comes down to the hero worship that sparked my bones when I hungered to be among dedicated people. Two years later, I returned, injured, hero-less, weary of government politics, cynical and angry that the world hit so hard, fearing the unwinding life before me. Overcome with lost innocence, I long for African nights. I turn the half-dollar over and over in my hand; Kennedy's engraved face disappearing and reappearing in the moonlight.

Downtown

♦

FRANCO STEPS through the doorway of our apartment dressed in his usual "deacon" clothes — topcoat over a crumpled dark suit, dirty shirt and tie; a half-buttoned cardigan shows under the suit jacket. "On to North Beach," he shouts.

I throw on a corduroy jacket over a dark green crew-neck, and we're off. We hail a cab near Fillmore and Webster.

"Downtown," Franco croons in a tuneful imitation of Petula Clark.

The taxi speeds us down Fillmore, turns a breaking right on Geary, right turn on Broadway, zip, through a tunnel whose yellow tiles cast an unearthly eerie glow inside the cab. On the other side we hit the neon brightness of North Beach plunged into the ice cream thick foggy air.

"Downtown," the cabby sings as he pulls the car to the curb on Grant.

"It-it's on me." Franco fumbles in his coat pocket for the fare. Light-headed with anticipation, he hands the driver a fistful of dollars. I shake my head.

"Don't worry," he says. He holds both arms out from his sides and turns round and round. "Get ready for the first fuckin' night of your life," he says.

We're standing on the tri-corner of Columbus, Grant and Broadway; neon lights flash in the background. Laughing young people dressed in sweaters and jackets, women with ribbons in their hair fill the streets. The world gushes with girlfriends and boyfriends. Up the street I see the convention town strip of rowdy neon busts and rumps. Topless Betty and Jane. Bottomless Alice and Tina. It's all there, and I'm part of it now.

"The heart," Franco gestures to the sky. "Where the blood gets pu-pumped. Right here on Kerouac Boulevard and Ferlingetti Lane. Ra-right here on Ginsberg Avenue, San Francisco, California, USA. And don't you forget it, Mi-Mr. Peace Corps, do-gooder, save the poor."

I can barely believe myself. I'm the boy who gaped at magazine pictures of cities and supposed I would die before I got here, or worse, live out my life in a town with one fire station, where the afternoon freight train stops Main Street traffic everyday, where everyone knows everyone else, and would slowly squeeze me into a little old man. My first big city!

Franco grabs my arm and pulls me across the street.

"What do you have against the Peace Corps?" I ask. I want to contain my excitement.

"No one ever came to save me from po-poverty." He tightens his grip.

"So there's the rub," I say.

"Oh, we weren't as poor as your poor, poor Ethiopians. Really, we were . . . we were . . . rich as the jewel in an Ethiop's ear." Franco's smile crinkles the corners of his eyes and stretches the skin of his face, which nearly erases the pockmarks.

"Poor here becomes rich over there." I shake off Franco's grasp.

"No world problems tonight," he says.

We walk a few doors to a marquee, which reads, "THE COMMISSION — Live Improvisational Theater."

"Wait'll you get a load of this." Franco leads the way.

The lobby throbs with young people. Along one mirrored wall a bartender opens beers and mixes drinks. Framed photos of the players take up another wall. The crowd murmurs. I follow to where a surly sergeant-at-arms stands outside the door to the inner sanctum. I recognize the tattooed biceps of Joe, the stud we met in Wayne's loft with Claire. Under the glare of the lobby lights, his face pasty white, his dingy brown hair carefully combed into a ducktail. Fury radiates from his stance. The guy could be a sentinel in a silent movie..

"Hey, Joe," Franco calls with good cheer.

Joe, a head shorter than Franco, turns slowly.

"You remember Gil," Franco hops from one foot to the other.

Joe makes no sign.

Franco continues, "Wayne said to tell you we're his guests."

Thin-lipped Joe looks around the room without the slightest re-action. Franco and I look down, humbly bowing to the commander and chief. When this fact has been emphasized with another hop or two, Joe opens the door just wide enough for us to slip through.

"Thanks, Joe," I say over my shoulder.

Inside the large room, waitresses in short black skirts and check-ered blouses clean up with busy cool after the early show, rearranging tables and lighting candles. The stage climbs out from the dark as my eyes adjust. The dusky air, being drained by exhaust fans, smells of beer and smoke.

I stand next to Franco, my eyes going from object to object. I remember the excitement of bedtime stories, waiting for the next word from my mother's lips. I'm flushed with the same sense of mystery in this crypt of make-believe.

"Over here," Franco points to a table near the front.

An attractive waitress with short blonde hair, an even shorter skirt, and a distant smile saunters over to our table. "What'll you have?"

Franco eyes the waitress from head to foot, "A Bud, for me."

"I'll have a Dewar's, neat," I say, hoping she'd recognize that I'd traveled.

She takes no notice, and shrugs away our admiring looks.

41

Franco raises his Groucho eyebrows toward the her departing derriere. I pretend to hardly notice her.

"What's a' matter?" Franco says. "You scared of girls?"

"Weaned on a pickle," I say, making a face.

"I'll give *her* a pickle."

I force a laugh, holding back, denying my excitement. The echoes of silence in hushed theaters and houses of God make me afraid I'll suddenly scream to drown my own thoughts. Every breath threatens to burst a balloon of anticipation. I want to put my hand over my ears before it pops. I rotate this way and that with searchlight eyes, looking into every cranny of the theater, inspecting each chair, the lighting booth, a table for two in a distant corner, an exit sign, anything to take me away from these dreadful feelings of delight. I'm really not worth all this.

What would Kennedy think of this whirligig? This smoky saloon with booze and glamorous girls and who knows what else. While he lived a life to serve the country and bring the world closer to peace and taught me likewise, here I'm about to let myself be drowned in liquor and laughs and women. Oh, he'd be turning in his grave to see my excitement in this puny theater, about to enjoy myself while so many have nothing. What about the Ethiopians I left behind? Many would never ride in a taxi or go to school, would live their entire life without entering a theater. What about those who toil daily through lifetimes of frustration and suffering? What right do I have to be here? Wait now! What foolishness? Lincoln died in a theater. I have seen how life beats people beyond help and salvation; how we're all blinded, destined to live the life we're born into. I experienced the impossibly meager wish to help. Don't I need to get on with my life? What would Kennedy think?

Our drinks are curtly set before us just as the tattooed arm of Joe opens the door to the group of rollicking young people waiting in the lobby. They flood in, dazed by the lights, taking in the newness of the place, picking their seats, talking excitedly, bringing the place alive. Watching them, I'm an old-timer. I must deserve to be excited too, but I'm not sure. After a few sips, I let down my guard. My eyes follow the waitresses moving between the tables. Just before the door closes, I see Claire slip past Joe into a seat.

Soon the lights dim, bringing a gasp of hushed tones to the audience. A youthful announcer's voice: "TO OPEN OUR SHOW TONIGHT, LADIES AND GENTLEMEN, PLEASE WELCOME THE COUNTRY GUITAR STYLING OF WAYNE TELLER."

The spotlight bursts on Wayne. A shaggy figure in a red cowboy shirt, jeans and western boots, standing center stage, guitar poised off to one side. I can barely make out his wispy beard. His lone figure armed with only a guitar bends forward into the two microphones. My heart jumps with the first sparking notes. I melt into the music as he leans forward into the microphone. "Will the circle be unbroken/ Bye and bye lord, bye and bye."

The audience orders drinks.

"There's a better home a-waiting/ In the sky, lord, in the sky," Wayne croons in a clear tenor. The audience talks, settling in, mostly ignoring Wayne.

I'm enveloped in this familiar song. I lean back in admiration. "By and by, lord, by and by," I sing to Franco.

"By and by?" Franco waves a hand with sly deprecation.

Not the sentiments city-boy Franco understands. For a moment I'm lost between the pull of this old song and the Shakespearian tastes of my new friend. "By and by is easily said," I tell Franco.

Franco raises an eyebrow, shakes his head "yes," and marks a point in the air. "By and by, lord, by and by."

Wayne begins another song. "All of my love/All of my kissin'/ You don't know what you've been missin'/ Oh boy, when you're with me, oh boy!"

Right away the audience perks up. "Looky there, m'boy, he speaks pop 'by and by.'" Franco claps me on the back during the Buddy Holly tune.

The audience stops to listen, hooting and applauding, rapping on tables. Following this tune, Wayne strums and croons another few pop numbers, and another country "train whistle" tune. Perspiration mats his blond hair to his forehead. He steps in front of the microphones and takes a large bow, then announces in a reluctant drawl, "I'm gonna end with one of my favorites, "Under the Double Eagle March" by Josef Franz Wagner and frequently played by John Philip Sousa."

Wayne neatly steps in back of the microphones, hoists the guitar to his chest, thrusts the box out to his side, taking aim. The notes catch a snare drum riding the curve of the song's melody through a cadence of marching warriors. Wayne's left hand flies up and down the fingerboard while his right hand hovers on the wings of a hummingbird. The notes burst faster than machine gun bullets rippling through the crowd, catching everyone with buckshot.

The fierce staccato trills grab my spirit. He's a one-man band. We don't know whether to tap our feet or get up and step out. Wayne plays the piece through in spectacular fashion so that every ear, every eye in the place focuses on his guitar flashing in the light. Then, he plays the march again, double time, with incredible speed. The melody soars. Wayne's face grim with concentration, the sweet smile retracted behind his tight lips and wispy mustache. The notes resound, rat-a-tat-tat, ricocheting off the walls, zinging over shoulders, filling the entire room with the singular motion of breath-holding speed, on and on, a panzer attack on the soul. Everyone, waitresses, the sound and light men, even Joe, stop and listen.

I'm overcome with admiration — and jealous, too. Here plays a brilliance I'd never heard in person. I knew this man, had been to his house. The crowd detonates a barrage of applause. I'm positively joyful being inside this world. I clap and clap. Wayne bends forward in a slight bow. I can't stop clapping until the announcer's voice booms, "WAYNE TELLER, LADIES AND GENTLEMEN, WAYNE TELLER." Wayne takes another bow, this time bobbing up with a wise smile. The spotlight and applause fades.

The lights come up half amid the buzz and excitement. The waitresses ply the crowd for drink orders. Franco hails another round.

After a pause, the lights dim again.

"LADIES AND GENTLEMEN. WELCOME TO THE COMMISSION. FROM HERE ON OUT YOU'RE AT YOUR OWN RISK.

WE KEEP NO DOCTOR IN THE HOUSE. ANYONE GIGGLING, SNICKERING OR HOLDING BACK LAUGHTER WILL BE ESCORTED FROM THE ROOM BY THE MEN IN WHITE COATS STATIONED AT THE EXITS."

Franco looks over at me with a smile of expectation. His long legs stretch out under the table. He leans back with ease. Our lives have had no other purpose than to bring us to this moment. "This beats sitting in a room and reading a book," Franco tells me.

I think I'm hearing a different guy from the one in my Shakespeare class. Hooked on great expectations, I'm caught up in some half-memory of Kennedy's promise. What worry stirs, along with the thrill of wonderful moments about to unfold? Perhaps a prophecy from the past will reveal itself in the darkened theater? I look to Franco for reassurance, still smiling without his usual cynical air. I can't get my mind to go where I want. A funereal presence in the thin darkness explodes in prehistoric magic. My heart halts on thoughts of death in this strange, shrouded place.

"'We fought like Greeks,/what the hell./We loved like Romans,/tough to tell./Doesn't matter/for those who fell," I said to Franco on a whim. "Ginsberg wrote that, I think, I don't know."

"Yeah," Franco says. "It was Ginsberg."

I just made that up! So, having learned Franco's tricks, I have snuck it past the master. A lipless smile lights my wily lie.

Illumination floods the stage. Three men, two in black tails, one in white, stand next to a tall woman with long, blonde hair in a white evening gown. She beams herself to the audience — a most beautiful woman, with a wide face, classic mouth and nose, luminous skin. A slight turn to her upper lip gives her a kind of knowing expression.

"That's Karen," Franco whispers.

I yawn to cover an audible sigh while I imagine where I must have seen her before, perhaps in a dream or on a billboard. Her large, striking hazel eyes, her face light and charming. She must have the brain of a mannequin, my mind tells me. She's so poised and perfect, I can see the ice steaming from her bare shoulders. I fear this Isis sort of woman, who could rob me of myself. I discover a mole near her lower lip. Her nose seems a bit large. A hint of haughty disdain hunches her shoulder. I could easily dislike her.

Music! The Blue Danube Waltz from an upright piano near the side of the stage. The foursome turn to each other. Man in black tux bows to woman in white, man in white tux bows to man in black tux. The two couples begin to dance up and down the stage. The audience laughs at the sight of two men dancing together with swallowtails flapping. Then the stage goes dark.

The show commences. Several short skits and song. I judge them all funny, whether or not they make me laugh. I want them to be funny with exuberant punch lines making fun of local customs and politics.

The lights go dark, and a thin actor with a mustache, red-blond hair and a large mouth addresses the audience. "That's my buddy, Victor," Franco whispers.

Victor begins, "Because of the cheap tickets, we can't afford a writer. So, we need your help. Let's have some suggestions for a skit for Karen and J.B.

"They're all funny, man they're very funny." Franco injects. "Wait'll you see J.B., he has the knack to make people laugh. He's the stocky, wolfish fellow with a square, mobile face and round body — the same guy we all know from 8th grade, right?"

First, a place? Victor calls out.

The audience hesitates.

"Vietnam," someone calls from the back.

"A topic?" Victor snaps.

The lights at half, the audience looks around. "Every dog has his day," someone says, finally.

"Okay, now an article of clothing."

From the back of the room comes a whiskey voice, "Lingerie." Choked laughs and titters.

"Finally, a character from history." Victor asks.

After a long minute, another voice, "Robin Hood."

The three have a moment of communal consultation, and then J.B. and Karen step forward.

46

Karen and J.B move up and down as if riding a galloping horse.

KAREN
(coughing)
There must be one around here somewhere.

J.B.
(also coughing)
I saw one last week, over there, but now it's a burned out tree stump.

KAREN
Well, it's gone now.

J.B.
I hate it when the jungle catches fire.

KAREN.
Now, it's over there by that tree. Hey, a funny peasant in pajamas.

J.B.
That's the habadasher/longerie-er/gun-seller. Very French.

VICTOR
*(speaks with French accent, mimes dressing
and undressing imaginary people)*
Quite true. Lingerie, guns? What can I do for vu?

KAREN
Weren't you by that tree the other day?

VICTOR
This is my shop, by this tree. Zee L'mericans bombed my last tree, over there.

47

J.B.

I thought the baker was over by that tree.

VICTOR

Alas, zee baker is baked. He vas a commie spy.

KAREN

A simple mistake.

VICTOR

I might have been by that tree last week. Hard to find the same tree every day, when zee forest is on fire.

KAREN.

It would be easier if you rode a dog.

VICTOR

A dog, a dog, my kingdom for a dog.

The stage goes dark. A big surprised laugh spreads through the theater. They were clever. They had gotten everything in. I surrender in admiration.

Other small skits of larger themes follow, fueled by similar suggestions from the audience. The laughter becomes louder and warmer. Cadences of light and dark open and close each sketch. Whenever there's a lull, Victor or J.B. or one of the others pulls an imaginary pistol from an imaginary holster and shoots a compatriot. The "wounded" actor falls.

All the while, I can't take my eyes off Karen. I deny over and over in my muttered inner dialogue that she attracts me. Damn if I want to admit any attraction.

"Karen's something, isn't she?" Franco says after a sketch about the first woman president visiting Vietnam.

"I suppose. If you like that type." I reply, arched.

"She's married to Joe." Franco replies.

"You're kidding me." Ah — there's the rub. Married to the doorman with blood dripping down his arm? The goon who fell out of the loft with Claire and climbed back into The Wild Bunch.

"They got a kid together, but they don't live together."

"God!" I couldn't help but snicker under my breath.

"He hit her once too often, maybe. They were young," Franco whispers.

"She likes to get knocked around some so she won't feel guilty for being an iceberg," I say a little too loud. The revelation tempers my thoughts about Karen. I wave my arm signaling the waitress for another round.

The cast reminds me of "The Little Engine That Could," chugging from skit to skit. I admire how quick they are, how they change characters. Could I hope to get up and do these things? How better to go through life than to become an excuse for laughter. I sigh. A career in the theater. The thought of teaching suffocates me. God, maybe I could become Wayne, a simple musician. On the cliff edge of my student days, I'm desperate to find my balance before plunging into a future I cannot fathom. Life matters less since Ethiopia. The Peace Corps had that effect on me. Forget "To be or not to be?" What do I do with the next minute? That's my question. Every conventional thought of the future smothers me. Maybe I could become a traveling minstrel and find a life among actors. The thought spooks me. All these talented people, how could I possibly fit in.

I'm so lost in my own thoughts that I jump when the stage lights come on full. The actors stand side by side, bowing, the audience clapping, whistling and hooting. The "Blue Danube Waltz" plays again. The group pairs off and dances into the darkness to enthusiastic clapping and whistling.

Bang! The house lights flood the audience. Show over.

Blinking in the light, I'm let down a bit. I don't want the show to end. Franco and I continue to sit. The audience, buzzing and tottering in a haze of good cheer, trundles out the door. In the piercing light, the quaint theater walls now look cracked and grim. The smell of beer and cigarette smoke curdles the air. We're left with ordinary, chipped and uneven Formica tables, the chairs scratched and in need of mending. The carpet worn and ragged in places. Even the waitresses lose their glamour. Their uniforms made of cheap cloth, their painted faces young, and in the harsh light, lose allure. The evening's enchantment drains away with the smoke.

"Let's go backstage." Franco says, raising his eyebrows.

"Can we?" I hesitate.

"Sure. I know most of 'em," Franco says.

As the crowd leaves, a few people hang back. Claire still sitting, is nursing a drink. She waves to Franco.

"Claire used to waitress here," Franco confides, gulping the last of his beer. "She's jealous of Karen."

"Karen?"

"The one you don't like, but like up there." Franco points to the stage.

"You mean the one with the ice chip on her shoulder? That's Karen?"

"Yeah, Claire and Karen were waitresses together. They went to acting workshops together. Now, Karen's a regular leaving Claire still in the workshops."

"Oh."

"That's why Karen and Joe busted up. Now she's one of the regulars, and he's the doorman. Know what I mean?"

"A loser."

"I go to the workshops, sometimes, too. You ought'a come."

"Don't you have to audition or something?" I ask.

"Not if you know someone like me." Franco stands and stretches. "Let's go."

Franco walks right up on stage past the stagehands unplugging wires and putting away props. I follow behind on little cat feet, worshipful of the pulpit. We walk through the very same door the actors used getting on and off stage. I close the door silently to find myself backstage in a cramped area of struts and props. Coats and hats and scarves hang on a row of hooks. Each object retains its stage-glow. Crumpled tuxedos, a gown thrown over chairs; the cowboy hat, the soldier hat, the pants and shoes, strewn like a child's room. So, I am learning about conjuring magic.

I turn to find the daring hazel eyes of Karen watching. She looks away when I look back. She appears more beautiful than on stage. I can see she's a regular person. I look away while she busies herself packing costumes.

"Hey Victor," Franco moves away from me toward the actor.

I'm out of place in the hubbub, light on my feet, afraid that someone will grab me by the shoulder and tell me I don't belong there. These characters, these actors move about in various stages of undress. The place functions as one big dressing room. Not what I'd pictured. My wits work slowly; I'm swimming underwater. I look around for Franco and instead look directly into the eyes of Karen.

"Hey!" She throws her head, motioning me toward her. "You look like you need something to do. Help me with this." She's trying to fit a bundle of dresses into a garment bag.

As I walk over, she looks up from her struggle and gives me a quick grateful smile. A regular smile. The smile of a young girl, naked and unafraid. I take the bag and hold it up for her. I inhale her perfume.

"Thanks," she says, reaching inside and straightening the hangers. She takes her time, arranging them just right. "I wasn't getting anywhere by myself. Perfect. I couldn't have asked for a better . . . ."

"Call me Gizmo?" I say. "Usually, I'm a coat tree, but I'm trying to branch out."

Karen screws her face into comical look. "Bad joke, but you'll do fine. If you could make yourself into one of those hotel bellhops — you can help me to my car." She hands me a green leather suitcase.

"Well," I hesitate, "sure." She looks older close up. I find my dislike melting. Maybe she's genuine in real life. I try to restrain my eagerness. Part of the show, I assure myself. I look around. "I came with Franco," I say.

"Franco? He's back in the closet with the boys, I'll bet. He'll never miss you."

"The closet?"

"Oh, the boys' dressing room."

"You mean they have dressing rooms . . .. Other than this one?"

"They don't dress in them of course because they're all exhibitionist." Karen points toward an alcove with a black door.

"I better tell Franco I'm going outside."

Holding the garment bag and suitcase, I walk over and push the door open. Victor and Joe are sitting in chairs. I'm amazed to see what looks like a religious ceremony going on. Victor is holding a lighted candle, and Joe, a spoon. Franco is kneeling between them, his left shirtsleeve rolled up. A rubber band is tied around his bicep. In his right hand he's holding a syringe. Wayne peers over Victor's shoulder at me, and Franco looks around at me staring through the door. With an impatient look, he shakes his head and waves me away with the hand holding the syringe, as if blessing me.

I close the door in an instant, unsure of what I saw. I try not to make sense of the scene. I turn toward Karen, who is staring me down.

"Oh, so you found them," she says walking toward me. "The real theater's right here. You ought to come more often."

The look on Franco's face blazes in my memory. "Leave me alone," it said, "not fit for your tender, squeamish flesh." My face flushes. I'm not sure I want to hang with them, but I hate being left out.

Karen throws a maroon cape over her shoulders. Carrying her bags, I follow her out a side door and through the darkened lobby into the street under the marquee.

"Didn't the big boys ask you to come in and play?"

"What do you mean?"

Karen laughed, "Oh, nothing. You're too nice to play with those boys. My car's up here." She points up the block.

Outside, the air is cool. I sling the garment bag over my shoulder. Karen pulls the cape close about her. Not an hour after midnight the neon lights have ebbed; rolling fog covers the ancient Barbary coast. The earlier carefree aura of the streets has given way to a somber mood. Up the street, even the blazing lights of the neon tit-palaces have flagged. Men in overcoats, hunched against the chill, hurry along on desperate errands.

Karen unlocks the door of a red Volvo.

My mind returns to the theater with Franco and Joe and the others. I want to hang back with them, all the same I'm exhilarated with this woman in the deserted night.

"Put that in the back seat," she says.

"Sure."

Karen holds the door while I lean into the back and carefully lay the bag across the seat. Straightening up, we come face to face. She puts her arms around my neck and kisses me full on the lips.

"Oh," she says, "What a surprise."

I'm speechless.

Karen slides into the driver's seat, "Get in, I'll drive you home."

The Ticket to Ride

♦

KAREN LIVES in the downstairs apartment of an old, three story Victorian on Oak Street near the entrance to the Bay Bridge.

Rather than ring me in, she comes out of the ground-floor apartment and peers through the outside door to the vestibule next to the stairs. She smiles that innocent smile, beginning at the corners of her mouth and traveling to the corners of her eyes, flooding the feathery hazel with a touch of brown warmth. Her eyes seem to change color in the light. I can't believe I'm standing here looking at her through a mere pane of glass. She quick opens the door and motions me in. I pause, not wanting the moment to end so soon, afraid to go inside, approach her, be closer to her. I have a feeling of death, a thought of death, a welcoming of oblivion, like a coming shock. Honestly I would turn and outrun my eagerness, but I am already short of breath.

Karen is all mystery in her straight jeans and a white-on-white embroidered Mexican blouse. Her hair hangs loose past her shoulders. The strands are dark now, thicker too. Sexual breezes stirs. Is this the same woman from the other night? Wasn't she blonde? Oh, no. This is someone else. She looks so unlike she did when I first saw her with blonde curls A wig! She was wearing a wig the night I met her. Right about her all along. Her face is the same. At least I think so. She touches her cheek to mine without a word. "Come in," she whispers. Her fresh perfume erases any doubt. To the left of a long hallway a door is partially open. Karen motions me inside.

I walk into a long flat with a hallway leading to other rooms and a kitchen beyond. The living room is lit by a poster of Che Guevara on one wall and on an adjacent wall a matching poster of Huey Newton in a black beret, seated in a fan shaped wicker throne, spear upright in his left hand, a rifle in his right, a relaxed almost inviting look on his face. "This is my natural heritage man," Newton seems to be saying. "Wanna fight about it?" The last face I expected to see with this Karen. She is so different than I thought. I spy a rocking chair in the corner, but I choose to sit on a floor cushion, feeling sharp in a new khaki Army shirt and my favorite jeans. I pull a joint — a gift from Wayne — from my shirt pocket and hold it up in a question.

Karen shakes her head, no.

"I thought we could take a walk, or something." I have trouble finding the pocket, and with an awkward push kind of crush the joint back into the pocket.

"You want to leave already." she says, shading her smile.

What now, I wonder? I feel as restless as the other night at Wayne's apartment. I have no idea what to do with this stranger on a Saturday afternoon?

Karen moves to a record player on a small mahogany table. She moves with natural flair, with more grace than I saw on the stage — as if she had let go of something. She chooses pop music, which I don't recognize, creepy falsetto voices. She sits, deliberate and comical, on a cushion opposite me.

The music winds around my mind and sways me this way and that. I try not to stare at the fine bones and translucent skin of Karen's face with the faint outline of a blue vein at her temples. I am rapt by her beauty. An inquiring, sensuous look passes between us. My gaze falters as the silence begins to tremble in my eyes.

Though I sense a softening in her attitude, to keep from staring too hard, I explore the room. A red and black Mexican blanket with Thunderbird designs hangs from the wall opposite Che. A child's ragged doll, a panda and a red and yellow fire truck lay on the window seat. Plants line the windowsill and large dried flowers in two tall vases frame the fireplace. I become aware of the strong, sweet aroma of incense, the very same smell of Wayne's apartment a few nights before. A small wooden table has a tableau of what appears mimeographed pamphlets, and thin booklets. Orderly but disordered. Intriguing, this actress-cum -woman with the wall posters.

My eyes return to Karen while the music covers me with a faint sheen that I'm surprised to enjoy. I seem lost in the juvenile music with the bouncy phrasing.

Ain't that a shame, I sing to myself.

The moment widens into five, making me uneasy. I try to remember the sound of Karen's voice.

Silence.

Karen stands without so much as a glance and walks out of the room.

In her absence my mind flies to possibilities. She refused the marijuana, the peace pipe, the currency of these people. I'd come armed, but am now disarmed. We have nothing to say to each other. She's a rag bone, a giant step up from me on the ladder of cool. Searching the place again, I cannot find one book save for the thin pamphlets on the small table. I want to run out of there before she tosses me out for lack of words. I take a sideways glance at the poster of Che, the poster of Huey. What could they mean in a household along with nursery toys? I've seen these posters in the apartments of students from school. I'd seen them in poster shops springing up on Haight Street. *Hey, hey, hey; Che all the way*, I cluck to myself. What was Che doing arming the peasants while I served in the Peace Corps? Could they be compatible? This revolutionary who forsook the oath to do no harm, had alarmed the people instead of teaching them. Was there no time to teach? Wasn't that the way to arm the people? Franco is right, I feel my squareness. You arm the people by arming the people. There's no reason to wait until the rift between rich and poor, black and white is so deep and apparent. In the presence of these posters staring down on me, I feel ignorant as an Ethiopian farmer who'd never seen the inside of a school.

Karen returns with a plate of cookies. Oh, now she's a mom, I muse. I'm home from school and we have cookies. Maybe I'm Santa Claus. Her smile charms me, but homemade cookies? Now what? I'd prefer a walk. Outside I could feel the breeze of freedom and then after a decent time, I could opt out, walk her home and retreat. She's so different than the other night. Her eyes open wide this afternoon. "Want to try one these?" she asks as she offers up the plate and takes one herself. We eat the cookies together, ritual bite for bite.

I've heard about cookies. I'll be ready for the turn on, or this high thing.

After a time, I'm relieved to be in my right mind. What do you know? A cookie is a cookie. Karen plays another record, a classical piece. Did the room shake slightly? A San Francisco earthquake? She turns to me — a far away, Mona Lisa gaze. Very calm and collected, she sits cross-legged.

Instead of my usual plod among possibilities, my mind finds its Pegasus, rises in a cloudless sky. I ride the wild steed. My cape flying full, one hand loose on the horse's neck the other hand casually holding the reins; I'm working out the design of a new existence. First, I ride one horse until another horse shows up. Then, I ride on, thought to thought, star to star, changing horses, riding to every corner of the universe. A pony express of the mind. I have found the ticket to ride.

Karen, who covers a laugh escaping her mouth, awakens me from this reverie.

"What?" I hear her say something. I bend closer. "What?" I ask again.

Karen shakes her head, speaking a silent phrase that spills purple flower petals on the carpet.

Searching for an explanation, a picture floats across my mind of an old black man in a white beard riding a raft. It's Jim, from my dreams. I laugh. The laugh becomes a small bird that flies over Karen's ear to the window seat next to the panda.

Round, fat music notes float out of the record player. I spy Yogi Bear playing the piano. Look at me. Inside a cartoon. Am I really? Or, am I merely rambling about in the world of a new reality? This thing I've heard so much about over the last months. What about the mushroom people creeping up from Texas. Do I see mushrooms growing from the carpet? Those sparklers appear like a dancing chorus line. Mushroom caps come dancing right across my line of vision,.

Quick as a thought, a quote of floating notes changes shape into round guitars and pianos. Trombones and saxophones flash inside neon musical staffs. More notes spring from the record player in a rainbow arc, splashing across the room into a spillway of colors. I try to listen, but see instead. I try to keep from laughing, but the laughter drops from my mouth in pink and purple flowers.

"Too much, man." I grin wide-eyed.

"The Book of Revelation" plays me for some cosmic joke, unraveling note-by-note.

Pastel colors, green gardens in summer, shimmer in the heat of my gaze. Time has burst full on when the heavens open. My God, what's all this? The cookie? The carpet explodes into moving kaleidoscopic colors. Rainbows pulse from the table giving light to dancing guitar chords shaped like football players.

Fear rises in my belly as I squat on my haunches trying to get up. "All right, lay it on me," I address the universe. "And by the way," I add. "What's the price?"

"No price," Jim smiles direct at me. I'm gonna show you. That why we letting you in for free."

"Thanks, but northing's for free." I say.

"You got the ticket to ride, my man." The warmth of Jim's voice persuades me, as his person begins to dissolve.

"Say," I yell after him, "who are you, really?"

A breeze ripples the feather in the old man's hat. "I am you," he says. Whoosh — he is gone.

I relax and close my eyes. I see myself wandering through a forest. Old-timey banjo music rings through the trees. There in front of me stands old Jim, now a minstrel in powdered black face over black face, motioning me down a winding path of piano keys. Musical notes with balloon smiles pop on and off.

I find myself on a bluff above the Ohio River lying in the grass near the edge of a golf course — a boyhood refuge on lone summer afternoons. I've telescoped my hands together and pretend to look though a lens, sweeping the landscape this way and that, until I've blocked every smoke stack and telephone wire from view.

I imagine myself many hundreds of years ago, in those green and verdant days when the native Americans traveled this river in canoes. I calm myself with fantasies that I had lived among them, and wandered through the forests, taking my living from the land and the river.

Now, in this cartoon fairyland, I watch myself walk among the very same trees; I spot the stone-cut faces of native tribes who haunt me. From that childhood bluff, I behold a plague of Redcoats pulling oars in open boats down from Fort Pitt. They land on the embankment and hack away the forests, skirmish with the local tribes. They promise peace with gifts of blankets and smallpox inoculations; and decimate the Mound Builders and Mingo's of the region, driving the remnants of the tribes — women, children and old men — down the river into extinction. I am filled with grief over dying native peoples along the riverbank, drowning with them in my own shame, unable to save a single child.

To keep from dying right there in Karen's living room, I jump forward to the days of the Underground Railroad. From my perch overlooking the river, I watch myself help escaped slaves onto boats that take them across the Ohio to freedom. There I stand with the old man holding the tiller, steering one of the boats filled with runaways through choking Civil War smoke.

A barge floats by carrying the clay of 300 years of dark, oozing guilt. The old man motions me to reach in and scoop up some of the gunk. I smear the thick mud on my face with both hands. I flash a glance toward the poster of Huey who now seems to be looking the other way.

A spike of panic pierces my mind. I have lost myself. I'm filled with apprehension. Trying to touch my eyes, to see if they're open or shut, I can't locate my fingers, my arm? Inside this anxiety, I try to concentrate on opening my eyes or closing them, the opposite of what I'm doing. I strain to find some part of my body while the brown bumptious face of the old man mocks. "What body? Inside — outside. What the difference, my man? Leave your body behind and enjoy the ride."

I am choked with cold terror.

Out of desperation I give myself to the music, only to witness a hundred motorcycles pounding rhythms of multicolored lightning across the midnight sky of my mind. A spinning landscape of colored glass lulls me into a dream. The colors soften to liquid reds and blues, a languid jukebox flowing in a wide unhurried river. I lay on the grassy embankment of my youth in a haze of contentment watching the mosaic of colors pass. I am gripped by deep assurances that I belong in this profound spiritual panorama. At last. I am the infant brought into this world with the thump of certainty. Where did doubt set in? I chew on a blade of grass. The river flows in a current of bliss carrying me into far off peace. I rest in this cocoon of my mind until I hear thunder. The lights explode into a volcano of sparking lava against a pale pink sky. Fireballs and mortar shells fall from the war movies of my youth.

I inhabit a world of unspeakable danger. Tales of the Crypt and Horror Comics cram my brain. Creatures grab with long fingernails and leering faces, lumbering through the long nights of childhood, slashing, gashing, searing and dismembering everything in their path. Heroes from Combat Comics heave grenades, charging hill and bunker, storming beaches, assault me. I am taken prisoner and tortured; I refuse to talk, going ever deeper into my unconscious resisting physical pain and the tirades of tormentors. I am caught on the embankment as the explosions become fiercer. This time my desperate trying yields the dawning sense of my arm. With great effort among the bursting shells, the labored tenant of my own mind manages to wriggle my fingers and slip them on. I open my eyes to escape the horror.

Gil, the real Gil, bounces back into the world shivering with the cold wind whistling through the atoms of my flesh. A hand touches a distant part of my body. My head rests on Karen's lap. She caresses the furrows across my brow playing a melody on my forehead. The bashful boy is bathed in the green sea of healing light coming from her touch. Her eyes call me into the great meadow of her loving heart.

The room has become a garden. Each object blooms. The floor lamp grows into a fern. The carpet sprouts into a field of wildflowers, the curtains an arbor of trees. The fierce posters and the panda pulse and glow, beckoning — Che with a smile and Huey with a naughty-boy charm. Each and every object grows leaves and flowers, beautiful and ridiculous, a radio bush, the table and record player blossoming into an apple tree.

I close my eyes with great effort on this unsettling world of glowing plants. I am inside the Paramount Theater where my father would leave me for a Saturday double feature. Joining in hundreds of war movies and westerns, I would jump into the screen and live among the heroes. I saved the squad, saved the fort, saved the wagon train full of women and children, and in the process killed the Nazis, shot the Japanese, and murdered the Indians. Each adventure of slaughter added a drop to my shame.

Trying to move, I gasp. I am drowning. A gloating green octopus surfaces from the lagoon of my unconscious. Fierce tentacles thrash at me, sucking my blood, ripping hairs from flesh, exposing that apple of guilt in my throat, holding before me the terror of my poor boy's mirrored self.

"Karen," I strain. "Save me." My eyes stare into her astonished face. The sound of my voice brings my body awake into a fit of sexual desire, burning in the grip of passion – I can't move.

I crouch behind jungle fronds, lusting after Karen's body. I crawl through the underbrush of a deep forest waiting to pounce and taste her creamy flesh. Very carefully I trace the round bottoms and nipples of her breasts resting in her white blouse, down her slim hips over the tight jeans outlining the perfect V between her thighs; her body beckons. In the midst of me, a huge hole, desperate and obsessive, ignites a fuse. My penis senses a target. My brain waves pull Karen into the electro-chemical grasp of my desire. But I can't move. Saliva dribbles from the corners of my mouth.

From Karen's lap, my lapsed boy stares into her eyes. She returns my gaze with deep concern on her face. What a relief. I snuggle into her breasts, feasting in the tingling of sex. My mouth nudges against her, tasting the bland cotton and the softness of her bra-less breast. I suckle her through the cloth making a wet spot. She caresses my babes head and pulls me closer pressing my face full force against her bosom. She begins to unbutton her blouse. My eyes follow her descending hand with each button, watching the widening slit of her blouse expose the expanse of her white skin. My tongue flicks around the rounded hill of her breast straining at the cloth. Impatient, I wait for her full breast, moving my lips across and up the mound to the pink folds of her nipple and taste the sublime warmth and freshness of her skin. My lips form instinctive sucking motions. My eyes close to the tranquil glowing lights of subdued rolling colors, moist green and peaceful blue ocean of dreams. I am home. Finally.

"THWAAKK! GRRIINNGG! THUNNKK!"

A loud crash. The sound of a thousand breaking mirrors. I hear the clang, but my lips cling to the nipple while my mind holds onto the dream. Slowly, one eye opens and strains toward the sound. Big G.I. Joe from Combat Comics throws the door open.

Karen yelps toward this huge figure filling up the doorway. Slowly, with fuzzy awareness, I recognize tattooed Joe, Karen's husband, the same goon who came down the loft stairs with Claire, dressed in jeans and a black t-shirt, standing in gigantic storm trooper boots. I remember Franco's warning about Karen's husband. Still I keep my lips attached to Karen's breast. Unwilling to let go, I continue to suck, one eye closed, content to end my life there. In one breath, Karen snatches the tit from my straining lips. My head bounces on the floor. My eyes open. The contents of the room careen around my brain, propelled by screeching guitar music knifing through my body.

"My God," a voice in my head screams, "Her husband! Serious business."

I sense Karen jumping to her feet while this hulking comic book character troops through the doorway, causing the room to rattle. "Stand," my drunken, dazed brain commands. "Stand." Before I find my feet and hands, they find me, pushing me up. Blinking in the light, the floor becomes an amusement park ride. I reach out to the table holding the record player that has grown into an apple tree, trying to steady myself. I'm about to fall with outstretched arms, when the room stops.

Dead silence. The walls glow. I sense movement in the border of gold and black curlicues painted around the crown molding, now transformed into snakes. The mouth of each snake clamped onto the tail of the one in front. I sicken from the diamond design of their skin and the ruby glow of their eyes. Ancient mosaics crawl around the wall. I struggle to wrench my focus from the ceiling to the terror of GI Joe's glare.

Karen poses in innocence, hands cupped over her mouth. The nipple of one breast peeks from her unbuttoned blouse. GI Joe stands with hands on hips, legs spread, waiting for reasons. No one breathes. The mosaic of snakes forms a frame around us. We stand frozen in time and space, blazing with colors inside a painting by Van Gogh entitled, "The Adulterers Found." From my peripheral vision, I perceive this scene hanging in a museum. Curious people pass. They have no eyes, but sniff the situation, reacting with compassion, indifference or humor before they go on.

Inside this frame of snakes, nothing moves. I assume the infant in his crib trying to make sense of my surroundings. My mind takes up with the panda bear on the window seat, growing it to a huge height. The toy truck sounds a bell in my head. The room chatters with voices, trapping me.

We spring from this painting in the stroke of an eyelash.

Roland, the kid, who is two or three, in jeans and a black t-shirt, toddles into the room. Open mouthed, gurgling and clapping, the boy screams with pleasure as he runs toward his mother's exposed tit. Karen's hands set about buttoning her blouse. The kid's footprints smolder.

In a silent movie, G.I. Joe moves closer, raising his right arm. My feet, of their own accord, turn. I run toward the front door over the smoking footprints, but GI Joe blocks the way. I turn the other way, racing down the dark hallway toward the kitchen. Running, running, running, I await the explosion and the excruciating pain of being splintered apart by one of G.I. Joe's grenades. I want to stop and turn around to face my own death, but my feet won't allow me even this. I run down the long hallway, much longer than I remembered, into the dark, seeking the dim light from the kitchen ahead. I can hear the big galumphing boots in pursuit.

Headlines flash through my mind in black and white, "DRUG DAD GRENADES RIVAL TO DEATH," "DOPE CULT INITIATION LEADS TO DEATH OF NEOPHYTE," "EVIDENCE THAT DRUGS CAUSE USERS TO EXPLODE."

I release my life right there, ready to fade out to oblivion. I want to crumple to the floor somewhere in this endless hallway and give in to inevitable death. Poor me, as I count the years of my short life and long for the lush warmth of death. I want to give in, but my mind says, *No! Run you fool.* My calf muscles flex and extend, carrying me forward. My heart says stop and face the enemy, but I can't stop.

My mind chatters on, horrified to face death, *I'm too young. I haven't lived yet. Don't take me.* All the wayward predictions from my father have proved true. Here in the first test of my manhood, I fall into a pure panic. What great Indian warrior, what sauntering soldier of fortune, what young man with the promise of greatness would fail to turn and face death squarely? I run, knowing I can no longer claim these dreams. I have become what I condemned of my own father, a simple human running in fear.

I careen off a wall in the dusky hallway, slowing down. Maybe I can turn and face my tormentor, but my shoulders freeze in the cold breeze of death. If I turn, I would surely melt in the heat of death's breath. Running again, I bump against a telephone stand

and bruise my wrist. I slam against the door jamb leading into the kitchen where I spy a large knife on the sink board. My mind says, *Run, boy, run. Nobody ever killed death*, but I pick up the knife anyway, heading for the back door. I jiggle the latch with death waiting to lay his bony hand on my shoulder.

I turn to discover GI Joe, two feet away, staring through the eerie white mask of death. Joe grabs me by the arm holding the knife. We struggle for a moment, pushing and shoving. I break away, screaming. I wave the knife, then lunge forward, kicking Joe in the groin, sending him reeling and screaming back into the dark hallway.

I can't get the door open. With the knife in one hand, I turn the doorknob, and kick at the bottom. In one last effort, I push hard with my shoulder. The door flies open, springing me outside, where I stumble on the concrete porch, missing the step down, tumbling through the air. Suspended, I see Death's plan. I fall toward the concrete holding the kitchen knife. Expecting a cloud of poisonous gas from behind, *Gilbert Stone now comes to death by his own hand.* I struggle to change my tack in mid-air. No course remains but to come down. Death's bony face, curious and peaceful, looms in front of me with the message to turn the knife on myself .

I give up completely in this suspended moment, curled in a ball with the tip of the knife pressed to my heart. The cement courtyard pulls me to earth. I await under the expert eye of mighty Death for the force of the fall to jam the knife through my heart.

At the last second, before crashing to the cement, a strong even voice cracks the word, "NO!" through the air. The voice resonates through my backbone from tibia to brain, slams me with such force it wrenches me around in the air, pulling the knife away, causing me to land on my butt with a gush of breath. Still, the force of the fall causes the knife to gash across my left arm cutting through my shirt and causing a broad line of blood to appear instantly.

The sight of the blood brings me to some sense. I'm a paratrooper landing in a rice paddy in Vietnam, full of enemies, dark sloping eyes closing in; bounding to my feet, I crouch with the knife poised for an attack.

Slowly, I turn. Empty porch. No one in the doorway. I move in a complete circle, the stalked enemy, alone in the October courtyard, bathed in the fierce afternoon sun. The kitchen door swings silent on its hinges.

Blood seeps from my arm. In control, the soldier rips off the shirt, wrapping the wound. I glance around to find a way out. A high wooden fence surrounds the courtyard. A padlocked door seals the alleyway. My choice — either the door to Karen's, or a stairway to the apartment above. The shirt has stopped the flow of blood. Dazed with the sunlight filtering through neighboring trees, I wonder if I've already passed to the other side.

I have deserted Karen. I turn to go inside, but the thought of returning sickens my spent youth. My heart hammers with guilt that I do not possess the courage to save Karen. I remember the last fight with my father before leaving for the Peace Corps, when the old man accused me of running away, of being afraid to go on with my life. That same tone rings in my guilty head, "You're no man."

The fear comes back. I'm caged and crazed to find a way out. The light hurts my eyes causing me to a squint. My feet and legs bounce, frantic to run. My arm throbs.

Without another thought, I bound up the battleship gray stairs to the apartment above and knock. In a moment a middle-aged woman in faded gray opens the door. She looks me over, calm in her chenille robe, unsurprised, a guest half expected.

"I gotta get out," I manage.

The woman nods when I barge into the kitchen where her husband, in an undershirt, sits in front of a plate of buttered toast and jam. He looks up surprised. I run out of the kitchen, down the hallway toward the front of the apartment and the front door.

The woman follows right behind, telling me in a mothering tone, "Careful now, careful."

I open the couple's apartment door, run down the stairs, past the entrance to Karen's apartment, through the vestibule, down the front steps and into the street. A blast of white heat from the harsh sun reflects from the pavement.

Not a soul haunts the sidewalk. Not a single car whizzes down the street toward the Bay Bridge.

Stranded in this white-hot no-mans-land, I run toward Fillmore with the staggering gait of a wounded primate. I catch a glimpse of myself reflected in a window that stops me short. I appear hulking, disheveled, in a white t-shirt, one arm wrapped in a bloody rag, my other hand still clutching the knife. My thoughts shoot back to Karen in that sun-soaked room with G.I. Joe about to kill us both. My memory remains fuzzy. I can't believe the blood on the knife. I have morphed into a wastrel, a murderer, a fugitive from death.

Vaguely I remember the fight and then running away. Did I defend myself and kill Karen's husband? From the very bottom of my intestines, a scream of fear fights to my consciousness. Remorse floods my eyes. Had I killed, without intention, in the flower of my youth, on an innocent afternoon?

I throw down the knife, stand dumb watching the blade bounce into the street. Then my eye catches the blood-soaked sleeve wrapped around my arm. *More evidence.* I see a flash of pain rising from the wound. I suffer a hundred movie scenes of jealous husbands. Did one of these take place moments ago with GI Joe lying wounded and bleeding? I cannot remember. I look toward Karen's house, waiting for the sound of sirens. No sound. No movement. Not a soul around. The sun beats down on my head. The waves of heat shimmer off the pavement. I am flattened dough baked in desert sands. No wind. I feel like I'm being watched.

Not a stir in the city streets. In bright silence, I suspect that I am the last man on earth. Feeling naked in the flimsy t-shirt, I lumber toward Fillmore. A part of me wants to run. The police may arrive, but I can't move my body faster.

At the corner of Fillmore, I turn right and shamble down the hill. Still, I don't see a soul on the street. An eerie sense floats along with the light. *Someone is watching me.* Beings from another planet have landed. Everyone deserted except Gilbert Stone — the last man remaining. Nowhere is there a living soul to be seen — yet I feel eyes sweeping over me.

I don't know where to go. I've forgotten where I live. I wander, looking for someone to point out where I belong. Not one soul. The buildings sag in silence. I'm alone in the world. My arm hurts. My wracked knee aches. I push on down Fillmore looking into the empty shops. Not one body comes into view. No one anywhere. No traffic. I am alone. I am watched. I am the last man on earth.

Time and the River

◆

MOST DAYS I CANNOT find the energy to leave my room. I lay corpse-like on the mattress or pull the scarred maple chair to the window where the only relief for my scratchy eyes is the dome of the sky. Inside the spreading dusk, the San Francisco fog edges up the hill to Alamo Square. Birds flit from trees to phone wires. Hooded figures float among the maples and juniper bushes buying and selling nickel bags. I try to follow the communion, but the figures remain in shadows. The long strawberry sunset soaks my spirit. I lay down. Didn't I just see Kennedy in the park yesterday? The bell in my head rings. I believe I must be ordained, but lack the courage and stamina to stand up and face it all.

When Franco ventures into the room I ignore him. The usual Franco, fierce and demanding, has softened in the last weeks as he has watched my darkening spirit. I detect a faint trace of sympathy as he stands in the doorway with suspicion on his lips. I play it for all its worth, sulking on the mattress ... unwilling to move, strangled by lack of desire to live in the world. I refuse to recognize myself. Dread pulls at the threads of my discouraged mind; I fear some sort of recovery from my death flight. I fear a wing of light may soon carry me from this sick bed, and then what?

"Hey man," Franco says, finally. "What's happening?"

I have nothing to say.

Franco waits. He tries again, "Gil, man, what's up?" He crosses his arms over his chest.

I pretend deep thought or perhaps catatonia. Refusing to answer, a lump of resentment forms in my throat.

Dylan on the record player, "Ain't gonna work on Maggie's farm no more . . . ."

Franco moves to the foot of the mattress. I sense my older friend's irritation. I know I must laugh or make some sign I'm alive. Franco shifts from one foot to the other, his face is red, "Come on, man." He holds out a space for Gil to come around, but I continue to beat the silence.

"You're stretching the rope, mother." Franco's voice is patronizing. "You haven't talked to anyone in a month. I don't buy it. Come on, talk to me."

I turn toward him.

"Look Gilbert-baby," Franco says, "pull yourself out of this. We're watching the revolution."

"Yeah," I mouth a slow breathy response. "I'm gonna take my physical, man. I'm in training."

"You gotta talk, god-damn you. Didn't I show you the ropes, man." Franco puts his hands on his hips. "You think you're the only one who wants to stop the war."

"I'm trying to remember how to talk," I say. "I don't think you understand when I talk it's all . . . all your friends when they talk they're so cool."

"You're gonna go ca-crazy, stayin' in your room all 'a the time," Franco says with an earnest inflection while looking into my pupils.

"I'm OK," I say.

"Look, man," Franco starts in again, "We've been schoolmates and buddies. We were friends before any of this hippie revolution. You got to give up this act of despair."

"I got the same chances as any soldiers burning like candles in the jungles," I say. "Did I tell you I'm gonna take my physical?"

"You gonna become another one of these street people out there, wandering around sleeping in the park.

"I'm gonna join the Army, man. I'm all set."

Franco sits on the edge of the mattress. We sit in silence, looking out the window into the last spread of burning sunset.

After a time, Franco speaks up, "I got a ship, man. As soon as the semester is over, man, I'm outta' here. Same no-draft status as being in school." He pauses for a space to let me speak, then goes on, "Shuttling around the Indian Ocean for three or four months, maybe more." Another pause. "Right away when I signed on, a ton of weight fell off my back, man. It's like a summer job. I'll be back by the fall. I have a few days and then I'm gone."

I knew of Franco's plans, but the news strikes me cold and lonely.

"Yeah," I say after awhile.

"It's not the end of the world, Gil. Let's celebrate tonight. You takin' your physical and me my ship." Franco moves toward the door. "I'll treat you to dinner in North Beach. Around 8:00 . . .. I scored some Owsley. You all right, man?

"Sure, man. Everything's up to date in Kansas City," I say. My insides ache, rasping and bitter. "It's OK, Franco, buddy. I'm in great shape. The world's come around. Did ya hear? Soon's the politicians sit down and talk, they're gonna stop killin' grandmothers and children. It's all right, man. I'm gonna stay in my storm cellar here until duty calls. Everything's OK. A-1, tip-top. Ship-shape, Franco, old buddy. You run along now and grab your boat. Give 'em my regards. Tell 'em I'm glad they're moppin' up, givin' 'em foreign aid and Vaseline and artificial limbs and stuff. If I get the call maybe I'll see ya from behind one of those rubber trees. Catch yer boat. Don't be late. They're lookin' for all that good Coca Cola an' Snickers bars to celebrate. Have a good trip, Franco old boy, see ya' when you get back. We'll get a job up on Montgomery Street, sellin' stocks for Dow and Dupont. When the war's done, we'll get back to normal you know."

Franco stands up and heads to the door, "Cut the bullshit Gil."
He turns toward me, "You're falling out of your mind with war, man.
That's a black and white movie."

I move. First one hand, and then the other. One leg, then the
other leg. I lean forward and use my hands to push myself up slowly.
I swivel to where Franco is glaring from the doorway.

"Purple Owsley?" I hang a long pause while I look around the
room. When my gaze fixes on him I can't help myself, "Let's celebrate
then, old man. You in the Navy and me in the Army. The two of us
goin' off to feed the guys and kill the Congs."

"Listen, motherfucker," Franco leans forward, "I'm gonna chip
paint, and sleep and work on my thesis, and paint, and chip, and
stand watch and work on my thesis. Same thing as everyone else."

"Yeah? And every paint chip is a dead Cong," I crack. "You chip
away everyday and pretty soon there's no more Congs."

"Paint is paint, Gil, for Christ's sake. That's where you're screwed
up. You na-need to get out of the room and look around. Not so
good here, either. Let me show you. They're ka-killing Congs in
your own back yard."

"Sure, sure. Everyone's killing peasants in pajamas. It's all the
rage. Why should we act differently?"

"I don't have to convince you I'm not a soldier, man. I know who
I am. I'm human, like everyone else."

"That's your trouble," I shoot back. "You *are* like everyone else." In
theatrical mode, I watch my words slam into Franco's face and punch
through his eyes. Franco, who claims to be a free spirit descended
from the beats, flinches. I see him close up through my stilted eyes.
"You're a lost soul, like the rest."

"You're the General, man." Franco snipes back. "You plowed 'em
under in your make-believe war over in Africa. Ain't that just holy
and great." A grim look crosses his face, hollow and unsmiling. "I'm
livin' in the 'November of my soul', man. I have got to get out of
here."

"You go from the protest lines to feeding the soldiers so they can
kill more Congs."

Franco gets a little rattled behind his patchy beard and mousy brown hair. He shrugs. "I'm gettin' out of Dodge, man."

"You're copping out,"

"Three or four months on the open sea. The salt wind scrapes me clean. Combat pay in the war zone. I'm gonna make enough money to come back and open a hippie miniature golf course over in Marin."

I stand, not amused. "You're a fuckin' soldier, just like the rest," I tell him.

A bone-handled hunting knife in a brown leather sheath, a gift from my brother, rests next to a bible and a worn copy of *Siddhartha* on the overturned milk crate next to the mattress.

"Merchant sailors don't kill," Franco says. "You're fucking scared, aren't you?"

"You freak me out, Franco." I pace the floor. At least I'm out of bed with agitation. With a solemn pacing limp, I aim to wound, "Protesting the war and then delivering war supplies?" I pick up the knife and slap it across my palm.

Franco folds his arms, "The whole economy's involved, man. I march in the marches, and I work when I need the money."

"You're a phony," I shoot back. The bare words out of my mouth, spinning in the air stun him. For effect, I withdraw the knife from its cover and point it toward Franco. "You're fucking right I'm scared," I say.

"So, that makes everything better?" Franco eyes the knife almost as a dare.

"Do you wonder if I'm capable of using this."

"You're a killer, really, you know that, Gil? Always ready to go over the top." Franco stays anchored with his arms across his chest.

"Hey man the war's just beginning for me," I say.

"Don't count on it," Franco's says with enthusiasm.

I step toward Franco, "I kill you with my knife and I'm hung for murder. I kill a Vietnamese and I'm a hero."

"War is a kind of perverse freedom, man." Franco's goading voice rings in my ears.

I slap the side of the knife across my hand and run the blade over the inside of my fingers. *What am I doing? How far must I take this to convince myself I'm sane.* "Do I now understand Van Gogh? So easy to do in the right frame of mind."

"Of course, the right frame of mind is everything," Franco says.

"Out in the jungle, if a little girl or an old woman hunting up firewood scared me, and I'm in the killin' frame of mind, I might shoot them or run them right through with my bayonet." I see blood dripping into wet rice paddies.

"Such holier than thou bullshit," Franco puts his hands in his pockets; he's posing without a defense. "If you were in the right frame of mind," he repeats.

He's daring me, I think. "The politicians torture us into obedience with guilt and pride." I move closer to Franco.

He's glowering. "You can say that." Franco contemplates the knife. "Come on stick me with your knife if you can find the guts."

"When you're in enough pain, you'll kill anyone they tell you to," I say, wondering how much pain undergirds my numbness.

"Maybe," Franco says. "Maybe some people will kill." A touch of concern comes into his face. "Maybe we'll have one of these freak happenings you read about in the paper."

I place the tip of the knife against Franco's breast-bone, surprised to feel the pulse of his beating heart.

Franco does not move, "The downtrodden work the power button, too."

"The American Generals want everyone to have red splotchy faces with thin lips and bushy brows," I say as I increase my pressure on the knife and Franco sways backward. "Hamlet proves right. 'To be or not to be?' The phrase resists the rust of repetition, don't you think?"

"That's the first question," Franco replies. "What about the question that follows?" A glint flashes in his eyes.

I lessen the pressure on the knife. "What's that?" I ask, withdrawing the knife.

"The one Hamlet never asked." Franco catches me with the hook of his intellect. "What's the next question?"

I place the tip of the knife back on Franco's breast. "If I had to guess . . .," I stop. "I don't want to hear about Hamlet."

"Guess like your life depends on it," Franco says. "Could you run me through, right here, right now? You in a killing frame of mind?"

"It's your life that depends on it," I answer.

Franco heaves a sigh, "I would say his second question has to be, 'What will I do, if I choose to be?'"

I pull the knife away, and throw it. It brushes past Franco's ear, then the blade clangs against the closed door, bounces, and sticks into the hardwood floor.

Franco touches his hand to his ear, checking his fingers for blood, but does not miss a beat. "And ss-so what, my man?"

"I see it all happening. That's the pain. The pros and cons forcing me to one side or the other. The Generals haul my ass over to Vietnam and plant me under some rubber tree to get shot at, killed or maimed. And my honorable buddy Franco here, and Franco is an honorable man, guiltless and in no danger, my clean buddy Franco will deliver me Coca Cola and Snickers bars, so I can die with the taste of home on my lips. That could drive a guy crazy, honorable buddy, clean buddy Franco. That's what."

Self-righteous and indignant, I glare at the pockmarks standing at attention on Franco's reddening face. He turns and moves toward the door. As I turn a flash from the mirror catches my bony body in a torn T-shirt and faded jeans.

I manage to change the record before lying down, then resume the coffin pose and vacant stare through the ceiling.

Franco tries for a light tone. "Just the same, tonight we celebrate. Your physical and my departure."

"Maybe, man, maybe," I say, lazy, spent and angry as Franco leaves the room.

Longing for uncomplicated Africa passes through my body sweeping away the grime of this civilization. Voices drag me backward among crazy thoughts and heroic wishes. I cannot escape. I'm ordained in the blood of the lamb.

The Bells of Rhymney

◆

IN THE FOLLOWING WEEKS, somber and silent I attend classes take notes, go to the library, try to write a paper comparing Hamlet's attitude toward his mother and Ophelia, which sounds sexy, but leaves me cold. I can't seem to get a full breath. I no longer care about Hamlet; I don't care about Gertrude; not even Ophelia, who sometimes gave me a hard on. On the page or on the stage the thrill of Shakespeare's words cannot compare to the hallucinogenic visions and marvelous musings of my unmoored mind to access the entertaining fantasies of Denmark's court. The drugs have turned my mind into a television set — without having to move from my mattress.

I'm restless in the house on Steiner Street. Returning to my square, lifeless room each afternoon, a room with not one picture on the wall. Only the spines of books stare back at me from their various positions around the room — on the floor, on the desk stacked on a spare chair, placed randomly on the dresser, stacked under the window sill, on either side of the mattress. I'm oppressed by the ordinariness of the slanting ceiling and musty contents of this attic room — the mattress, the third-hand 1950s scratched maple desk and chair, and the bureau with a framed, foggy mirror.

I barely talk to a soul either at school or at home. I have cut myself off.

I watch from a perch inside the mirror, trapped by my deepest fears. I struggle to get out into the eternal sun-filled air. I open the window to catch a breeze, sweet to my nostrils, but I can't move. My thoughts weigh a ton. I cannot keep my head up. I yearn to be out — out of the race, out of the way, out of the running, out of demands, out of the ceaseless desires for more, out of the hunt, out of the wishes.

I am desperate to be free of the parade of to-dos to get ready for next day when the to-dos would be due and I would have not only to work on those due, but also on the to-do's for the following day; paying my dues, compounding my dues until God knows when, and then, there would come the dues-day.

The run-up, the run-in, the test, the paper, the end of the semester, the summer, the new semester, the new teachers, the new books, the new people — over and over. To do or not to do? That is my question. And stumbling between the weedy rows of all that I must hoe, are the weary, leaden feelings I must lug along. Must I begin and do it all over again? I am overwhelmed.

On the other side of the mirror, I read assignments without enthusiasm before going out to the basketball court. I'm irritable and unsteady, taking on a gloomy mood around Franco, refusing to join in the usual joking banter. I stop smoking. I ignore the guitar leaning in the corner, pass up several chances to visit Wayne.

I hear nothing about Karen or Joe. The thought of that Sunday afternoon chills my teeth and brings soreness to my soul.

I care to do nothing but go to the window and stare at the park in hopes of finding some sign of Kennedy's wake, some recognition my life might begin a new mission, something fresh and breezy that will sweep me into a new world. I long for that lurid and soul quashing afternoon with Karen to have reborn me in some way, for the memory of Kennedy . . . to free me for triumph.

I have decided not to go.

I'm trying to be happy about dodging the draft.

I've decided.

Have I decided?

Should I call it dodging? That's what they called it in WWII. My father went, but this is different. In Vietnam we are the aggressor. I made my mind up. I will not fight. I would drown in the mud. I'd served as a teacher in the Peace Corps. In spite of these two years, they would make me go and fight, too. But teaching was my contribution, recognized or not by the government, I'd taught for democracy. Now they wanted me to go and kill for democracy. I will not go. I will take a chance with my sanity. I will be marked down as a coward and a freak.

But I don't care.

But I do care. I will not go and kill people who do not threaten me. I will not fight on the whim of political diplomacy. It might not save me, but I will not be ushered into the hereafter with the heart of a stranger on the tip of a bayonet. I will not beat the government, but I will not lose my life and rightness.

Why not celebrate this very small decision? I could not call it a victory because I am losing some shred of myself as well, some nut and bolt of my sanity that I can never replace, some youthful grace and fearlessness, the full faith and belief that the great protector, destiny itself, would never allow me to pass into harm's way. Now, in my decision to triumph over the government I make myself vulnerable for the remains of my life.

A flash of the Ethiopian dream cuts my mind, the one I dreamed at the school for the blind the night before my life changed. I remember the children running . . . but I can't remember the dream. They were after me is all I remember, everyone is always after me.

Then, I muse about Karen, about the afternoon with her. Recreating her, her smile, her open fierceness. What I have been missing all of my life — fierceness. How she greeted me, warmed to me. I think about what if we'd just had a normal afternoon. No drugs, no kid, no separated husband, no death and no folly. What if we'd been like a movie, a young man and a young woman together on a Saturday afternoon? A walk in the park. What then? Too boring for the movies. Just about right for life, ever dramatic in its molting of the moment, lump in the throat, unexpected, true-to-life dreams, unlike movies.

What might have come about? Perhaps romance. A very sweet woman, exciting, intriguing with her posters of Che and Huey, Black Panthers for background. Her budding career as an actress. Just the right amount of mystery and fierce rebellion. I could dream about Karen without getting depressed. Her face floats before me. Her white cotton blouse, her breasts, her body, the tight V of her jeans, her smells, her smooth skin, her bright smile, her fierce eyes, her openness, her desires.

> O what will you give me?
> Say the sad bells of Rhymney,
> Is there hope for the future?
> Cry the brown bells of Merthyr.

"What?" I ask of the old tune. "What can you tell me?"

"Shame on you," another voice.

"Are you out of your mind? You didn't even get laid, man," a pigeon voice chimes. "Forget about that woman. She ain't for you. That kind will play you for a sucker, man. How bent on self-destruction are you? Get up now and walk, just like Jesus tells us. Jesus was a Jew, just like you. Get up and walk."

These voices, this Greek chorus that inhabits my mind. These chiming, rhyming tones that spin the atoms of my mind, shout the opposite of what I'm doing, what can be done. These negative voices — not to save me, but to save themselves, their haughty opinions, their prejudiced judgments, their common wants and needs, their degraded, unlearned comments on a world that does not concern them. Invented voices, wind-swept words, blowing through my mind, distorting my own thoughts, random voices that come from some other space-driven dream, not my own, worn-out words floating on clouds of these citizen bands I'm always trying to avoid. Family voices chiding, biting, cutting at my own warm rational desires.

How can I do anything else but lay on my bed staring through the ceiling. In thrall to a paralysis of guilt and shame. I'm aware of a vanished sense of purpose since moving in with Franco. I'm back in the mode that lacks ambition similar to how I felt when leaving Ethiopia. Flashes of green eucalyptus and pine baked into countryside shoot through my head. The village of Sebata, the trees, the small Arab bets where I would silently buy cigarettes, the food stalls, the fragrant tea shops all remain branded onto the landscape of my mind. Often I find myself wandering down its main street to the gravel driveway that leads to the school. Often I remember the men who rolled barrels of water up the hill from the small stream that served as the village water supply. When the school built a pump at the stream and put these same men out of work, some sabotaged the pump. Now, I feel bad for the men whose livelihood we took away with a simple water pump. What had the Peace Corps done there?

And then the dream. I'm trying to remember how the dream ended. We were all trying to help. That was the dream, the day he died. We were all trying, out of breath, puffing. Looking to the left, looking to the right, looking in back. We were all there trying, as the wages of war were brewing we knew not where. War is always breaking out. Peace is always trying. The dream got to me, but I have forgotten it again.

"Let's face it man, you're a lost ship." An inside voice, almost imperceptible, distant, familiar, coming from a roaring, spinning machine.

"You're depressed young man and you better shake yourself out of it." Is it the voice of Mrs. McCoy, my sixth grade teacher? She grew African violets on the windowsill. Is that what I went to fulfill? African violets?

"Your idealism done flown the coop, man. You need a transfusion," a vague black voice intones.

"Go to law school, Gil." My father's voice. "Go to . . ."

"You'd never make it through the first month. You don't have the strength." My high school voice.

"You're not smart enough." The childhood voice.

"You used up your idealism in the Peace Corps," say the voices of teachers.

"Become a corporation man. Teachers don't make enough money," says the voice of my father.

"Fuck the government." The voice of Franco. In my head?

"Forget the law. What about this insane war in Vietnam growing every day?" says a voice of my future. What kinda law is that?

"Go make some money. Go ahead. This market won't last forever," say the voices of my uncles.

"When will a sense of ambition return?" says my own worried voice.

"You're lost, my man." A bright flicker of red and a bluish flame spins through my brain, revealing Old Jim grinning, leaning on a pole. "I'm gonna fix you up, my man. I got a road to liberate yo' mind."

He stands at a path through an English garden similar to the one fronting Wayne's house. "Come on, my man, follow me. There's more to this world than meets the eye." Jim winks and disappears.

I take hold of Old Jim's message with sly arrogance. I'll become indestructible, a superman who knows no fear. I'll claim power . . . control. I'll be safe at last.

I try to fathom the accents of Old Jim, "We can turn the world on its ear."

For the first time in weeks I pick up my guitar with pleasure—

> O what will you give me?
> Say the sad bells of Rhymney,
> Is there hope for the future?
> Cry the brown bells of Merthyr,
> Who made the mine owner?
> Say the black bells of Rhondda,
> And who robbed the miner?
> Cry the grim bells of Blaina.

They will plunder willy-nilly
Cry the bells of Caerphilly,
They have fangs, they have teeth
Say the loud bells of Neathe.

Put the vandals in court
Say the bells of Newport,
All would be well if, if, if
Cry the green bells of Cardiff,
Why so worried, sisters, why?
Sang the silver bells of Wye,
And what will you give me?
Say the sad bells of Rhymney.

And then, another voice, the melodic tenor of Franco startles me. Is it real, from the living room or just another figment?

Come all you young fellas so young and so fine,
Seek not your fortune in the dark dreary mine.
It'll form as a habit and seep in your soul
'til the stream of your blood runs black as the coal.
It's dark as a dungeon . . .

"You gotta sing about the people, Gil, baby. You can't sing about bells." Franco pushes through the half-closed door towing a friend. "This here's Lenny."

I lay down the guitar, startled to see a stranger. I look to Franco with a half lemon, half quizzical look.

"I told you about Lenny the Traveler . . . who gave me the hash pipe from Nepal." Franco spreads his arms and motions toward Lenny. "In the flesh."

I size up Lenny, who resembles an elf, with wisps of brown hair hanging over his ears and an expression of no comment on his lips. He is wearing black silk Chinese slippers, a pair of faded-red jeans and a yellow pajama top over his thin torso. I try hard to hide my surprise at a prominent red dot painted on Lenny's nose, but I stare nonetheless.

"Hiya." Lenny squints and gives a wave. He holds a small vinyl suitcase in the other hand.

"Lenny an' me grew up together," Franco explains. "Lenny's gonna stay in my room for a couple days. I'm staying over at Lorraine's." Franco had been keeping company with Lorraine lately, a classmate who lived nearby.

"Glad to meetcha." I extend a hand.

Lenny nods in place of a handshake.

Handshakes are uncool. I forgot.

Beyond the doorway, behind Lenny, I detect a slight movement.

Franco hesitates, then goes to the door and brings in a pale girl, 17 perhaps, who looks 13. She's the exact height of Lenny, dressed in loose pants and black Chinese slippers, a white blouse under a worn yellow sweater. She, too, has a red dot painted on her nose. She smiles through drawn lips.

"Meet Lenny's old lady, Libby." Franco brings her into the room. She carries an identical vinyl suitcase. "They're gonna stay here a few days," Franco grins, "You don't mind, huh?"

"I guess not," I let out.

After an awkward moment, Lenny brings out a curious hand-carved ivory pipe and a chunk of hash. "Try some of this," he says.

Lenny walks into the living room. Libby and Franco follow.

I hesitate, but join them, shuffling from my room. They sit around the Formica coffee table, Libby on the floor, Franco and Lenny on the vinyl couch under the skylight. I lean against the wall. Each round I take my puff, reluctant, diffident, but puff I do, handing the pipe to Libby without looking. The ritual plays out in silence.

Lenny opens his bag and pulls out a piece of cloth that he unrolls and holds against the wall for all to see. The hand-embroidered sign proclaims, "As you meander the curvy road of life — drift proud, chew well and leave no turn unstoned."

Lenny laughs a naughty, forced laugh as he tapes the cloth sign to the wall.

I try to raise an eyebrow when I notice a patch on the sleeve of Lenny's pajama top that reads, "Grain Ranger."

I move my head back and forth a few times, muttering. No one pays attention.

Libby grins a wide Yogi-bear grin.

Lenny points to the Grain Ranger patch on his arm and grins back. "Help prevent forest fires," he says.

I wonder how Lenny knew I'd been thinking of a bear.

Franco and Libby laugh and snort.

These folks appear somewhat strange, I comment to myself. "You look pretty straight to them," a voice in my head replies.

"Remember the Two Thousand Year Old Man?" Franco asks Lenny.

"Back then, a good job could of been watching the clouds?" Lenny says.

"Let 'em all go to hell but Cave 7," Franco says, breaking into laughter, causing Lenny and Libby to snigger and laugh.

I try a laugh too, but I don't get the joke. "What's that mean?" I ask, but no one hears.

"Welcome to Cave 7," says Lenny. "Right here."

"Let 'em all go to hell but Cave 7." Franco repeats.

After the hash expires, Franco nods to Lenny and Libby. The three walk toward Franco's room, leaving me leaning against the wall. I'm abandoned, watching them disappear down the hall into a fog. I retreat to my room, plop on the bed, stoned into a dreary aimlessness.

ALONE, MY MIND MARVELS at voices in my head. Have they been there all the time? They don't sound out of place, but I can't remember them. Hadn't I just been answering to voices an hour ago? Of course, they haunted me, but I never listened to their incessant whisper before. But now, the Greek chorus in my mind chants in earnest unison, "Face it man, you're lost. You're depressed young man. Idealism is gone, man. You need somethin' else now. Go to law school."

"Not that grind," I respond.

"You're too dumb. You spent your idealism in the Peace Corps. Now, wake up. You're a natural corporate man. Let's get the government." This war's killing us. Make the cash."

"No ambition. I can't make cash in a country that's killing women and children."

"You're lost, man, you need to get fixed. More to this world than meets the eye, meets the I, meets the eye."

My mind explodes. A weird high-pitched blender sound enters the sudden baroque room of my head. I doubt if I can study. The thought of reading a book nauseates me. I can't curl my hand around the guitar either, so I settle for drifting off while the objects in the room dissolve into an album of misty colors.

I awaken suddenly. God, my mouth is as dry as beans. Lenny is knocking.

He pokes his head through the doorway, nods toward the kitchen. "Food," he says in his silent way, leaving the word "food" hang in the air.

I rub my eyes and follow Lenny to the kitchen where four neat place settings are laid. In the center of the table steam hovers over bowls of rice and vegetables. Entering the kitchen, I shiver, cold and groggy, wondering where I've been the last few hours.

"Good food," Libby grins. Lenny and Libby grin. Chopsticks replace forks on a folded paper napkin next to each plate.

I look for the three bears to show up any time.

"Those red dots painted on your noses for a reason or do you have a type of measles?" I ask — a wisecrack I immediately regret.

Lenny and Libby giggle.

"Dig in." Lenny reaches for the bowl of rice. Libby spoons vegetables onto my plate, broccoli, carrots, cauliflower, greens and red cabbage. Lenny puts several spoonfuls of golden brown rice onto my plate before serving himself.

The plates filled, Libby murmurs, "Giver of life, Giver of light, we thank you for your bounty, Amen."

"Amen," Lenny agrees.

"Franco didn't show?" I venture after a minute of fumbling with my chopsticks.

"Uh huh." Lenny scoops up the vegetables and rice.

I thought he'd show. I damn Franco for abandoning me with these two weirdos. He could've stayed for dinner the first night.

Franco, I am learning, has a way of leaving me hanging in the air on one of his jerry-rigged schemes, never quite revealing all the details. Several times Franco planned to meet me, and then didn't show. One time we were going to a play and I arrived early and bought tickets — and Franco never turned up.

I notice that Lenny and Libby chew on their first mouthful for a long time. Whatever food I'm able to balance between the two sticks falls on the way to my mouth. After several tries, I retrieve a fork from the drawer, deliver a forkful of the vegetables directly into my mouth and start chewing, too. My mouthful doesn't last. Lenny and Libby are still chewing on their first bite. I take another. The rice, dark and hardy, tastes of exotic spices; the steamed vegetables taste bland except for a little soy sauce. Before I can chew more than a few times, the food slides down my throat.

"Every mouthful 40 times," Lenny tells me after finishing a mouthful.

"Forty times." Libby adds.

"Forty times?" I repeat. I take another mouthful and count each clenching of my incisors. Before number seven, my left hand starts on the next forkful. Chewing and chewing, I notice my mind looking around the room for something else to do. Hey, I'm observing the workings of my own mind. Now, if I'm the one watching my mind, who's thinking the thoughts? Oh, man, what a split.

Libby keeps her eyes down. Lenny chews with his eyes closed. I chew with renewed energy . . . 37, 38, 39, 40. I swallow the lukewarm mush trying not to taste.

The meal continues in silence, but for the sounds of chewing. Lenny and Libby look up from time to time, grinning. Watching the muscles of Lenny's jaw work the food, I concede these two brim with soul.

"Franco's not gonna show," I say.

"Musta got hung up," Lenny says between mouthfuls. "He's takin' care'a some business up on Haight." Lenny has a twangy Eastern Shore accent.

"What kinda business?"

"Hey man, we all got business." Lenny tweezes a chunk of broccoli in his chopsticks and fills his mouth.

Lenny's comment has a mocking effect on me. I wonder, *do I have business?*

Lenny and Libby talk me into chewing one mouthful of food 40 times. I can't believe I surrender, even though it makes sense. These people shock me and attract me. I never met people so determined to live outside the mainstream. If I let them, they could possibly teach me to see the world differently. Since my return from the Peace Corps, I have sensed that the world is falling to pieces. When I met Franco, the direction of my life changed. I had been planning to become a teacher, maybe a college professor, find a wife and have a family, but Lenny, Libby, and Franco's other friends track away from society.

Really, I don't think I can put up with this. I feel alarmed, but I can't put my finger on the feeling. I'd better start looking for another place to live while I can. *If Lenny can convince me to chew a mouthful of food 40 times, what next? A red dot on my nose?*

My chewing is interrupted by Lenny.

"We're not gonna hurt you, man," he says. "We're lookin' to make another kind of space, cause the one we come from turned out fucked. Uh, hah?" Lenny returns to chewing, demonstrating again that he could read my mind.

Libby raises her eyebrows and grins.

These friends of Franco scare me.

The conversation continues . . .

Gil: "I lived in Ethiopia. They got problems over there, real problems. It's different, too. Real different."

Libby: "Why'd you go over there, man?"

Gil: "To help."

Lenny chuckles, hoots to himself: "We're the ones need help."

Libby: "We have great injustice here at home, we need cataclysmic justice on the order of a flood."

Lenny: "It's the same here as there, man. Ignorance and greed. People play the same, man. The strong ones dominate the weak and take what they want. It don't take no genius to see that."

Gil: "We're at least making some progress here, man, and OK, we're working on the problems." (I could grasp the great injustice of the world while I lived in Ethiopia, but I don't want to think hard about home. I don't want to hear these bozos put the Land of the Free into the incinerator. We have problems, all right. I heard it all before. Why listen to these two? Too much chewing.)

Libby (throwing me a "don't you get it look"): "We need something."

Gil: "Wait. Look at all the freedom we have — all the social mobility."

Libby: "What do we do with the freedom. That's the problem. We keep doing the same old stuff. Greed and wars, feast and famine."

Lenny: "Things ain't got much better since the Bible. If we don't start making a new world, the whole thing's gonna blow up. Look at our parents, fearful from the depression, terrified from the war, making and spending money hand over fist."

Lenny (pointing his chopsticks): "We're their trained acrobats, man."

Libby: "We're draining the earth to make trinkets. Do we make progress if half the world starves and the other half eats too much?"

Lenny looks up from his plate and stops chewing, "Everyone's wearing plastic doodads on their lapels and cruising around in these cars, big as shrimp boats. We're burning up the earth's blood."

Libby: "They're hawking our heritage. Another war now, to destroy our generation."

Lenny: "We have to start a New World, man. Make things different right here, man? You went all the way over to Africa. Now you got to do something here, man. You mighta' just as well stayed over there and lived on the government."

Gil: "I don't know, what can we do?"

Lenny: "The first thing we got to do? STOP. Just stop everything. You dig? Stop the little things — like buying and selling and accumulatin' money and bribing people. We got to get everybody to stop. Then we got to stop the big things."

Gil: "What do we do if we stop buying and selling?"

Libby: "Trade. Barter. Get rid of money."

Lenny: "Money remains the root of all evil. The very root. That's what it says in the Bible, man."

Libby: If we don't cut out the rotting roots of this society, there's no hope."

Lenny: "They got the final word in these bombs, man. You can have hope with bows and arrows, but not with the stuff these guys have. And they'll use it, man. They proved it."

Gil: "The death of Kennedy proved there's no hope for the brave and the true, no hope for the ones who want to make a better world. don't know. The world's been goin' on like this for a long time. There's nothing we can do to turn it around. I tried, man, I know. Over in Ethiopia — all over the world, man. They just want to come here and live like we do. I swear."

Lenny: "That's because the backward-looking types and the ones who want to make bigger bucks stop us at every turn. We got to change these boys. We got to make 'em see the light. We got to turn 'em all on. We got to get to the money people and show them we can live without it. You grow me food, I'll build you a house. Like that. We don't need middlemen. We're a country of middlemen – middlemen for the middlemen, everyone taking a little off the top. So we're all slaves, man, slaves."

Gil-thinking: Maybe these pajama people in Chinese slippers with a dot on their nose can show me the light after all. How else would I ever see it? Am I in school to learn how to teach children to become their parents? Force them to become part of the long human chain to buy more trinkets so they can hold up their end of the gallows? We gotta find more. Maybe these two know. We've got to change direction.

These freaks in San Francisco don't accept the world that's been handed to them . . . like I did. What about Kennedy now? Here's the crises. What the hell did he talk about? Did I listen, really? What rot. What bullshit. What did he do about this country? Sending us off to Africa when we should have been sent down south to register voters and into the cities to teach. Just romance pure and simple that lured me to Africa and led me away from the disgrace in my own country? I never thought about here. The Peace Corps a diversion? Oh, man? So, Kennedy, what the fuck? What do I do now? Franco is right. But what about these people. They're different. They don't understand about the dream.

Gil: "What about God?

Libby: "What kind of God allows humans to slaughter in his own garden?" That's their God. They bought him from some ancient market and force us to believe — that's the true mystery?"

Lenny: "There's endless mysteries, man. We should figure' out the mysteries."

I must admit that this new way to see life makes sense. I don't need convincing, I just need to be free. I hear their righteous words. I've been converted. Let me join with these anti-forces, because I feel changes in the wind. Far out, man.

The meal takes about 45 minutes. My jaws ache.

"Good food." Libby lays her chopsticks across her plate.

I'm fighting my growing admiration for these two. They're right . . . a new kind of world. Important what you put into your body, good whole food, not the plastic canned and frozen vegetables I grew up on.

"Eating's nourishment for the soul." Libby touches her chopsticks delicately, averting her eyes. "Fuel for our temple."

She's a pretty woman, small boned, with her brown hair cut short, the fine features of her face thin and aching, she wears her vulnerability without reservation, open and a little hostile.

93

In spite of my doubts, I am swept away with great energy as I help Libby clear the table. I wash the dishes, rinsing each one with care. I take charge of the wooden chopsticks, drying each one and standing them in a cup. I wipe up the crumbs from the table, and scour the sink and drain board. After Lenny and Libby retire to Franco's room I empty the two large cupboards over the counter, wipe off the shelves with a sponge and wash each cup and dish. I mop the floor and consider washing the kitchen walls. I finish with a sense of home.

I return to my room and close my eyes, and watch a faint array of colors drift through my mind. Nourished and serene, I nestle in the bed, comfortable with my own thoughts.

About nine o'clock Lenny comes into my room to share a joint. He sits on the corner of the mattress. "A stranger is the furthest part of yourself," Lenny tells me. The sound of Lenny's voice and his far off smile fades into sleep.

I am startled awake in the cold light of stars shining through the bare window. Where have I been? Swimming in another strange country? Hammering, hammering in slow motion, under water. I'm building a house. I'm wet with perspiration – a rain of confusion. Drowning, I remember drowning, gasping. "I have to breathe," I whisper into the eerie starlight. I lay on top of the blanket, struggling with a scrap of guilt for still being dressed in my jeans and shirt in the middle of the night.

An anxious thought confirms that I have turned a bend in the road and discover myself moving in the opposite direction from the one I'd been traveling. I undress in the cool San Francisco night feeling light and strange and apart from my old self; I crawl between the sheets. Pin pricks of distress surface behind my closed eyes. What if this new life turns into a mask for real life. Could this be a mistake? Franco and his bizarre friends have lost all sense of ambition. Why am I here among them? I feel helpless to move out of the grasp of this new life. Shouldn't I struggle to get away from these people?

"Come on," the voice of Old Jim from the river asks. "Where's your sense of adventure?" Jim the runaway of adventure?

"These people may prove dangerous," I think.

"There's no danger here," Old Jim says. This shadow, the voice of my companion, urges me to break out of my old life.

"You ring like danger," I say aloud.

The shadow laughs softly, "You have no trust, that's your problem. You see the door, but never walk through. You always be on the outside."

"I don't care what's on the other side."

"Oh, indeed you do. More than anything, you care. You want to be part of what's on the other side. I say, let's go find what's there."

"*No*," I think hard into the cloud of my thoughts.

"You know you can't resist," this shadow voice smiles. "Let me paint you a mural."

A flash of green Ethiopian mountains. The city of Addis breaks into my consciousness. Women laboring under bundles of wood crowd the dusty city streets. Beggars, lepers without fingers and noses. Crying children plagued with flies. A world of poor people struggle for food. Scenes of wars, women and children fried in gas chambers. A slide show of mankind marches through countless slaughters, a murderous rampage from the caveman to this very moment in the flaming jungles of Vietnam. This shadow paints the Guernica of my soul.

"*Must be something better on the other side of that door,*" I think.

"To step through this door be your destiny," shadow Jim whispers.

"*Leave me alone.*" I bury my head under the pillow. I long for a joint to help me return to the point when Jim visited just hours before. I could wake Lenny, but no, how uncool. Am I crazy? Getting addicted to this stuff? My palms sweat.

"The company you keep marks the direction of your life," my father warns.

I imagine Lenny offering my father a joint and painting a dot on his nose. No charge, Mr. Stone. An honor to paint a dot on the nose of a veteran, sir.

I can't remember being high. I close my eyes, trying to conjure high with my mind, but that doesn't work.

Childhood fears haunt me among the swaying trees outside the window. Wispy creatures with angular faces glide through the dark.

In frustration, I throw off the covers and sit up determined to go over to Haight Street to find something to smoke. I move into the dark living room, peering down the hall hoping to see a light under Lenny's door. No luck.

I creep back to my bed where I turn from one side to the other. I count raindrops, offer perorations to God. After hours of wrestling with angels and other beings, I toss and turn then fall into a fitful sleep.

Waking, I turn from the window, pull my pillow over my eyes, but can't sleep. Finally I roll off the mattress and pull on a pair of jeans. Morning light has broken. Not a stir in the house.

In the kitchen, I punch a spoon through a biscuit of shredded wheat. The voices return.

"Oh, what will you give me," say the bells of Rhymney

"Shame. You're outta your mind."

"Do I know that voice?"

"Face it man, you got no cool." The hip voice I purloined from paperback Kerouac in high school, but never dared whisper aloud.

"You need a transfusion."

"Who?" I wonder.

"Make a plan and follow it." My father's voice mixes into the marble swirls.

"You're not good enough. This smug doubt."

"If I could strangle that voice."

"Fuck the law. They've got us killing babies in the name of the law, fer Christ's sake."

"My voice or Franco's, or Lenny?"

"Oh, what will you give me, say the bells of Rhymney."

"I'll give you everything," I say out loud through a mouthful.

"Look out you murdering fools. We're gonna stop ya," I gurgle, pleased to hear the vigor of my words.

Spooning the sweet crackling wheat into my mouth, I am aware of an awkward affection for Franco and Lenny and Libby. These people arrived in my life to rescue me from wishing the world were a better place, by changing the way the world lives beginning with myself. I'm not in the Peace Corps, lonely witness to the rugged and uneven burdens of existence. I'm putting my own life on the line, living the way I believe. I can't keep the smile from spreading across my face. I have begun the passage toward my birthright.

I finish the bowl of cereal and, rather than give up the moment, have another. The fatigue of the long night fades. While I dawdle on the second bowl, Lenny comes out of the back bedroom and waves on his way to the bathroom. On his return trip, he ducks into his room and returns in a blink holding up a joint with the trace of a smile on his lips.

"Thanks," I say, taking it. "I believe you're reading my mind."

Lenny presents a broad grin and scampers to the back.

I eye the joint all the way to my room, rolling it between my fingers, feeling the uneven heft of it, and place the lumpy caterpillar on my desk. I sprawl on the bed and pick up a textbook, *Teaching the Difficult Student,* Channel and Louey, and open to the bookmark.

Glancing over to the desk, I spy the joint, then try to bring my attention back to the book. I read a paragraph. My eyes return to the joint. Christ, it's seven a.m. Back to the book, I pick up a pen and look for a sentence to underline.

Ten minutes later I jump up, light the joint with a sheepish glance toward the door, and take a long deep inhale . . . and then another. I put the joint out with a spot of saliva between my fingers, copying Franco. After that first rush, a little unsteady, I sense flying out of clouds, heave a sigh. Lying on the bed, I take a few more breaths, place my hands behind my head and stare out the window beyond the trees; the sky's bluer, it swallows me whole.

The phone rings — I spring from my smoky reverie.

"Hey, man, Mr. Gilbert Stone?" asks a voice with a ring of familiarity.

"It's seven in the morning. Who's this?" I ask.

"Better check your watch, pal, it's almost ten."

"God, I'm late." I recognize Noonan's voice, then doubt myself.

"Name's Busby, Ernie Johns gave me your number."

The familiarity of the voice continues, insistent in my head.

"Sounds like Noonan," I say into the line. "Noonan from the Peace Corps."

"Noonan's dead."

"Dead?"

"Yeah, dead. Hate to break it to you like this, pal."

"Sure, and I'm talkin' to Santa Clause in hell."

"Noonan's dead, I'm tellin' you. I'm his old friend, Busby, an' I wanna meetcha. Can I come 'round."

"Here? I'm late for class."

"I'm in the Fillmore District somewhere. What's the address? Won't take long, just to say hello."

"Steiner Street. 814 Steiner."

"See you in 10 minutes."

In less than five, the doorbell rings.

I buzz the caller in and walk down to the second-floor landing, waiting for him idly with my hands in my pockets.

He huffs and puffs his way up the stairs, under some heavy burden.

"Jesus Christ, I'm gonna get a fuckin' nosebleed," he says.

I recognize that it is Noonan right off, but there's something different about him. He carries a heavy Army duffel bag over his shoulder, red hair sticking out from under a black slouch hat. His stocky body draped in an Army trench coat, pulled tight with the belt and buckle fastened. Under the coat, I spot trendy jeans. Noonan's wearing cowboy boots.

Following up the stairs behind my former Peace Corps buddy two young women who appear to be twins; they sport identical denim outfits and cowboy boots, long blond hair parted in the middle, and blank, noncommittal looks on thin Aryan faces.

Noonan looks over his shoulder, past the two girls, down the stairwell craning his neck before he turns to me. "Busby, here." He extends his hand. "That fart Noonan told me all about you. Says, you're a real swell guy. One of the best. Tells me you were in the Lincoln brigade together. I can rely on you."

I force a wry smile, ready, for the sake of old-times, to go along with his story. I examine this made-over character, and take in the two girls who stand behind Noonan-Busby on the top step before the landing. Noonan appears thinner, his face redder than I remember, sunken, hollow cheeks, without any trace of boyish fat.

"Noonan, you arrogant son-of-a-bitch. I thought you were in Boston."

I stretch my mouth into a grin, resisting my accustomed subservient mode. After nearly two years Noonan still casts a shadow of unworthiness between me and the sun, confounding my right to feel first in my own heart, but I buck the memory in me. I'm almost excited to see him.

"Busby's the name, fella. Noonan died in Cambridge, in Harvard Yard, among the ruins of those ancient red brick buildings. Puked himself to death. Right on the steps of the library. Died in my arms."

I lead the way up the winding staircase into the attic apartment.

"Jesus," Noonan puffs, "you livin' with Rapunzel or something?"

The girls — ladies in waiting — follow.

"Meet Moonstroke and Weebie," Noonan says entering the apartment and dropping the duffel bag in the same breath. Looking around the room, he removes his hat to reveal the full glory of his red hair. "Man, a hippie pad."

"Who you tryin' to fool, Noonan?"

"I'm on the run, man." Noonan puts his finger to his lips and glances over his shoulder. "The Draft Board's been trying to suck Noonan into the Vietnam action," he whispers. "Noonan's a dead man."

I shake my head. "I know whatcha mean, man," I reply with a trace of sympathy.

"Busby's the name. Busby from Berkeley. Old Noonan, what a guy, old times in Africa, old shakes, stories for the grandchildren."

I relax, surveying the outlandish fellow Noonan has become, with a red ponytail dangling from the back of his head.

"Whatcha got in that bag there, Mr. Busby?" I ask, curiously, and feeling strangely superior to this old nemesis, in my own place with him wanting something from *me*, "Wanna crash up here with the Rapunzels?"

"I got a proposition here, man," Noonan says, kicking the duffel bag. "You got a place where I can look out on the street?"

I usher him into my front bedroom with the view of Alamo Park.

Noonan goes to the window. He leans on both palms and scans the street from right to left.

"Nothin'," he says. "I knew I lost 'em . . . can't be too careful."

"Who you lookin' for?" I ask.

"Gotta be careful in this business," Noonan says, turning and walking into the living room. He slaps Weebie on the behind and kicks the duffel.

Weebie jumps. "Fuck you," she says.

The three of us circle the duffel bag as if paying homage to some kind of Stonehenge monument.

"I need a place to keep this for awhile," Noonan finally says.

"Old Army gear?"

Moonstroke brushes back her straight blond hair, and hands-to-mouth covers a laugh.

"Kind of," Noonan-Busby says. "No fooling, listen up."

My dislike of Noonan returns with the redhead's brusque manner. I didn't like him and I don't like him, good old days or not.

"I got some merchandise in here and I need a place to stash it for a while."

"What kind of merchandise?" I catch the drift.

"Some Mexican weed I came upon in my travels." Noonan keeps his eyes on the duffel, "Need a place to stash it for awhile."

He then walks down the long hallway toward the back bedroom, peers into the kitchen, opens the door to the loo, opens the narrow broom closet.

"Perfect," he says.

"Illegal contraband in my house?" I ask. "Your illegal drugs?"

"Hey, you gotta live like an outlaw to have a righteous life these days." Noonan pulls out a key on a chain hanging around his neck, squats down and opens the padlock.

I look around to see if anyone from the house is lurking.

Noonan opens the bag and fishes around inside.

Instead of considering this proposal, I begin to wonder if Noonan is more tuned to the people living in the house than I am. They're all dropping the last letters of words, liked they dropped a class; trying to sound tough, pretending they're from the street, inflecting their tones with Black slang. Noonan sounds like Lenny and Franco now. No more Harvard. No more Boston charming, cutting Irish upper crust accents. Everyone's just down home these days. Just folks. Imagine that. Even Noonan morphed into one of them.

Noonan pulls a package the size of a brick wrapped in plastic from the duffel. "Look at this stuff, man," he says holding the parcel up. He pulls out a pocketknife and cuts a generous piece off the brick, handing it to me.

"About a third of a key. Payment for keeping the shit in your closet for a few days until the heat backs off."

"What heat?" I ask.

"Oh, I don't know, I got people followin' me."

"So they follow you *here*?"

"Naw, I give 'em the slip before I got here. Nobody there when I looked out the window."

"I don't know, man," I stammer, handing back the cut package, half in cellophane with the rough edge of twigs and stems sticking out. "I don't know."

"You'd do a favor for your old buddy Noonan, if he wasn't dead, man. He'd remain much obliged if you'd do the same for me."

"I don't know, man," I squirm.

He pushes the dope back to me, "You scared of pigs and war mongers? Noonan told me I could count on you to stand up against the mindless ogres of the world. Lincoln Brigade, he said. You're a righteous guy if you get past all the do-gooding, you-go-before-me, sentimental, one-world, crap."

"I don't know, man," I say yet again.

"So, it's a deal," Noonan says, shaking my hand.

"A couple days," I relent.

There I stand, just as my father warned, playing with my future in the blink of an eye. No thought of the consequences. With a Harvard man, no less. Police raids, time in jail. Shame in the family. *What am I thinking?* The powers that be are slaughtering women and children on the other side of the world? Who gives a fuck about these murdering bastards and their laws?

"Sure thing," says Noonan, wrapping up the remains of the brick, and stuffing it back in the duffel bag. He snaps the padlock shut, hoists the bag, carries it down the hall and throws it into the broom closet.

"Wow, man," Weebe says.

"Good deed, man," Moonstroke tells me, her eyes catching me in a cautious flirt.

"Let's make like a sprocket and change gears," Noonan says as he hands me a joint the size of a cigar.

Heading down the stairs with the girls in tow, he waves and shouts, "See you in a couple days," before slamming the door.

I KEEP MY FIRST STASH of marijuana cleaned and wrapped inside a hand-painted Mexican box in the top drawer of my scratched maple desk. In my comings and goings, I smoke moderately in the evenings, allowing myself to drift off. When I smoke during the day, it takes a toke to clear my mind, never allowing the grass to interfere with studying, going to class, or shooting baskets. I pick up the guitar again, some evenings smoking half a joint while I pick out chords and croon folk tunes.

IN THE NEXT WEEKS, Lenny and Libby weave a trail of grains, vegetables and tofu through my life. I witnesses the two of them become stranger every day. Next to "Grain Ranger" on the sleeves of their pajama tops, Libby adds hand-sewn patches that read "Vegetable Villains," and "Rice Renegades." The red dots on their noses never fade. The pair of them become smaller and thinner in their loose clothes and Chinese slippers — they are like a pair of wind-up mice as they scurry about their business. More like twins than ever, they laugh in tiny squeaks, clapping their hands together in miniature movements.

Libby paints scenes in a large, watercolor pad from *Alice in Wonderland* and other children's books, or occasionally of episodes from Haight Street. My favorite, which I invite her to tack on the living room wall, shows two shadowy figures exchanging something in a doorway.

Lenny has retired from the life of a seaman and become secretive. I suspect he sells a little dope here and there, though he doesn't appear to do anything much more than bop around in his pajamas.

Though I begin to respect Lenny and Libby, I find difficulty accepting they have taken up permanent residence in the back bedroom.

"Hey man, you're always over to Lorraine's anymore," I finally say to Franco. "I thought we were roommates."

"We are, man but I got this thing going, you know."

FRANCO BRINGS ANOTHER fellow up to the apartment. "This guy's Bucky," he tells me.

Short with a small paunch, balding, Bucky has a square open face with the skin pulled tight around his jaw bone, and a scrappy, no-nonsense expression. He saunters into my room, his hands stuck into the pockets of his jeans and his head angled up. He flashes a guarded half-smile.

Open and easy in my own room, I shake Bucky's hand and show him a wide-open smile.

"Whatcha got behind that shit-eating grin?" Bucky asks.

"Just me." I feel my face get hot.

"Is that you, or that smile you?"

"I guess it's all me." I have no idea how to answer.

Franco interrupts, "Bucky's a poet, always lookin' for the truth."

"I'll try not to smile so big when you're around," I say. I'm trying to salvage my pride with cynicism again.

"Smiles don't interest me." Bucky looks around the room.

"Bucky's gonna stay in the back room with Lenny and Libby for a couple days. That all right with you?" Franco asks.

"I hoped we could have a couple more people stayin' here. It's kinda empty sometimes," I say, acid burning my insides.

"Hey, I hope you're not being sarcastic," Bucky says. He talks fast, not stopping for a breath. "Us sensitive types have a hard time around sarcasm. I puke a lot when there's sarcasm in the air. I like real sincere sincerity in the people around me, kind of a cushion, you know, like my mother's house. My mother has lots of cushions around. Sincerity makes me feel down to home. On the other hand, so many people think they're being ironic when they're being sarcastic, you know. Sarcasm turns on different wheels than irony. I can live with irony, but sincerity works best. You know why?"

I shake my head, still unsure of how to take this guy.

"I thought you might be interested, seeing how you're lookin' for truth, like me." Bucky gives me a big shit-eating grin. "When you're really sincere, it allows the people around you to be free. I think you'd agree it's important for people to do whatever they want, right?"

He turns toward Franco.

"Take Franco here," Bucky goes on. "I remember when he was afraid to stay out late and run around with the guys. But a bunch of us surrounded him with sincerity in our formative years, and today, — he's free as a bird. Not afraid to do anything, ain't that right, Franco. That's what sincerity will do for you." Bucky's eyes grow bigger. "It's not the sincerity itself, you see, it's the freedom it gives you. Ain't that right Franco?"

Franco fidgets toward the door.

What happened to my budding friendship with Franco? I wonder, feeling pissed and abandoned among Franco's lost childhood friends. I fell under the power of this fellow, Franco. Lenny and Libby curbed his ebullience, now this. I'm a prisoner.

Bucky wipes a hand on his jeans and holds it out to me. "You an' me'll talk about life. I can tell you're a real deep type," he says.

Franco winks, heading for the door.

I plop on my bed. The burn in my stomach is flaring. *Another stranger moving in.* This guy could have dropped off-the-wall from some germ infested library latrine. *I have no doubt Bucky will camp with them for more than a few days. I never bargained for these characters moving into my own space.*

On the other hand, meeting new people improves life.

I squirm, wanting to welcome these folks in spite of my unease, and now I'm not so sure about Lenny and Libby. Maybe they know something I don't. They live inside of secrets. I sense a sinister air about them. All these friends of Franco grew up big-city kids. Maybe they can teach me how to hang tough.

I close the door and steal to the desk drawer, withdrawing a joint from my stash. Slowly, secretly, I light the thin cigarette and savor the smoke. I retire to the bed and close my eyes, sinking into the luxurious cloud of drifting thoughts. The tension lifts from my body. I'm no longer bothered by new people in the house. "No big deal," I murmur, drifting off.

THE POPULATION OF THE HOUSE increases over the next months. People keep showing up. Some stay, some move on. Friends of Lenny and Franco, friends of Bucky, friends of friends. Crash becomes the operative word. "Mind if I crash here tonight?" They flop on the living room floor. "Can I crash for a couple days?" They use the shower and toilet, file in and out of the kitchen.

I keep to my room, worried, puzzled, opening the door a crack, venturing out to meet some of these itinerants, smoke a joint and retreat. I peer into my books under the harsh ceiling light, like a visitor, trying not to hear the restless sound of sleepers in the living room. I'm afraid the strangeness of these folks will begin to rub off on my own skin; I'm afraid becoming part this outlandish clan makes me a freak. I promise myself to get out and find another place, but I'm powerless to move. My limbs feel like concrete. I conceal my fear behind a wall of smoke.

One fellow, calling himself Indian Johnny, stays for weeks. He sits on the floor near the couch in the living room with his legs folded Indian-style, and sways with the breeze that whistles through the cracks in the skylight. He wears his fine, light-brown hair, long — down to his shoulders with a red bandanna wrapped around his forehead, Comanche style. He never utters more than a few words, never smiles, talks using make-believe sign language. He possesses an inexhaustible supply of weed, passing it out to whomever comes by.

The day after Indian Johnny disappeared, I knock on the part open door to Lenny's room and lean against the door-jamb. Lenny is siting on Franco's bed cleaning an ounce of grass in a shoe box lid. Libby sits next to him drawing. Bucky, the usual model of chatty, seems morose and reclusive. He huddles in the corner by the window reading and making notes on *The Decline and Fall of the Roman Empire,* a book he carries with him most times. *He must use speed,* I suspect.

"Its gotta stop." My voice cracks. "No more people in this house."

"Sure thing," Lenny says. Libby keeps her head down and nods.

There's an attitude in their acceptance, though. I pick up a look passing from Lenny to Libby that says, 'You don't know what's happening here, man. You're gonna act a square all your life.

"I thought all these people were your friends," Bucky says.

"Sure," Lenny repeats, "no more people."

Not knowing what else to say, I return to my room.

I'm a fool, I tell myself. I'm desperate to rest easy with this crazy life growing around me, but I have no idea how. Am I a hippie, a bohemian or am I crazy? Lenny and Libby have the right idea. I should stay cool and watch the parade, but these grotesque characters with shaggy hair, ragged clothes and no place to live unnerve me. I'm becoming transient myself with all the traipsing in out of the house. I feel sorry for them, but I dislike them; I see them headed straight to the garbage dump of society.

The next afternoon Bucky and a black fellow come struggling up the twisting staircase carrying a huge TV set that they manage to push and pull, sweating and groaning, into the living room. I watch from the doorway of my room. The cabinet and screen seem in good shape. They situate the set in the corner where Indian Johnny sat.

"This here's Lester," Bucky says. "Lester fixes anything's got wires."

Lester, standing behind the TV grins, showing a mouthful of crooked teeth. Overcome by the radiance of Lester's smile, I recognize a friend. I walk over to him and reach out my hand. "Glad to meet you." I smile for the first time in weeks.

"Lester and I is walkin' along," Bucky affecting his best street-wise accent, "an' we seen this here TV, over on McAllister near Fillmore, settin' by the curb, and I says to Lester, I bet you can fix this 'n. An' he says, maybe I can, but how we gonna get it back?' An' jus' then, one o' my buddies comes by in his cab, and I run out in the street and hail him down, an' we manage to load it into the trunk, and man here it is, and we got ourselves a TV. I bet anything Lester can make it work."

Why do these people insist on pretending they've been brought up in the street, when they're middle class? I steam behind my homogenized mid-west accent.

"We'll see now, we'll see," Lester says. Rubbing his goatee, he looks inside the rear of the set.

Lester manages to fix the TV — it picks up one channel. That night he sleeps on the living room floor. The next day, he shows up with a shopping bag and moves into the only unoccupied spot in the house, the kitchen.

A week or so after that, Wayne and Claire break up. Claire tells Wayne he has to move out so Joe can move in. Wayne, who pretends not to care, moves in with his guitar, a box of cooking utensils and a folding cot. He sleeps in the small alcove next to the stove.

That evening I lay on my bed counting the people and struggling with the notion to pick myself up and find another place. Lenny, Libby and Bucky live in the back bedroom, Lester and Wayne in the kitchen. Franco sleeps on the couch when he doesn't stay with Lorraine. A rag-tag assortment of strangers and semi-regulars crash on the living room floor. Noonan and his girls stop by every day or so to remove some of his stash from the hall closet and sometimes bed down on the hall floor.

Most mornings I wade through a full house to wait my turn for the bathroom. I'm ready to burst. *How did I get into this?* I smoke a joint to calm down. *Two people are sleeping in the kitchen!* A house filled with drifters.

I anticipate disaster, though I still maintain my own room because I pay half the rent.

Maybe it's not so bad after all. I don't mind having people around sometimes . . . I want all of them to like me. I want to be a member of Franco and Lenny and Bucky and Wayne's club.

I crawl inside my bubble of smoke where I've become comfortable, and from that vague and detached head of the pin, I determine to examine these transient lives parading before me.

Day by day I vow to make peace with these strangers.

> O what will you give me?
> Say the sad bells of Rhymney
> Is there hope for the future?
> Cry the brown bells of Merthyr,
> Who made the mine owner?
> Say the black bells of Rhondda,
> And who robbed the miner?
> Cry the grim bells of Blaina.

My mind projects the answers on my wall during the slow hours after midnight when the drama unfolds in the shadows of Shadrack and Abednego filing into Nebuchadnezzar's furnace, wrestling with angels. We have all come together in San Francisco to found a generation in the coming millennium, a generation destined to restructure the genes of society and teach the world how to live together. Far out, man!

Part II

Roll Over Beethoven

◆

IN EARLY NOVEMBER as the cherry-colored sun descends behind Alamo Park, Lenny bounds up the winding staircase into the communal attic apartment. "Look-it this! Look-it this!"

In the living room Wayne and I roast inside a haze of smoke. I'm leaning against the door-jamb of my room, Wayne is sitting on the floor with his back against the couch noodling on his guitar.

Lenny turns to me, rejoicing in a high, eager voice, "Groovy, eh?" as he flourishes a large fancy poster: "BENEFIT FOR THE SAN FRANCISCO MIME TROUPE." "It's a big benefit with bands and everything." I've never heard such enthusiasm from Lenny.

The gleaming poster features wavy lettering over swatches of fall colors with scattering leaves behind gold and red lettering. "FEATURING," it reads: "THE JEFFERSON AIRPLANE, FUGS, SANDY BULL, and the JOHN HANDY QUINTET." In the foreground a lone mime tips his hat.

I pass Lenny the circulating joint then take the poster in both hands, and examine the picture at arms-length like some long lost Egyptian papyrus.

I have difficulty making out the weird lettering at the top, but recognize the familiar style. "Very nice," I say.

"Libby done it." Lenny affects his most down-home ungrammatical speech in order to emphasize the poster's far-reaching importance. "So we got us this here big 'un to keep." He holds out a fistful of smaller handouts featuring the same design on red paper. I hold up the big poster for Wayne to see.

"Far out, man." Wayne says.

"It's gonna be groovy." Lenny beams.

ON FRIDAY NIGHT, the gang congregates in the apartment on Steiner Street. Lenny and Libby are sporting matching yellow pajama tops, featuring last year's Christmas holly and red berries. Wayne and Claire, together again, arrive decked out — Claire, as a deb from the 1920s with her hair up and a blue velvet dress, and Wayne, a cowboy wearing a red Western shirt with silver studs and spangles. Lorraine and Franco come up the stairs hand-in-hand. She, pretty and shy with light brown hair and a ready smile, is laced up in a frilly antique dress. Bucky and Lester are in their usual t-shirts, jeans and boots, and I have gone for my brown suede jacket, western shirt and striped britches.

We are standing around grinning and joshing in a cloud of good humor when Busby shows up in a bowler hat and tweed suit with his two sequined lady friends, Moonstroke and Weebie, in long cotton dresses, hoop earrings and lace-up boots. As he passes me he looks over his shoulder and swears to me that he had ditched the cops.

We walk in a group toward the Fillmore a few blocks away stoned and excited. The merry troupe, arm in arm, sing and skip down Steiner, flushed with a sense of something about to happen. Turning a corner, we are stopped short by a thousand, maybe two thousand people lining the block around Geary and up Fillmore waiting to get inside, two and three people abreast. Wayne whistles.

"Blows your mind, " Lenny says, eying the throng.

"Hey, far out, man." Bucky cocks his head toward the huge queue. "I never seen this kinda thing. It's a monster."

The assembled masses, most in their 20s, sport youth, flaming and bright. Many are got-up in costumes — painted Indian faces, pirates with earrings and tattoos — but most are wearing costumes much like ours. There is a strange symmetry, an otherworldly, ortho-dox match that casts a oneness over the whole of us. Not a business jacket, shirt or tie to be seen.

The cheerful crowd, a singular animal, eager and spirited, bucks against the gate, impatient to enter.

To my surprise, I feel as hopeful as the day I arrived at Peace Corps training, when I first realized how I'd struggled to be among these people, pursued them in dreams, and finally now find myself fit and ready for travel.

They are spread before me: a bubbling, rolling force, a seam of color along Geary Street and around the corner for blocks and blocks. My little band walks along the snaking line to find the end, sporting a jaunty air, joking and gaping. Camaraderie lingers in the crisp November air. I find an unexpected bond among my houseful of outcasts.

"Do you smell it?" Busby jabs me in the ribs.

He smells grass blowing in the wind. This amounts to more than smoking in the woodshed; this smoke floats on danger. Where had these people come from?

Franco, squiring Lorraine by the elbows nods, "We're among freaks." He points toward a tall fellow wearing pajama bottoms, with his bare chest painted in tattoo designs. "Queequeg!" Franco punches me on the arm.

The line moves fast in fascination with everyone cast into the good nature of the emerging glow. We buy tickets and walk up one flight. Libby's poster is plastered on every available wall. The sheer number of them bring a festive, leaf-strewn gaiety to the entourage. Libby tries to keep a straight face. Holding her hand, Lenny is bop-ping up the stairs in his Chinese slippers. Clanging rock music rolls into the scruffy lobby. The anteroom opens to a narrow hallway. I hang back at one of several large doors leading to a room the size of a high school gymnasium. No seats. People stand, listening to the music with their arms folded. Against the far end, a stage looms, rigged with a mountain of speakers and wires.

A young girl with long brown hair and wearing jeans sings and shouts, backed by a ragged group of musicians whose long hair, jeans and cowboy boots brings them right down from the stage with their siren of thundering music spiked with a twisting thread of electric guitar. The group has the improbable name of Jefferson Airplane. I had seen the group at the Matrix — surprised at the audacity of their name, the spark of their music and their complete ease with outlaw lyrics. The crackling, rhythmic music sounds new and moves my body in outrageous, impatient, uncontrollable and hidden desires.

The auditorium smolders. Lamps from the balcony project swirling images on the floor and ceiling, setting off the crowd in flashing radiance. Spinning and turning, gyrating to the music without touching each other, a few couples are gradually swept up by the driving rhythm flooding the floor with vigorous force drawing in others. Raising temperatures, exploding kinetic energy into dynamic waves of bouncy, bending, flexing movement. The beat infuses the very air of the dank building and transforms the ancient catacomb of the Filmore from of the tame juking days of grandfathers into an arena of young bodies, aborning the exuberant snaking sexual revolution of a new nature of beings.

My mind stops. Dancers skip across the light-splashed floor. I shout to Franco above the music, "Too far out, man, too weird."

"Very far out," Franco looks around. "Here's the jewel in your Ethiop's ear," he says above the music.

The words "weird" and "strange" fit. For no apparent reason other than I can no longer contain the expression of my energy and power, I hug Franco and Lorraine. I dance with them for a few moments, allowing myself to be caught up in the whirling lights, hidden and yet found inside this effervescent throng.

"Who thought this stuff up?" I look from Franco to Lorraine to Wayne to Lenny. "Whose brainchild?" I ask.

The music pounds and staggers me into a trance. Looking around this great whirl, I fantasize that President Kennedy is standing just

114

inside the large paneled doors, peering in on the multicolored throng. He is dressed in a tuxedo, taking it all in. Perhaps he stopped by on his way to a political dinner, a car waiting for him curbside while he comes up for a look-see at this new catch in the framework. What is he thinking? Does he feel the excitement? Does he understand the power rocking though this hall? Is he keen enough to feel the booming changes? I believe that Kennedy recognizes this generation. He looks around and wonders how he might use this fierce rolling energy to put things right.

Many in the crowd listen to the music in small groups, watching the wild dancers driven by the music into frantic rhythms. I sense bodies from an exotic tribe tramping out the rhythm of a new world. The music intensifies. More dancers move to the center of the floor riding the beat of a wild new rock and roll. Lights flash, bouncing around the room in a whirling star-drenched sky.

Franco and Lorraine sway and twitch in tune with the people around them.

Though I try to hold back, my body stirs. I tap my feet, swoosh and sway. I am carried off with others dancing by themselves, drifting near the center; chased by lights; the music tugging and pulling.

I find myself dancing in rock-and-roll sync next to a beauty with long auburn hair. Our eyes do not meet, though a smile flickers when we come close.

I follow her elastic body. She has done herself up in a long dress of shimmering white, with blue flowers that flash in the light. Her arms and body whirl in modern dervish moves. I'm impressed and then charmed.

I keep dancing, hoping she will stick around. After bobbing and weaving in an intricate and sometimes awkward shuffle, I point to myself and mouth, "Me Gil."

"Suzanne," she whispers between the notes. She demonstrates a graceful little turn, strutting back to face me with a devilish smile that knocks me back into a shuffling, self-conscious imitation. After watching Suzanne for a time, I aim for a semblance of grace. She holds her body erect with her long neck and smile flickering in the light. Our eyes catch. She twirls with flair, her arms, legs and torso moving in the right places. She's an ethereal vision, an amulet of magical effect gliding on the lights, her body a perfect expression of herself.

Once, when I lose myself in the beat, drifting off on my own, in and out of the other dancers, Suzanne pulls me back, drawing this long-time non-dancer close to her. Sensuality grips me in a bump and grind released by the music. I'm the Elvis of my school days — banned from the waist down.

I catch sight of Lenny and Libby through the flashing lights, moving together in a half rhythm, bending their legs and bouncing. Looking closer to see their painted faces, Lenny shows his big bear grin, and bops over to me, "Ain't this groovy, man?"

"Yeah," I nod, the only words I can rouse. "Yeah."

I'm absorbed in Suzanne's long, slim body moving around me. For much of the time, I bounce and shuffle while my upper body remains stiff. Never finding what to do with my arms, I finally come to a compromise by letting them hang loose as a kind of ballast to my careening body.

Suzanne, self-assured, senses my awkwardness and moves closer, takes my hands and we dance together for a while, until she lets go and whirls away.

We dance for more than an hour while the Jefferson Airplane pumps. We even dance some to the Fugs. When the John Handy Quintet comes on, playing jazz, the dancing stops. The crowd listens.

I stand in back of Suzanne, sometimes touching her arm with my chest. Once, when she turns and flashes her smile, I dare to place my hand on her shoulder, then let it linger for a moment.

While the quintet plays, Suzanne takes my hand and we walk in semi-darkness examining the crowd. Suzanne moves in long strides, dramatic and determined. "We live inside the museum," she whispers.

"We ride through the park," she says swinging our arms together. "We discover aliens. We watch leaves falling from trees."

I am lured by this woman who is so straightforward and alive, aware of her nonsense, but unafraid to allow the child in her to

116

reign. I make out her face in the uneven light – high cheekbones, a thin prominent nose and wide mouth. Her thick hair, parted in the middle, falls well past her shoulders. Her eyes gleam, though the color remains hidden in the shadowy hall. I could almost set sail with this pussycat pulling at my owl strings.

"Are we there yet?"

"There's no there. We're dancing." She whispers the secret.

"I thought we were walking."

"We're dancing." She flickers with an eager girlish grin and squeezes my hand, continuing to lead through the maze of people scattered across the floor.

I'm becoming a prince in her glow; my excitement pulses with the flash of the lights.

"This is not walking," she enunciates schoolgirl correct. "This is dancing. Dancing is dancing and walking is dancing." She skips two steps, "Skipping is dancing."

"Everything is dancing," I venture.

"You have it."

When the Jefferson Airplane strikes up again, the crowd resumes the fury of the dance. Suzanne takes my hand with a sad turn of her lip, and a farewell look in her eyes, blows me a kiss and dances off among the lights. She must have decided to take a turn around the floor.

When I lose sight of her, panic overtakes me. I roller skate around to find her, then run, peering through the uneven pulsing lights into each face that might be hers. Moved and flustered by my attachment, I move about the floor, dancing and walking, somber and unhappy, looking, wondering why she's left. I remember that funny half-smile she showed walking hand-in-hand around the floor. I've lost her. I stand in the middle of the mash of dancers with my hands on my hips; the lights flash around like sparklers, the music beats and blasts, the dancers whirl and spin. A sick sense fizzes in my stomach. She might have left the hall. I fight the urge to run down to the street to find her. On and on I search for her face among the ruins of the evening.

A moment later, a tap on my shoulder. Expecting to see Franco or Lenny, I find Suzanne. She has followed behind me the whole time. I grab her shoulders with both hands and pull her to me. I clasp her a bit roughly, tightly. Her body responds, her arms close around my shoulders.

"Don't do that again," I say, trying to sound mock stern. "Don't ever leave me," I breath into her ear. "Don't ever." I hold her tenderly for a moment before I release her. We dance for a while sideways looking at each other until we fall into a close dance without a word.

When the dancing slows, we move to the edge of the circle of lights. Hand-in-hand, we leave the crowded music floor. In the lobby Suzanne snatches her purse and shawl from the cloakroom, and then down the stairs we run, and out into the fog-drenched San Francisco night.

We preserve an echoing silence crossing Geary. Already after midnight, the street rings with emptiness. When we reach Sutter, Suzanne points, "Thataway," and we turn up the hill.

We walk for another block before I pull a box of Marlborough's from my jacket pocket, picking the joint I had stashed inside. I stop under a streetlight and strike a match, cupping my hands and taking two full inhales before I hold it out to Suzanne.

"I don't smoke."

"Oh?" I am perplexed with this woman.

"I'm a dancer," she explains.

"I used to be a basketball player."

"Well, you won't hit many baskets with that."

"Make," I say, "make many baskets."

"Do you weave?" she asks.

"Oh yes," I respond in my single foreign accent. "I weave many baskets to sell into zee Bazaar."

"I suspect something bizarre about you," she says.

"I won't be bizarre if you smoke this," I venture.

"You won't make many baskets with that."

"Zey love zem in zee Bazaar."

"Then don't smoke that stuff," she says.

A pause. A longer space. Then, nothing. When I cannot stand another moment of silence, I stub out the joint, and drop the remains into my jacket pocket.

"OK," I say.

"Now you can make zee baskets." She points to a little side street that goes up a steep hill with one dim street light. "Here."

Several houses up, across from a small weedy lot that peeks down on the bay, Suzanne opens a gate. "Here we are."

She leads me past the large house in front, down a narrow path to the side, through a well-trimmed garden, and into a patio facing a little square house. A light shines on a concrete stoop with an iron railing radiating a flash of deja vu.

Suzanne leans against the door for a moment, perhaps deciding what to do next. A force moves through me compelling me to encircle her in my arms. Her eyes grow large and clear, the most astonishing shade of aqua green. I kiss her lips, lingering for a moment. God, this must be the one.

"Is that a good night kiss?" she asks.

"Whatever you like," I answer. A faint vision of Karen's face passes through my mind.

"Come in for a cup of tea." Suzanne squints and opens the door. "No lock?"

"Nothing in here." She switches on the light to reveal a large square room, empty except for two large sitting cushions and a small table in the corner. "Welcome to my studio," she declares. "I came out here last month from New York to join The Dancers Workshop. A group you never heard of." She wrinkles her nose and narrows her eyes. "Shoes off," she says. She kneels, kicking off her shoes. "You, too," she mocks with a stern look, "I aim to keep this floor perfect."

I lean against the door, pulling off my boots, "Socks, too?"

"Your option."

"So, you're a real dancer." I check for holes in my socks, and when I find none, decide to keep them. "I mean, you dance for a living."

"Sometimes I dance. Sometimes I teach. Sometimes I wait tables. It's all dance."

"Like walking?" I survey the burnished wood floor and newly painted walls. A large mirror leans in one corner next to a window that looks out on the garden still lit by the stoop light.

"Isn't it lovely?" She pirouettes and skips around the room trailing a shawl of rainbow colors. "All mine," she exclaims joyfully. "All mine." She switches on a radio, coloring the room with music, continuing to cavort, twirling and whirling, spinning and reeling, dancing around and around the room. Tuned to the pop station, the radio sings out a song I'd never heard of from a group I'd never heard of. A melodic high toned group croons a moody song, "California. Dreamin' in California," something like that.

"Man, we made it," I say, referring the lyric while watching Suzanne waltz around the floor. She amuses me. Creates fragile feelings in my stomach and fingers, and in fact all of my nerve endings I've never known before. To my surprise, her movements delight me. I long to join her as she prances around the floor, but I'm afraid away from the dark auditorium and pounding music. The song, the long autumnal, melancholy notes mirror my own feelings of reaching out to no avail. To this stranger? I cannot help myself. I would have all of her, and here I am in this room with her as if I've known her all of my life. I have no idea how to move, and yet I must.

"That was the Mamas and Papas," the DJ intones over the air. "with a single from their album, hot off the press, *If You Can Believe Your Eyes and Ears*. And if you can folks . . . this group's going places. 'California Dreamin'' . . . the Mamas and Papas . . . and here we are ahead of the pack. All ready here in sunny Northern California, light years ahead of the world . . . we're already here. What a song, what a group . . . they read my mind . . . I know they'll be reading yours."

Hadn't I just thought that. Hadn't I just told Suzanne that we are lucky to be here already. I'm hearing my own thoughts mirrored over the radio.

Suzanne pulls me into her dance. She skates around the wooden floor sliding her feet in long strides, making a whirring sound. I follow as best I can. When she makes a leap, I try an awkward jump;. She turns, I twist. She whirls, I spin. She flies, I hop. She pirouettes,

120

I jump. Suzanne gambols, I struggle. Round and around the room I follow, my movements awkward and wobbly in the large, empty space.

Suzanne slows and leads me to the cushions in the corner, and sits me down. "You better stick to weaving baskets." She tumbles gracefully into my arms.

She lies with her head on my chest, her arms draped over my shoulders. I hold her lightly, my chest beating and swelling; I kiss the top of her head. She murmurs and wriggles.

I am bewildered and confused. I'm not ready to meet the love of my life, don't want to think about it; I'm only aware of the need to smoke up that stub in my pocket, but dare not disturb her. I am suffering with misty pangs of fear and longing. I have no idea how to court this woman. My hope is to not to have to fight for her love. I fear trying to win her, because I fear I will lose her. I wish all the uncertainty would be over so I won't have to ache this way. I want to get out of this somehow, but don't want to leave. I know, too, that dealing with this brier patch would be much easier if I could only smoke that tiny bit of grass tucked into my jacket pocket.

In a moment, Suzanne wriggles out of my grasp, kisses my neck and stands.

"I've rested enough. Tea?" She springs through a door to a tiny kitchen painted bright yellow, with a small sink, hot plate and a half-fridge. "Cozy, eh?"

I watch, helpless, while she puts a kettle on, watch the graceful curve of her neck. She fills the pot, her long arms reach to the sink and then the cabinet. I'm aroused and cover my groin with my jacket. I resist walking over and putting my arms around her — but finally give in. While she fishes tea bags from a glass jar on the counter, I turn her around and kiss her. Suzanne returns my kiss with a passion that surprises me. We kiss and embrace until the kettle sings.

Suzanne turns the light and the kettle off, and leads me into a narrow room off the kitchen big enough for a mattress on the floor.

She pulls me down and holds me. "My boudoir. Am I too forward?"

In the half-light coming from the studio, I find myself in the presence of a giant cutout of Spiderman taking up the entire wall facing the bed, "Friend of yours?"

"My father. So don't even try to get away."

"Wouldn't think of it." I pull her close.

She responds with spirited embraces and long kisses. Susanne's warmth presses out the cold hovering over my shoulder.

We hold our bodies together for the first thrilling expression of finding one another. She moans. We explore. Slowly, we reach for more.

I hold her lightly, feeling the strength of her arms, the solidness of her back. A veil of reserve comes over us as we touch tentatively, caressing in soft strokes the complete newness of the other's body. Breathless, pulse pounding, light and pure.

Overcome by shyness, I keep my face close to her's so our eyes won't meet. I'm drowning in a tide of conflicting emotions. Too soon. I want her. I don't need her. We must have been together for a thousand years. I shudder, am afraid. I cannot live without her. I'm intimidated by her intensity. I am cautious because she does not once refuse me — not when I kiss her, or run my hand over her body or touch her breasts or pass my hand between her thighs. Each time she returns my touch, my kiss, with her own. I've never been with a woman like this. I'm unsure. Perhaps I've already gotten in too deep. Out of breath, I stop. Holding her close, I fix my stare on Spiderman.

Suzanne reads my mind. "Don't worry," she whispers, "Dancers love too soon, too much. We're not afraid of passion. Don't worry."

"I love you," I breath. "I don't know," I say unable to hold back my doubt.

"Yes." Suzanne tightens her arms, enfolding me with remarkable strength, holding nothing back, locking her arms around me. She crushes me to her, wringing every doubt, every negative thought from my body. The fastness of her embrace ignites my own vigor. My body echoes her touch, jumping the synapses of my nerves all the way to my soul.

We release each other with moans and sighs, falling back and savoring the relaxation flowing into our muscles. Then, she tugs the top button of my shirt. I lay on my back while she undoes button after button, and nestles her warm mouth inside my shirt, kissing my nipples, running her lips over my chest, kissing me all over, darting her wet tongue into my umbilical cavity.

She undoes the buckle of my belt. She pulls the metal snap and unzips my britches, sliding them down my legs and touching with tremulous hands the bulge of my penis through my shorts. She removes my socks and then my pants. She bends over my feet and kisses them. Moving her head back and forth she caressing my body with her long, languorous hair.

She stands and slips out of her dress seizing my eyes in the remnant of flickering light. Her slim body, a pale shadow, darts back to the mattress where she draws the cool comforter over us both. Lying in the hollow of my arms, her breasts resting against my chest, her breathing comes from deep inside her throat. Our nakedness touches, settling in to each other. I cannot remember a time when I did not know Suzanne, stunned with the thought we have known this secret for a thousand years.

I kiss the top of her head, and her forehead; I kiss her cheeks and run my lips over her chin and down into the hollow of her throat, along the delicate curved bone down to her breasts where I wet each bud with my tongue and kiss them both, causing Suzanne to giggle.

"Am I a road to be traveled? Come here," she says, pulling my face to her lips.

We make love in a flurry, in a flicker we are close and riding the moment. The sound rocks us, the moonlight seeping into the small room. Shadows play with us. We are inside and bestride each other. Surprised, happy, not knowing why. We are wanting, sharing We are riding the light. The sounds, the full cry of desire, we relent, fallen and furious in the attack. Catching the light and laughing at last. We move through the circle of light, rocking and shuddering, moving past our bodies, desperate to hit upon the core, tearing the barriers, and then, holding on no more, the long glide shooting the wide expanse, sparking into the golden glow. The moment for me is muffled and hoarse. The moment for Suzanne loud and serious and frightening.

My breath escaping in gasps, her moaning spreading. We lie close. The quick breaths, the denial of what happened. The raft of peace we cling to.

We lay for some time motionless, before I slip over to Suzanne's side. Quiet drifts, surrounding us in a light, serene sleep. My hand lay on her thigh. Her arm stretches over her head touching my hair. I turn on my side and whisper into her ear, "I love you." I want the phrase to be more, but can conjure nothing romantic.

"Yes," she breathes.

I fall onto my back staring hard to see through the roof. I remain motionless for a few moments before my legs burn for movement. I don't want to shift for fear of disturbing Suzanne. A cramp in my back causes me to turn on my side.

"Are you restless?" she asks, still awake.

"No," I whisper.

"You're restless."

"I'm keyed up."

"Oh? I'm very tired. So much dancing."

I wait, counting breaths, trying to drift off, but my eyes will not stay shut. "I'll be right back."

"Don't go."

"I can't sleep."

I pull on my trousers and shirt, and maneuver over the clothes on the floor, through the kitchen to the studio where I grab my jacket, and step outside to the stoop. I shiver in the San Francisco chill as I pull on my jacket.

The fog has cleared and I gape through the little entrance at a small strip of lights that float along the dusky harbor. Leaning against the railing, under the pale stars, I light the half joint. I inhale deep mouthfuls of the sticky smoke, holding each puff. I smoke until the bolt of velvet lightening strikes my brain. I relax. The night darkens, the stars brighten and the world pulls me closer.

I take out a Marlboro, and mull over the day with each smoky breath. I'm among the luckiest people. I am wise and sure and quick.

Stubbing out the cigarette, I tiptoe inside; in a moment, lying beside Suzanne breathing softly, I am fast asleep.

Hell No, We Won't Go

◆

HAIGHT-ASHBURY IS ROARING with red, white and blue psychedelic posters. Mocking the famous Fillmore concert ads, antiwar messages ring out in cryptic waves of twisted, hallucinatory script: STOP THE WAR!! MAKE LOVE NOT WAR!! NO MORE WAR!!

The Berkeley Vietnam Day Committee is planning a giant gathering for peace. Along with old-time lefties, many big guns have promised to speak for peace. Local rock bands determined to bust their strings.

Following the rally, a march on the Oakland waterfront is scheduled to disrupt shipments of troops and war materials intended for Vietnam. A rumor floats about that antiwar activists plan to bomb the Oakland Naval Base.

SUZANNE AND I have our first squabble.

"Why must you refuse to take part in a demonstration? You're being amoral," I tell her,

"And get blown up? That's not why I'm in San Francisco. Anyway, I have a secret to tell you."

"Don't change the subject."

I suspect a truth — whether I can admit it or not — I am trapped by the life-style of my unruly gang of roommates. I want to win over these cool, grass-and-acid dropouts to stop-the-war politics. They think I'm a square and want to leave the system . . . not make it better. I see them as naive and ignorant in their myopic view of the world. And now I must move apolitical Suzanne as well.

We sit, legs folded, on my mattress and face each other.

"You believe Big Brother, our government. But if we don't speak out, who will?"

Suzanne pulls a pillow onto her lap and hugs it to her breasts. "The government knows lots of people object to the war. Why don't they shut it down?"

"Don't be naive, Suzanne."

She sticks out her tongue. "I am not naive. And now your boys steal explosives to scare everyone? Your anti-war people act worse than politicians."

"That's just what the government wants you to believe."

"You don't know me very well. Or you wouldn't try to force me into going."

Suzanne goes on to tell me that her father is a retired Air Force pilot from the Strategic Air Command.

I comment, "So he flew all over the world leaving vapor trails that quickly disappeared into the pockets of the wealthy manufacturing and oil barons. All right, then march with the napalm-droppers."

"Aha, you were just waiting to drop that on me, weren't you? When you're not numb on that dopey stuff you smoke, the few feelings you find worth expressing are outrage, anger and righteousness."

"Well, that's very observant. But I don't use these feelings against you."

"You're out to shame me into joining your pinko commie liberals. I should feel guilty because my father defended our country?"

"I never said that."

"Well, you think we're criminals. But I don't have to prove anything to you. I do not care about politics."

"This isn't politics. Napalm is not politics. Napalm is inhumane."

Did Jack have this problem with Jackie? No, she always agreed, I muse. That's what I want from Suzanne, agreement and understanding. It's enough that I must battle the likes of Franco, Lenny and Bucky — but also convince Suzanne? We're mates, for God's sake. But I see in her, and in other women, a stridency that outweighs moral wrong. *What would Jack say about this march? Doesn't matter.* No argument works on Suzanne. I beg her to be involved, but disinterest echoes with her every breath.

And now, quite sober, Suzanne napalms me back.

"My family didn't have such a great life defending this country," Suzanne says. She huffs at me, bringing up a great unspoken rock of childhood resentment. "You have no idea how hard it is to move every year, sometimes twice a year from base to base. No goodbyes to friends . . . in the middle of the night. We kept this country free so you can march your asses off and inform the world that our government is rotten."

"Suzanne."

Her eyes film over. "You keep quiet for once. We'd leave a town and drive for days and days to get to some other base in the middle of the night and then we were given a little bungalow that some other family moved out of hours or maybe weeks before, and that hasn't been cleaned and has no sheets or towels or even toilet paper." The tears spill. "Dirty dishes stacked in the sink. You try it someday, facing empty quarters some family's been yanked out of, their dishes left stuck together. Go out and march against that if you want to march against something."

I hand her the roll of toilet paper I use for tissues.

"Thanks. Some nights I would wake before first light and watch my father in his Martian flight suit. I never understood how he could get up and dress in the pitch dark. I pretended to be asleep while he stood over me to silently say goodbye, and then I would hear the car pull out and he'd be gone . . . for days."

"Come on, Suzanne. Your father earned good pay, early retirement. Cradle-to-grave insurance and shelter for his family."

"You don't know what it was like, Gil! You don't know how it weighed on my mother and brothers and me. We never kept any friends. I went to nine different schools before high school. After awhile we never even made friends . . . we knew that we were going to leave anyway."

"What's that have to do with burning villages of women and children?"

Suzanne gives me a blank stare.

"Come on, I'm not blaming you."

She pulls at the roll of toilet paper trying to find the perforations.

"I'm sorry." She wipes her eyes. "It's so sad."

"I'm sorry. I'm sad, too."

"We were a band of Gypsies. All the pilots were my uncles. They were decent people, doing an important job."

I begin to wonder what happened to my Peace Corps idealism. It doesn't seem very peaceful anymore. I'm more ashamed of my time spent teaching than I care to admit. I never mention Ethiopia anymore, and have yet to tell Suzanne stories about my time there. What is happening to me? Is my spirit flagging? I'm sick of myself and my righteous feelings. But how else can I be? Do pilots dream about explosions, phosphorus, napalm dropped on innocents. Do they dream about exploding people? They must dream . . . they're people. We are an ignorant bunch. I must include myself, I know, but I don't feel ignorant. I feel like I know. I feel like I have been burned to death in the jungles a thousand times. How do you tell people that? I don't dream like I did in Ethiopia. I can't remember one dream from that time.

"Pilots are just people." Suzanne squints at me. She knows how to draw my attention back. She reads my thoughts, tries to read my secrets, but only to make me love her own people. "They have barbecues and weddings and funerals. Many funerals," she says. "You don't know."

Like a father, I know. I know, I've been seared in the jungles a thousand times. I smell a barbecue of human flesh. I've been told I'm too sensitive a thousand times.

"OK, Suzanne, tell me more."

"I loved the parties. My parents gave great parties. I'd dance through on my way to bed. The good fairy. I would touch their glasses with my wand to turn whiskey into an elixir to keep them happy and safe. And if they drank a little too much, they deserved it, especially my father. Pilots need to drink. It's a lot of stress doing everything right all the time, keeping a plane up and on course. One switch that's not switched and there you go. I heard about it plenty and knew it happened. Off duty they let down their hair. He took me to all his friends funerals, just so I'd know his responsibilities. And now your protesters plan to use dynamite and on our own boys. That's the worst thing I ever heard."

"That's a rumor spread by the government to frighten people off."

She blows her nose. "The Vietnamese have been fighting each other for a thousand years."

"With slings and arrows, not B-52's and napalm."

She strokes my cheek. "You just want to go around looking at all the pretty girls."

"Oh, right, every thing's a dance to you, even a peace march."

"Not true." She pouts. "I believe the war's wrong."

"Then, my dove, why object to march?"

"I don't know. Now you'll miss what I had to tell you."

"What's that?" I respond, relieved to change the subject.

She looks away. "I had something special to tell you."

"Come on, tell me."

"No."

I dry her cheeks "I'll listen closely."

She hits me with the pillow. "You don't deserve it."

"I don't doubt that a bit."

"I wish you wouldn't agree with me when I say something foolish like that."

"I'm trying to understand why you won't go with me."

"That's not enough."

"What's not enough?"

"You have to forgive me."

"For what?"

"For growing up with those boors."

"The pilots? Well, all right. I forgive you, but you had no choice." She lies down on the mattress.

"You have to mean it."

"OK, I mean it. Well?"

I wait.

"I'm not ready," she says.

The whole apartment echoes with emptiness.

"We're all alone," I tell her.

"I'm falling in love with you, that's all," she says as she slices a quick look at me.

"Well, that's wonderful. And the best thing I've ever heard."

"It's not very romantic the way I said it. I should've told you while we were making love."

"Suzanne, I'm overcome. It's wonderful. I love you, too."

"I didn't mean to tell you in the middle of an argument. I should have told you when you were deep inside me. That's when I feel it most."

"We're just having a disagreement, not an argument. Happens to all couples."

"I didn't want to start a quarrel. And I know you disapprove of my family. Even I took off from it, didn't I?"

"Now that's foolish. Yes, I hate the fact that we kill innocent people. Your father and your brothers joined the war almost with no choice, that's all. Now just lie down and turn over."

I massage her shoulders and shoulder blades.

"This is almost like having sex," she says. "So I guess it's all right that I told you. Help me take my top off. And besides, demonstrations aren't any fun."

"Oh, my dear, I'll let you have the last word on anything."

Ah, so you don't forgive me after all. Okay. But this demonstration could be dangerous."

"Not if a lot of people show up."

"Gil," she tells the pillow, striking it, "I just don't want you to get your head bashed in."

"That's just rumors. You have the most beautiful back. And front."

"Then who stole the dynamite?"

"Gelignite."

"Well then gelignite."

"I didn't. Does this help down here?"

"Someone did and someone could use it."

"The pigs are trying to scare everyone off, honey."

"But no one knows for sure?"

"I'm not worried."

"Not worried? That's taking the easy way out, Paul McCartney told me."

"Yes, my day tripper."

"See, the Beatles quote me."

"But when the whole country blinds itself, that's takin' the easy way out too."

"You're the day tripper, Buster Brown. I shouldn't even be letting you do this to me."

"Do what?"

"Excite me so I can't think."

"I'm going, sweetheart, with you or without. Now be serious."

"I'll go to keep an eye on you."

"Keep an eye on me?"

"You'll need help and a nurse. I'll pack the first aid kit."

"Is that right?"

"Right, Buster Brown."

"After knowing me for a matter of weeks, you think I need a nurse?"

"First night I saw you I said 'this boy needs looking after.'" She tells the pillow, "Saddest sight I ever saw."

"Suzanne, this is serious. Some big people will be there."

"All right. I'll go. Don't go on about it."

"Oooh!" I cry, taking a bullet. I grab my stomach, and crumple over her.

"Where does it hurt?" she asks.

"Right here."

She pulls up my shirt and blows a raspberry on my stomach

"Oh, the horror, the horror!" I cry, and hug her.

"All right, maybe something else will help. As long as your hands are there, unhook me."

I strip off her bra and we lay quietly in each other's arms.

"Does this help?" she asks.

"You are the one," I whisper. "You are the dancer of all my dreams."

"Seriously? I think you have to prove big statements like that."

"We've been together almost every day since we met."

"You're hard to fight off."

"You are some graceful article, Isadora."

"Well, I had to come all the way out here for my lessons."

"Let me look at you. I will surely die if I ever lose you."

"Good to see you perking up again."

Desperation Waltz

◆

I WAKE UP RESTLESS. Manic. Empowered. My day of deliverance is here. My eyes glow as the very hour of liberation draws near. Heroes come to end the war.

Along with this elation, though, is the half hidden notion that on some days my life falls out of control. Squinting into the corner I can see the used parts piling up, but I ignore these shreds of my psyche and scraps of my thrown off life.

I have a few hours to convince my indifferent Cave 7 room-mates to join the Berkeley demonstration. In jeans and T-shirt, and a comradely mood I nod to Lester, awake on his cot behind the couch where Wayne sits smoking. Franco lies comatose wrapped in a blanket near the TV. Busby shivers bleary-eyed in his sleeping bag next to the stairs.

I gesture to an imaginary audience. "Full house," I say.

"I'll raise you five," Wayne says.

After brushing my teeth, I rouse the front room.

"OK, you guys. Who's up for Berkeley?"

Wayne sips his cup of tea, and yawns.

135

Lester sits up and yawns.

"Good luck, man," Lenny sings out from the kitchen where he and Libby are cooking Wheatina.

Libby looks out at me and shakes her fist, "Go, man."

I hector and hound my fellow potheads. "Time to saddle up for the big Berkeley demonstration against Johnson's war. Today we ride, gentlemen!"

Why I must rev myself up this way is a mystery; I can't resist this urge to flog my fellows as I feel my life becoming unmanageable. In just a few months, Suzanne has become my only touchstone. Oh, what a paper-thin life. What a straw. Where is the solid life I was led to believe would be mine? I know the protest is futile and I have sworn off politics many times, but I can't help myself. Something big, a mind-blower looms before me and I'm drunk with hatred of Johnson and McNamara. They will go down in infamy. Johnson must push ten million rocks up ten million mountains to win release from my vengeance. True, I can find no sensible reasons for being incensed. The war has not grabbed me. Why am I agonizing so? But I can't live doing nothing, and the lack of a world view in these attic potheads staggers my pork chop brain. One last glance at my psyche shivering in the corner and I head out into the wilderness of these ignorant fellows. In truth, I am bewildered.

I wheedle, sweet talk, and stick the war up their noses. Over the last weeks I tacked up rally posters in the living room and kitchen and notes on the TV — no takers. No stoner dropout draws a breath of recognition.

I back Franco against a wall. "Does your mother deserve to live or die?"

"Be-before or after I was born?"

"Right now."

"Well, sh-she's already here."

"But you hate her? You hate all she stands for in her old-fashioned Midwestern corn-belt way. Why not have her removed?"

"It's a ca-capital offense."

"So she differs in her ignorant way from ignorant, rice-growing Vietnamese mothers of draft-age sons?"

"No, I don't suppose she does."

"Then, off with her head."

"Yeah, sounds right. O-off with her head."

"Hi- ho, the witch is dead!" I sing.

"Hey, why don't y-you talk about your own mother? Leave mine and her draft-age son out of it. We haven't killed anyone l-lately."

Franco's stutter seems to be worse. It's a sign, I think.

My eyes roll up. "These days not speaking up makes you an accessory. This rally gives us a chance to fry Johnson and McNamara."

"And their mothers? All right, I'll go. But only to observe, not to stop the war."

Franco convinced, I barge into the back bedroom to face Bucky who lies reading *Gibbon's The Decline and Fall of the Roman Empire.*

"Hey, do we help the common man from declining and falling?"

"I don't trust politicos, man. They bring everyone down."

"They're all we have. We're gotta stick it to Johnson and Mc-Namara."

"This is the TV version of a war that's been goin' on a thousand years."

"Real people burned, skin scorched and puffed into flame, and dying horrible, inconsolable napalm deaths. That's not Disneyland."

"You're a dreamer, Gil. Worse than a dreamer, a zealot. You remember them from the Bible? You insist on morality." He holds up his book, "This guy is right. Now, it's we who have succumbed to a loss of civic virtue. Why not let us savage Americans be savages? We all die anyway, man."

"I'm sorry for you, man."

Bucky goes back to his Bible. "Hey man, what do I know? You guys may end the war this afternoon. You don't need me." He looks up. "The world is already created. It says so right in the Bible. Created just like this. It ain't never gonna change, man. Get stoned, man, and drop the world. You could get hit by a brick any day of the week." He slams the book to the floor. "Wham! Just like that"

I smack my hand. "We're gonna pin those fuckers against the wall and milk all that Texas steer blood out of 'em."

"Oh? Sure." Bucky picks up his book.

"We're gonna put our asses on the line. We're gonna march to the docks, man, and picket the U.S. bomb and napalm armada."

Bucky's eyes fix on me. "They'll command their minions to shoot the whole lot of you, little man, before they let you blow one gear off their machine. It's billions beyond belief at stake. Wise up. Gil, baby. But have it your way. Me, I'm gonna go over to Golden Gate Park this afternoon, drop some acid and commune with nature." He throws me a two-finger salute. "You be the hero."

I wince at Bucky's sure-fire rejection. He may be right, but I cannot contain myself. "We're gonna defoliate the Congress. We're gonna search and destroy the purveyors of napalm and agent orange. We're gonna stop the fucking war right now." Then I stride into every room trying to shake each house-mate into sanity.

Before leaving, I walk into the back bedroom, take a pillow off the bed and slam it into Bucky's head. As the pillow slides to the floor, Bucky looks up with a shit-eating grin.

"OK, Samson. Pull down the pillars. But remember the price, man," he adds as I walk from the room.

These uncooperative kooks I live with often lighten my mood and lessen my desire to crap out on a mattress for days at a time. Suzanne, my dancer, lifts my moods with her smiles, her irregular and succulent beauty and her lissome dancer's energy and flashing green eyes. Be happy and go lucky, she tells me as she dips and turns. She urges me to break free from my diseased dark moods.

I wonder whether my withdrawal from her lately stems from my fear that I will infect her. I'm sure that the less she knows about me, the longer she'll stay. I must endure her lonely silence about my psychotropic moods. She looks after me with irresistible impulsiveness. This, of course, only makes me feel more moody. But, after all, she's a woman and has enough to bear. That incubus in the corner, Ghelderode's "schmerz," the one eying me from some distant future with fear and disdain. I would lose that if I could. Let Suzanne dance it away, let Franco analyze it away. I would not pay any mind if I could hide the thing under an old umbrella, but the loosely wrapped mummy has become a sly companion, looming at me during restless nights, through the awakenings and wanderings of the watery dark; the dreamer transformed into the dreamed. I would beat it with a stick if only I could.

ON THE BUS TO BERKELEY, I sit between Suzanne and Franco unable to keep from bursting. Swinging onto the Bay Bridge my excitement builds, surely something really big will take place before day's end. Playful, I embrace both companions, kiss Suzanne's cheek, and Franco's too.

"Pardon me, sir," Franco says. "Do I know you? Or have you lost all sense of decorum in public? This is not a rock concert, it's far more serious, such as dying from gelignite."

Anxiety jabs at me. I gasp, feel timid; then I switch to a somber mood.

I remember Jack. His steady gaze, the empowerment he gave off the first time I saw him at college. I bonded with Jack's openness, his will to bring the world to a better place. Could I be wrong?

I keep an eye out for heroes along the route.

"Look, you guys. Someday you'll tell your grandchildren: I demonstrated the afternoon they stopped the war. I stood up and helped turn the tide."

"Not if we're blown up, or have our skulls cracked open by the pigs," Franco says.

Suzanne, facing the window, "I don't march, or even stay, if there's any threat of a bomb. Not me, Buster."

"I don't believe anything so mean will happen in Oakland, California, USA," I say.

"I'm just along for the ride, I'm shipping out, man," Franco says, leaning into me. "Gonna see the war close up. Like Francis Scott Key witnessed the Revolution. I'll know what's going on by the color of their flags."

I taste motor exhaust and study Franco in the early sunshine. *If his ship sinks I'll remember this day with him.*

We arrive in Berkeley late in the morning. Down Shattuck toward the university we hear the echo of far-off loudspeakers. Students throng and hurry down the street.

"Come on," I say.

Suzanne grips my hand, "Let's grab a bite."

"But we're already late!"

"I didn't get breakfast."

Franco heads into the Mediterranium Cafe.

Suzanne says as she follows Franco, "Look, this is gonna be all day, so we have time, and I'll frazzle, starving in the sun all afternoon."

I'm about to go on without them when I spy Jack's pea coat. The old salt stands, hands in pockets, leaning against a tree and eying the crowd. I'm stunned, but not surprised. I nod and Kennedy nods back.

I join my friends as they step to the counter for croissants and cappuccino and bring them outside. Once seated, I start to enjoy the spectacle from their regal table in the sun as the University students parade by. I feel so much older and wiser than these shaggy undergrads.

"It's a warehouse for adolescents," I declare.

Franco says, "If we could only find some way to market 'em."

"Johnson has," I say. "Freeze-dried cannon fodder for the war machine."

Suzanne's nose wrinkles at my nonsense. "Not these kids. These kids will stay in school 'til the war's over, like you guys."

"They're still tryin' to draft me," I say in a muffled voice as if the draft board may have wired the cafe patio. I've not told this sister and daughter of the Air Force about my physical at the Induction Center coming up in a couple weeks or so.

"How can this protest work?" she asks. "The power brokers will never listen. You guys preach to the choir. This will never dull one spark of the war."

"Sure it will." I grip her shoulder, "We'll protest 'til they hear us. We're gonna nail those blood-letters in Congress. We're about to go over the top."

Toward noon we fall in with students and near students in jeans and work shirts or chinos with plaid sport shirts and dirty bucks Most are college kids, rarely a suit to be seen. Freaks from San Francisco in bandannas, tie-dyes and Army surplus smell of hot dogs and coffee.

Cops in squads gape at the flood. They stand firm, fiddling with batons behind their backs in a most casual, assured manner.

"Colorful enough?" I squeeze Suzanne's arm. "Isn't this dance too?"

I suffer her look of haughty contempt and lack of interest. One of the enemy, she's here only to humor me, though stopping the war has her sympathies. Furthest from my mind is what I know to be true — Suzanne is there to take care of me.

The hoard turns down Dwight Way and approaches the rally site on a scrubby broad field.

Hundreds now turn into thousands on the grass. Many carry placards, "Get out of Vietnam," "Stop the War." Not earthshaking. Not mind blowing – square anti-war fare. Official and semi-official folks hover on the edge of a large platform while a band sets up over to the side.

A young long-hair in jeans and matching jean-jacket speaks. All ignore this orator's ministerial TV harangue. A distorted sound system riding the wind breaks the phrases to pieces so they must be caught and rebuilt in the streaming sunshine. A large banner over the stage in giant uneven black letters that drip splotches of red paint says "Stop the War Now."

Leading my friends into the back rows my adrenalin pumps. The crowd breathes mild curiosity. No lame speaker will keep me from stopping the war, I decide, as I hush small groups who insist on talking. "Listen, listen! Women and children burn as we speak."

In denim, famed Mario Savio grips the mike. He voices the same argument in the wind, broken pieces that rise and twist. Savio trusts no one over thirty and his voice's sharp edge achieves the crowd's full attention. He speaks firm into the microphone, "There is a time when the operation of the machine becomes so odious, makes you so sick at heart, that you can't take part. You can't even passively take part! And you've got to put your bodies upon the gears and upon the wheels, upon the levers, upon all the apparatus and you've got to make it stop!"

Soon, his voice too, trails off and he leaves the platform without firing up the crowd.

Who's next? What firebrand can they concoct?

Amid shuffle and confusion a local rock group takes the stage. Muffled by the speakers their name sounds like "Ho Jo the Free Flow Fish" ... or something. In long hair and bandannas these freaks ring with political consciousness.

> Yeah, come on all of you big strong men,
> Uncle Sam needs your help again.
> He's got himself in a terrible jam
> Way down yonder in Vietnam
> So put down your books and pick up a gun,
> We're gonna have a whole lot of fun.

I clap and sigh, "Finally, a little life."

The weeping politicos and comatose freaks band as brothers, all in the same park. The elements of the two movements merge. I see the plan stir. Out of disorder springs strength to stop the war. I'm sure of it. *I've found our real Peace Corps, Jack.*

I look at the people around from my own little self-declared platform.

"We're gonna smash the powers of an insane government," I hear myself say aloud. "Johnson bends the world to his will with nuclear weapons, and cuts off arms and legs in the name of liberty. We'll hang that fucker." I smile and grind Johnson and McNamra in my fist.

Franco, arms folded, eyes me like I'm a mad man. "Tell 'em, General Gil."

Jumbled, my emotions agonize. The romance of resistance rises in me. I must empower my generation to stop the war. I look about. Dare I speak the word "peace"? Fright shakes me as the group on stage sings out.

> And it's one, two, three
> What are we fighting for?
> Don't ask me, I don't give a damn,
> Next stop is Vietnam;
> And it's five, six, seven,
> Open up the pearly gates,
> Well there ain't no time to wonder why,
> Whoopee! we're all gonna die.

Yes, I'm at a boil, agitated in this frying pan sunshine, this ornery predicament, this know-nothing, care nothing crowd. Wry First Lieutenant John Fitzgerald Kennedy in his dark blue Naval uniform stands off to the side. He understands my love for our country, its opportunities and shuns the shopworn lobbyists, the grist of the military-industrial complex that burns villages in far away countries. Jack would never let this war happen. You understand me, Jack. I have come to our demonstration. So what if I'm confused. I don't know all the facts. Maybe they'll fight this bogus war for a thousand years. But it's not the American way, Jack, not decent, so help us stop the massacre. I need a peace gun to slay these monsters.

Suzanne picks a spot on the grass to sit that is so far back our small group can't make out the speaker's face. She's no hippie and could attend afternoon tea at the White House wearing a long Salvation Army skirt and a sheer scarf round her throat.

Once seated, we have to look around the latecomers passing in front of us as if it's a ball game. I crane my neck forward and to the side, but must settle for hearing. Each speaker pitches the same themes and harangues the crowd or the government. Deep in their shrill tirades I detect my own nuclear unconscious, my duck-and-cover under the desk or a race down marble hallways to the school basement.

Speakers prime the crowd for the march. Gelignite rumors hang in the air. Tensions mount. Cops are expected in force. Heads to be busted.

Then the wind carries the sound of slow rolling thunder. Engines whine nearby. My heart stops. Here come the cops. The crowd braces for an assault.

More the wonder when I spy Ken Kesey's psychedelic school bus coming toward the rally shepherded by Hells Angels on motorcycles. The bus weaves from side to side down the street. The destination box on the old bus reads FURTHUR. The word MAGIC is painted in red on the bumper. Faces smeared in shades of red, blue and orange, Kesey's Merry Pranksters hang out the windows. The rally lifts on the fresh blood of Kesey's arrival.

" Hurrah!" I shout.

Suzanne looks off and sings "Que Sera, Sera" to herself.

Loud speakers on the bus blare sounds of helicopters, bursting shells and machine guns. Bodies in battle fatigues sprawl on the hood and spray the crowd with magic bullets. More Pranksters shoot toy rifles and pistols out the windows. Bodies outfitted in American flag shirts dart and throw smoke bombs. One suntanned Prankster has a target painted on his back. Some dance in black pajamas with army patches and hop about with toy weapons; others sport battle fatigues, and painted faces. All shout and scream as they invade and take over this serious antiwar rally. A second bus speaker spits out music over-layed with tapes of harsh military phrases, "Get the gooks. Get the gooks. Pilot to bombardier. Pilot to tail gunner. Waste the motherfuckers, shoot 'em." Another amplifier belches out machine gun fire along with comic book war noises — boooom, bwaaak, rhaaaar, ka-boom, boom. A search and destroy mission explodes as opera in front of us all.

Franco asks. "Are these the Mewwy Pwanksters, Daddy?"

Amid the uproar my eye falls upon a lone figure in an orange jumpsuit and a German spiked military helmet who crouches on the bus roof poised to chop down the crowd. Kesey! He has no weapon but his short muscular body, and no intent but to bend these young minds toward some as yet undelivered goal he alone can see. I sense a fierce need to commandeer the crowd and provide new direction. This is Kesey's Moses moment. He keeps reading the sky and knows something. Will he come as Wotan — some half-god from a cuckoo's nest, or as Captain Ahab out on bail from yet another drug bust? Kesey has become the Great White Whale itself. Out front and here to show the way. My God, what will he say? The crowd's heartbeat rises . . . but with a sense of foreboding. No one expected this monstrous assault.

Overjoyed I shout, "This is too much man, there he is. The real Kesey."

My hero has arrived, he whom I can follow over the top.

I point, "Look, man, look! That's the real thing. All the rest of this is bullshit. This is big! These logistical walkie-talkie guys on stage won't stop the war, man, Kasey's gonna do it. We got to follow him to the brink."

Doubt flashes through my mind, but I can't help myself. These weirdoes compel me to line up with him. No one else so pulls me into his orbit. Maybe I should flee these crazies. But I have no will to resist his call.

"Look at 'em, man, look at 'em. Kesey brought the war here, not the words."

I'm jumping up and down as Suzanne pats the grass, her eyes say "settle down." I glance at Franco and knows he's not a comrade. I raise my imaginary machine gun and shoot at the crowd right along with the Pranksters as I sing out with them from Dylan's *Ballad of a Thin Man*, "But something is happening here and you don't know what it is, do you, Mr. Jones?"

Suzanne and Franco grow uneasy with my antics. Her look beseeches me. Meanwhile I march inside a *Combat* comic book.

What's come over me? I once told Franco, the urge to go over the top catapults me to a height where I am no longer myself. My strangled throat leaves me speechless. One time I lost control when I watched my father — trim in uniform — board a train to go off to World War II. I cried for three days . . . would not eat.

A childhood vision of an issue of *Combat* sticks in my fore-brain, "Take the next hill whatever the cost. Go over the top." I whirl with fear and desire.

Now I'm dancing in an ever-widening circle and people are moving away from me. I prance with my imaginary machine gun, blasting the crowd and still singing, "Something's happening, but you don't know what it is!"

On stage The Fish continue to wail Country Joe McDonald's "*I Feel Like I'm Fixin' to Die Rag*":

> Come on Wall Street, don't move slow,
> Why man, this is war-au-go-go
> There's plenty good money to be made
> By supplying the Army with the tools of the trade,
> Just hope and pray that if they drop the bomb,
> They drop it on the Viet Cong.

Disgorging from their Day-Glo bus, Kesey's horde attacks the park in costumes from outer space, and sprays magic bullets from toy guns.

Suzanne takes my arm. "Calm down soldier boy, you're on the wrong team." Her eyes track me with fear.

In my own fear, I want to be someone forever unlike myself, someone who accepts. I want to die in Suzanne's arms and forever be free, but I cannot muster the spirit. I do not know how.

"For God's sake Gil, what's come over you?"

How to tell her all this? Here, at this moment. All I want to do is cry for forgiveness for I know not what?

I grin and squeeze her hand, then break off. I slough off any time to reassure her . . . then mow down those standing nearby. Suzanne watches in fright as she wrings her hands anxiously. I fear she is aging years, but I am powerless to stop myself.

The platform rally plods on. The Pranksters park their bus near some bushes and armed with wind-up machine guns, amble into the crowd. The congregation falls back. The speaker, a certified victim of the Nazi régime whose family perished during World War II, and now wears a black-and-white camp uniform, struggles to speak and hold the crowd's attention by ignoring Kesey and his Pranksters.

"We got a war right here," I yell, and dance with my gun, darting in and out of the crowd. "I am a Marine with the Pranksters."

Suzanne's look tells me, "You may stop the war, but you're killing us. Just kill the bad guys."

Franco sneers from on high. "Mow 'em down, Audie Murphy."

I'm sorry I'm making Suzanne and Franco so uneasy, but I can't help myself. I wonder about Franco, who won't join me. I've been trained to avoid the otherness of life in order to keep myself safe. I'm ready to charge and fight in this guerrilla theater.

The crowd stares, cold or sweet-smiling or gleeful. Soon, I catch the attention of Pranksters in American flag uniforms. They stalk me. Three of the flag-zombies herd me into their midst. Good thing I'm fighting in safe old Berkeley, USA. If I'd landed in the jungle, stalked by the cunning enemy, I'd be dead. In this moment I know all I want to know of the war in Vietnam.

Two of the Day-Glo crazies chase me in and out of the unset-tled crowd. They wrestle me to the ground. One fellow with long, blondish hair clamps my wrist. "In case of capture, take this," he says and grins. Two orange capsules drop into my hand. Then, still crouching in tall grass the Pranksters shove off.

The crowd's great skeptical mind wanders back to the speakers. I hide behind a group of oldsters, professors maybe and their families, who look amused, and yet ignore me. I study the capsules and slip them into my shirt pocket.

In his orange jumpsuit and laughable spiked helmet, Kesey shifts from foot to foot near the platform. His Wotan persona is unaccustomed to waiting, and light years ahead of them all. He folds his arms and gazes into the crowd. I am dying of hunger for his speech to set the universe aglow.

I GO FLAT AS the afternoon fades. I flop down and lie on my back, look up into the cloudless blue and hope to lose my weariness from being on maneuvers all day. I lack energy to look for Suzanne and Franco and hope they find me. After a time I sit up, fold my legs and just belong, secure in spite of the crowd close around, or the dreary speakers and the sun glaring down.

Everything's all right. They'll stop this war. They near the bunker. They shall reclaim the good old USA from the bad new USA. Let the bush burn on the mountain once again. Has Kesey been ordained to throw out the false gods?

My fingers touch the pocketed orange pills.

Or does Bucky's smirk hold the truth? Must we endure this war until it ends? War or no war, this slaughter of innocents has to stop. Or what does civilization amount to?

My hopes dull by the time Kesey gets the mike. Pranksters with guitars, horns and a flute join their leader on the platform. A musical speech? What a freak. This will shake up the squares. Hard to believe Kesey's is allowed up there to speak, his presence an outrage as these vest-pocket minds face his flaming orange. The helmet's gone and they see the warrior king's thinning blond hair. Not the hair of Michelangelo's Moses.

Their equipment plugged in, the Pranksters tune up and hash around free form, at first a coffeehouse poetry-reading kind of music, but then senseless notes piddle out and get dumped on the ground. Kesey pulls out a harmonica and plays still more random organ notes. No talk, just notes. The crowd tenses. What's he up to? They await his words, not plunkety-plunk and mouth organ phlegm. What happened to Moses here? I'm antsy, afraid for Kesey and my own belief in him. They want him to speak against the war and he just poses as this curbside harmonic busker. Gotta hand it to Kesey, he keeps you guessing, a light year ahead. Come on, Ken, bust loose!

The harmonica groans on, no hint of stopping. Annoyed, I stand.

Kesey says something but it's impossible to make out through speaker distortion. He speaks again and I hear or think I hear, "Fuck it." Kesey goes back to his harmonica.

"Fuck it?" I ask.

Far out, but what's he mean? Oh, the wily one will turn us on.

When Kesey stops playing the second time, I listen hard.

"There's one thing we can do," Kesey says softly as his mouthorgan taps the mike. "Walk away from this war and say 'Fuck it.'"

Did my ears hear "Fuck it"?

"You got to walk away and say fuck it," Kesey says again.

Walk away? He's putting us on. He must have a power card up his sleeve. I'm disarmed. My heroes don't walk away and say, "Fuck it." I want something more than 'Fuck it'.

I mutter to those around me, "What kind of hero says this?"

My anger rises. "Diddle on the mouthorgan while Rome burns, motherfucker?"

I flounder and seethe in a hell of a fix. *What's Kesey doing? Saying "Walk away from it?"* The true believer lapses, bewildered. The crowd droops. Bewildered, I look about for Suzanne and Franco.

HERO-LESS, EMPTY AND ALONE, weary of the rally, the war, the harmonica, and Kesey the dopester. Life spills in a heap before me. Kesey and the Pranksters go on with their hopeless crap, but I can't listen.

I spy Suzanne through the sparse crowd. She joins me and without a word takes my hand. I can't even look at her.

She shouts over to Franco a few yards away. "Now, isn't this guy something?"

Did she means me or Kesey? I can't quite decide. Maybe she means me, so I break away with a laugh and once more spray the crowd with gunfire.

"Great!" I yell. "Put a real gun in my hand. Take me to the trenches. Fuck it, fuck it, and fuck it!"

I rock with anger. I want to punish the whole bunch. Repulsion for the drugged-out Kesey and his groupies overwhelm me. My hero, for Christ's sake, turns up and tells me to walk away.

Kesey and his Pranksters leave the stage to puzzlement and half-hearted applause. Another speaker prepares the crowd for the march, but Kesey has unsettled them.

Franco says. "Not to rain on your parade, Gil, b-but I'm heading back."

The curious mill around the Pranksters' bus. Close-up the bus slips into a kindergarten finger-paint war with every inch smeared and splattered with Day-Glo orange, blue, green and blood red. The Pranksters swarm, aliens from another planet, but now look more homemade Halloween than galactic.

I drop Suzanne's hand and push into the crowd. Kesey, in orange, stands by a crude American Eagle painted on the bus. His big jaw juts more than usual and holds a winner's smile. I walk up to him and raise my rifle. I point the make-believe gun at Kesey's forehead. "This one's for you, old man. CaaPoww!" I spit at the legend himself. "You're dead, old man. Fuck it. Fuck you."

I ram my fist into the air, "Here's lookin' at you, Ho."

The great Kesey smiles like a Buddha, and looks right past my quaking fist.

Solemn, I turn and walk back to Franco and Suzanne, who wait near Shattuck.

We move up the street, silent among students and freaks; my gut is ripped.

I reach in my shirt pocket, pull out the pills and open my hand to show Franco the two orange capsules. "Hey, look. Our legacy from the dead hero." Without thought I take one, and offer him the other. Half a block down Shattuck we swallow the capsules in unison.

"You got it from the horse's ass," Bucky will tell me later, and hold up a *Chronicle* with Kesey's picture. "I tell you, the guy's working for the Pentagon,".

Suzanne hangs out at Cave 7 for the evening. She refuses to abandon me as I pass through a strange new phase of deep silence, falling into my cubist brain and hopping about in Picasso-land on the Prankster's orange pill.

An Egg's an Egg for A' That

♦

IT'S A COOL AND FRAGRANT SPRING evening as my hippie clan gathers in the slant-roof attic living room of Cave 7.

I've come to my senses over these strange people.

I've given up my gripes to Franco — or anyone — about this house of strangers, and I do not try to stem its flow and growth. Tension fades as my tolerance builds affection.

I accept Lenny's post-midnight footsteps on the thin-carpeted stairs.

I find I care about Libby's welfare and worry about her back room coughing flares.

Franco's broken agreements and flitting from house to house bother me no more.

Bucky treats me as a refugee from a boarding school. So what? I smile and chat about the decline and fall of the American empire.

Busby — no longer Noonan — has fallen out of our Ethiopian adventure, and has warped into another paranoid dope dealer.

I have accepted my home and have come to terms on Steiner Street. I roar, "Let 'em all go to hell but Cave 7," in silence. Chuckles cross my mind's eye view of this world. I think of myself as a liberal fellow now, accepted into this world.

I still jump when someone walks into my room, become flustered when I can't find a pen, scream when Bucky is boorish at the table — throwing his napkin, walking out of the kitchen without a thought to help clean up.

But I push these frustrations down my esophagus, past my breastplate, down further into the nerves surrounding my gut where they form a low level growl of electric current waiting to leap out. Though I use a lot of energy to keep these seeping emotions down where they burn dully among the smoky canticles of my unconscious, I do not recognize this inner song and so I fight the false war, but I don't tell Franco that or he will walk out of the room, muttering about my Freudian bowels . . ..

Wayne sleeps in the kitchen, Lester behind the couch. I love them both. Wayne practices guitar runs by the hour, which used to drive me crazy.

I cook now, often bake bread or boil large pots of brown rice and vegetables that feed their numbers.

My angel, Lester, the house electrical genius, remains our only earner and steady supporter of food and rent; a lad always pleasant, interested in others, never alarmed and ever retiring about himself.

I make a separate peace with these souls. Yes it's true, I could not get along with my God-given Midwestern family and its beliefs and customs, but now I've joined a family I can bond with and face the world.

I may drop out of grad school and join the real planet. A degree offers me nothing. I bide my time. I might move to the country with Suzanne and raise chickens on a backwoods ranch once I've beaten the draft. In this, my young life, dropping out might prove prudent.

I begin to accept "cool," "far out" and "groovy" as my inner state of mind.

THESE THOUGHTS flit through my recently remade mind as the commune assembles for our modern hippie family evening at home.

Suzanne and I sit on the living room's worn Persian rug and watch the single-channel TV.

Helicopter locusts land on rice paddies and napalm burns the jungles of Vietnam. Foot soldiers in full battle gear leap and charge into villages of thatched huts as Vietnamese flee in horror. Toothless old women gape and old men in baggy pants and pajama shirts quake while rude soldiers push them aside, search for arms and the enemy. Weapons chatter with bombs bursting in air. Serious young news correspondents, short-haired and handsome in spotless jungle camouflage shirts, precise in their toothy objectivity, report from the scorched outposts of Southeast Asia as the sun sets beyond San Francisco's fading strawberry sky.

Eucalyptus and pine scents from Alamo Park drift in through the open skylight. The smells mingle with two fresh loaves of Wayne's macrobiotic bread that sit on the coffee table by an open jar of apple butter. Lenny passes a large joint. High on speed Bucky trudges in from the back bedroom, sweating and red-faced. He sits and looks grateful for people. Libby on the floor looking devilish as she searches for something in the room she might paint or decorate. Paul Butterfield, blue and sassy, spins on the record player.

Lenny, on his knees, is cleaning grass. His fingers crush the sticky buds into the lid of a shoe-box. He slopes the lid, pushing the leaves to the top with an open matchbook cover, winnowing the golden brown flakes while the seeds roll to the bottom making a pleasant drumming sound. The pile of fresh weed, acrid and faintly musty, swells our hearts as keen as any flag.

Wayne taps his foot to the music, cuts thick slices of bread and passes them around. He brings surprising strength to the house. Upright as Whitman, his bearing puts us all on best behavior.

Lester hangs in a corner and rewires a hi-fi, looking up from time to time, his smile everlasting and good-hearted.

Libby chooses to make over the TV cabinet with psychedelic flowers of orange and blue and gold, and lets her brush lick tongues of flame onto the tube's four corners.

Lester laughs. "My TV's gone awful fancy."

Libby's return smile offers wry crinkles.

I sprawl on the rug with Suzanne who is wearing a flowery skirt over dancer's leotards. We spend most nights at her place, but to-night I have revealed her to the family. She passes on the marijuana. I offer her the joint each round, but Catholic Suzanne waves it on with a papal blessing.

REGULARLY SHE LETS me know of her unease with drugs and hippies, and at every chance calls my friends "zippies" or "drippies." She tells me: "You're a grad student and very, very different from these castoffs. You and I know the world has more to offer than these gaudy little druggies ever dream of."

I have come to believe that these are the very same troublemak-ers who will change the world, and reckon Suzanne needs this first contact with my friends and the culture crystallizing around us before she shares my own gloomy admiration. My friends, I explain to her, hope to extend the ethic of "smoke and cool" to embrace the world. "We break bread and new ground for the war-weary slaves of modern society," I say. "We make no judgments, sweetheart. We give everyone space to do their own thing. Our spiritual outlook embraces the world. We refuse to suffer the same guilt our parents suffer. Watch us stuff peace and freedom down the throats of the planet's rednecks."

"Your friends are not grounded," Suzanne says. "Where they stand, there's no ground, Sweetheart."

"Dangerous accusations from the child of a fly boy," I say. "Just like your old man, *we* are redefining a new ground, Honey."

BUCKY, BURLY AND CONTRARY, now unfurls a page of his free verse about the fall of the American empire and the coming wipe out of the hippies of Haight Street, and about the final radiation of mankind in general.

Breathless Lester, half-hidden behind wires and switches, after some coaxing, tells of his childhood in upstate New York, where he turned out to be the youngest son in an interracial marriage that gave birth to eight white children and a lone black Lester. A story listened to in hushed silence even through the comical parts.

Laurence Olivier — Franco —passes through the room, his eyes awash, dark and brooding,

Lenny, secretive and opaque, unfolds childhood horror tales of friends who have run away from home and come back with an arm chopped off by a railroad car, or been kidnapped and sold to gypsy caravans. He adds, "And it's all the righteous truth, man."

Busby shows up in a trench coat, jeans, and cowboy boots with a red ponytail dangling from under his slouch hat, and carrying a new suitcase. His twin associates follow him up the winding staircase.

"Man, what is this, a hippie convention?"

Moonstroke and Weebie, more airy and drug-drenched than seen before, shuck long, velvet coats to show off the new fad of dark stockings and miniskirts. A spangled vest covers Moonstroke's dark see-through blouse. Weebie in a ruffled tuxedo shirt with ruby studs over her own see-through blouse keeps her voice more reserved than Moonstroke's frenetic chatter. Weebie may lack her sister's glow, but gives off a strong cool charm.

Busby rakes the stairwell for shadows.

"I swear a car full of pigs tailed us from Oakland. I drove around North Beach for half-an-hour to give 'em the slip."

He peers from face to face through the smoke and makes sure he knows everyone.

The twins sandwich Wayne between them on the vinyl couch. He wiggles his ass and notes that both are braless behind their little vests.

Later Busby tells me in my bedroom, as he looks out the window to check out the park across the street, "I got to get some refuge."

His voice thickens. "Hey man, there's people loitering in the park."

"It's a park. People loiter."

"I gotta stash this," he says of his suitcase and heads for the usual closet.

Back in the living room he sits by me on the floor, pulls out a cigar-size joint and says to Suzanne, "Let's try some of this. But I warn you stay seated for the five or ten minutes after your first toke."

Busby grins showing the space between his two front teeth, a smile that I remember from a thousand years ago in Ethiopia.

The Steiner Street house has become Busby's dope warehouse. Despite his grandstanding, I'm grateful for my old friend's generosity, but I try to cover my resentment, alarm and fright that Busby's taking advantage of us all, and putting us in danger. If we get burned, we will deal with it using Franco's philosophy, "Whatever happens, happens."

Suzanne whispers. "He's so weird. I can't believe he's your friend." She glares at the twins, smoking in tandem, vests loose and skirts high.

"Hey, Generalissimo," I call across to Franco who is crouching in the corner, a hostage to the pungent cloud of grass, "Let's hear from Denmark's Paisley Prince,"

Hearing his name, Franco returns from some faraway place, blinks and looks over with a puzzled smile.

"Hey, Lord Olivier," Bucky says. "Where's the prince?"

After a moment, Franco stands, exhales smoke through his nostrils and speaks:

Ghosts of my father's war call me. I am here.

With an off-center English accent he pauses a dramatic beat, then continues:

Omelet, Bad Egg of Denmark, the Great Pretender to the throne.

Placing his booted-foot on the corner of the coffee table, he raises his hand, and presents his own "Hamlet, Prince of Denmark:"

This day, my father's ghost with grave propriety has come upon me crying, youth unworthy of our Great Society. Unworthy to follow the traditions of Hannibal and Alexander the Great, you wretched weak descendants of Greek warrior states. Pathetic sons to Rome's legions. Inferior to the Kings of Spain who defeated the Moors and tended the Inquisition.

Miserable progeny of Russian Czars and Austro-Hungarian princes. You coward sons of the brave soldiers who defended our rights from exploding Kamikazes, and annihilated the anal fixations of Hitler's Nazis.

What duties have you spurned ingrates, refusing a decent day's work and a piece of the action in future stakes. This ghost reminds that you obsess with earnest politicians, breeding canker sores of fantastic suspicions. When you cry peace, it reeks of disgrace.

You mock the plain good sense of your betters, while binding yourself in youth's ignorant fetters. Indeed, the officers of authority see quite well the youth of this country camped before the gates of Hell.

However, told I this ghost, do not fear youth with its sweet breath. Fear instead impotent old men obsessed, gloried in destruction and the weapons of death. Go stuff thy own revenge.

These mighty tools of combat already did exist, bequeathed as Christmas toys and birthday gifts, brought to our tender childhood play to wean us from our mother's breast and senses. We cut our teeth on metal guns and barbed wire fences.

Now I slay my father's ghost, turning this fight upon its rightful hosts. Wherefore I propose, we take these aging warmongers, imprison them on Maggie's farm and let them hold congress. Give them planes and bombs and rifles. Let these politicians and Generals choose up sides to murder each other over trifles.

Wagging his finger, Franco looks around the room.

With all due respect to my father's charter, who called me Omelet in exalted honor, me thinks this dripping egg on the face of Denmark's elders smells rotten?

Lenny looks up from his shoe box lid, "Far out, man."

"We'll put 'em all up there," Bucky chimes in, "Johnson, Mc-Namara, and Ho Chi Min. Chairman Mau Mau and Khrushchev. The whole lot of do-badders and mad-hatters."

"Don't forget the factories that make tanks and mortars," Libby says, applying more paint to the TV, "and the ones who make napalm."

"All of them." Franco says, asserting his accent. "The military-industrial complex and the Freudian-inferiority complex — all these politicians, and assorted warriors who make their fortunes from the blood of our brothers. We will take them prisoner and run their asses up the flagpole. The whole a gang of the old farts over thirty."

"Far out!" Lenny pours the clean grass into a large baggie, moves over to Libby, now painting the TV, and picks up a brush.

"Here, here. Hail the chief." The audience joins amid claps all around.

Franco sits down exhilarated.

"Right on!" I cry.

Suzanne kicks me.

"Far out!" Lenny says and looks up, so pleased.

And Busby's pot at last zonks Franco off his feet and onto the rug.

Bucky grins. "Hail Franco! Make the world safe for bureaucracy."

Suzanne grabs Franco's arm, "What about our boys dying for you, you bastards? And for all of you stoned pinheads making a game of war. You all want to make *us* out the bad guys. But what about those foreign butchers? Should they go free?"

Suzanne is in tears. I try to hold her, but she shakes off my hands and fights her sobs with all her strength. Guilt fills me as I watch her back heave in the silent room. Still, my pride bonds with the righteous rage of my confederates.

Gasping, she rises onto her elbows. "What gets me is. . . is that you don't care about our boys, the ones we went to school with, who are laying down their lives." She screams, "What's going on with you people? How can you live in this stinking smoke and talk like children who don't know any better? People I know are dying so you can do whatever you please. When do you talk about that?" She closes her mouth and looks past me to Franco.

Franco gives off a quiet grin, "Wow! What a grip, and she talks, too."

Caught in the middle, I sigh and want to protect her, but I don't want to care anymore. I am embarrassed by her outburst. I want to live by the hippie command — cool at any cost, man. This isn't cool. My Suzanne can't handle it.

Everyone looks away. Again I try to wrap my arms around her, but again she shakes me off.

"This war is a TV joke," I say to her back.

She wriggles up to sit on the floor. "A joke? What's wrong with you? First you shout to heaven against napalm and then you say it's a TV farce?"

"I mean it's a mercenary war."

"Oh, really? You don't want me to cry because your dope fiend friends won't like me. These, these cowards!" She turns to the others, "All of you are afraid to fight and you want Gil to join you. Well, you people have terrified Gil! You've sucked him in until he's frightened of you all! His mind's so twisted living here. He'll squander our love for you dope-smoking morons."

Silence floats about the room, crushing the smoke.

Suzanne gazes blind at the TV tube where Libby has just painted "FUCK YOU" in red, white and blue.

Wayne stands up. "It's been a righteous evening." He nods at the TV. "We'll get those mothers in the end." He grins and walks toward his sack in the kitchen.

Libby puts her paints away. Lenny wipes the brushes with a piece of cloth.

Franco leaves for Lorraine's.

Busby, after looking out the front window and the back window, motions his sisters in tow to follow down the curving staircase.

Suzanne goes into my bedroom. I'm afraid she'll get her wrap and go home. After a moment I follow and lead her to my mattress.

Her knees give way and she curls onto the bed facing the wall. Her back shudders. I stroke her shoulder.

"Now your friends won't like me," she tells the wall.

"I like you."

"How can you like me?"

"Oh, they think you're very courageous . . . because you proved it right here in enemy territory. If I had a medal I give it to you."

"Oh, keep quiet. And hold me."

We lie together, but soon I'm lost in less complicated times, in Ethiopia, with my Peace Corps buddies, and quarts of Melotti beer with injera and wot. We talk about our work — how to build schools and teach essay writing — and less about politics, how to get better textbooks. We worked for change inside the system.

Now, it seems, every thing's upside down and turned to greed and ignorance and tens of thousands slog toward death in Vietnam. It's all wrong today. Not like my father's war.

This is a war fought for the wealthy. But Suzanne doesn't grasp it, can't think it through. I won't be cannon fodder.

I rub her arm as she goes under.

How can Kennedy help as the issues fog over? I long for his approval. Should I stay clean and run with the straight arrows? Or have I pissed that away? I'll never get into law school or be admitted to the bar or become a civil rights lawyer. Or what if I had to go on the run for some civil disruption? How would she cope, being with a hunted fugitive? The shame to her family. Maybe we could go to St. Louis or Chicago, move into a clean neighborhood, find a stable job. But as what?

I move to light a cigarette as Suzanne wakes and turns to me in shadow and moonlight. Pale green eyes bore into me.

"You're a drug addict and clumsy and can't dance. You live with riff-raff. You stand up for everything my family and I are against. You're a coward and an intellectual bully and a fraud as a citizen and afraid to fight for your country. You fear you will lose me. Somehow I still love you and even find you wonderful for some reason way beyond my understanding."

"It's pretty clear then. I should be taken out and shot. And you should do it."

"See? That's why I love you."

"Because I'm a smart-ass?"

"No. Because you're a hopeless little boy in a great big world and need me."

Gil Fights Vietnam

◆

BY THE TIME I STEP off the bus in front of the Oakland Army Induction Center, the sour taste of drugs whacks me in back of my eyeballs. I stumble to the front of the square granite building that's bigger than the Pentagon itself.

From the steps I can see several yellow school buses pull into the parking lot and let out streams of husky high school seniors, each one carrying a gym bag — every one of them bigger than the last — joking, snorting, gung-ho comrades. "Give me the gooks," I hear buzzing around their heads. "Give us the sons-of-bitches and we'll fry 'em for lunch." These big, milk-and-beef-fed hulks hail straight from the gyms and football fields of high school, and are headed to the killing fields. *God how I hate them. God, how I wish I could be one of them.*

Across the street a string of cops sets up crowd control; they drag out gray and black wooden sawhorses from the back of a police van. Behind the barricade, a group of fifteen or twenty protesters meander around. This disorganized bunch of young men in beards, sandals and scruffy coats and women with denim jackets thrown

165

over spring dresses distress me by their slovenly appearance, and yet they remain my people. Some hold placards reading "Love Not War" and "Stop the War Now." Others, holding cardboard cups of morning coffee, watch the police carry the heavy barriers into place.

AMONG THE CROWD Gil spots President Kennedy, dressed in a Naval officer's overcoat and leaning against a tree. He's smoking a cigarette and looking very casual. Gil catches his eye — there's a flash that hints of work to do. He can tell his Navy hero approves of his intentions.

He sees, too, that wily, fat men, Tycoons, have come to film him. For some time now — he cannot remember exactly for how long, they have come along with photographers lugging cameras and lights from newspapers and magazines, who point their cameras at him from the shadows.

I WALK UP THE STEPS to the large steel and glass doors and enter. There I make out hallways filled with bomb smoke. Once inside, I unbutton my pea coat and sling it over my shoulder. I'm late for my scheduled appointment and must go through with the next group. This means sitting on hard school chairs among my fellow inductees, and staring into a gray marble hallway that reminds me of grade school corridors that led to destiny itself. My head swims. I chirp to loosen up and then lose myself in the marble swirls of the floor.

After a time, a dour-faced general in a very pressed Army uniform hands round a sheaf of forms and ratty, tooth-marked ballpoint pens. "Fill them out," he tells the group sitting pensive and morose. He does not observe my luminous red pants, or painted face and earring, or notice that I'm wearing two different shoes and socks. My costume, it appears, won't keep me out of the Army.

I fill out the form in a babyish scrawl, sometimes printing, sometimes scratching out script. I misspell words, put "Pagan" down for religion, and "still running" for race. For number of children, I write "3 billion." When it comes to high school, I scratch out the word "school;" and for occupation, I write "gook killer." For years of education, I enter "More than you." They want the address of every place I've ever lived so I scrawl: "22 Rue Morgue, Paris; Saint James Infirmary; tree house near apple orchard on Hill's dairy farm — two years; dust bowl and vicinity — three years; storm cellar in Kansas — one and a half hours."

As I finish the first side of the form, the class of '67 comes trekking in from the yellow school buses. They grow bigger in the cavernous hallway, joking with each other, busting their buttons to be taking their Army physical. They're ready to fight, ready to get out of the small town sling and see the world. In secret I join in their glee. One big galoot called Grease with a shaved head must be the captain of the football team.

"Hey, Grease," they call, "How about for 'YEARS OF EDUCATION' we put 'zero,' huh?"

"Hey Grease, fill out my form, man, I forget how to write."

"Hey Grease, when we gettin' the guns?"

Grease doesn't say anything, makes a couple of grunts when he sits down in earnest to figure out his forms.

I go back to filling out my own form, frightened for a moment that these gung-ho high school bombers will catch my getup and kick the shit out of me. I keep my eyes lowered waiting for a wise-ass remark, but no one takes any notice.

I finish my addresses.

After a time, the dour general returns. "Okay, stop. If you haven't completed ya' forms, do it later. We're gonna take a written test now. Get in line, follow me, and bring ya' forms wid ya," he says.

I follow the football players down the marble hallway. They gape and stumble, grim as prisoners of war, bedraggled and out of line in jeans and checkered shirts, chinos, and button-down collars. Dressed the same as the people from the demonstration a few weeks before. Still, no one notices my two different shoes and socks. A couple of the guys ahead of me punch each other in the ribs.

To these guys it's another march to assembly or study hall, but to me, it's war. Brought up in a small town, educated in the public school system, means that I'm already trained to kill . . . but my mind plans how to flunk the test. They will score my test and know right off that I'm illiterate.

The 50 or so recruits and I shuffle into a small room. We squeeze inside another set of school chairs with tables. The impatient general passes out tests and pencils to everyone. "Now I want no cheatin' on this," he says "you be good guys and do it yourselves, cause we don't give you no grade here. We use it to classify ya', is all." Passing out the pencils, he says, "an' if I do catch yer cheatin', it'll be all the harder in basic. I'll see to it." He laughs a cool, ghoulish laugh that leaves no doubt he can indeed see to it.

Once everyone has tests and pencils, he tells us to complete every question, even if we have to guess. Fair enough.

I begin by spelling my name wrong, "gilbertte" and in all small letters. Attacking the multiple choice questions, I choose "D" for the first five answers without reading them. For the rest, I read each question, and choose the second most likely wrong answer. No easy matter. One out of every seven or eight questions I check a right answer.

As the General paces back and forth scouting the rows for cheaters, I start feeling paranoid. I feel myself go pale. I'm frightened. *Do I really want to fail this test? Do I want to get out of going to a war that I'm trained for? Maybe I've made a mistake. These results become permanent parts of my record. What if I want to be an FBI man someday, or a Senator or even run for President? The FBI would check on me to find that I'd failed my Army physical. Do I want to continue this ruse? I could plead sick and return a straight arrow. There's still time. The answer is, "Yes, I want to continue the ruse." I refuse to join a human turkey-shoot. I'm determined not to come home with one or two arms or legs missing, or worse. You kidding me? I read* The Sun Also Rises. *In an eye-blink of clarity between the fog of drugs and the stark terror of the very strong arm of the Armed Forces, I decide that if God exists, He would not send me to some small God-forsaken country to kill people I don't know or dislike, nor take the chance they will kill, or even worse, dismember me. I shall help God decide.*

I spend the last ten minutes of the test praying to a God who may or may not be there, who may or may not be listening, and if listening, may or may not help me according to what else revolves through His mind today. I pray to this theological indeterminate, that if He gets me out of this now, I shall do something of His own choosing very, very good for Him some time and some place in the future.

With my head bowed over the pages of questions and the pencil poised in my hand, I go over this plan with the God of my childhood, the God of my fears and the God whom I suspect may be an insurance executive. Even as the dour general collects the pencils and tests, I pray with fervor, more than ever before in my life, through my fears, like a child.

NEXT, HERDED INTO a tile locker room and presented with a key attached to an elastic band to wear around our wrist — we draftees are instructed to dress in our gym clothes or if we have failed to bring them, down to our undershirt and jockey shorts. Then, half naked, we stand in line with hundreds of others.

Non-coms pass out paper slippers and rough white towels, and then lead us out of the dressing room and down a hallway along a white painted line. "Wait here with the others. Don't talk."

Out of the air they have picked up more recruits numbering in the hundreds shifting from foot to foot, as if pulled from the clatter of an early crowd at a football game.

The line moves toward a room where a swinging door swallows one under-shirted newbie after another. As I get closer, I glimpse white-jacketed male attendants.

Closer yet, I see them taking blood — the part I hate most. I can't stand needles. I am brooding about the needles when I have a thought: *Go with it. When they show the needles, I'll faint, fall right there on the white line painted over the marble. They'll be convinced I'm too delicate to go into battle.*

Getting to the door, I hold my breath. Inside, an assembly line of nurses and attendants in white jackets sit behind a low counter attempting to take blood and keep the formation moving. One attendant swabs alcohol on the arm, the next sticks in the needle, the next draws the blood and the last one pulls the needle out. Then, out the door to the next test.

Standing inside the door, I'm preparing to drop, when the fellow in front of me lets out a big moan, and , wham, falls flat to the floor. The one in front of him falls and the guy in front of him, too. I turn around and the fellow in back of me falls and another one in back of him. Up the line two fall together, holding hands. I look around. Ten or twelve recruits have passed out.

From behind the counter an entourage of white-jackets climbs over bodies with clubs and starts prodding the boys on the floor. "Come on, come on, get up you saps, you think we was born yesterday. The sight of a little blood scare you? Wait till you see where you're goin'." They stick these kids in the ribs and smack their arms until the raw recruits get up and fall back in line.

So much for fainting. I settle for a mere scream when they put the needle in my arm.

Next the line shuffles on down to the hearing test, where I then stand half-naked, holding my sheaf of records in a manila envelope, shifting from one foot to the other . . . for 45 minutes.

Finally I'm called to go inside a small, soundproof room and put on earphones. "Raise your hand every time you hear a sound," a young man with a beardless face tells me. I raise my hand and keep it up. He smiles. He keeps a big grin on his face the whole time. The technician marks his chart. He looks up. He looks down. My hand remains hoist. He looks around and then up again, he looks down and makes a mark. He keeps his head down for a long moment, then looks up. My hand floats. He looks down and makes a mark. He peeks up. My hand has not moved. He makes another mark. When he turns the machine off, my hand stays put. He makes another few marks, and says, "Next." My hand hangs in the air as I leave the room.

The inspection of feet and hands is a terse look — front and back, tops and soles. Three people in white coats peering over feet. No one says a word.

The line proceeds through another swinging door. Someone says, "It's time to box with the doc." We move to a small cubicle with a white cloth curtain for a door.

When it's my turn behind the curtain I am forced to lie down on a piece of slippery paper on a cold Naugahyde table, and wait for the examining doctor. He comes in looking younger than me.

This can't be a doctor. I swear he's the fucking guy who was just in front of me in line. That's it! They give you a long white jacket and a stethoscope and you examine the guy in back of you. That's how they do it!

The doctor and I begin to box — he smacks a cold stethoscope to my chest, grabs my left hand to take a pulse, pushes me forward for a few punishing sit-ups, lays four hard taps to my sternum, and finally, hammers on my knees.

He even has a joke. "I know I can get a rise out of you," he laughs, pushing me down on the table to listen to my heart again.

"Is it still beating?" I ask.

No laugh. He lifts my right arm over my head, and punches my ribs. "Cough," he says.

"How can I keep from it?" I ask.

"Stand up," he commands, putting his hand under my balls. "Cough."

I follow instructions, all the time trying to remember what the "doc" is doing so I can do it to the fellow behind.

When the match ends, he wins.

I volunteer to help fill in his chart.

No laugh. He puts down a few stray marks in random boxes on my form and waves me on to the next station . . . through more swinging doors, down another hall into a gigantic gymnasium.

"Push ups, how many can you do?"

"One," I tell the pudgy gym instructor in a T-shirt and sweat pants. "I don't have to show you, I know I can do one, so put me down for one and we'll call it a day."

He won't take my word. "Do it," he says, "Do two, and I'll put down three."

I manage one, very, very, slowly, then rest my body on the cold wooden floor. "I told you," I say matter of factly.

"Yeah," he says, "I'm puttin' down a hundred."

"Thanks," I respond. "You're cute."

Next, they have a machine that measures your heartbeat. Two young, white boys in white uniforms tape electric wires to my chest and wrists that are connected to a shiny black metal machine with meters. They instruct me to place my hands behind my head, squat down, then hop up, "Ten times."

"I prefer to read poetry," I reply. The two technicians, one big and blond with a squint and a smaller one with thin, balding hair and drooping lips, roll their eyes.

"Poetry will get my heart beating much faster than these uncivilized exercises," I explain. "I am not a bear."

"Get down and do these squat-thrusts," the big one says directly.

"Cooperate," the other one says.

"You're missing the point," I explain patiently, "If you insist on divining the state of my heart, measure me while I recite some of Ezra Pound's lesser known cantos."

Cooperate," the big one says, and pushes me down on my haunches.

"To be or not to be," I say from my position on the floor.

"Yeah, yeah, yeah," the big one says distractedly, "now jump up."

"I can't," I say.

The smaller one boots me in the butt. I hop up.

"That's one," the big guy says.

"Eyes I dare not meet in dreams." I hop again.

After a few more of these encounters, the line receives an invitation to lunch. In a giant cafeteria, they give each one of us a chit and we go through the line. We get the "B" lunch, no choices. Tomato soup, crackers in cellophane, two hot dogs with brown buns, ketchup, mustard or relish, lime Jell-O with floating banana slices on a piece of lettuce, half-pint of milk, rice pudding.

We sit in a corner away from the people who work in the building. Turned into weary issues of raw-recruits, exhaustion surrounds us.

No one says much. Even the giant home-bred farm boys from the school bus flag into submission, although a towhead with a bony nose sticks a hot dog in his ear before he eats it. No one laughs or says a word. They reel from a long morning of needles and tests and instructions and doing what someone else tells them. After lunch, in a minor act of defiance, the one they call Grease picks up his rice pudding and turns it over on the metal tray. The fellow with the hot dog in his ear leans over, scoops it up with his spoon, and eats it down. No one laughs.

After ten minutes we are herded out in the hall for more waiting, more tests, more following the white line from this room to another room. Urine tests, X-rays, grip tests, earwax examinations, tension tests. Then back to the gym, with little testing stations tended by more young, muscular Army men in tight T-shirts.

First, they make me walk on a raised rail in my bare feet. I can't do it. I keep falling off. I can't walk one step.

The two muscled PE -instructor types at this challenge become frustrated watching me. "We gotta write something," one says. "Everyone walks two or three steps, buddy."

After the eighth or tenth try, I sit down on the wooden floor and refuse to try again.

"Put down zero," I tell them.

The fair-haired German-looking young man in glasses and an Army cap, glares. "No one ever got a zero on this test."

"I'm the first," I say pleasantly.

"Your fakin," his partner, a rougher type, says. "I've had about enough of you."

"They're gonna put you in jail," the one with the cap says with delight.

Because I can't walk on this fucking rail?" I say, getting angry.

"You're fakin' it buddy. Anyone can do two steps on this thing."

The big guy demonstrates, walking his two elephant feet along the bar.

I try again. No success. "See," I say, "I'm the kind of guy that can't find his balance."

"Move along, move along," the one with the cap says, "I'm puttin' you down for ten steps."

"You'll walk on the water when them gooks start shootin'," his partner laughs.

I move around the gym to the next series of tests that I can't perform. The rope climb, my favorite . . . I can't get off the ground. I hang limp as a possum with my knees brushing the floor.

The recruiter couldn't care less. "Next," he says without looking up, writing down a number.

I manage to do nothing and less on the gym floor. By my own calculations I have scored minus 23 points in the dozen or so tests scattered around. I figure I'm winning, but I'm getting tired.

I stand in this big gymnasium with hundreds of stripped and vulnerable young men in towels and shorts. They succumb to their animal trainers as so many monkeys put through paces.

GIL'S CHEMICAL-FILLED BRAIN begins to paint his keepers' faces with extraordinary contortions. Each new, creased expression oozes into hideous flashing colors. Faces reflect dark, bruised purples, scorching masks of red smoking clay with the empty eyes of morticians; arms reach out in flashing cobalt green. Creature howls burn his ears. Devils roast singed black cats. Snake skin tattoos creep along their arms and legs. Fingernails grow into claws and bodies assume chilling serpentine movements. All about him leather-skinned, comic book horrors of dinosaurs and Gila monsters sear him with fiery forked tongues.

He sees death all around him both in the testers and those being tested. He is surrounded by ordinary, common death. These ghoulish guides exude the decaying colors of mundane death, the dry parched skin, the ogling faces and clutching tentacles of commonplace ordinary death. Not colored by the grand mystery of death, not heightened by the gospel promise of release, not moved by the great transition to glory, they present mere shadows of death reported in the local paper. Grace eludes them. They come spewing poison droplets propelled on pencil points . . . but he is prepared . . .

his childhood public school training in the art of aggressive defense comes to the fore.

Then Gilbert Stone screams out with revolting intent. "Ahhhhhhhhhhh! You bastards," he yells through the tight straining cords of his throat. "You sons of bitches," he shouts. "You baby killers. Slaughterers of old women. Bounty hunters for the devil," he roars. "Destroyers of the Republic, Murders of decency and hope. Ahhhhhhhhhhhhhh!"

A snapping sound cracks at the stem of his brain. He screams again in the stillness, his throat catching in the raw effort, "Murderers." The sound wrenches out of his bowels. "Motherfucking murderers," he curses leaving his body convulsing, shaking and quivering.

Beasts with scorched skin and plastic eyes turn toward him. A huge body-processing creature squints at this tick upon its balls.

Gil screams again, "You murderers." In the stillness, his throat catches in the effort.

Five fire-breathing monsters with dinosaur heads come toward him. Their claws reach out and clutch the wayward child, pulling him down on a mat. He waits for them to tear him apart, to split his flesh with their sharp claws, to rip out his eyes. His body tenses, ready to be hacked to ribbons.

THEIR FIRST CONTACT feels soft on my arms and ribs. My eyes blink, and my vision changes. No creatures. No murderers. What do you know? Standing before me: Archie, Jughead, Reggie and Betty. And Veronica, too. They murmur, "He's disturbed about something. Gentle, now. He must have been holding this back for years. Let's go on a picnic, what do you say, Betty, and take this guy along."

"He's all mine," Betty pipes up.

"Let him rest," Reggie says. "We'll send the chauffeur."

"What chauffeur?" Jughead asks.

"My father's chauffeur, of course, you bonehead," Reggie says uncharitably.

"Let him rest", Betty says, soothingly.

"He can go with us," Archie says "What do you say, soldier?"

My mouth tightens. Lying there on the floor, no words form on my dry lips.

"Well, we're going to leave this up to you boys," Veronica says, flashing her eyes with a very big smile. "Come on Betty, let's go powder our nose and meet the boys later."

"Good idea," Betty says, "and be sure to bring that cute soldier boy along with you." Then she turns back to me with a provocative look.

"OK," Archie replies, "we'll meet you down at the Float Shop."

The three of them, Archie, Reggie and Jughead very gently and kindly pick me up from the mat and lead me out of the gymnasium. For the first time I notice that everyone in white T-shirts and shorts, towels slung over their shoulders watch and smile.

I walk out with Archie on one arm, Reggie on the other, and Jughead with his walking stick leading the way. The entire gym goes mad with clapping and cheering. I soon accept the applause being right and proper. I nod to the crowd.

Grand and full of good humor, my three new friends escort me to an impressive office, where they assure me that I am about to have a good meeting with a very important person. They lead me into the office and sit me down.

The nameplate on the desk reads, "Irwin Solberg, MD."

Archie, Jughead and Reggie take their leave, reminding me to meet them later. "Don't forget, Betty invited you," Reggie says, winking goodbye.

"You take care, now," Archie says, "See ya later."

"Don't take no wooden nickels," Jughead snorts.

Then, I am alone with Irwin Solberg, MD, who looks quizzically at me. More boxing with the doc? I match his look. Seeing myself being sized up, I stare back. For a long moment I gawk openly.

The doc glances at my hands, and I perceive a game of body language assessment has begun. I note the casual state of the doc's arm placed on the edge of his desk. He does a hard take of my face.

I cross my legs and nod to the doc's open notebook and fancy fountain pen.

The doc counters with a glare to my nose.

I cross with a series of quick glances to the phone and the tape recorder and then to the bookshelves, making sure the young doc follows my line of vision.

Dr. Solberg counters with a peek over the desk at my half-naked body. The long moment turns into five.

I ogle the officer's jacket and round tan service cap on the coat rack.

The doc winks.

I close both eyes for a moment.

Irwin clears his throat.

I uncrosses my legs.

The doc leans forward on both arms.

I inch my chair back with a squeak.

The doc smiles.

I thin my lips.

"Well," the doc says, finally.

I am startled.

Irwin Solberg, M.D., not much older than I am, must be right out of a residency, doing his time in the Army before he settles into a lucrative practice analyzing the wives of lawyers and businessmen. He has a full beard hiding a round, plump face that will be fat soon. He's the kid that didn't play sports, afraid to get his clothes dirty, overcompensating by being a whiz in school, with much prodding and nagging from his parents who put him straight through college and medical school, while keeping him in unsoilable pants. No doubt a rabid fan of the Baltimore Colts or the Chicago Cubs.

"Well," he says again, with the slight catch in his throat, "what brings you here?"

"Wanna change places?" I ask. "See for yourself?"

"That's not possible, do you think?" Dr. Solberg, jacketless, but dressed in army khaki with a matching tie, comments, solicitous.

After a moment, I say, "To have a tryst with a psychiatrist, to test his wits and turn his brain in twists, has always been my ardent wish, before I have to cut my wrists," I tell him. *A little nursery rhyming will bring to mind case studies he read in psychiatry school. I can hear the antenna of the doctor's brain turn.*

"Do you like to rhyme?" Dr. Solberg asks.

"A rhyme in time saves what's mine." I say.

"Could you tell me what that means?" Doc Solberg asks tentatively.

"I don't know, it matches."

"I understand you had some things to say in the gymnasium," he reports.

"Yes," I answer, "and they all listened for a change. Isn't that just grand? And then my friends Archie, Jughead and Reggie brought me here to talk to you."

"What do you want to tell me?" Solberg asks.

"It's time for you to do the talking," I say.

"What do you want me to say?"

"That I don't belong in the Army. I'm crazy. I don't cooperate. I'm spaced-out on drugs. I'm an undesirable. I'm belligerent. I have bad genes. I am not quality cannon fodder and I would cause the Army more trouble than I am worth. In short, I'm a bad risk. 4F material."

"You sound pretty coherent right now, Mr. . . . ," he counters, looking at my folder. ". . . Stone."

"So what," I say, "I don't want to go."

"I can't just tell the Army you're not fit."

"Why not?" I ask, "You're not gonna go. What's the difference between you and me . . . four years of med school, a sleepless internship and a highfalutin' residency. So, you can stand the sight of blood. What the fuck, man. I can't, and I ain't goin'. You give me your hat, we'll change sides of the desk and you go."

"That's not possible," Dr. Solberg says.

I can make out the guilt building behind the doc's eyeballs.

"Why not?" I hammer. I stand up, walk over to the coat rack and don the military jacket and cap . . . both too big. I turn and salute. "How's this? They'll never know, Irwin," I say as I begin to move around toward his side of the desk.

The good doctor affects calm; him being no stranger to obtuse behavior, having studied myriad cases, and, no doubt, having attended numerous lectures and symposiums on these phenomenon, he refuses to react.

"Come on, Irwing," I urge, now moving next to him, "Er ... wing ...." I sing into his ear, "Erwing, we're going to change places now."

"Well, Mr. Stone," Irwin says, addressing the empty chair in front of his desk, "what would you do if I agree to change places with you?"

"I'd give you a 4F and send you on your way," I say without hesitation. "I'd give everyone a 4F."

"Wouldn't the Army be suspicious of me giving everyone a 4F?"

"They're already suspicious, Erwing," I say brightly, pacing in back of the doc's chair. "That's the nature of this machine you're part of. Can you imagine a fork without tines, Erwing? The nature of a fork demands tines to stick meat with. The nature of the Army demands suspicions to stick you with."

"Why should I give you a 4F, Mr. Stone?"

"I'm incompetent, sir, a head job, unbalanced, crazy, if you like. So I don't have to fight if I don't want to. And I don't want to, and neither do you, Erwing Solberg, MD — Muddled Dictator. I'll be glad to take off your coat and hat and sit down in that empty chair and give you a lot of good reasons, and some minor cooperation, if you'll give me a 4F, sir."

"Sit down Mr. Stone, and we'll talk about it."

I take the chair, still wearing Solberg's officer's cap and jacket. "Should I describe my hallucinations?" I venture a good-will gesture toward his profession.

"If you care to," he says, pitching the note of a doctor. Dr. Solberg glances over to his pen. He's itching to pick it up, holding himself back with discomfort.

"I'm not making this up. I'm divining your thoughts. It's a simple concept." I continue: "The filtering effect of my mental aberration has grown mind antlers from my brain that picks up every vibration in my surroundings, turning them into true pictures of their essence," I tell the doctor directly. "I can read minds. However, I prefer the term, "reading essences. I often talk to animals, rocks, pencils, lamps, art objects, shoes and toasters, and although most inanimate objects have little to say except repeating their function, I have spoken with shoes that remember where they walked. A toaster may repeat the word toaster, and do I want toast, and how dark or light I might want my toast, and to pay attention when it pops the toast so it won't get cold. I have also talked to a lamp that lived the life of a vase and had an interesting history including back to the scooping of clay from the earth and what went on around there for centuries in the mud, and shaped and put in a kiln and who created the vase and stored it, and how after many years it turned into a lamp and ended there in my friend's house, happy most of the time except for the excessive amount of dust in the air. So you see, everything has a conscious history. Not mere human beings. Everything in the universe has a degree of awareness about itself. It's us humans that keep declaring we're so unique. But then," I add "in a way we're no different than the toaster or the lamp. Reciting our function over and over."

I pause for the doctor to take this in. "I suppose," I continue, "that you plead ignorance of these phenomenon and I must content myself with crazy in the conventional sense — say outlandish things, that I am Christ saving the world, seeing things that aren't there, and hearing voices, cowering in front of fire hydrants and claiming means to destroy the world. Nuts. That's how you psychiatrists train. Limited in imagination, your mind strapped into the robes of arcane mania. You have formed distorted models. Nuts. None of you knows what's nuts.

"Nuts just want to be loved and saved from the emotional massacre of this bone crushing, marrow sucking society to which you have sworn allegiance. But you've taken nuts and made a business out of it. Families, clinics, medical schools, whole institutions, hospitals, and couch upholsterers have become dependent on the economic consequences of nuts. Home mortgages and college educations depend on keeping people nuts. So, if I am to be declared nuts, I must play it the old boring way of Erwing Solberg and his teachers. I need to keep convincing all of you over and over that I'm nuts."

I stand for dramatic effect and stare right down the doctor's eye sockets, "Right now, nuts proves my sanity, my ticket to keeping my legs and arms intact, shrapnel out of my face, my eyesight, my balls, and my head balanced. And finally, because I hate this war. They kill people for political ideals. All right, so I'm a trained killer. I grew up that way. So, I want to change.

"Irwin Solberg doesn't want to kill Asian women and children either, or send young men to their deaths, but he must in order to save his own skin. Look, Erwing," I say, sitting back down, "let me level with you. I am gay. I could corrupt the whole Army. Don't send me."

"You don't appear to be gay," Solberg counters.

"Wanna hold my hand?" I ask. "Wanna hold my prick?"

"Lots of young men tell me they're gay, Mr. Stone. Frankly, I don't care. You appear to be strong enough to fight, or serve in some capacity in the Army no matter what your sexual expression. You do have a lot to say about politics and philosophy. Tell me more about yourself, Mr. Stone."

"Okay," I say, a little weary. "I'm chicken." Whereupon I squat down on the floor squawking and clucking, duck-walking around flapping my arms. I detect laughter behind the doctor's eyes.

He titters. He can scarce keep from putting his hand to his mouth. He picks up the pen for some sense of decorum.

I might win on pure amusement.

"Erwing, the fishmonger, son of the fishmonger, Erwing." I cackle and cluck, and bounce around on the floor.

After several minutes of cackling, including one stint trying to lay an egg, Dr. Solberg relents, "Okay," he says, "enough of this."

Under the doc's breath, I hear the word, "bullshit," but I have reached the man under the uniform, under the surgical gown, the grandson of immigrant farmers and traders from Vladivostok.

"Okay," the doctor says again, "Sit down in the chair and we'll talk about a 1Y."

"What's that?" I ask, jumping into the chair and folding my hands in my lap.

"It means, you're exempt for six months, and then the Army has the right to call you back for another physical."

"Not good enough," I cluck.

I'm about to assume the chicken posture.

"Sit down and shut up," Solberg says, rising from his chair. "Do you think I am on a goddamn picnic? Why would I want to send you to some country I never heard of until two years ago?"

I sit meekly. Not a cackle escapes my lips.

Irwin Solberg continues, "Mr. Stone, I'm not going to send you anywhere you don't want to go, though this does not turn on my decision alone. I'm going to recommend that the Army manage without you. But for the Army's reasons, not yours. Catch the difference, Mr. Stone. Do you believe you're the sole person entering this office to play Hamlet, Mr. Stone?"

The doctor sits down. "I don't think you're crazy, Mr. Stone, any more than Hamlet proved crazy. I think you're discontent, therefore you would object to any sort of authority whether for your good or not. Perhaps if the Army, on my recommendation refuses you, Mr. Stone, the very weapons you claim to save your life here, may lead to a calamity worse than taking your chances on fighting for your country."

The doctor leans forward and picks up his pen again, "Now hand me your file."

I grab the file from the corner of the desk and hand it over. Looking through the first few pages allows the doctor to slip back into his official role, and when he regains composure he marks some boxes and writes several sentences. On another page he makes several more marks, and then signs his name. He hands the file back to me. "Okay, Mr. Stone, it's done. Out the door and to your left. Give this to the clerk at the end of the hall."

"Is that all?" I ask in astonishment.

"That's all," Dr. Irwin Solberg says with a plump smile.

"You mean, I'm out?"

"You're out, Stone."

"You mean, I'm free to go?"

"Down the hall to the clerk."

I stand up and take the file.

"Thank you Dr. Solberg," I stammer. Likening the moment as an unwary gift.

I hesitate, grateful in spite of myself.

I'm a freed inmate feeling so light on my feet that I almost fall turning toward the door. For some reason, I'm reluctant to leave the room. Though I'm about to be released, I have a vague feeling of not being satisfied. I want the doctor to declare to the world that I belong somewhere else. I want total certification of crazy, so I'm divorced from a world making war on women and children.

Wobbling out of the psychiatrist's office I realize Solberg and the Army have taken something I did not wish to give.

I present my file to the clerk who checks my name off a list.

"OK," he says. "Go down the hall to your right and claim your clothes."

"That's all?" I ask again.

"You'll get a letter," the clerk replies absently.

I move like a stick in the wind as I walk to the dressing room. I try to hold on to the patina of craziness, to get a handle on the defiance I exhibited at the beginning of the day; a broken thread of connection lingers.

A few others are in the locker room, yet no one is saying a word. Not even the locker door squeaks when I open it.

I dress without thinking.

The freed prisoner trudges back through the marble corridors, back from destiny. The vapor of drugs drifts through my brain. A high whining sound clangs in my ears and echoes from the marble floors. My eyeballs are near popping. My vision blurs and passes into tiny colored dots. Neon signs flash across my brain. I walk into a wall of fog and open my eyes. At the end of the corridor I walk through the door.

A police squad has cordoned off the noisy crowd gathered across from the Induction Center. I button the black anchor buttons of my pea coat. My eyes ache and my head swirls in a haze. A light rain falls on the dreary Oakland streets through the approaching twilight. I pull my collar up and turn toward the bus stop.

When the crowd recognizes me, they shout. The muffled words blow on the wind, "Hell no, he won't go Hell no, he won't go!" They cheer.

AMONG THE CROWD Gil sees Kennedy, now dressed in a Navy raincoat. He's smoking and looking very casual. Gil catches his Admiral's eye, who flashes a look that confirms that the work has been done. He can tell that Kennedy approves of how he handled himself today.

Photographers snap photos and the Tycoons with their cameras whirring, motion Gil to remain on the steps for a moment more. A phalanx of lights reflects off the wet street. Newly recognized, he pretends not to notice the crew running past the police barriers to film him coming down the stairs. Their lenses, like gun barrels, light the new star in their cross hairs sure as any sniper in the jungles of Vietnam. When he reaches the bottom step, he stops and pulls a cigarette from his inside pocket. Cupping a lit match, he takes the first inhale and looks directly into the camera for a James Dean moment before he exhales and turns away.

He suspects that the Tycoons have entered into cahoots with the government. He has seen this sort of thing before where ordinary people turn into wolves. He recognizes the director and his crew from North Beach cafés where they filmed him when he came inside from walking the foggy streets. He reads the obscene intentions in their eyes. They don't comprehend his work with Kennedy and the Elder Brothers. No matter how they butcher the message, the story will get out. The world may be brought to the brink, but the peace will come. He lets them film him as he goes about his business. These righteous Tycoons will share out-takes with the Feds to crucify him one day, but for now they have no idea what he is about. That's why they need him.

Into the Land of the Dead

♦

AT THE CORNER OF OAK AND STEINER Streets I stagger into thick woods. Up the little hill I pass three- and four-story Victorian houses that fade into leafy forest. Twigs crack and snap as I trip over a woodland floor. I fall and fall again in this psychic shift from sidewalk to thick underbrush. And now I smell smoke from some far inferno.

A narrow path leads me stunned and frightened through dense ferns. Could this be Ras Dashan or Mount Moriah? Surely I will come back to Steiner Street around some turn, and yet I'm trapped in the turmoil of the message from Oakland, of days — or was it weeks — ago.

Maybe the naive Irwin Solberg, M.D was right proclaiming that I would be inclined to live an oblique, desultory life. That I have, in fact, lost my youth, given it up by refusing to fight the war of my generation. *Oh, lost. Oh, lost. And, lost again.*

I run for untold hours trying to find my way back to Steiner Street. I duck under branches and tumble into underbrush. Switches and nettles tear my shirt. I gasp for breath, stagger, and again run until night descends. I've become a prisoner of the path, unable to turn back. The maddening smoke thickens. A whistle sounds in my head.

HOPE FADES. Numb with struggle, Gil's breath frosts in deep clouds as a steep shale path leads down into fragrant cedars. Hurling himself over roots and logs and shifting scree, he dodges rocks and fallen limbs. Bushes scratch his legs bloody. He's lost his shoes. He cools his face with handfuls of ferns. He is swallowed whole by the forest.

Days or weeks pass.

For a few restless hours he sleeps in thick overhanging undergrowth, and then runs again with no direction but the sharp winding path. Time fades and his sense loosens. Finally, when he can run no further, overcome with terror, he pitches out of the deep shade of poplars and ash into a waist-high savanna of grasses. Lost and despairing, he comes to a rushing river in near darkness under a bleeding sun. His eyes are red and sore in their sockets. He makes out a long file of dusty figures tramping along a narrow road toward some far dull light.

Dreaminess overtakes him. His eyes close as he slumps onto the grass and huddles against his knees; eventually he sleeps with the sound of rushing water seeping into his dreams..

He plunges into fitful visions of smoky creatures that bray and howl. They toast each other with jeweled cups of blood. "Wake, you mortal, Gilbert! Awake you fool!"

His eyes are jerked open. Despite the heat he's chilled from shoulders to shins. He shivers as over the tops of tall grasses he watches the endless parade of tattered souls marching on. Beyond this mournful pageant the river swirls and gushes past deep and forbidding rocky banks.

Hanging back, he follows these limp figures as they sway and scuttle at a ragged pace. The smell of fear hangs in the air. Could they be refugees from some bombed city driven to this cruel end of the earth? In shabby gowns their bony and lifeless bodies radiate despair. Children who fall out of this silent lumbering crew get smacked back into the narrow herd.

Gil shudders at their fate and chokes in the heat and sulfur smell. None of these pale beings spot him, even as he pushes through them, aiming to avoid their destiny.

At the river he reaches a cove where rough stairs covered with patchy moss, lead down through rocks to the water's edge. Spray refreshes him for a moment and he flashes on why he's here. But this burst dies before he can grasp its shape or meaning.

Rocks shoulder up through the water to form swift channels along the bank. A high-pitched hum wavers in the air. He blanches as sun dazzles the rough chop of the dark river. Far out, the current streaks green and blue. Further still, mists lift and rise like ghosts mingling on the waters. As he walks along, the river rushes and calls.

The pageant above moves off into the distance.

He can grab no notion about what he's doing here. No motive takes shape, and so he wanders mindless up the rocky beach. The wind whips up as he steps onto an outcrop carpeted with dark green seaweed and moss. He moves out on the promontory to the water's steady rush.

A boat of some sort glides out of far mist. Closer, he spots a dark figure on a raft, and through the wind and mist Gil calls, "Hey! Hey! Hey!"

A deep gravel voice chants back:

Whaata yu call? Whaata yu call?
Whaat yu call me fur? Whaata yu call?
Whaata yu call? Whaata yu call?
Whaat yu call me fur? Whaata yu call?
Whaata yu call . . .

Eying Gil, a large black man in a half-crushed top hat poles his large raft up to the rock. A black rose stuck into his hat band jars a memory Gil can't quite place. The big man looks Gil up and down and glares. Then, with a hand on his wooden pole, this familiar presence rests his other on a hip and laughs. "What you doin' here?" he asks. "You up to no good, or you lost?"

Gil's foggy mind catches at his soundless words. "I'm here for you to take me to the other side."

The raft-man indulges Gil. "The other side? Other side o' what?"

"The other side, sir. I have business over there."

The smile widens on a shot of gold tooth and Gil spies the gleam of a gold earring under his tipped brim. What's more, his black rose gives off a fruitiness Gil can smell from the shore.

"Oh, we all have business, one time or another." The man's hat tilts at the endless figures stumbling the road above the bank. "But why'nt you go with the others?"

"Can't you see? I'm not one of them." Gil says.

"Oh, no? Then you got no business here, my frien.'"

"I'm supposed to be here. I just don't remember why." Then his brain lights up. "You must know me! I saw you just months ago at Karen's house. You owned a barge, then."

"A barge? I don't know no Karen. My name's Jim and I been at this raft ten thousand years, and bound to be here ten thousand more." The man's ancient face approaches kindness and questions Gil's sanity. "Well, sir, you have stumbled into some place where you just better not be. Got no right here, you see — and dangerous to boot."

"Look, I am not crazy! I know where I am and why I'm here. I'm beginning to get a handle on this." Gil looks to the far mist. From over the fog bank a face takes focus and a likeness rises. "Jack! I'm here to find Jack."

"You never find your Jack this way. This way forbidden to living folks like you."

"I promise you, Jim. There's a damn good reason I came all this way."

"Good reason!" he laughs. Deep crows-feet frame his dark eyes. "You got no reason here, no rhyme neither. You in trouble, my man. I don't rightly know how to explain."

"Trouble, man? What could be more trouble than living in the world?"

Old Jim rubs his patchy beard. "You sure don't make a lot of sense. I can't take you where you wanting to go, 'cause it's only one way to get there." He nods toward the line of souls hobbling upriver. "And you not be one of them."

"Even so I know you're supposed to take me. You wouldn't be here if not."

"And how you know that?"

"Jim, let's not argue. Be a friend, just take me across, then point the way where to find him."

"Oh, now you think you talkin' like some frien' of mine. Well, you got no rights, and I can't do nothin' for you."

"I have no God damned idea who the devil you think I am." Gil wipes an ash flake from his tongue. "But then why did you come when I called?"

"That's my job! But I don't deal with fakes, boy. I do the special cases. I do accidents, unexpected deaths, murder, people of note and the like. They usually be small groups and my raft get them across quicker than the ferry. Then there's important people, too. I take them sometime. Saints and martyrs — but they ain't too many these days."

"Consider me a saint. Only a saint would do what I'm doing."

"Saints not be the cynical kind."

"I am not cynical! I'm here to save those still alive."

Jim's face lifts to the sky and he sings out, "As above, so below!" He rocks forward on his toes and drives his pole into the water as if to make off.

"Captain Jim, I'm not here to argue. Take me or I'll swim across."

The captain fixes Gil with steady black eyes. "You gonna swim?"

"It seems I must. I'm here to find Jack and find Jack I will." Gil looks across the forbidding waters and imagines flailing through waves of murky water and fading into deep green mists beyond. He remembers hills and thick forest he's already traveled. He rests a foot on the water.

"If you drown, then I take you across."

"I won't drown."

"You associatin' with the wrong kind'a people. Talk to yourself an' you talkin' to a fool."

"You must have taken him — the last President, he died of a gunshot wound. I've come to bring him back. It's been done. People come back from this place, and I aim to bring him back."

Jim shifts his pole from one hand to the other. "Who that you say?"

The water calms a bit. The horizon brightens and for a moment the mist lifts. He spies a far shore.

"You know who I mean." Gil edges closer to the raft. His heart pounds, "I'll trade you my soul."

Jim snickers and then laughs. "You got nothing I want, frien'. I'm here for the people that need me to be here. You want to throw your life away, and eternity, too? I can show you how to get outta' here. If you go back, this'll be nothing more than a dream."

"I've come too far. I can almost see him across there. What difference does it make who you take across?"

"No difference."

"Then, why not me?"

"Ignorance led you here, not fate, my man. Press your luck, break the laws. Hell be the consequence." Jim rests his arms across his chest, still clutching the pole.

"That's interesting," Gil says and wades out next to the raft. "But I'll find him and bring him back. That's my fate."

Blue mists glimmer and call from the far banks.

Jim takes a hitch on his overalls, his face all angles and shadows. "I advise you — only two ways to get over there. The sure way be dying. Crossing the river right here dangerous to the immortal self. Since I been here no man ever rescue a soul from Death. Never, of the live souls I cross, I warn you, does any return."

Holding onto the raft with its slow waver in the fast flowing current, Gil wades nearer to him. His bare feet are cold and almost numb on crabbed rocks.

"Shit."

Gil has stepped on something sharp. He looks down, pulls up a blood-streaked foot across his knee and watches a slow red drip.

"What you want to do that for? What you want to go and walk on them razor rocks? You don't need to prove you're a mortal to me."

Somehow the blood allows Gil to feel brazen and unafraid. "To see if I can walk on water. What a surprise."

Jim confesses, "I sometimes take a person across. I find them half-blind wandering the shore. They don't know where they landed or even who they be. They lost the power of speech. They raving too, maybe forever. Never even see me when I take them over. They just crazy, while you as I see as not-so crazy . . . yet, young man."

Fear halts Gil's breath. *Am I making a mistake? Am I this crazy?*

"Let me tell you somethin' for your trouble. By dyin' there be a chance for rebirth, but crossing the river alive condemn a man to eternal wandering. Since I been here Death never let no one return by the river."

"In the good book, one came back," Gil says, raising an eyebrow.

Jim pauses. He looks over his shoulder and raises his pole. "I'll take you across if you insist," he mutters, and turns distant. "That's my job, but no mortal returns unchanged." His voice hovers over the water. "Changed for the worst."

Swaths of green and red mists color the sky. Fear tightens around Gil's heart as he remembers his old life. The risk of losing himself in this cold and watery land seeps into his bones, but hero-longing swallows him whole. The nerves in his belly shatter into a pile of sinking despair at the desolate memory of losing Kennedy.

Hoisting himself onto the raft Gil loses his footing and falls to his knees. Jim grabs his shoulder to steady him. The raft, though sturdy, proves no more than rough driftwood planks lashed with rope. One bare mast supports a faded rag of sailcloth.

Jim, almost sympathetic now in the heat of his efforts, poles them out into the blue-green waters until a wind comes up. They sail into a deep orange sunset as Gil shivers in the fog, seated with his knees drawn up.

A vision of Kennedy, his hard wrought last Civil Rights address and his breathtaking speech at Houston fill Gil, and he hears again the awesome pledge to place a man on the Moon. These were the last life clips the Peace Corps Volunteer saw of Kennedy. There on the raft in unknown waters at the edge of the world, Gil resolves to pull Kennedy back into the clatter. Better to forfeit his soul, Gil thinks, than slog on through the desolate life of a hungry ghost.

Dark waves rise and melt as suddenly jagged rocks jut above the tide.

Jim digs the pole into the rocky bottom. "Not too late to turn back. No one be the wiser. Live out your days. When you die, then you cross in the natural order."

Jim's tone encourages Gil as he shivers, and perhaps the breeze of Death itself prickles him.

They pole now through hard water that ripples past submerged rocks. From time to time Jim turns, as if Gil might find a change of mind. But Gil's jaw clenches. They cruise into gloom. Sulfurous fog with a dark casino glow shrouds the raft, hides the mast's rags and even Jim as he poles them forward. At times the mist surprises with rare steamy warmth, and at others cold fog cuts at Gil's skin. Now wind churns vapor so thickened that it seems they lose all sense of course. Jim poles on, untroubled by murk. Gil's fears lift; he foresees returning with Jack.

As the fog parts they draw closer to a black, sandy beach with bushes and forest beyond. Jim's stern face turns to Gil only once as they approach. "You be here now, alone and forgotten. You outta your world and nothing be as you take it to be. Believe me, soldier, I rather work at my pole a thousand years than find myself abandoned ashore like you."

Gil looks Jim straight in the eye and smells the black rose in his hat band as he claps the raft-man's shoulder.

"Thank you, Jim. I'll be back with my friend or I won't be back at all."

Jim's look suggests this refugee might be crazy enough to achieve something despite himself.

Gil slides off the raft and into the bowels of Hades and splashes through sulfur-smelling water onto black sand. In his shame and fear of this adventure, Gil expects a spray of bullets to cut him down as in some childhood war movie, but his ears ring only with singing silence.

His eyes widen in light that filters up from wet sand. Dimness claims him. He strains to see. No sun shines here, but each object and grain of sand casts its own faint glow. A tree trunk winks on and off and troubles his sight.

"A shipwrecked sailor," he shouts, "Ahoy!" just to hear a sound, but his voice lacks body — a whisper in space without substance. Nothing in his vision stays steady. Liquid shapes quick as spilled mercury slip in and out of form. The movable landscape dazzles. Cedars and pines sway in oven heat. Mountains along the horizon disappear and reappear in craggy silhouette. The endless dizzy dreamscape only slows when he looks into the far distance. He sinks, shaky and faint, into cold black sand. The work to make sense of the place drains him. He crawls up the beach. Blue bursts of light cross the sky. He feels captive to a vast midnight.

Gil gathers himself and plods up from the dark shore to small thickets of dark dwarf lilac bushes near the edge of a swaying forest. Small petals waver and glow, embers that brighten and die in muted shades of ash. He looks about. New colors hang high above and a stronger smell of yellow sulfur glows against a blood-red sky. Everything he sees has its own backdrop. There is no wind, a silent, still force saturates the space like a dead calm at sea.

He envisions a crazy dark dance of misshapen creatures. Hollow sounds click and whistle. *Am I asleep?* He is nearly overcome by a deep desire to open his eyes, but his lids already stretch wide as they cast across the sky.

He strains to hold back his thoughts. Covering his eyes, he fights past the fire bursts and flows of crashing volcanic landscape. His stomach rides a carnival wheel. With his head lowered, he shields his eyes from the glowering sky and stares beyond at a quaking forest swaying like the twisting legs of giant puppets in a mummer's play.

His feelings of loss mingle with this landscape of darkness and despair as he cradles himself in bleak loneliness. Creeping among his bones is a sharp sense of being home, his spirit having roosted on this deserted shore all along, far from ambition among the shapes and colors and people moving through cities. *Should he scream for*

Jim with his unbearable bodiless voice to take him from this cinder where blackness glimmers and crunches underfoot? Must he crawl to find his way, this hero's hat a mere illusion? Here he lay fallen on a deserted beach, a washed out vagabond.

GIL LIES IN AGONY UNTIL he senses movement. His heart leaps. He spies a woman of stern bearing among nearby bushes. He recognizes Death's Wife at once and makes out long white hair piled in a bun and ornamented with a single black rose. As she glances at him, Gil sees that even with white hair Death keeps her in the blush of youth. She collects mandrake roots and choke berries, perhaps for pies or medicines, and drops them into the skirt of her apron. Death has a wife? Do they play cards on slow nights? He rises and plods along the beach toward her.

"I'm here to ask a favor of Death!" Gil declares in what voice he can muster, but as she looks up from berry-picking an ash-green bush he senses at once that his words lack substance.

"Forget favors," she tells Gil over her shoulder, a voice bodiless and brush-dry as she goes about picking. "Avoid him, sonny, or lose all your valuables."

"Well, I have to chance that. I've come for a favor I must ask."

She draws back at the heavy blood-shock of a living voice unlike any she's used to. "You should not have come," she tells him. "Didn't the boatman warn you?"

"Oh yes! he says, "but you see, Madame, things play out worse where I come from and all courage has vanished."

She draws back even more as she shakes her aged, steel-streaked hair and turns her smooth face and fierce features directly at Gil. Her eyes penetrate, perhaps kill. Her fearful beauty and raging eyes take him in, "Death hears pleas all day long. You think only the dying want to live? Even the dead beg. These fools crawl across deserts and coral reefs for one last breath. As if one sigh would lift them to Paradise! My husband brokers no deals and yearns only for our palace of shadows, away from these snivelers on their knees. Do you think he lacks feeling while these supplicants flood him with prayers and entreaties? There is pleading enough in the world where he must go every day to toil his trade. When he returns he eases his weariness tending to his garden without the whine of strangers begging favors."

Gil finds her hard to look at, but stands breathless before her ancient beauty, "I can only believe Death intends me for this very journey. He spared me once. Ask him."

"You traveled far to find this isn't far enough," the harsh wife responds and turns back to her berry-picking, which Gil finds a relief. "He spares many lives for the moment," she says into the bush. "Do not consider yourself rare. He takes them all in time. You have been warned."

"What else can we living expect but surrender? But I insist he'll know me. And will answer for the good of the world; Madame! I know he will. After all, do these roses not give off a good odor in his garden?"

"It's better you don't bank on a rosy future."

"I knew you had some humor somewhere in you, however black."

"Mister, Death does not operate like some genie in a bottle. He and I, we have a quiet life here. . . . Hold my apron for a moment while I empty these berries into the basket. . . . So when strangers show up and hope to buy back their old sensations for a promise or two, he treats them roughly. Of course, we rarely see a blood-man like you. . . . Please, watch where you stand. I'm afraid you may crush my foot." She laughs a forced laugh, which Gil interprets as her highest level of humor. "And if possible, young man, please speak more softly."

"I see you are wearing a black rose in your hair. I've never smelled a black rose up close. Do they smell differently from other roses?

"Indeed they do."

"May I smell yours?"

She plucks the flower from her hair and hands it to Gil. "Keep it, I have more — and more coming."

He lifts it to his nose . . . it is a deep fragrant flush of a bloom with a hint of fruit, fresh as a garden. He reels, half drunk.

"Many thanks, ma'am. It's wonderful."

She sweeps small stems from her apron and lifts her basket. Leaving Gil, she says, "He'll be along."

"Madame!" Gil cries. I shall remember your kindness, and your beauty."

Her limestone stare weighs his boyish idiocy with silence.

OH-H GOD, HOW SHABBY his torn clothes feel to him as he watches her leave. His wet ragged pants and damp shirt are pasted to his quivering body; his hair straggles to his shoulders. Is he some hippie Robinson Crusoe? *I have no fucking shoes, only this rose, fragrant and repellent, now in my buttonhole.*

Gil, with a severed feeling of being estranged from himself, a complete other entity, walks into dark woods. Oak and birch trees rest in everlasting deep autumn. Large trees with bare limbs stand and twist with witches' arms and skinless fingers. Brownish leaves mat the floor.

Passing through the trees he reaches a clearing overlooking a vast valley. At a crossroads a bearded old man, thin and frail, watches him draw near. The corners of the man's thin lips curl with a silent snarl. Wind rises. He wears a railroad engineer's cap, faded gabardine pants and a checkered shirt, its collar frayed. Old ghosts speak from his aura, and Gil merely senses a voice in the bodiless speech of dreams.

The old man eyes Gil's approach and croaks, "Whatta you want?"

Gil is relieved Death does not probe with the full force of his gaze. "I'm here to see you!"

Death stares at Gil's chest and stands listening. The old man's everyday pretense shocks the immigrant boy who backs off as a cough wheezes and fiddles in his chest.

Death raises a hand to his ear, "What's that? What?" He hears Gil's heart, but not his voice.

"I am here," Gil begins, drags down a big breath and then his mind goes blank. "I'm here," he says again as if beginning an essay in Mrs. McCoy's sixth-grade class. Here Gil stands for a second time talking to old Death; him as real and solid before the young man as this nether world allows, and Gil is speechless. He tries to look at this creature square and forthright. . . just the way his Mother taught him.

"Would you," Gil begins, but stammers as his voice cracks. "Would you rekindle the life of Kennedy?" he sings out trying to dam the springing tears. His head shakes and he covers his face. For all his feelings of loss he had never cried because of Kennedy's death, but hard tears now shake him. "He died too young!" Gil bawls as the storm-sky scatters his words. "He had much to give, sir! We need him! We had a chance, a chance," Gil croaks, "we had a chance to build." Like a child, he sobs and between sobs asks Death, "Don't you believe we must have a better world?"

"Really?" Death says, but not straight at the boy.

Unmoved. Annoyed, Gil thinks. *Impatient. Wants to get home to his wife and garden?*

"Would you . . .?" Gil asks through the wet slag of tears. "Would you give Kennedy life again?"

Death's hoarse voice cracks, "Kennedy A? Kennedy B? We got a lot of Kennedy's . . . although never enough . . .."

"Oh, God, you know the one I mean. Please don't play with me." Anger rises toward this frail, crafty fellow though Gil warns himself to take care and now fights for a deep breath. "You know the one, damn it."

"I suppose I do." Death's head tilts, a bit coy. "Yes, he's here, young man. But do you know who you're talking to? "

Light flashes and thunder hammers across the sky creating a stark projection of Death, caped in black with scythe held in bony fingers, white skull pursed on smiling teeth . . . a huge glowering figure against the steel gray sky. Fright shakes Gil as the image fades. He's the harmless farmer, the train engineer talking with a young man at this country crossroad.

"Wonderful show," Gil says, hiding his fear. "You know how to wake a guy. Do I surprise you, coming here like this?" He looks about the countryside yet feels he's at Steiner and Oak. "Do I approach a crossroad, sir? I feel something familiar about it."

"You name it and we'll call it yours, young man, although I am not liable to surprise from your discounted myths. Your sort continues to grope to these shores, hungry mouths wide, and then turn back, once you find no sustaining light. You retreat, but later come again as I call you. Being here and granted a short chat does not make you special. Don't prolong your pretensions."

This speech does not follow the well-spoken Death scenes in an Ingmar Bergman film. *He's confusing me on purpose?* "A philosopher, sir! I should expect that, shouldn't I?"

Gray hair sprouts from under his cap and Gil imagines a bald head beneath. Death at this crossroad carries a garden spade, tapping it lightly against his palm.

"I am what you see," Death says and gives a conquering laugh that rattles the storm-sky, his Halloween mask now a white glow that again fades into mock flesh and lightens Gil's heartbeat.

Gil gulps a breath. "You must remember me. You chased me down a hallway just days or weeks ago. You showed me your face; turned me from certain destruction, cushioned my fall. You could have taken me then but gave me another chance. Why?"

"There's no one here who didn't come when I called." His spade motions toward his endless fields of tombstones. Patient arms cross against Death's chest as he falls silent.

Silence doesn't become this chatty devil Gil thinks, only to remember that his mind is being read by this humorless specter. *Am I so naive that I believe this Sunday school teacher pose? Of course, the old man has been at this a long time with many changes of costume.*

"You have made exceptions," Gil presses.

"It's not me who makes the exceptions. My work merely parts the way when the soul tires."

"So then, you taught Moses," Gil says surprised at his own smart remark.

"Moses? Do I know this Moses?" Something final lingers in Death's answer. Has he suffered Gil long enough? Lost interest in trifling with him?

A great dread of losing contact with Death rises in Gil's chest. He is bound to the old man by fear. *But am I sane?* The question enters his mind for the first time. How can he stay captive to this absurd belief? Even if he's dreaming, what is he fighting? His own light will fade all too soon. Why did he put himself in harm's way? Restoring one person to a world already mad could never make the slightest difference to anyone toiling through life. America and the planet would stay just as lurid and ruthless as ever.

"Will you give me permission to bring him back?"

"You?"

"I'm a bright fellow and in my right mind."

"You think you're Christ? Or maybe your Kennedy resembles Lazarus?"

"The remedies of Christ do not take in my world, as you must see every day. We need a master politician to turn ignorance into peace."

"Well, boy, all my guests agree to be here. They find truth here nine times over and have no desire to return to your world. At first, they affect being frightened, but most cry out, happy to escape. That's the God's honest truth. Once here, life loses its hold on you. But you, young man, dodge the truth. You haven't lived among us for some time. And what's more haven't lived in the world long enough to know your ass from a hole in the ground. You should not have come to me. I cannot help you. I am just as you see me, a mere workman, some tired figment who takes no pleasure in his job."

Gil looks past this phantom to a dry river bed of tombstones in the valley below. Winding lanes lace rolling hills; mossy graves and hedgerows; white monuments and mausoleums rise and scatter and ripple past human sight in this infinite cemetery of cosmic breadth. What mighty spirit demands this funereal craft and handiwork even here halfway to hell?

"He will not be interested in you," Death says, almost kindly.

Gil fears he must no longer lay open his weaknesses, and plain-voiced he says, "Then let me speak with him and change his mind."

"Ha! You find yourself powerless here, just as in the world." He turns about with arm outstretched. "I do not provide a dwelling place, only a rest stop before the soul moves on. Those aren't graves, they're beds mocked up for humans to age like wine. You might call this winter hay in the big barn."

Christ, Gil thinks, *this ripe old man could pull out a chomp of chewing tobacco and harp on the weather.* The old scourge trailing miles from Ingmar's rare and exalted being.

"Look, you've made exceptions! I know you have. So how can I bring him back?" Gil is surprised by his purpose and enthusiasm. He no longer fears the unknown.

Death takes a deep breath. "Sonny, the dead themselves make exceptions, things you don't know about. You perform a fool's errand to venture here when you know so little. The dangers become far more treacherous than what you imagine, and beside them, death becomes petty."

"Are you the Devil?"

"Me? Hell, no." Death laughs with a sneer. "That phantom drifter. That quitting creature who comes and goes. Hell, he don't know himself if he's the Devil. I am Death," he says, "ever present where you come from, here and beyond. I am a calling creature. I call you from one world into the next."

Again, clouds roil amid muted thunder to spawn lightening streaks across the sky.

"Then if you're not the Devil you must be a compassionate being! You also must know the great distress in my world when you took him. Look, you have something, a beautiful wife, a rose garden — and no fear of dying. So just let me have a talk with him."

"Do you think you inhabit the only world? We function as a way station here, can't you grasp that? You boast of your damned world! I'll tell you, it's no more than spinning dots that you agree to call a habitation. This world's the beginning, sonny, beyond the hatchery of time and matter! The journey begins here. God help you fools."

"Okay, okay, whatever you say. But we live and breathe and have in our being great pain and joy. We look upon you as a thief in the night that steals children and robs families and beats our dreams into dust. You are the mystery. You are the tempting fate."

Death strokes his whiskers. "We have no clue to your spiked religion. Like young Keats with his nightingale."

In an almost whisper, Gil recites:

> Darkling I listen: and, for many a time
> I have been half in love with easeful Death,
> Call'd him soft names in many a mused rhyme,
> To take into the air my quiet breath;
> Now more than ever seems it rich to die,
> To cease upon the midnight with no pain,
> While thou are pouring forth thy soul abroad
> In such an ecstasy.

A question peers through the eyes of Death. Gil has moved this phantom, who disdains compassion. Death reminds him of a rummy who can't help himself, doing his job, feinting left, feinting right. And now, Gil cannot help but see Death as part of himself.

"Could you call Kennedy? "

"I could." Death shifts his stance. Slaps his spade against his palm. Looks to the mountain.

"Will you call him then?"

"Why should I? Who sent you to disturb the dead?" His shoulder rises and dismisses Gil. "But say I allow you an interview. Let you see what he has to say. Most of his class has started up the mountain. He's disoriented and far more disturbed than you can know. Still can't believe he's here." A wisp of smile rises. "You know, I could bury you now, if I cared to. It would save time later when I'm slated to come for you. "

Fangs of light stab the landscape. Thunder rattles against distant hills.

Gil shudders, but he damps down the fear. He is unafraid for the first time in his life. "To be or not to be," he pronounces, "that is the question."

"Tell him that, sonny, although he may not even speak to you. He ponders, he broods. He moans sometimes. He's been here too long. Doesn't believe he's here, but even so refuses to leave. Hides in his old office. We've many like him. You're all the same here, buddy boy, everybody brooding and frightened, maybe hiding in a burrow or wandering about looking for lost bones. A next life? They don't know! Old scarecrow scenes of religious horror still terrify them. Folks hide and howl when it's all too clear they dragged these bags of horrors with them. I tire of these 'fraidy-cats.' They'll be the death of me." Death ventures no smile.

"Go on down," he continues, and points a finger bone toward the bottom of foothills leading up to the mountain. "I couldn't care less what you do, fella. But it's overcrowded down where he is. See if you can get him up off his ass." He points his spade with displeasure. "He's right over there."

Gil peers into a haze that rises from low-lying ground near the forest. He makes out a crazy quilt of hedgerows and stone walls mounded with earth. Damp specters float among the stones. Do they smell? None too appetizing a search. Afar he spies Old Glory. "In the American Cemetery?" Gil asks.

Death taps the spade lightly. "I have to plant more trees. Go on, go on. Don't just stand around. Everyone's busy here, can't you see?"

"I'm off and many thanks."

The old man shakes his head with a grunt of a laugh that has no glee, only a cagey sheen.

GIL SURVEYS the vast potter's field that rushes up at him in black and white. Small burial plots rupture and bleed into color, shifting with thousands of immortal specters — bare human forms — going about their business, pacing back and forth in stoned fear. Gil stumbles into their midst, wobbly on his feet, and down a dim lane plain as a country road . . . *might some creature leap from behind a bush? But how can he be harmed here in Death's domain?* He regains his calm center — cold and calm, yet uncomfortable, edgy, and threatening to panic at any moment . . . playing tricks against his weedy mind.

What if this horror film proves real? *Does he even exist here?*

He steps from gravel onto grass, barefoot on cold ground. The clammy emptiness of the place chills him. These specters are sheer in the flickering midnight, and ignore the living being among them as they move along rapt by their own quandaries. Gil shudders and lurches forward. Some of the others flutter in small worlds about their tombs, or hover, or lie down and lift their heads to look about, eyes round and stealthy. Many look horrified . . . of what Gil can't tell.

AS A COMPASS HE PICTURES the remembered Kennedy and holds that image before him. Soon he comes upon a figure seated on a large marble rock, looking much like Rodin's "Thinker." Burnt and broken slats from numberless speaking platforms strew this grave site with its gas-lit Eternal Flame. Above the figure float faded shreds of red, white and blue bunting. Printed black slogans crowd him like a murder of crows. A battered placard stuck to the marble rock says, almost mocking: All the Way with JFK.

Deep in thought, if not mourning, his head supported by his hands, Kennedy sits unmindful of the debris skipping about. At times he looks toward a mountain so gargantuan its heights fade into mist. His restless leg moves and flexes his foot. He turns from the topless mountain and drops back into deep thought, chin propped on a fist for moment, then his anxious clasped hands lower and lie gripped between his knees as he rocks back and forth.

"Ooh!" Gil's soul cries for this familiar side view leaves him gasping. A hard slow pound in Gil's chest chokes him as he watches Kennedy swell in the heaviness of Death. The cathedral candles of Gil's nerves flame and flutter. Tears rise but freeze in his skull. He stands before this figure and coaxes tears but finds himself a mere tourist at mourning. Kennedy looks up with death-doll eyes.

Gil cannot read them, but in shock he faces the man he seeks. Could it be? This deep thinker mirrors the man Gil imagined. His breath skips. The massive head dwarfs a thin, bony body. Even his striking jaw juts bolder than in photos; the skin drawn taut; his forehead creased deep as his hair sweeps back in a small wave. A curious expression gazes out from under a mental barricade — a defensive air Gil sensed from pictures. The President has no eyebrows. Worry hovers at the corners of his mouth. He reads thoughts of despair, and yet unconcern, underscored by a stab of humor, deliberating impatience but with a measured lock on the moment. So young, Gil thinks, as all youth flees him.

"What's that smell?" Kennedy asks.

"Uh, life, sir."

Gil plucks the black rose from his lapel and holds it up to Kennedy on his rock.

The man himself leans down and sniffs. Some earnest notion crosses his face. A gaze of recognition? He studies the wavy, black petals and then looks at Gil full on. Rises! Slips from his marble rock and stands before the young returned Peace Corps Volunteer, who is an inch or so taller. The two stare face to face and Gil senses the President is ready to seek him out.

Kennedy's thoughts encircle Gil, who passes into the dead president's world where he stands in a warm room smart with framed pictures, a large desk, papers, a pair of couches and several chairs. A rocker waits by a window overlooking a large lawn and a white city — the room and view are part of the man's inner being. Gil's eyes narrow to keep him in view — not let him slip away. Has he somehow taken me into a memory of the Oval Office?

"Sir," Gil manages to mouth while looking at the famous rocker. "How's your back, sir?"

The older man holds out his hand, and as Gil's grip goes right through, he says, "I'm just getting started on my day, young man. So I don't have much time. You have some business with me?"

"Mr. President, sir," he says, a boyish lilt cracking his voice.

"I know you!" Kennedy says, "aren't you a long way from home?"

"Yes. My name is Gil and I was in the Peace Corps."

"I shook your hand on the lawn, Gil. I remember it well. It was very hot day in August and you were on your way to some place." He pauses. "Going to Africa, I believe. Of course. I was so busy, but I gladly spared the time! What greater gift could I have given to the youth — the promise of the world?"

How can he remember me on the White House lawn? This must be a trick of my mind, the whole thing is a dream. If I am about to leap from the bridge of my own psyche, let it be in a beautiful place with trees and sparkling blue waters, not here in some wood-paneled office conjured by my own mind.

"What is it that you wish from me, young man? I have only a few minutes."

"Well, sir," Gil ventures, "I've come to find you down here."

"Down here?"

Gil notes the wry smile the President has flashed on television in the past — when losing a thread of translation and needing a cue — something to catch hold of. How agreeable a smile for a man of such significance.

"I didn't know we were down anywhere," he says. "Not when I look out this window. Do you feel quite right, young man?"

"What business do you do, sir — day to day, you know — being in Hades? Do you recognize where we are, sir!"

"I miss your drift. And no need to call me 'sir.' Call me Jack. Many call me Jack — even people here in this office . I want everyone to call me Jack — it's short and I recall it with affection."

"Okay, sir. Jack." Gil's stomach turns a little queasy. "I've come a long way over the past few days . . . and may have been here even longer, but I can't measure time down here. I've come with a purpose and now it's hard to remember . . . I'm a bit wonder struck, sir. Jack, sir. I'm struck speechless by being here, and as I say, don't believe I'm really here." Gil fires off a hearty cough and clears his chest. I'm ready to leave after my unpardonable lack of notice without an invitation if you prefer."

"Well, you're here, Gil. Why not stay? Do we have some business?"

"Sir! Jack. My original intention, my reason for seeking you out — after you fell off the planet so to say — and being known for your intentions of creating better times —I came intent on inviting you back . . . or even kidnapping you from down here where you're not needed . . . and taking you back to our lost and forsaken world. But now, I'm not sure what my purpose might be, and of course you're well situated here ... beautiful office, great view!"

"Yes, and I have a rose garden you know. Black roses, now that I think of it that smell just like yours."

"It's a shame to bother you while you're thinking, and with me at such a loss and my intention kind of fading. And then, of course, meeting you in person shakes my soul and I'm not sure I should have started this enterprise and might just as well have stayed up on Steiner Street and worked in a bank or the insurance industry. You were my hero, but now in this place ... heroes seem out of place ... you know? I feel I should take the very good advice of Jim, the boatman, and Death himself to declare this entire gloomy episode a dream ... and get on with life in my world ... in your absence, you know, and push on like everyone else after your departure ... let things decline to their natural order so to speak. Do you know what I mean?"

"Young man, you seem deeply confused ... much as I was in the Solomon Islands when my unlighted torpedo boat was rammed by a Japanese destroyer in deep darkness far after midnight and torn from under me. I felt much like you at this very moment. But then, although I had a bad back, I set out and swam three and a half miles to shore while towing my injured crewman. I've had no time for confusion since grade school and never did, not for a moment. I grew up nurtured on pressure, and those around me did not tolerate confusion. In 1940, when I was twenty-three, I published *Why England Slept*, a straightforward exposition without a moment of mystification or perplexity. So pack up your confusion, Gil, and give me straight out why you're here. You can do it. As I said."

"Jack, Sir. Well, I'm here to return you to the world, so you can bring about a truer world, true to the intent and destiny of human kind, that is, let the sun shine through. The confidence! What I can't seem to articulate is ... peace! Bring peace to the world. Solid gut-calming peace. Do you need a more straightforward explanation?"

"Need for what?"

"For convincing you to return to the world, sir. Setting Johnson aside and getting you into your old ergonomic chair in the Oval Office as you lift the world onto your shoulders and let John, Junior crawl under your desk as he pleases. I could stay here in your stead, sir, Jack, sir, if that's what it would take sir."

"I find you an amusing chap! Do you really think you could engineer some kind of escape? I'm not even sure where I am, frankly, or how I got here. What's more, my back pain has eased."

"Engineer, sir?"

"How would we get away?"

"I came this far, sir. I could maybe talk us back or think us back the same way I got here. And of course you as the resurrected President would carry a lot of weight."

"I believe, young man, Gil, you don't really know me, and if you did you might not be so set on revising history. Certain qualities in men do not change. Want a look?"

"A look at what, Jack?"

"A look at this city from its back rooms." He walks to the window. Visit that.

Gil looks toward the Capital beyond and senses that it rolls in shame and guilt, but looks heaven-sent while paper changes hands, as oil rigs rise afar and reputations fall. Not a temperate moment to be had.

"Do you think I want to go back, young man?" the slain president asks. "I still have a feeling for boating and nature and so on, but to live in the world as my old self? Where shame and guilt rustle the fallen leaves. Nothing to appeal to a sober eye. Desire fills the flowing fountains. Sweat falling from the lords and ladies. Do you think I want to go back? And I can't go forward either! I believe I must stay put, though no one before you ever urged my return to the world. Look at that world!"

"That's what I mean, Jack, sir. I want you to revisit your compassion! Your great heart! Your creation of the Peace Corps. *Ich bin ein Berliner!* Return you to the world so you can finish the work you began."

"Ha! You have my sympathy, Gil, but no. Going back doesn't give me the edge."

"But you were the edge, Jack."

"No, I provided the button . . . merely the lapel pin. A playboy son of an ambitious father. I carried out orders. But . . . I have an idea! *You* go back. You be my missionary! You carry out our plan to bring the Peace Corps to the world and make the whole planet a fair playing field. I'll help you, and Sargent Shriver and all my friends will pitch in. I'll send directions by your dreams. And I'll arrange the necessary minions to aid you. I'll do for you what my father did for me."

"But me, Jack? We need *you*, sir, the miracle. You command the eyes and hearts of billions around the planet who admire America. No one knows me, sir. It's your personal vision, sir, your rising that'll shock the world into peace."

"I will appear to you, son, and direct your every move. I can no longer travel the old path. If you go back and do my bidding, I can move along from here and find my own peace. You know, I'm — I'm lost in thought here with my ass stuck to this big marble rock — well, you saw it."

"But, sir, even with your well-informed aid I cannot do in the world what you can. As you know, I'm half-blind with indecisiveness."

"You must know, young Gil, the world rewards blindness. The world is too busy to look deeply into the mirror. I would never have gotten where I am without blind reflection. That and the curse of my childhood privilege set the stage."

At this point Kennedy approaches a door across the room. He nods for Gil to follow, but Gil hesitates. Whatever he's about to be shown he doesn't want to see. Kennedy's face reflects sober remorse opening this dark corridor. Gil follows into half-light. Further inside, the ex-president turns lucid, "I still spend much of my time off of the rock here. Though this office soothes my vanity, these twisted chambers draw my remorse."

Gil watches Kennedy move forward. The shadow of his hero shrinks in stature and thickens. As he moves past walls covered with writing the old man's hair whitens and grows wilder before he stops and turns to Gil.

"Do you want to go further? A rich life provides overwhelming advantage. One assumes it's natural to live over the top — you understand, I'm sure . . . and if you don't it's recorded here on these walls."

Gil follows as they walk further down the shadowed and widening hallway; they brush by rows of papery bodies dangling by their necks, their skin like stretched fabric. "Don't mind these; they're old omens from ancient times. Beside, I meant no harm, only fun."

"Alive once?" Gil peeps.

"Oh, yes, players of bit parts in ages past, on to better things now, no doubt. Now look, as my stand-in, young Gil, you must harden up — live in the company of attitude. Yes, I know right from wrong, but fame becomes its own reward casting itself in a pitched battle with the humble virtues. You are not a scholar of the French Revolution, I assume — that was the last time the people understood who they were pitted against. Since then it's mere pacing in circles and rascals trading places with rascals."

"Jack, sir, you surprise me. All this doesn't sound like you."

"How do I sound in private without benefit of speech writers? Coy? Like an ordinary man? Like the arrogant Boston aristocrat that I am?"

"That's not the JFK I know, sir."

Near the end of the passage, they come into a cold, cement-walled chamber, dark as a fossil preserved in amber, with narrow cement benches hewn from the walls where assorted foul and stinking men sit naked in a sauna of cigar smoke.

"We rode high on my father's millions. Can you dream of such fearless liberty to do as you wish with any man or woman? A world paid for and protected — never a mistake or second thought.

"And these my father's minions caught up in their trades. Now, of course, when it's too late, I feel guilty on their behalf. Their brains bleed old straw. I wanted to shake free of their advice and hungers, but my muscles froze into knots. I'm paying for human coin I spent without compunction. I'm more along the lines of what Mrs. Roosevelt said of me, 'as someone who understands what courage is and admires it, but has not quite the independence to have it.'"

"I don't recognize you, Jack, sir. I knew many worthy men and women deeply drawn to you and your vision during my Peace Corps days. Not just Volunteers, but the government types, lawyers and such who helped you run the show. Sargent Shriver, for Christ's sake, Moyers and Wofford. The Harvard professors, the great intellects from California and Chicago, the well-meaning career government workers who claimed your vision, the colorful roisters and politicos from Boston, the simple faithful and great unknown workers from the Church, sir!"

"These old men are mere departed buddies of my old man, who set the stone long before I accrued the refinement to attract the worthy crew you mention."

"Well I came upon you on your rock, Jack, looking damned agonized. I took your suffering and remorse for how you were robbed of your rightful place. Now, you tell me it's your own mistakes. It's true I know only the public person — but nonetheless you continue to inspire millions and carry so many of us along with you. You may have greater self-awareness, but you don't know what's going on right now in your old world.

"There's a war they say you started that my generation is taxed to finish in Vietnam. They accuse you of being a war monger, you, the originator of the Peace Corps. You are a cipher to me now, Jack. "Although you've never been to Addis Ababa or dreamed of children leaping over cliffs, come back with me. Bring us your righteous vision. You must return to lead."

The dead President mounts the rock near the entrance to his library. Gil stands, looking up to him.

In the silence between them, Gil takes a last chance. "I remember you striding out of the Portico of the White House to greet your hundreds of Volunteers headed all over the world. Your right hand in your pocket, your slight smile. I remember my pride as if going off to Gettysburg to fight for the Union. And you spoke with genuine warmth, wanting to join me to teach so very far away.

"I remember your manner, and the way your lips spoke with such reserved grace and formed words that propelled our hearts forward. You urged us to go out and learn about the world and then come home and tell how the world truly lives — to make a difference on this planet.

"You covered us with honest idealism, and we were inspired and while we were all living among those we sought to help, we found ourselves robbed of you and the great river of your light and enthusiasm, and things fell apart; dreams collapsed into ugliness against our strongest desires. We were washed away in the aftermath, carried off by the judgments of lesser men who invaded the fine buildings and granite halls of our capital.

"So I came to bring you back and restore what we lost. Leaderless, we founder in the stench of Vietnam. We have fallen on the sword of drugs and addiction.

"I remember you well speaking to us and sending us out into the world from the White House. It must have been the last true day of my life."

The dead president sits listening intently, but is lost, pensive even. He seems almost eager to take his mind off himself, and yet his fingers begin drumming on his knees. "There must be better days ahead, Gil. Even if I were to go with you now, where would I return?"

The murdered president's expression lapses into wary puzzlement. "See for yourself?" He declares with a thrust of his chin.

Gil follows his line of sight. "I can't see, Jack.

"You can't see the mêlée — over there?"

"No, sir. I've come to bring you back to the living."

Kennedy claps Gil's shoulder and fixes him in a blue dazzle. At once energy surges through Gil.

Looking again, Gil observes a bloody mist above an ocean of graves. The field swells and wrinkles. Gullies and stands of trees rise and fall where farms once stood. Bright sun blazes on small wooden bunkers built behind boulders; small forts dot the hills. Great phalanxes of soldiers in close formation attack columns of troops in rags . . . more costumes than uniforms, and each man carries a weapon: a giant spear, bow and arrows, musket, rifle, machine gun, grenade, club, hatchet, knife or sword. These weapons also litter vast fields with the detritus of bloody battles since before civilization . . . green sod soaked in red blood.

The skirmishes mix in a brew of gunfire and razor-edged blades, with the soldiers in all manner of combat dress . . . tunics of bright gold, heavy body armor and camouflage fatigues, but their shins are only flesh and bone with feet blown away as they crash footless toward encounters in a mash of columned and random soldiers assaying bands of marauders, each slashing the other to ribbons in a great operatic scene of blood and confusion, horrible bawling of "Mama, mama, mama," crashing bombs and bursting smoke. Men fall and rise again and trade spears for cartridge belts. Arrows sing through the sky and bullets spark and ring off ancient armor. No man seems to comprehend his enemy while he shoots and plunges forward in blind limbo. The feral forces fall and tumble and rise again. Blue silhouettes lie in death throes, crumpled and pleading. But none stay dead. All bleed into another war behind another weapon, recreating through a new character. White-hot pain shimmers across electric air, the wounded squeal and act out fresh raptures at a new death. A lull in one place breeds horror in another. Some enemies in smart uniforms stand aside and guide this sportive dying and shrieking until they too rise, bound, bombed and blown away. Gil is witness to a blood-swept eternity that tears the lenses from his eyes. And still it does not stop. Victims cough and gag with disbelief, blood splashes from mouths and body wounds as agony twists faces. Shrieks curdle the air. Body parts litter the ground. Blood drenches the sun and smears trees. Suffering and disbelief gleam on the eyeballs of the lifeless.

Gil turns away, but still he sees bloody visions. Vomit groans against his throat yet nothing comes. He screams, falls and beats the ground. Moments pass until he regains consciousness. Kennedy barely notices as he stands on his rock seduced by the Guernica before him.

"Better for me not to see," Gil manages.

"Too hard on you, Gil? Look away, then, but you cannot deny the crush of horror humankind maintains."

Gil takes in Kennedy's profile. The ever-photographed face, worn now, thinner, paler, with lined forehead, his mask mournful, jaw still earnest. Uneasy he looks over Gil's shoulder as he towers over Gil on this rock in front of his library.

"Jack," Gil says, finally. "Sir, I've traveled this long distance to help restore you to the world."

Kennedy shifts a bit, but does not look at the younger man. Does he search for a memory of the world?

"Sir. Let us return."

"Return?"

"To restore your vision, Sir. To save the world, Jack."

"I never wanted to be a savior," Kennedy says quietly. He looks at Gil square on. "You be the savior. I have decided to go up the mountain. You've helped dislodge me from this rock."

"Me?"

"Your talk of return shows me what I must do. Your world is a fading memory. But I will be with you young Gil because we are all of one soul. I'll guide you with signs and miracles, and wherever you look, that's where you can find me. I'll send followers from the mountains and warriors across the seas. Where there's strife and injustice, and nations lose their peace, where people are not free to speak their mind, I'll lead you with portents and warnings, Gil, a seagull or the clang of a buoy. Where your legions suffer for their rights, I'll be there with you. I'll be with you. We begin with peace, Gil. Now, you must leave me."

IN A FLASH GIL FINDS HIMSELF alone. He is stung with the old pain of abandon as he stands on the bank of the Styx where Old Jim is awaiting with his raft. Wet, black sand coats his bleeding feet. The trees behind him hide the scenes he's just inhabited. Clouds scorch the horizon and he smells faint traces of sulfur from afar. He is weary from travel and his head pounds. His eyes ache, sucked dry as a bone.

213

He is feeling like an old fool, spent, past trying to pry dreams from the tombs of death.

"You be the first I take back," Jim says, a kindly dip in his voice. "Where the man you come for?"

"I couldn't convince him, though I'm not through yet."

"You the luckiest man I know. Best not try again." Jim picks up his pole and pushes them into the waves.

Gil's spirit falters as they begin to cross the wide, dark river. He eyes his failure on the receding shoreline like a crow that has lost its prey. Empty, he watches as Jim pushes against the rocky shore, and soon they are caught in a tide that pulls them into mist and beyond. Far out they break into sunlight.

Gil mulls over Kennedy's words of promise — how the departed hero will find a way to guide him in the world. He'll contact me. Excitement stirs. Schemes spin across his mind, as Jim poles mid-river.

When Gil strides off the raft on the return shore he reaches to shake Jim's hard hand. "Thanks, Jim. You saved my life."

"It's only my job — though you give me a moment or two. I think you got a break from the Old Guy — a gift few mortals merit. But you used up your luck son. Stay away from this river, you hear?"

As Gil walks up from the embankment, through the parade of staggering frightened ghosts, he begins to feel his success. He is drenched in the mist and drenched as well in the spirit of the man. He has returned with a writ of promise. He has snatched a rare reprieve from Death, and will bring the ringing truth back to the world.

Gil smells the richness of the black rose as the aroma lifts from the blossom in his hand. He marches forward euphoric, saved, hatched from the golden bloom of righteousness and directed at last on the road to Damascus.

Part III

Visitors

♦

THE HIPPIE COMMUNE inhabiting the high attic apartment on Steiner Street has dissolved. I watched it disappear before my eyes, fading like the slipping sunset.

Franco shipped out to carry war supplies to Vietnam.

One day I returned home and Lenny and Libby were gone without a word, their room empty.

Bucky moved across the park with Annie, his sometime girlfriend.

Lester went to live with a sick brother who needs him.

Wayne and Claire's healthy new baby came into the world on Waller Street.

Busby collected his perennial stash from the hallway closet and dropped out of sight with his Gucci bag and twin bunnies. They're holed-up somewhere in the Mission.

ABANDONED BY FRIENDS who were strangers, I mourn my loss and move into a cheap row of apartments on Garden Street across from the Cassidy & Schreiber Mortuary. Daylight filters through the wooden slats of my new, two-room garret. Wind whistles through chinks in the window frame. During the dark and damp San Francisco winter, the only heat comes from the gas stove stinking in the kitchen.

From this place I decide that my journey will begin in earnest.

GIL BECOMES POWERLESS as his abilities of speech slip away. He prefers silence and the truths of the voices in his head. His trips to the local super market begin to include the theft of a brick of cheese secreted under his pea coat. People peer at him as if spying from behind a thick glass window. Some days he cannot find his shadow in the noon sun. He begins to intuit people's thoughts by simply gazing at them during his long walks through the city's streets and alleys. He detects the coming calamities that threaten the future. The rising tide of his courage brings on waves of certainty against these grave forecasts.

Kennedy has seen it all coming and now he is providing a way for Gil to combat the dark forces with his mind.

Elder Brothers appear at first only as voices. Later these voices materialize all over San Francisco as large serious men with beards and big-boned bodies in jeans, plaid shirts and heavy boots. They are Kennedy's minions. Though they wear no uniforms nor monk's robes, Gil spies these book-carrying monastics who make strong-minded strides down the paths of Golden Gate Park. They sit in cafés on Haight Street and at coffeehouses in North Beach. They recreate down by the bay sipping tea and playing chess, talking only with each other.

He realizes that he's known these Brothers since childhood, when they held out candles in the dark and whispered to him. He remembers no time when their voices did not speak. They stood and watched behind his mother while she read bedtime stories. They comforted him when his father went away to war. They hovered behind the drawn curtain of the Ark of the Covenant. They escorted him past dark cemeteries when he'd been kept after school. And now these watchers have appeared to testify to the truth of his mission. He and these sainted ones will bring peace.

Wherever he wanders, slipping into a café for a rest and a coffee, Gil finds Brothers talking or engrossed in thick books. He yearns to lock eyes with them, but they turn from him before he can speak. At times one of them will flash him a look so intense and deep that he chokes. Or a Brother may pierce his breast with a gleam from the world beyond that shocks his joints. In time, some of these wise ones begin to recognize Gil. A slight nod from one, then another, but he's forbidden to approach. Reasons, their looks say, will come later.

He knows these Elder Brothers come to infuse humans with new spirit, and that Jack himself sent them, for Gil sees his face shine from the Mountain when they show up.

"Pay attention," Jack's face floats before him, "for these Brothers, now immortal, once were as you. They come to guide humankind."

But can he trust such thoughts? He worries and looks over his shoulder for a speaker. His heart skips as he rounds corners and tries to crush all doubt. He feels his body lift as these bold ones shift some secret knowledge his way through hints and finger waving. However he is but their servant as their mysteries stay mysteries even when they allow that he might be called upon to serve them.

As he walks and listens the path opens before him in their divine voices. The Brothers have perhaps chosen him to lead the way into the coming Millennium. Of all pilgrims in this golden city he has been led here for this special purpose. Why else do they whisper to him in shadows? They have watched over him since childhood.

When he objects and falls to his knees in his stinking, wind-whistling room, the Brothers remind him that he is specially prepared for this mission. They cite the mental and emotional tortures of his childhood such as his fear of teachers and cemeteries born of constant loss and abandonment. They insist his suffering must go on as he faces cruelty all around and sinks deeper into the world. The hardships he witnessed during his time in Ethiopia, when led there by Jack, did not fall upon him by mere chance. On the street today the looks of ill will, the mockery that he meets arise for him to overcome, while he leads the world toward peace. The voices of the Brothers reverberate in his head. "We have come," they murmur.

"We who save must suffer," the Brothers tell him, "We have come to guide you."

He can doubt himself no longer. He surrenders his mind up to the control of these Brothers. He no longer questions their authority. Messages shoot through his brain in washes of energy from far forces beyond the universe. They impress upon him the need for total secrecy about his mission, for if the plan is made known, spirits from other realms will wreck their true purpose in the coming Millennium.

This is not a mission he accepts with a full heart. He pleads with the Brothers. He is unworthy. He's unstable. His mind, narrow and unlearned. His body thin and weak. He desires only to be just another sailor out for a walk in the park. He confesses his fears. But the voices keep on and he cannot deny the promise they bring. They know so much about him already.

Some among the Brothers argue that Gil's not fit, though many insist he's well trained. Some, meeting him in the park riddle him with doubtful stares. Among the hordes of exotic hippies dressed in vests and jeans, hand sewn shirts and beads, shawls, long dresses and head-scarves, the Brothers appear as workers in ordinary seamen or lumberjack clothing. In time they will judge his fitness . . . and perhaps discard him.

Kennedy tells him from afar and without showing himself, "If you pass the trials set before you to save the earth, then you will receive the keys of redemption. You will be bathed free of all flaws and rewarded both in this world and the next. Together we shall claim our places on the Mountain. If you fail, you will live out your days in vagabond rags, know no peace as the world itself remains in chaos."

From a distance the Brothers direct him. He follows signals they pump through his mind. Flash-card faces of bearded holy men light his brain. Kennedy thinking on his Rock haunts him. Grainy voices of old men croon, and urge him into the streets. Some days they soothe his confusion, but most days they crack his ears when he makes a wrong move. They give no back-up and less help. They insist he must break free on his own.

As fog and drizzle glide under the Golden Gate Bridge, and night brings the smell of the ocean, he's happiest at their bidding. He pulls the knit cap and pea coat close as his boots strike the shiny cement. Though the Brothers' directions become difficult, a fine mist of moth figures and angels hovers about his body. Wondrous powers protect him as he makes his rounds. When he buys a pack of cigarettes, like he used to do in Ethiopia, counting out the money strains his understanding. He cannot tell the shiny coins apart. A handful of change over the counter brings suspicion from clerks who hand back coins or wait for more money as his fingers stiffen into squat bananas.

At times he spots Kennedy in his pea coat, cigarette at his side as he leans against a park tree, or even spiffy in his officer's blues standing by a hotel entrance as Gil, disheveled and shamed, passes by, and Kennedy eyes him otherworldly and intense. A nod from the great man lets him know he's headed in the right direction, and a wink warns of action ahead. "See," say the voices, "Kennedy watches you do your job. He's with you every step of the way. Right there in the streets, so fear no trouble. You are safe. He approves. He approves very much."

But now The Tycoons show up in earnest. At first Gil can't fathom why these old men are watching him. He intuits they have bribed someone to betray the reason he exists. Or did Franco or Busby somehow give him away? These wily Tycoons know only that he's the lead actor in the drama unfolding in San Francisco. They don't know his true mission. Now he begins to understand why they trained their cameras on him when he came out of the Induction Center. His James Dean smile hooked them through the roofs of their mouths. Now he understands their curious glances as he enters North Beach coffee shops. As they get close, their stale cigar smell chokes him.

Stout and bald, these older Hollywood stereotypes chew cigars for power. Jaws gape and thick fingers point to him from the screen porch above the courtyard behind his place on Garden Street. Their long lenses peer through his kitchen window and prick him. When he moves to the front room he catches their glint from the mortuary across the alley. They'd wake the dead to grab him with their lens.

At night they camp on the rooftop of the building next door and in the dark seek him out. X-rays pierce his walls, sweep his naked skin. The crew chatters while it chews at his every move. Attended by a raft of blonds in miniskirts Cecil B. himself often directs.

They film him day and night, even his dreams, and hope to unearth the secret reasons for his moves through the streets. They dog him in hopes that his soul can be sold for a great profit. They sense from clues, such as the interest of the Brothers, that by following him they will capture the very ticket-worthy creation of the Millennium of Peace.

Do their dull-wits grasp the meaning of this drama? Filming his life, without knowing his true role, fulfills their ignorance. Though he can't escape these schemers, he keeps his secrets in utter silence, even from Suzanne. This drives the wordless Tycoons crazy. De Mille himself makes demands similar to the parade of teachers who dogged his silences throughout his school career.

He returns to Garden Street only late at night, to sleep. He spends days and nights listening to the tune of the Brothers' directions. The Tycoons follow him in trucks or cars, spy on him from rooftops, and trail him along streets, onto buses and cafeterias. Tripping over each other to pack up their cases and cameras to follow him, they remind him of Keystone Cops bumping about on their stubby legs.

These clueless Tycoons lately let him know they require tricks. He should be clever. They lust to sell tickets while he fills with dread and fear he'll slip off into the cracks of his mind. They pursue him on a stage winding from North Beach to the Haight to the Tenderloin and back again. He ducks past windows, in and out of doorways, keeping close to buildings. Cars and buses try to knock him over. Cops give him wary looks and sometimes ask where he's going. He stops old ladies and bends to talk with their dogs. He may help dog and mistress cross the street. He helps lost tourists find addresses. He directs others to restaurants and theaters. He is helpful and keeps practice as a good angel.

"Action! Action," The Tycoons shout. "More action!"

Do they want me to tear my heart out?

He often despairs when calling out to the Brothers, because they never listen. For days he walks the streets according to their directions without seeing them. Out of the blue they surround him in shops and cafés along Haight Street. They eye him in bars and coffee hangouts in North Beach and in stores and restaurants on Post and Sutter.

He wanders from one trap to another, sits in a corner and hovers over a cup of coffee, waiting for hours to be known and fully charged with his duties.

They direct him with sign language or sometimes they hold up cue cards with a word or two in black letters. Often when he follows an inner command from the Brothers a Tycoon throws up his hands and walks off in disgust. Such grimy moguls care little about him. When he calls out, they don't answer. They are not friendly; have no wish to contact him. They only care to probe his secret moves, render him mere camera fodder. Sooner or later they must pay so he can eat. He assumes the contracts will be signed later.

As he walks the Elder Brothers often confirm that he is the Chosen One. He sees himself robed and afloat on mountainous white clouds. He pleads with the Great Lords to choose someone of moral strength and character, but they take no notice. Are they blind to his unworthiness? His lack of ambition? They plug their ears. They train him ever more intently for the great work.

They insist he walk the misty night past lighted windows of Victorian houses where common souls rest in the comfort of warm rooms. He passes restaurants and theaters, bakeries and laundries, parking lots and topless bar, back alleys, sheltered bus stops and shiny cafeterias.

While he walks, he sings to the Brothers the silent song they taught, "OM MA, OM MA OM."

Walking, these Brothers assure him, changes the world.

"Do not tell your secrets," they caution. "Though you have yet to understand, each step saves a thousand souls."

He walks with unceasing hope that the next corner, the next turn will reveal the Brothers waiting in joy with open arms to lead him to his reward.

The days pass into weeks, each step becomes more painful, and each coffee shop where he waits alone turns out to be empty of acceptance.

When he's drained and can walk no more, he traipses back to Garden Street and in his front room falls onto the mattress. He no longer follows clocks. He wakes with a start, to find no sense of time or place. The noon siren tells him of the day, the mortuary neon, of night.

At all times he is protected by the Brothers and Kennedy himself. The plan becomes clear. He begins the work of making the world safe. Kennedy will bring about the Millennium of Peace. He walks in the bliss of such knowledge. Despite his hunger for food, Gil's inner ear stays tuned to the voices that command him from corner to corner.

The Tycoons, grumpy and stinking, follow with their cameras. They entice him with women and promise riches if he reveals his true work. Though he is tempted because of his growing frailty, he remains true to the promise of the Brothers and the Millennium and will not betray the secrets of his soul. Soon, the Brothers assure him, he will speak truth to the multitudes.

Gil's Vision

◆

"A MUTATION OF THE RACE alters the world for all time."

Gil smiles and mouths these words to all who will listen. His strange, sly smile signals to anyone who looks closely that he is up to something.

His vision builds his imagination to bursting. He burns to lead these children and save humanity. Guided by the Elder Brothers, he dares to bring his flock into the pastures of heaven.

He spits at buses full of tourists gawking at pedestrians along Haight Street. These nylon, polyester puffy people, disfigured by flour and sugar and desk bound jobs, now in beehive hairdos, plaid shirts under suspenders and with cameras swinging about their necks like inverted nooses, are relatives from Dubuque and Hoboken. They don't suspect the mounted revolution in this sainted city of San Francisco.

Could Gil be the only one who understands the times and divines the import of the coming Millennium? Where are the Great Ones? Where is Jesus? Where are the Buddha and Moses? Is Mohamed asleep? Can't they hear the great cry of the world? Must they stay mute? Or God ignore human misery? Where are they? Is Gil the only one to prepare this city's horde of lost and angry children for the great trek from the wilderness? "You must till the soil," the voices whisper. "Nurture the seed, water the desert." Gil feels terror and cringes as he realizes that the Elder Brothers have prepared him for this very task.

IN THE EVENING I decide to go to the Fillmore and state my case. I ponder *should I call Suzanne and make a date to pick her up*, but I put the phone down, thinking the Brothers would prefer that I go without her. *She won't mind.* Instead, I send her a telepathic message that she should not expect me . . . I have more important work to do than go out on a date and dance the night into oblivion.

I imagine myself standing before a multitude of hippie kids in a field as I once dreamed of catching my students from jumping off the cliff's edge in Ethiopia, and they looked up to me for the answers. Now I must come through for these lost and lonely. These years will extend my commitment in Ethiopia, where I tried to further the cause.

I forget Suzanne.

I turn on the rock radio station and smoke a joint.

I take my time in the shower, and towel myself pink, trim my beard, select my best jeans, and slip into a loose-fitting blue shirt scrolled with flowers. And finally, I pull on my brand-new cowboy boots. Before I leave the shabby green apartment on Garden Street, I drop a tab of acid.

Hippies crowd the Fillmore entrance, unable to get inside. No Friday night for the past couple of years has gone without an open dance in that auditorium, but this night holds a special anniversary celebration . . . invited guests only!

A pretty girl wearing Indian beads inside the box office apologizes, "Want to buy a ticket for tomorrow night?"

I am outraged. Already the hippie leaders like Bill Graham have elevated themselves to "invited guests only." We, who began the revolution, must stay outside on the very anniversary of our ascension.

I decide I must speak of this to the crowd. Walking out into the mass of disappointed hippies milling about on the street, a voice in my head sends me around to the side entrance where heavy band equipment is carried in. I wait for the doors to open.

A couple of roadies, in classic western duds and handlebar mustaches, come out and stand by the doors, smoking.

When I walk over to them, they offer me a J. I share it with them, and when they go back inside, I join them. They give me a knowing look. A voice confides, "We have sent these gentlemen to usher you inside."

Electric guitars screech endless riffs. Strobe lights stab and jangle the music. Moonbeams and amoebic splotches float on the walls. The spiky-haired guitarists often get lost in their spidery runs. The beat seduces. My body must move. Pierced eardrums crumble my brain. Guitar screams destroy all thought. When the music stops, echoes bounce around my brain.

"Get up there on the stage and speak," the Brothers urge me. "We will provide the words."

During the change of bands I climb up on the stage and stand among the litter of amplifiers, speakers and the bewildering tangle of instruments.

Butterflies churn my stomach. Even so, I climb over the sprawl of wires inside an electric buzz of flashing lights, and look out on the swaying crowd. I lift a mike from its pole, assume a Lincolnesque stance, clear my throat for attention and wait for the words to start. I eye the crowd from wall to wall, yet the Brothers are silent. I wait for a note to be struck and my words to be delivered.

Two security guards come up and take me by the arms. A third removes the microphone from my hand. The three of them escort me down from the stage and through the crowd to the back of the hall where Bill Graham, in a V-neck sweater, stands with a clipboard. He glares with the indignation of a department store clerk catching a thief. "Who is this guy? No one said he could hijack the stage. Give him to the cops. He's trespassing."

IN THE FRONT ENTRANCEWAY Suzanne appears from nowhere and taps the blue-shirted security guard on the shoulder. She points to Gil, "He's my husband. He gets out of hand, sometimes. He's spaced out, is all. I'll take him home." She grabs Gil's arm.

One guard winks and Suzanne leads him stumbling down the same stairs they descended arm-in-arm on the first night they met.

A Whiter Shade of Pale

♦

SUZANNE PRODS ME, "Move into my place."

"Naw, it wouldn't be so good for us just now," I tell her.

"Why not?"

"We should stay like this," I sigh and try a smile.

The long slog back from meeting Kennedy has burdened my spirit. The acid stomach, the burning headaches, the lightening-like pains shimmering through my brain have drained the fire from inside. I cannot see past the four walls of my shrinking room. If I were to wake one morning as an insect I would welcome the distraction. There is no cover for me here. I am lost and abandoned on Garden Street.

We sit on the ratty mattress in the front room. She takes my head in her hands, tries for eye contact, and says, "I don't feel we're together anymore."

"I have things to do now." I'm irritated that she doesn't know better than to bug me about being together. "When I'm done, we'll get married, and go off and have a kid."

"Sure, just like that. Any old place by the side of the road – right after you do what you have to do."

"We can go up to your Uncle's in Mendocino, and get back to nature and raise goats. Suzanne, I don't expect you to understand, but I have important work to do here first." I'm unwilling to speak of my mournful destiny. I dare not reveal my secrets. Once when I spoke to her of the Brotherhood and the Tycoons, she mocked me. I can't trust her with new revelations.

"I'm sorry you don't know who I am," I say.

We are sitting back to back, turned away from each other.

She folds her arms. "I know who you are, Mr. Gilbert Stone. You're like everyone else."

"I am, and I am not. There are great forces working here. Greater than you know, Suzanne. This is the cusp of the new Millennium, right here in San Francisco. Try to understand this. A great miracle is about to unfold in this city. And I see now that I must get along even with the Tycoons. These are powerful forces at work."

"Oh? You're going to sit and watch powerful forces working?"

"I have been called. All right, it sounds fantastic, but look around you. Why are we all here, even you? Because something gigantic is about to take place. You don't have to believe me. Just look around. Sooner or later it'll come to you."

"So who or what is calling you, Gil? Tell me who. Tell me what."

I strive to stay silent, but cannot hold back. "I've been chosen and from my earliest days have had this calling. I've never lived a moment when I was not totally aware that my every thought and move prepared me for my calling — and for a task that would benefit the world."

She turns, now facing my back, "Chosen? For what? You can tell me."

"Well, I'm trusting that you'll believe me."

She tries to smile, "Gil, no one's been chosen since the Bible. Tell me, do you think you're flipping out? Some of your friends from Steiner think so."

"What if it's necessary to leave the beaten path? And go out of the ordinary? To achieve something that will last. I find that I must do just that. We're forging a new race. We are going to bring about a new and better Millennium."

"Honey, this is dangerous talk. People will think you're out of your mind."

"You believe the warmongers are in their right minds?" I get up and raise the bamboo window shade, letting in a blast of morning sun. I feel helpless before the light. "We are the Dawn Warriors, Suzanne, riding to meet the Night Destroyers. In a way, darling, I see myself leading a group of lost children — my generation."

Suzanne pulls at my jeans. "Well, let's not fight. We don't have to disagree."

"This is not a fight. I tell you what I'm here to do and you don't believe me."

"It's not that I don't believe you. It just sounds so outlandish." Suzanne stands and holds my shoulders. "Maybe you haven't told me everything, so I just can't understand. If you could explain a little more, I would think better of all this mystic hoopla."

"You imagine I'm out of my mind?"

"No."

"Then what are you afraid of?"

"Not everyone is going to understand."

"Do you understand?"

"I'm not sure. You say so much. S-s-sometimes you sound psychotic."

"When?"

She copies my matter-of-factness, "When we first met you were different."

"All this time, you never knew me? Well, that's true. I did keep things from you. Now, I'm telling you who I am. But you refuse to see."

"I'm serious, but right now you're confusing me because you're confused."

I stroke her arm, "You won't be confused if you believe me."

"You talk to people who aren't there, Gil. I've heard you."

I turn and stare out the window.

"That's great!"

She slaps her thigh, "You talk to people who aren't there, but you won't talk to people who are."

She shakes my shoulders until I can't look away from her.

Hardly moved, I study her with half-closed eyes. For a moment, she disappears into the sunlight. A moment later the corner of my eye catches the gleam of a camera lens.

"There!" I point to the roof of the mortuary. "They're up there with cameras, filming my life. Filming us, Suzanne."

She does not look where I point, just glares. "There's no one on that roof! No one is spying on you!"

"Oh, yes." I point again. "There, there.

Suzanne screams my name, punches me hard in the stomach and shouts into my face, "Wake up, Gil!"

She runs out the door and down the chipped green steps.

I follow and watch her run down the alley toward Divisidero. I yell after her, "Don't think they didn't film this little scene, Suzanne. You'll see," I shout. "You'll believe me when you see us up on the big screen!"

From my rickety porch I spot Kennedy in a pea coat standing at the end of the alley. He is smoking a cigarette as Suzanne runs past him. He catches my eye and nods, raising a fist. I am on the right track. He approves. He approves very much . . . though just now it's hard to believe.

The Fool on the Hill

◆

AS HE KNEELS ON THE GRASS, head in hand, Gil pleads to the God he summoned while filling out his application at the Army Induction center. "Today, I invoke the politicians and commanders who call upon me to do by stealth what they cannot accomplish with their mighty weapons and paltry political skills. To those who insist I lead, but refuse to think twice about putting me in harm's way, to those who lie and lust after far-fetched fantasies of victory, to those earthly disciples who tamper with and distort the shining words of my mysterious, love-filled God, I take umbrage. I preach wrath.

"Do not imagine that I am so crazy that I take my appointment as The One like some naive soul who fancies himself King Solomon or Moses in some former life, or Jesus for that matter.

"On the contrary, I have demanded proof. Daily, I challenge the stinking Tycoons who plague my life. In frustration I revolt against these insane voices who have taken over my mind. Using great patience and care, I have joined rigorous debates with the Elder Brothers of Kennedy who invade my world. I protest over

233

and over that they mistake me for someone else. For days I dismiss their directions. I run from them and hide, but each time they find me and begin again with their righteous babble to charm me back to their cause.

"Each night, following their commands exhausts me. I sweat, stinking in my pea coat, walking the streets alone with the crush of pain spanning my mind. Back and forth across the city of the millennium, I stand at the top of Lafayette Park to incant the words they feed me.

"But you, to whom I trusted my faith and reason, have forsaken me as sure as these cunning Tycoons and Kennedy's deceitful minions. I swear never again to work on their behalf. I can't take it anymore. I beseech you this final mercy on my lonely quest," he prays to the God of his childhood. "Tell them to leave me alone. I am nobody's savior. I yearn to be just another sailor walking his girl in the park."

A moment later the Brothers' voices protest, "No, no, don't be discouraged." They urge him into the street once again to walk his lonely nights away. "No, No. You are The One. We promise you. You have come here at this time, in this place to save the world. You are the Chosen One."

"Prove it," Gil says, weary now of their game. Wishing for death. "How do you expect me to believe I am The One?"

A patient voice makes clear, "You are the living proof. Every day, we show you how to save the world. Soon you will be the Anointed. And then all doubt will vanish."

"No! You only torture me. I walk and listen and you torture me."

"Sit on this bench and calm down. We will give you proof. We are your true friends, trust us."

"I trust no one. Give me money so I can buy food and pay the rent."

No answer, only a humming signal that they approve of his request. He's just where they want him, he knows. But their talking tires him. Whenever he asks for proof, they fall into patient, measured silence.

He's still angry and jumps up and circles the bench. "Why do you torture me? If I am truly The One, then you should feed me."

No answer. He is the perfect dupe of these Brothers.

"I'll go to the Tycoons," he threatens. "They will feed me. They appreciate me and will reward me."

"The Tycoons want only to cash in on your suffering."

"But at least they know I need to eat."

"You will be fed from your usual sources. Your body does not concern us. We purify your soul."

"But I need more help."

"We give you what you need."

"No! I can't eat words. Feed me! Am I less than the Israelites who received God-given manna?"

"In time you will see," they call.

Silence falls, Gil's brain is an empty beehive. Now he's alone and afraid. Loneliness grips him. He regrets the way he's talked to the Holy Brothers.

There is no sign of Kennedy. Meek and unsure, he walks back to the bench, sits and waits for them to take over his mind. Nothing. Only leaves overhead are rustling. Far away children are at play. In the distance traffic whirs. Life is dull and without bearing.

He pleads to the voices, "Forgive me, Brothers. I am genuine and sorrowful for my ingratitude and lack of respect."

Silence.

Gil stands and circles the bench. He stands on the bench. He stands on one leg and then hops down. He lays down on the bench and covers his eyes. He rolls off the bench and the ground bangs his knee. He lays there for some time, grips his knee and moans.

At last he opens his eyes, gets up and again sits on the bench. He waits. After a time, he spots Kennedy in his pea coat; he is leaning against a tree, in his hand a cigarette hangs at his side as he watches Gil horse around. He's embarrassed. He has been watching Gil all this time. He breathes deep and catches Gil's eye. He points his cigarette at Gil and casts him a wink that says Gil's anger is just and part of his training.

Will the voices reassure Gil? His brain remains an abandoned beehive. He panics.

"I will do as you command," he tells the voices.

Silence as he sits breathless.

"I am your servant."

An uncertain voice says, "You will only run from us again. You must believe that we are training you."

"See?" another tells him, "Kennedy watches and approves. He approves very much."

Gil's head bows, grateful the voices have returned. "I will do your bidding."

Now Gil spies the Tycoons slinking into the park. Already set up and rolling, they move down the slope toward him. When they focus in on him, he wants to get up and run.

"Sit still," a voice tells him.

Another joins in. "They are taking your portrait."

"Sometimes the Tycoons can be useful," the first voice adds.

"You must use these capricious pretenders," says another voice, "as they use you. Do something interesting."

Gil tries a cartwheel on the grass, but falls on his side. He tries again and this time falls backward and slams the small of his back. He tries to stand on his head, but falls over.

The failed athlete brushes grass from his pea coat and jeans. He walks straight up to the little group of Tycoons, two balding men chewing cigars and a tall blond woman in a sequined mini-dress; they stand behind the cameraman and soundman. Gil sticks his tongue out and makes a bulldog at the lens. These clowns love Gil's moves, jump about and wave him nearer. When he draws near, they move back and suck him across the grass toward a small grove. One holds up a neat sign lettered MORE.

Gil makes his hands into horns on either side of his head, becoming a charging bull. One mustached Tycoon waves his cigar and beside the camera mimes drawing a graceful bullfighter's cape. He sweeps and sweeps his cape. Joy surges as Gil lowers his head, hooves scrape the grass; he tosses his horns and charges.

After they've shot all they need of this little scene, his Tycoons draw back behind the camera, and slip into the grove of trees.

Gil is left charging in open space to the amusement of passers-by. They gawk as he growls, spits and lunges at them bull-like. He yells, whoops and snorts, and as they shake their heads he frightens them off.

They haven't understood the stakes for Gil. This is not play, but survival. These Tycoons filch some living part of him with each frame of film. He's angry and filled with rage, tricked. He will get these stinking Tycoons.

The Beatles' "The Fool on the Hill" runs through Gil's head. The song is about *him*. Each time he does something dim-brained that song gloats over him like a fleecy cloud. He is the fool on the hill. He knows the Beatles have spotted him, forlorn and alone, on Hippie Hill in Golden Gate Park as he follows the commands of the Elder Brothers. After having done cartwheels when the voices told him to be interesting, who knows what he did on Hippie Hill when the Beatles named him the Fool on the Hill.

GIL HAS A SPECIAL AFFINITY for John. They've been friends since childhood. During the war, with his father training in England, Gil's mother forced him stay at the kitchen table as she nagged about the starving children in Europe until he finished his plate and spooned down the peas and carrots or spinach and last dab of mashed potato. After he finally stuffed them down, and after listening to the radio and playing with his tin soldiers under the coffee table, and after his bath and being swept up in his mother's arms and carried off to bed, and after being read to by his uncle, the silly and childish bedtime stories that he pretended to ignore but loved — after that time, alone in his room in the dark with the black-out curtains clamped tightly over the window, after that time, in his dreams, that's where he would meet John.

Of course, John appeared to be a child of war-torn England, and a raggedy kid, but with great joy in his heart. After all, he recognized Gil. They gathered in their dreams to dance and play together — John and Gil and their friends from all over the world. Ten or a dozen of them frolicked every night, made their plans for the days to come.

They played flutes and often danced around a great meadow where all the world's children play. They chased each other in tall grass and patrolled the borders keeping an eye on the younger ones to make sure they don't wander off and fall over the edge of their dreams.

Later, they talked in earnest by a lovely pool surrounded by tall date palms. These half-grown men of his dreams do not play together like Gil's friends during daylight hours . . . in dreams they are different. They hold nothing back. A great fountain of joy splashes over them each night as they come together, blessing them with trust and love.

Since they sometimes play among the rocks and ruins of war they see the suffering of children of war. They enter into a pact that the dozen or so of them will someday band together and make certain that war and destruction cease to be. No more hungry, raggedy children, no more sorrow and fear. John becomes their leader. That glint in his eye knows just what to do.

NOW, GIL HAS *become* the Fool on the Hill, shamed and fearful that John will never recognize him. Mixed up with crass Tycoons and the demanding Brothers, and with Kennedy himself, caught in mazes of duty and denial, wanting to do the right thing, but no longer sure what needs to be done, Gil is a fool indeed, pieced together from bodiless voices that buzz in his beehive.

He cannot go back today on the vows of his childhood, vows that charge him day and night. He knows that Kennedy and the Elder Brothers chose him for the purity of his vows. Gil, along with John and the others know they can end war for all time. The prophets declare that if one earthly soul desires with all his heart to bring an end to war, eternal peace will be granted. Gil has no choice but to be that earthly soul.

He goes forth, fulfilling the prophecy with the guidance of Kennedy and the Brotherhood, and with the promises of John and the others, to bring about this great Millennium of Peace. He may be the Fool on the Hill, but he is not mad. He is not crazy, nor at the mercy of fantasies. Prophets have come before him and prophets will follow. He goes forth without fear. Kennedy and the Brothers show him the way.

"I am the way," Gil shouts, running out of the park. "I am the way."

Groceries

◆

IN THE GRASS, behind the trees lining Oak Street, the cameras grind away. Gil can barely make them out, but he knows they're filming from the back of a cream-colored Lincoln Continental.

AT DIVISIDERO, I GO into a small grocery much like the *Arab-bêtes* or stalls where I shopped in Ethiopia. The mustached Arab in white shirt, vest and head-wrap eyes me from behind the counter. My wild hair, beard and burning, bold eyes seem to bring suspicion. I flush and start to sweat.

The store sits squat and square, its four walls and narrow aisles are shelved with boxes and cans.

I'm hungry, but can't decide which package I want so I pace the aisles. Cheese and cold meats in a thick-glass cooler attract me. A rainbow of cans and boxes call to me. Beers in green and amber bottles pack another cooler are appealing. The choices overwhelm me.

There is a newspaper by the cash register that catches my eye. The Brothers have taught me to decipher answers to dilemmas from headlines. "SAVAGE OFFENSE MOUNTED," "Fierce Fighting in the Golan Heights," "CONGRESSIONAL HAWKS MEET, Deny Bombing of North." No clues here. The far left column head reads "LOSING WEIGHT CAN BE FUN"— that's the one! My hunger fades and there is no need for me to decide now. But a nameless desire remains.

I can see impatience building in the man behind the counter. *Buy something*. But I don't know what.

His eyes are saying, "Quick, a decision, hurry, buy something fast or I throw you out."

Anxiety now flashes out the back of my head. I'm growing warmer in my pea coat and loosen the top button.

The Arab's face doesn't change.

I wonder, *"Why don't you invite me to have a cup of tea. I would like to sit cross-legged and sip tea with you and discuss the world situation and perhaps gain a hint about your life.*

I now try now to choose something more to satisfy the Arab than to sate my inconstant hunger. *What does he want?*

I taste only the suspicions of the Arab. Feeling pressed, I pick up a package of rainbow fancy-fruit Life Savers. I lose my hand in my pocket until my fingertips touch the waiting coins. I draw out the change and some folded-over bills, and place two quarters, three pennies and two nickels next to the Life Savers.

The Arab's look quizzically at me, so I unfold a dollar and lay it next to the change.

The man rises from his seat on a milk box and shakes his head. He takes the quarter and rings fifteen cents on the cash register. He slides a dime toward the rest of the money and the Life Savers. "Doo much," he says with an accent.

Not quite understanding him, I glance at another newspaper with a number of pictures on the front page. There is a photo of young girl on a horse jumping a rail fence. Her black hat, riding breeches, boots and riding crop hold clues. She's so poised and eager in the grace of that jump. The title above the picture reads "The Grass Is Always Greener." A photo across the page depicts war and agony writhing in rubble from a bombed building. An old Asian woman with four skinny children is staring far off, dazed. The feet of a dead or dying body push into the picture's corner. I compare this with "The Grass Is Greener."

The Arab again says, "Doo much coin."

I nod toward the dollar and change next to the roll of Life Savers. "Enough?" he asks.

"Too much," the man says. His suspicions fade and he turns friendly.

"Ah, he recognizes me!

Good natured, the man says, "Put money in pocket."

Uh, but did I pay? I'm not sure. Did the cash register ring?

With patience the Arab opens the Life Savers for Gil and offers one. "Here."

It's clear he understands who I am. I take the fruity candy and suck it.

He waves again for me to take the money.

I obey by scraping the change into my palm and slipping it into a pocket. Then I offer the Arab a Life Saver, which he accepts, and with a smile and a wink pops the ring-shaped candy into his mouth. I get his meaning; this shopkeeper has known all along my true identity.

"Gud night," he says in his thick accent. As I walk out the door bells tinkle overhead.

I head down Divisidero, the sidewalk is deserted. I see the cream-colored Continental pass ... *maybe they're ready to talk to me.*

A lone woman looms in the distance. In the glare of streetlights I can't make out her face. She has the bold stride of someone I know. *Perhaps we will have coffee together and hash over world affairs, or perhaps she'll give me advice about this mission.* My hope grows. Is she someone from a long time ago? From a block away I see a flowing cape and long, breeze-blown light-colored hair, her head is down. *Is it Suzanne?* I close my eyes to form her face. When I open them she is gone.

Walking down Divisidero I read the signs aloud — "U.S. POST-AL SERVICE ... BEER AND WINE TO GO ... THE FRIENDLY BANK ... CANDY ... SHOE SHINE PARLOR ... DOUGHNUTS

... WHILE U WAIT ... C923326 ... FURNITURE OUTLET – REAL VALUE ... BY ORDER OF ... VOTE ... DRINK YAHOO ... ICE CREAM – BUY A GALLON ... KEYS MADE."

When I linger at a sign or am drawn to a particular one, I know the Divine Ones guide my eyes there for a cosmic reason.

I often hear snatches of talk from people on the street that lead me to a correct decision, or a line from a car radio broadcasts my true route. "FREE ESTIMATES ... FREE PARKING ... TOW AWAY ZONE ... DON'T CROSS ... BUS STOP ... CATS PAW ... GLOBE PAINT ... BAKING DONE ON PREMISES ... PLUMBING SUPPLIES." These clues from the Great Ones guide me. They map the salvation of the planet.

At Oak Street I spot Kennedy in his officer's overcoat, quite casual as he leans against a tree, cigarette at his side. I catch his hero's eye. It would be nice to stop and talk, tell him how faithful I am to his thoughts, but I'm shy.

Kennedy nods knowingly, but makes no gesture for me to stop. His lets me know that my work has been well done.

"See," the voices tell me, "Kennedy oversees your work. He approves. He approves very much."

My eyes, of their own accord, lift to a small sign whose neon reads "ROOMS." I understand that I am to go back to my two rooms on Garden Street.

I head home to work on the Sphinx and await further instructions.

The Sphinx

◆

AS I WALK DOWN THE NARROW ALLEY called Garden Street, I lean close to the mortuary wall. Near the closed funeral home garage, next to a parked hearse, Kennedy appears in a dark uniform, holding a hat in one hand and a cigar in the other. He is watching me approach. He seems to be noting my intensity. I am wary of this solitary figure as I try to pierce my hero's puzzled stare. The commander in chief says nothing, but nods knowingly to acknowledge that I am on the right track.

"See," the voices whisper, "Kennedy watches you do your job. He approves."

I think to invite him in, but know that he wouldn't come. The big man has other things to do. Just now I doubt he really approves, or that I'm doing a great job.

I skip across the alley and up the chipped green steps. I pluck the key from the mailbox under the telephone bill that I pretend isn't there. Inside, I raise the shade on the fading stars before I hit the mattress. For atmosphere I've taped a poster of the guru Satchidananda to one wall and nailed a Dylan album cover to another. From under the mattress I pull a plastic bag of loose weed and one rolled joint. I fall back and smoke. I'm drained. I don't eat or sleep, but lie on the mattress with my face to the wall musing on my predicament. *Every thing's hunky dory. Where is that last bit of muenster I smuggled out of the Shopway?*

All night I crisscrossed streets on orders from the Brothers. I attended to their every direction, but I now feel skinned and wretched. My toes burn and the balls of my feet swell tight in my shoes. Following orders, from first one voice then another, I walked up Geary until one said, "Turn around and walk back." I snaped-to on my heel, walked twenty paces until another voice commanded, "Stop! Turn around and go up to Van Ness." People passed me with strange looks.

When I could no longer abide the orders I ran into Zims and hid in the men's room. But when I came out, more directives pounded me. "Go this way." "Don't bump that woman." "Turn back." "Cross the street, quick, don't look back." "Walk fast, but don't run." "Go to the other corner, quick." "Turn around." "Go up Hyde." "Keep going." "We need you to do this." "You are cleansing this block." "You are making this street fit for the Millennium."

Lying on my bare mattress, I have no idea of the time, only the dark. A cigarette after the joint tastes flat and ratty. My mouth dries to balsa. I don't go into the kitchen; the Tycoons might poke their lenses through the window. They never want me to be out of their sight. But now I'm too thirst-ridden to care. I creep into the kitchen and gulp from the tap.

"The Sphinx" is my name for the unborn albatross about to un-fold its nascent wings that stands in the kitchen. I call it the Sphinx because though it is a bird and not a lion, it presents me riddles and answers my questions as it leads me on about the streets. Pieces of metal frame this sculpture I've formed from odd street scraps of wood, glass and other refuse. Now I must add a last touch that shows this chick will burst free and soar. These pieces I've joined create a memento to my endless travels through the streets, and a tribute to the peace I bring. I dip these bits of flotsam into a pot of melted lead on the stove and weld bits onto my growing bird. I pace and circle until this albatross pulls me into itself, where I will hear the whispers and the answers.

I build this bird at the Elder Brothers' command. At the right time the Sphinx will free the secrets of the Millennium and the world will become safe. The waiting may be hard to bear, they tell me, but, after all, I'm saving mankind. Worth the wait.

I should hammer the tiny, flat nail heads back into the flooring, as they keep riding up from the deteriorating linoleum, but the heads stick up just enough for me to walk around barefoot and feel pleasurable pain that doesn't quite pierce the soles of my feet. They make me feel like an Indian Rajah asleep on a bed of nails.

I have a shower in the bathroom off the kitchen. The water is so hot the windows steam up and I am inside a rain forest. With a red bandanna knotted around my long curling hair I'm transformed into a South American Indian living on mescaline and herbal roots. A painter's ladder leans in the corner where I sometimes perch above the lens probes of the nosy Tycoons.

Some days I'm used to these stinking cigar-chewers, other days, they drive me crazy. They have no idea that I'm carrying out the Brothers orders, but these raccoon Tycoons do not let me rest. They want to steal my secrets to make them even richer. Then they will junk me. I will disappear like glass colliding with a rock, then swept up into a dustbin.

The rock-n-roll music station gashes my brain.

I go about working on the Sphinx quite cautiously. Under direction, I join one piece of glass or metal to another. A cigarette hangs from my lips. The furrowed brow of the artist, the touch of the sensitive fingers, the tinge of divinity lighting my brain.

Now I join an old metal hinge to a hunk of wood I tore off an old bar sign. The Sphinx comforts me, as does the rice I eat when the Elder Brothers allow me.

I glue slivers of mirror to strips of metal painted green and blue and then attach the metal to the wrought iron base of an old floor lamp with melted lead. My Sphinx now has the breadth of a one-winged eagle, an American albatross. Her dazzle attracts and I crawl under her and lie down. I can feel the tiny nail heads against my back. I can see right through to the top of her and my mind is eased. What a soft cloud of comfort descends upon me.

But a Tycoon bobs up at the window over-looking the little backyard, taps on the pane grinning and waves me to get up. I'm frightened. They've never before come this close, or felt so real. Always before I knew I could handle them. Now they are coming for me in truth. And I've never been so lonely in my life. I would cry, but can't find the tears. In truth I long for even these ignorant Tycoons to contact me. I crave their wondrous looks that indeed I must be up to something cosmic and have come to make real contact. Yes, they will have to pay me, along with the Brothers. I cannot walk another mile; take another direction; dodge another camera or save another soul. Pain racks me. I lie on my bed of nails flat out of hope.

I leap to my feet. I won't live in this world. The remedy is in hand. I will take leave. I'll teach these grubbing Tycoons a lesson. Show these ungrateful Brothers — and Kennedy, too. Remind them all I cannot be treated lightly. Let them find another savior. I will kill myself to find my own rest. Murder my body and slap salvation in the face. I wish them all goodbye, Kennedy, the Brothers, the Tycoons, and Suzanne, my mother, my father, and my brother. I gladly leave them all for one moment's peace. I will show them the way.

Gil PULLS THE WATER-STAINED kitchen window shade all the way down. Then he turns on the wrought iron lamp, twisting the shade sideways as a spotlight. He steps between the shade and the bright light to appear as a shadow to the short-sighted, moldy Tycoons. They will regret not being kinder.

Ready to die, now, he dares them to film his dusky reflection from the courtyard and the camera on the roof of the mortuary. Nervous silence fills his skull. He removes a long, thin carving knife from the kitchen drawer, hunkers down before the light and waves the knife overhead, casting his image on the window shade transforming himself into a silent movie star. He senses the Tycoons shuddering outside. They must feel sorry for him. The Brothers come, sweet and full of regret. Do they believe he'll do away with himself? They're bewildered. He brandishes the blade at the shade again. Ah, fear fills these devil Tycoons. Who will they follow and torture when he's gone? Star in their movie? Who'll be their fool on the hill? He will die with his secrets. Oh, the cash they will lose!

Knife held high, he paces by the window as they film his ghost. He runs the blade across his neck. He jabs the blade close to his heart, They see that he is serious. "High Drama on High Nails." There's a title for these hungry Tycoons. Standing near the shade, he rips off his shirt and holds the knife close to his heart. He presses the sharp tip to his skin, and breathes slowly as they gawk and the cameras whir. They are egging him on! "Give us a great climax!" Gil presses the blade harder. More pressure will break his skin. "You are chicken," they smirk. Not a word from the Brothers.

Gil turns his body to compose a stark silhouette. He pretends to plunge the knife through his chest, feeling the cold steel on the skin between his arm and rib cage. he screams, bends and falls. Struggles to get up, then slumps into silence.

He lies there for some time, moving only slightly to adjust the location of the sharp nail heads on his body. The Tycoons breathe hard, surely he is dying. Sorry and guilty, they know their lack of kindness killed him.

Gil is all smiles. The Tycoons believe everything they see. Less easy to fool, the Brothers and Kennedy know he's alive though he remains still and silent. Let the Tycoons know death's blade in their guilty hearts. The Brothers laugh with him. The poor, baffled Tycoons, their cameras are food-less. He is almost sorry for them.

After a time he tires of the game, to say nothing of the nail heads, but knows that once the Tycoons find he's not dead they'll go on haunting. He pleads with the Brothers to rescue him from this hell.

"No," they tell their little savior, "you must continue the work."

He pleads with them, "Release me."

"Not yet," they croon, "you have much to learn."

"Tell me what you expect."

"Everything will be revealed," they repeat.

"How is he to accomplish this work?" "Be happy," they tell him, "for the work is great, the sacrifice is great and the reward will be greater still. More will be told," they say in joyous tones, "your fate is revealed in your every action."

GIL HAS LOST THE PICTURE of himself in this time, in this place, among these preparations for the Millennium. Choking on his confusion, charmed by the mysteries of the Brothers and strangled by the Tycoons, he falls to his knees under the shadow of the Sphinx, in awe of the work to be done. He's filled with the fear of his ancestors, imprisoned in a web of secrets. Watched, probed and tested in every thought and movement, never safe. He has become a mere actor caught up in the fine wheels and sprockets of a camera, cut and spliced to flicker across screens that would spill his essence out of his frail farting vessel into a heap of ravel.

Go Ask Alice

◆

"HOW WOULD YOU LIKE to head up my Peace Corps?" the boss asks Gil. The voice is quizzical in a paternal way, like it is offering an invitation to a celebration.

Gil is moved by the offer despite his wet discomfort as he opens his eyes to the bright sunshine seeping through the trees of Golden Gate Park. He makes out the dome of aqua-blue sky, shivers from the January cold, and stretches his sore limbs. He spent the night huddled in his pea coat under a eucalyptus tree in the Panhandle, cold and restless on the damp grass. His jeans are cold and clinging. *The Peace Corps?* He chews on his beard. Wandering memories of a sparkling JFK seated in the Oval Office tug from his dreams.

Then, crooning voices of the Elder Brothers salve his ears, "Look, look," they say, "today is the day."

A Christmas song floats into Gil's head. "Go tell it on the mountain, over the hills and everywhere. Go tell it on the mountain . . .."

"Today is the day," the Brothers' croon.

Yawning and rubbing his palms together, Gil watches a gaggle of preteen kids wrapped in blankets warming themselves around

251

burning trash barrels. Under the blankets these runaways wear raw rags and shiver in the cold dewy air. He walks over to the smoky barrels and holds his hands to the heat. He's so much older than these kids — and wiser. They do not know yet that he is ordained their leader. One or two give him a nod. He nods back a knowing nod. The fire scorches his face, singes his eyebrows. Smoke grates at his eyes. His jeans and pea coat steam. He's OK.

He's all right. Today is Gil's day. It's been promised. Look at him there, ready to take command. Gil's the man. But does he swagger? Hell no. Salt of the earth. The good boy, modest even.

When he can't stand the fire another minute, he heads toward Haight Street. The sidewalk is slick in the damp morning cold. On the corner of Masonic and Haight he stops in front of the Drugstore Cafe. Eying the red, white and blue sign over the door, Gil walks to the window and peeks inside; his eyes roam over the big brown glass bottles and other apparatus remaining from the drug emporium days. The glass cabinets that once housed pills, tinctures and ointments now display donuts and rolls. Someone shuffles back and forth behind the counter. It's about to open and he hungers for donuts and coffee.

Waiting, he bounces in his boots to keep warm and watches the street come to life. Only a few cars and early risers, neighborhood folk who still work for a living. More cars. More people. The houses of Haight-Ashbury, like suburban mothers, push their long-haired kids in beads and bandannas onto the street. Early morning hippies look like everyone else . . . tousled hair, sagging faces and sleep-drugged eyes. For a moment, Gil does not feel so very different, but then, of course his mission and his difference intercedes.

A tall fellow in powder-blue jeans, with long hair and a drooping mustache opens the cafe.

Gil crosses the floor of black and white octagonal tiles to the sweets case. The place bustles. He orders two coffees and six glazed donuts flaking with iced sugar. He wolfs down the first donut while the counterman draws his coffee. He eats a second still standing, waving a ten dollar bill he got from Suzanne, and gulps a hot coffee with his mouth full while pointing at two large cinnamon buns. He settles into a chair by the window, tears off hunks of half-done dough, chews and looks out the window, chews and tears and gulps more. He is skin and bone and gives up trying to remember when he last ate. No word from the Brothers. No Tycoons. No Jack, for that matter, after putting Gil in charge.

Gil fastens on two large men with full beards drinking coffee. Playing chess this early! He's guilty about wolfing down the donuts and buns. Just a chunk of bun sits on the wax paper. He feels guilty packing his stomach with white flour and sugar, but stuffs down that last sweet chunk. He swills his coffee dry, then sits staring at the chess geniuses. Large bearded faces rest on large arms and hands that weigh moves in silence. These two look like the Smith Brothers. Gil's heart starts to pump hard. The Brothers mean to keep an eye on him. At once he looks down, unworthy. Are they here to give him some sign? Will they allow him near? Head bowed, he's shamed by all the donuts he's eaten.

After a time, Gil looks up at them and though they don't react, he quickly looks away. Such faces shine and blind him. He becomes bolder and watches their large hands hover over each piece. Soon he allows himself a deep swift glimpse of their faces, so bent to the game. Does Gil dare go over and watch?

One of the men looks up at him. Poor Gil wants to duck. He wants to either approach these awesome souls, or better yet bolt out the door and be gone. He's paralyzed, but at last stands and heads to the men's room. Inside he reads wall scribbles: "Rimbaud eats colored glass" and "I stuffed Lucy's pussy with diamonds." He tries to move his bowels, but has nothing in them yet and can only pee. He washes his face and hands with rusty water, surely the blood of the Lamb and, though he's tempted to keep it, with grace slips his stained paper towel into the wastebasket.

Back in the cafe, he takes a breath, pounds his stomach, and strides right up to the chessboard. Neither Elder raises his beard. What the hell, he feels something courtly in his stance, as a kind of Norman Rockwell figure, a cheeky bum sucking up to two Blessed

Ones. Indeed, he is the Good Soldier in rags. "Hey fellas, what's to become of me?"

One Brother turns from his pieces. His bright inner beauty beams through Gil. A voice asks, "What are you doing here? Today is the day." The other Brother moves his rook and looks up, angered and grumpy. "You shouldn't be seen with us. It's too soon."

Gil steps back. "But what am I supposed to do?"

"You'll know soon enough." Grumpy says.

"Today is the day," Smiley boasts. "After today you'll know how to proceed point by point. But first, you must be summoned, then learn to suffer scorn. Only then will you be of help to us."

"Now, go!" The one who smiles, turns grave and places his hand on his king, as perhaps on Gil. Yes, he sends Gil on his conquest.

Both ask, "How can you doubt us now?"

AWED, GIL BACKS AWAY, gives a little bow and, dreamlike, floats out the door and into a crowd of long-haired hippies in bell-bottom jeans, tie-dyed shirts washed in greens and blues caught together in a giant crystal. Some come as wizards and soothsayers, some even as Spanish Pistoleers in cornered hats or dastard pirates draped in kerchiefs and cloaks.

He joins in the flow toward the Panhandle. Having already met with the chess-playing Brothers, Gil feels laden with importance. Surely this swell of hippies comes to escort him personally to the ceremony.

Lush rock rhythms pull them across Stanyan Street into Golden Gate Park for a very special day. Excited and eager the Tycoons wait for Gil behind the tall trees and today he even savors the worthiness of his life being committed to film. Does he detect a touch of reverence in their manner that hints of veneration as he comes to lead his generation into the Millennium?

The spectacle takes shape before him. He enters as the sun is climbing, the crowd lolling on the Polo Fields. He gazes from the sun's zenith upon the rush of warm bodies that dance and sing in his honor. Brothers and Sisters, colorful beyond words, fill the giant meadow, rise and heave as waves on a Kansas wheat field. He basks in triumph witnessing the chosen of the Millennium come together to beam their love thoughts to the world.

Painted faces burn in Bengali bursts of yellow and orange. Women dance in East India's wrap-around paisley dresses of purple and green. Carved sandalwood and deep-blue lapis lazuli earrings flash in the sun. The men parade their abundance of long hair and beards. Children — carried, wheeled and toddling — twist and gape. The bright San Francisco sun burns the grass and trees as heat waves shimmer and the lawn dances.

Expectant flower children by the thousands frolic and gambol on the grass, do somersaults and cartwheels, their eyes big as saucers. They stream from the Panhandle through the winding paths of Golden Gate Park, laugh and call out to strangers. Old-fashioned neighborliness floods them as if headed to a Nebraska barn raising or great Texas barbecue. Toe-dancing ballerinas mix with cowboys and East Indian maidens. They all come. More than Gil expected. The Brothers promise him: "More than twenty-five thousand believers!"

"I am here, Jack, your Peace Corps at my feet."

As Gil becomes part of the crowd, he spots Kennedy in a navy dress jacket leaning against a tree, watching the joy erupt. He smokes a fat Havana, and watches these children of his reign pass. Gil catches the old man's eye. A glance from the commander tells Gil he's on the right track. "See," the voices tell him, "Kennedy oversees your work. He approves. He approves very much."

The crowd settles onto the Polo Field grass. The Brothers gloat in Gil's ear, "Here are the children of a generation come to pipe their music before a world gone mad. This has been our dream from the beginning."

Gil heads for the east end of the field where a stage rises with microphones and banks of speakers. The Quicksilver Messenger Service bashes out an anthem. Guitars spike the ears of the dancers and invite them into a brave new world.

The strut of strident and self-righteous organizers says, "Look what we have done. We are changing the world."

Gil stands offside and oversees the presentation. For their Human Be-in, a word-play now fluid reality, they plan a few speeches, some music, and a mighty show of hippie power. Gil approves under the noonday sun.

The buzz deepens into a hush. Scrawny Paul Krassner, once a child prodigy of the violin and now a Realist of the antiwar movement, in a white, open-collar shirt comes to a mic and howls. "Howoo! Call me werewolf, you look beautiful out there." He leans forward, the embodiment of brass. "We have come to bury Caesar!" The crowd roars. "We have come to stick a giant Texas barbecue fork up the ass of Lyndon Johnson!"

The crowd sighs a yawn of approval.

"We have seen hundreds of our brothers come home in body bags. We have seen starving Vietnamese run from flaming villages. If we don't stop the Department of the Dead now it will ship more bombs and planes, more napalm, more flamethrowers overseas and more of our brothers to their deaths. Look into the cancerous eyes of the frightened old men in Congress. Do they have souls? Not one of them."

This is a playful, sweet crowd. The cancerous, frightened old men must have been this beautiful once. What happened to them? Can we be different?

"You are the savior," the Brothers remind Gil.

Gil beams upon the assembled while Krassner screeches on. "Our mighty nation has been perverted into a grotesque war machine. We are here to stop the machine. Stop the war. Stop the fucking war machine now."

The crowd flinches, but then responds, "Stop the machine . . . stop the machine . . . stop the fucking machine." The chant builds rolling volleys.

A young organizer walks over and whispers into Krassner's ear.

Krassner listens. A short muffled difference erupts. Then, shaking his head, Krassner turns to the microphone and drawls, "Guess what? This is not an antiwar rally. Welcome to the sweet-as-pie Human Be-in." He laughs, looks to the side where the organizers gather. "Now they tell me I'm not supposed to talk about the war. I'm only here to introduce the speakers . . . so fucking pardon me."

The crowd hoots back, "fucking, pardon me."

Gil watches from the side of the platform. The Elders instruct him, "Be ready to speak." He is assured they will put the right words in his mouth for he is the spiritual instructor of this gaudy human wheat field. Is he really ready to lead his flock? Gil raises a mighty wave of his steel arm. Soon, he shall reveal the Divine Plan to Krassner and these mongrel organizers.

A distant growl grows across the field, a rumble of engines. All eyes turn. From a ridge overlooking the meadow, a CinemaScope vision, as sweeping as a John Ford Comanche invasion, Hells' Angels on motorcycles — a hundred abreast and deep thunder toward them. Fear rolls over the crowd. Everything stops. Krassner, speechless, watches while this sea wave swoops down in a dark wing.

Gil stifles a strong urge to bolt as these fierce hellions roar full throttle into the dell.

"Do something," Gil's voices order. Gil wrings his bones for a way to prevent bloodshed. "Beam peaceful thoughts!" his voices demand. He beams and beams, "JOIN US IN PEACE."

A horde of Morlocks howl, launched from Satan's lap, motors smoking. They roar in straight from the center of hell itself. Smoke hovers around their shoulders. The crowd freezes while a great disaster unfolds upon the peaceful green meadow.

The Brothers beam a lion's heart into Gil to keep him from running.

Does Gil fear the fury of five hundred screaming warriors?

But never doubt the power of the Brothers. At the last moment, Gil steps forward and makes the demons heed his beamed instructions. The charging army of bikers break into two groups and encircle the crowd, then nose-in their front wheels at each end of the platform. Engines die in one rumbling roar. The massive riders dismount. It's high noon in Golden Gate Park.

Skulls stare from black leather jackets that flaunt American flags and winged devils. Sleeveless denim shirts show muscled arms dripping tattoos. Faces heavy with beards, sunglasses and long hair look set to maim with chains dangling from belts. Anger rolls from their shoulders. Their women dismount, also in leather and chic impregnable tight jeans.

The flower children, fearful as a Vietnamese peasant village, wait for the foreign invaders to stomp and quake the ground.

The assembly waits for Gil's voice.

At any moment these five hundred bikers could wade into the crowd with chains, knives and brass knuckles — but for Gil. He, the old man from the sea, the ancient seer, the speaker of truth to the powerful stands with his staff against the rude tide.

What? These Hells Angels want to join the renegade forces? They drift to the edge of the crowd, sit on the grass, and gaze baby-faced at the platform. They have come to be part of the Be-in, not to annihilate it. Relief trickles through the crowd as fear, thick as barbecue sauce, drains off.

Yes, it's true, Gil has calmed these angry Angels. The Brothers murmur about him, pleased. "The Miracle of the Bikers," they say. Moses down from the mount, his arms folded, he looks upon the assembled. Here, in one swift movement the Brothers reveal Gil's deathless, invincible preparation. The fearsome Angels have succumbed to form a wall of steel against those who would break up the Human Be-in. "Beware the informers," the Brothers warn.

Gil scans the crowd and finds federal smirks behind dark glasses and Hawaiian sport shirts, hirelings of the FBI and the CIA, their faces painted with fake hallucinogenic eyes. Among the crowd these capitalist tools work themselves into the goings-on only to report to the armaments hawkers who would have their own children clubbed and shot should they fail to marry the war machine.

Krassner quiets the crowd. "All right now. All right. Let's welcome our bipedal friends here. They've come to be with us, to show our united strength to the world." A roar goes up.

The Angels look about with an air of, "What? We never meant to cause a stir."

So cool, everybody here, even to us.

Krassner rants, "So let's get on with it! Now, I'm only supposed to be the master of ceremonies . . . I've used up my time . . . ain't that a fucking laugh? My own fuckheads censor me."

The crowd chants, "Let fuckhead speak. Let fuckhead speak. Speak, Krassner, speak!"

"All right, all right. It's a good thing they're my friends over there, or I stay up here 'til they drag me off. But I'm a nice guy . . . right? I'm going to introduce our next speaker, OK? But remember, we're not here to be gurued to sleep. So, listen to these prophets and psychedelic cowboys, but don't be fooled about why we're here and what we have to do . . . we're here to stop the war. We're here to shake loose the crusty scabs of the greedy war mongers . . . once again. Let's be quick about it.

"Now, let's hear from a poet of the first order, a patriot who once again looks upon the hungry minds of a down-trodden generation . . . and inspires them . . . Allen Ginsberg."

A great roar goes up.

Ginsberg climbs to the platform, a gramps before his time, with long, straggly hair and beard. He sports a spanking-new Nehru shirt under a brown business vest, red, Indian, silk pants, sandals, and a sparkling round, yellow skullcap. He springs onto the platform, a Russian bear unleashed by the gods. Laughing a few words to Krassner, he shambles over to the microphone.

"I'm stoned," he says right off. "Stoned on this beautiful day, on this array of brother- and sisterhood. You are beautiful out there. We are here today to witness a miracle. I see the power. I see the strength to choose love and peace over war and destruction."

The crowd calls back and sways with him.

"This is not an antiwar rally. This is a love rally. We know where the war is, and we refuse to participate. Maybe my friend Paul, the Realist, got carried away. He may even be correct, but we have discovered new ways to put the world right.

"We do not fight fire with fire. We follow a better way. We fight hatred with love, fight stupidity with love, fight fear with love, fight fight with love. We are doing everything our misguided brothers in power are afraid of doing. We are stone-aging them back to civilization."

At the word "stone," a roar smashes the sky. The gentle bear bends into the uplift, drops his arms and intones, "OM. OM. Join me," he shouts.

The crowd responds, "OM."

Ginsberg hums into the mike, "OM" and claps tiny finger cymbals and dances his bear dance.

"A little improvisational poem," he says to the crowd, unsteady on his feet. He turns to the others on the platform. "What do you think it takes to get up here? It takes a little white rabbit."

Ginsberg laughs a faraway laugh and looks to the sky in a frozen stance. Is he confused, what does he expect, a little white rabbit? Has he forgotten his whereabouts?

The poet comes back to himself.

"I want to read a poem in honor of today. I want to share this with those of you who think I quit this profession to use drugs and follow gurus. I am honored to read this poem I wrote last week on my way across this war-blown country of ours. You are the first to hear this." He laughs, "They won't let me read all of it. I had to pick out certain parts because they said it's too long, so here's what's left of it, liberal censorship and all."

He laughs and pulls several sheets of paper from his vest pocket. Wind whips the papers.

Ah, Jack, Gil remembers him pulling the pages of his inaugural address from his coat pocket and the wind playing the same game.

Ginsberg stands up tall, no longer the bear. Dignity broadens his stance as he lets the words rise and fall, seek heights, growl with deep rolling rhythms.

"From *Returning North of Vortex*," Ginsberg tells the crowd. He holds the pages against the wind as he reads:

> Red Guards battling country workers
> in Nanking
> Ho-Tei trembles,

Mao's death near,
Snow over Iowa
cornstalks on icy hills,
bus wheels murmuring in afternoon brilliance toward Council
Bluffs
hogs in sunlight, dead rabbits on asphalt
Booneville passed, Crane quiet,
highway empty — silence as
house doors open, food on table,
nobody home —
sign thru windshield
100 Miles More to the Missouri.

. . .

Detach yrself from Matter, & look about
at the bright snowy show of Iowa,
Earth & heaven mirroring
each other's light
tiny meat trucks rollin' downhill
toward deep Omaha.

. . .

"Meanwhile, under the influence of LSD
Veronica races through the fields
in an acute panic" —
Author Dal Curtis
In a violet box her big tits fall on snowy ground.
Gray ice floating down Missouri, sunset into Omaha
Bishop's Buffets, German Chocolate, wall to wall carpet
Om A Hah, Om Ah Hum

. . .

Let the Viet Cong win over the American Army!
Dice of Prophecy cast on the giant plains!
Drum march on airwaves, anger march in the mouth,
Xylophones & trumpets screaming thru American brain —
Our violence unabated after a year
in mid-America returned, I prophesy against

> this my own Nation
> enraptured in hypnotic war.
> And if it were my wish, we'd lose & our will
> be broken
> & our armies scattered as we've scattered the airy guerrillas
> of our own yellow imagination.
> Mothers weep & Sons be dumb
> your brothers & children murder
> the beautiful yellow bodies of Indochina
> . . .
> You pledge to God to send
> 100 or 10 or 2 or $1 a month to the
> Radio Bible Hour —
> The electric network selling itself:
> "The medium is the message"
> Even so, Come Lord Jesus!
> Straight thru Nebraska at Midnight . . ..

At last, as if he'd been holding the flutter pages captive, Ginsberg allows the sheets to flutter off with the wind.

Many in the crowd rise, clap and cheer.

"More, more, more," they shout.

"READ MORE! READ MORE!"

The poet answers, "I share my innermost feelings because that's my job, that's everyone's job. Listen! We're all One Being."

He goes on through large tears, "Why am I crying? Because all of us, every one of us, is part of the truth. They know it in India; they know we are all one. Even Columbus proves we are all one."

Gil follows the rise of Ginsberg's voice. *The heart of the poet is near.*

Ginsberg says, "Let us pray. Pray now before the haunches of the beast."

Gil prays to his inner voices. "Brotherhood unlock my throat, give me strength to speak truth into the heart of everyone present, touch each face, wipe the ash from every soul, let me serve to rise above the smallness of this life to bring the word of the Messiah, to cleanse the earth once and for all time. Open my throat Lord put the words there . . . Ahhhhhhhhhhhhh." Gil screams a silent scream.

On the platform, Ginsberg prays his Hindu mantra, "*Om Namah, Shivaya* [I offer to Shiva a respectful invocation of His Name.]." He chants and dances his Russian bear dance and claps his finger cymbals. "Om Namah Shivayah, Om Namah Shivayah," over and over and over until the crowd picks up the chant, and comes to its feet, dancing. Each part of the great meadow rises in small clusters to dance a jig or a shuffle, and chant, "Om Namah Shivayah . . . Om Namah Shivayah . . . Om Namah Shivayah."

The organizers grow uneasy.

Someone tells the band to start playing, but the music coming over the speakers cannot match the chanting flower folk.

The organizers look to each other. This is not their plan. Several more speakers are waiting. The crowd is out of hand.

"Om Namah Shivayah . . . Om Namah Shivayah."

The entire meadow of twenty-five thousand souls dances and chants. "Om Namah Shivayah . . . Om Namah Shivayah."

The organizers can't hear each other and shout among themselves while the chanting rises and dancing grows frenzied. "Om Namah Shivayah . . . Om Namah Shivayah . . . Om Namah Shivayah."

The organizers decide to stop the dancing and chanting before something god awful happens.

This must be the holy reenactment of Moses' descent from Mount Sinai bearing the word of God. This same power greeted the prophet carrying tablets from the unbearable face of Yahweh Himself. The power of his voice roused the people to this pitch, so that, trapped and enraptured with guilt, they threw down their idols, and renewed their covenant with the God of Abraham.

Gil's mouth and throat join the chant, inspired by the voices of the Brothers.

The organizers appoint Krassner to quell the crowd.

Frenzy sweeps in, a catharsis. "Om Namah Shivayah . . . Om Namah Shivayah."

Krassner goes to Ginsberg who transcends his bear posture and turns on the tips of his sandaled feet.

Chanting quakes the earth. "Om Namah Shivayah . . . Om Namah Shivayah . . . Om Namah Shivayah."

The poet wheels and chants as he wanders about the podium, heedless of Krassner, the organizers, and even the crowd.

"Om Namah Shivayah . . . Om Namah Shivayah."

Nothing works.

At last a calm young man with rimless glasses and wearing a red T-shirt hugs Ginsberg from behind around the belly and wrestles him from the platform.

"Om Namah Shivayah . . . Om Namah Shivayah."

The crowd dances in delirium. The frenzied crowd bumping up against one another, dizzy kids turning in wild circles. arms outstretched.

"Om Namah Shivayah . . . Om Namah Shivayah . . . Om Namah Shivayah"

At the last possible moment before the crowd detonates upward as holy dust, the featured speaker for the day, Timothy Leary, steps to the podium, serenely screws the mike higher and cups it in both hands, and says, with the lilt of an Irish lullaby, "Hush, you now. Hush and be quiet now with the wind. Let us all become the wind . . . now, dying down and rustling through the trees and the grass. Let us caress each other."

In the background the chant calms and settles, "Om Namah Shivayah . . . Om Namah . . . Om Namah "

"Let us be with one another, now. Let us gently begin to touch the hair and faces of the ones next to us, as we begin to come down like a once fierce Santa Ana and move to a lower force. Let us now listen to the silence that is the truth in the wind."

Lower, now, "Om Namah Shivayah . . . Om Namah.

"Let us begin to listen . . . whooooooooo . . . whooooooooo." he blows a low, rushing sound into the mike, "Whoooooooish . . . whoooooooish,"

Leary's powerful and pure voice settles as pollen on the chanters.

Slowly, the prayers dip and dim.

The crowd returns to itself. A silence, called by Leary's powerful strains settles on the meadow. The trees surrender and the very air itself pushes down on the crowd and gentles their soaring spirits as one great mind comes to its senses. A rolling wave crosses the meadow. All sit cross-legged and calm and await the speaker's words.

Hope swims and lifts Gil. *Has my whole life led to this moment?*

Leary stands tall, handsome and serene, a glowing Roman candle. The breeze ruffles his straight, white hair; his sea-blue eyes gaze at the throng. Excitement hovers over his white linen Indian guru suit. Wisps of hair cover his ears, peak from the back of his neck. He waits for a window in the crowd-buzz. He begins in a low tone, "Welcome Brothers and Sisters. Welcome to the first manifestation of the Brave New World."

A cheer rises.

"Thank you for this shower of love on this bright never-to-be-forgotten day."

Gil, too, looks out on the crowd. From ground level he drinks in the wine of this day of deliverance. The Brothers whisper, "Here is proof of your work, proof of the Millennium."

Leary's voice bounces onto the crowd. "I have come to bear witness to the great spiritual message of the ages. In the words of the Divine Seer who spoke before me, 'We are all one.' In the words of his friendly critic, Paul Krassner, 'We are up against the wall, motherfucker.'"

There is a great roar of approval for this adult who can say "motherfucker" from the podium.

"By accident or design we have learned of a reality greater than any of us were taught. We have come to see the truths spoken by all the great prophets . . . Lao Tse, Buddha, Mahavir, Shiva, Zoroaster, Moses, Jesus, Mohammed, Socrates, Pythagoras, St. Augustine . . . and how many more from every century and corner of mankind, from every language and folklore . . . those who have repeated these truths through the ages from the time of creation, until this very moment. They all say the same thing. "Know thyself. Love each other.

Laugh with each other. Do no harm. Do the bidding of God. How much time do we have left to practice these sacred values? These ancient doctrines are our only chance to survive. How much time do we have left to love ourselves and one another? How much time do we have to find peace on the planet?"

Huge shouts and clapping.

Rocking back and forth on his heels, Gil clasps his hands in an unconscious posture of prayer. He is mesmerized by Leary's bright white figure and rich voice springing from his deeps. *Here is proof,* Gil tells himself.

"Once again," Leary roars, "the powers that rule our world refuse to hear these venerable messages. And so our century has given birth to the great world wars. We have perfected the bow and arrow into the deadly dust of radioactive annihilation. I do not agree with my brother Paul that a devilish malice fires the pieties of this war. The world is out of control, trudging through the unconscious paces of the ages-old war-machine, mirroring the conflict inside the undisciplined mind of mankind." A peculiar curl forms on Leary's lips. A smirk of cosmic triumph heaps anger and resentment on the slaughterers. "The gigantic celestial scheme already exists in the mind of God," he continues. "Only our individual inward journey will bring the peace we long after. What is needed today is a creative act by each and everyone."

Leary's voice falls, "I have seen it. I have experienced peace for a time, and I come to tell you that peace exists — but peace will never be out there until we find peace in here." He beats his breast, his blue eyes aglow.

He raises his hand to grip those poised for his message, "I have talked with the trees . . . I have spoken with the dumb creatures of the earth. I have walked in worlds that have been unknown except to a handful of people down through the ages. I have been where very few have been . . . and I tell you the good news . . . a truer existence lives . . . a greater reality waits to be uncovered."

A door-latch unlocks inside Gil's head followed by thunder. Two huge doors slide apart and reveal a great blue sky fringed by high white clouds that stretch into eternity. Deep goodness smiles with unconditional love. "You are the leader. You are the leader. You are the leader," the Brothers drum.

Leary's ecstasy rises. "Where was electricity before being discovered? What about radio waves and ultra violet light? Always here, waiting to be discovered, their reality as simple as turning a corner. How do I know? Because I have traveled to worlds within worlds that we have never known. When van Leeuwenhoek discovered that polished glass could open the world of microorganisms, science began a new journey. Now, we have discovered chemical combinations to open unknown worlds.

"We too, must begin a new journey . . . the journey into consciousness. I am here to tell you. Forget them and their war. Go about your business. Life is a school. Learn from it. Refuse the false offer of riches. Go to the mountains and make a new life. Live together like children. Find nature. Finger-paint. Read the great prophets. Leave this craziness and start another world based on the urge that makes trees and flowers grow. We can live no longer in a loveless world. We can leave the cycle of killing and revenge.

"We have come to a crossing. A time to stand and tell the world, 'STOP! STOP!' We are going to build our own world, without fear, without guilt. The time has come, brothers and sisters, to STOP. The time has come to TURN ON, TUNE IN, AND DROP OUT. The time has come to go to the mountain and prepare to usher in the Age of Aquarius. The time has come to teach the generation of war, that another generation has come to take its place . . . a generation that holds a thousand years of peace in its heart. The time is now . . . brothers and sisters . . . TURN ON, TUNE IN, AND DROP OUT."

Gil falls under the spell. Now the Elder Brothers sing back to him. "These are the words you have been waiting for. Turn On, Tune In and Drop Out."

The phrase, borne on the lips of the crowd, becomes song and as rising smoke from a newly kindled fire, it repeats over and over, first in thin riffs, then swelling. A cathedral energy resounds and shakes everyone. The massive crowd heaves onto its feet as its sound builds.

Timothy Leary looks skyward into bright sun as his last words ride the crowd and all follow his gaze heavenward. Out of the blue, miraculous event, their combined stare crystallizes in thin air a small speck that grows to a ball falling and swelling.

All stand spellbound. It is now a great ball that is falling earthward, red and white against blue sky. The chant rises, "Turn On, Tune In, and Drop Out."

The colored ball becomes a parachute floating to earth. Mouths open, necks stretch, eyes widen at the chute. A figure dangles and rides the charged air and floats ever faster toward the meadow's middle . . . as with the Red Sea, the crowd parts.

The dangling man hits the ground tumbling and bounces to his feet wearing an orange jump suit with dashing white silk scarf and old-fashioned goggled aviator's cap. He unbuckles his harness and lets the wind take the chute while the crowd claps and cheers.

Amid the chanting, the chutist smiles from behind a thick mustache and plunges into the crowd as he brings forth handfuls of purple and orange pills.

The shouts and clapping go on as the wind kicks up and rumors blow through grass and trees.

The notorious underground chemist Owsley whose labs all over the West Coast turn out vast beds of LSD has fallen from heaven. He moves through the crowd, and from a bottomless supply, gives out, hands, passes, offers, places, divides, spreads and tosses into the air chemical gifts to the children of war's outstretched hands . . . his and Leary's blissful solution, their invitation to the mountain, a cosmic coating for the fears and judgments of the world, yes, a way out, a promise of new life.

As the flower children sing and dance, harmony and peace fill the air, and indeed a new day dawns. The answer has finally come. The Age of Aquarius falls upon the weary desert dwellers as a new Earth turns on, tunes in and drops out.

The Quicksilver Messenger Service, lazing at one end of the platform, plugs in its amps and roars. Stoned little groups dance with a vengeance.

Gil senses it is his time. Just a nod from Leary or a glance from one of the organizers would be enough to bring him to the stage. "You're next," the Brothers say. "It's your turn. Go on, Gilbert Stone, get up there."

Beside the platform Kennedy waits in his navy whites and rakish officers' hat. He claps to the roar of the rock band. Nods, urges Gil to deliver the message of the Brothers.

Gil walks gingerly up the steps when a tough-looking guy with a visor and wispy mustache grabs him by the elbow, "Where you think you're going?"

"Up there." Gil tries to push past.

The muscle holds his shoulders and pushes back. "You're not going up there. What makes you think you can go up there?"

Undaunted, Gil replies, "I'm the human be-in. I'm going to speak."

"Ooh, I thought you were Lyndon Johnson."

"I'm supposed to speak up there."

"Look, man, I don't know who you are. Leary was the last speaker and nobody can top him." He pushes Gil's chest hard with both hands once, and then again.

Gil stumbles and almost falls. He stands his ground while this rogue hippie advances on him again.

"Beat it, Skinny. You're stoned. Go sleep it off." He pushes Gil again.

Gil backs off a few steps. The voices whisper, "Don't let this jerk boss you around. This is a test!"

A test? Gil stands tall, though deeply confused, and cocks his head at this roughneck. But that only invites him.

"You're not listening to me," the bouncer says, and with his open hand smacks Gil hard on the cheek. Very hard.

The blow stings. He tastes blood. A fist this time, glances off his face. He rubs his mouth and finds a red smear.

"It's blood, motherfucker. Now leave or you'll get more."

Backing away, Gil wipes blood on his pea coat, and turning, catches his humiliation being filmed by the gleeful Tycoons. *Blood, how wonderful!*

Shocked, he staggers and begins to run. Dodging the throng, he heads down the path, back the way he had come hours before. He crosses Stanyon into the Panhandle, and at last he slows down. He rubs his beard as warm blood trickles from his nose. "Damn that guy. Damn that guy."

An Elder Brother asks, "You thought this mission would be easy? If salvation came easy, we'd be out of a job."

"He doesn't want to suffer," another says. "He expects to be accepted in one fell swoop."

"This is our time of teaching," a kinder voice tells him. "Let's not be too hard on him. He is the meteor of the war."

"He's not tough enough for this mission? Huh! And not very smart, either."

"We've made our choice. We can only go on."

"Tell him to clean his face."

Gil touches his bloody lips. He's a mess and the fool of the Tycoons. He's disgraced. *Whose are these voices who urge me on, and then make fun? Tell me to speak, when I'm not wanted?* They're no better than the Tycoons. He must shut them all out. "Leave me," he commands the Brothers. "Leave me." He'd been alone all day. "Leave me," he whispers to the wind.

His head clears, but with the voices gone, panic comes in cold flashes. There is no sign of the Tycoons.

How can I bring them back? Anything . . . I'll do anything.

A voice asks, "Anything?"

"Oh, yes."

"Okay then, first go to the drugstore and clean up in the men's room for a fresh message."

"Then," a second voice says, "he can have donuts and coffee and watch us play chess. How's that sound?"

"Then more lessons. Let's not go easy on him.".

Gil, still dazed, says, "Today was to be the day."

"Please, no bitterness. We respect you, of course. We never said what the day would bring. We said only that today is the day. And so it is. In time you will come to know what we mean."

The Tycoons are back, tracking him.

Gil nods and now talks aloud to the Brothers as he heads toward Haight Street. "You lied telling me to go up there, be an idiot, and now my mouth is all cut up. You are killing me, you liars. You are murdering me. You don't care about me. I'm through with you liars. There are no rewards." Gil doubles over and screams, "YOU DON'T CARE ABOUT ME! YOU ONLY HURT ME!"

Standing to full height, Gil shakes with anger. He cannot help himself. He jumps up and down in anguish and frustration, and runs through the Panhandle yelling and screaming. The Tycoons run after him, their tongues out with joy, cameras whirring.

Jack is waiting for him at his home corner of California and Divisidero. "You're my man," he tells Gil. "I believe you can handle this Peace Corps now. You've proven your mettle."

St. Dominic's Preview

◆

TODAY GIL WORKED ON THE SPHINX until he wept, trying to project his unwieldy sculpture into the stratosphere. Working the scraps of tarnished metal, wood and gleaming glass, wobbly on its spindly cast-iron legs from an old lamp, downcast in its demeanor, pasting and bending the shards of his nightly excursions into a soaring vision. He had hoped, through some miracle of regeneration, to incorporate the whole of the world's longings, the sum of humble human aspirations into one finely wrought transformation allowing anyone who looked upon his creation to annihilate all that was fearful, hateful, unclean and unnecessary. Faster even than a note of music, this sculpture would refract the light from a billion benevolent beings into one explosive light brighter even than Paul's blinding vision, a sacred sun so powerful every sentient being would be awakened by the radiance of the universe and come away cleansed, reborn without fear or rancor.

He has now given up in abject abdication, foiled and frustrated, the poisonous taste of lead on his lips, the rumbling in his stomach shrieking desolation like he may die at any moment, crushed to death by his own ignorance, his light extinguished beyond grace; swallowed before his time into the grinding gears of the cosmos; absolutely dismissed from the triumphs of the universe, beyond his petty understanding. He sputters, utterly unworthy of the next breath.

Oh please, an Elder Brother tickles his ear with laughter. Aren't you the lucky one, Sir Gil with all that vision and talent at your fingertips.

Not amused, Gil slaps his head. Surely he must die now by the hand of the great Golden Gate. He must fly from the lowly height he has achieved in his forlorn and bewildered life. He must leap from the greatest of all American clichés onto the pounding cement of far western waters, the wailing wall of the damned.

But the Brothers only chortle. They declare his tepid interest in his own death as a laughing matter. They screech as he once again tries to take the easy way out. "Dump yourself and you will only have to come back and start over in worse conditions, with more hindrances and less mercy, less insight," they tell him. "We will bring you back as a clown or boudoir inspector, you will never learn to add or subtract. An ignorant crooner, you will wander with a troupe of vagrant jugglers and entertainers. No one will take you serious. You don't know enough to take your own life. You have no idea where to take it. In time you will drop like a rock. Until then, take our directions."

The Brothers' words strike him with their hilarity and delight at his fix.

He moves to the mattress in the musty front room, takes out a joint, lights it, and takes a drag. Thin curls of smoke drift up and mingle with motes of dust swimming in the sunlight. He floats with them. He relaxes all burdens. He longs for great things to happen, to pull the muscles of his loose body taunt; he prays to recoil the unwinding strings of his shoddy mind. But his spirit prepares for death. He has arrived.

The Brothers continue to chuckle.

He will march to the other side of town, walk out onto the great orange bridge and make it his own pedestal of expiation. He will present his breathing body to their mute gaze and become one with them. Time to go sucker?

The Brothers come back at him, "Time to sell your life for a song".

What good is it, this constant back and forth, with the godly voices, the constant threat of my fellows, and the small recompense of the great adoration. He must go and he must go soon.

"You are a chicken-hearted ranger," they insist. "Stop this nonsense. Listen to us and we will make you anointed and adored."

When the anthem of vituperation, "Like a Rolling Stone" rocks from the radio, Gil stands as if called to attention and these same Monks, those who mock him now, the same who pushed him to abashment in Golden Gate Park, lead him out the door and down Garden Street into bright sun. A lens catches his turn up Divisadero Street. He will give them a show. He takes long strides. His boots strike the hot pavement.

The afternoon city lies deserted. Only a few unemployed walk the streets. Cars with wives and kids whiz by.

Outside Reno's Hamburgers, teen boys, menacing in their desultory idleness, eye Gil with barely masked threats. The Brothers tell him to cross the street. These slicked back boys with cigarette packs tucked under the their short-sleeve tee shirts look hungry for something he doesn't understand. He would like to talk with them, find out their thoughts, but he feels shapeless, and besides he is on a mission to quench the gods.

"You act like a child," the Brothers chide, "why talk to these miscreants? They cannot help you."

Walking swiftly up the long hill toward the ocean, he moves on toward his rendezvous with the bridge. Near a park at the corner of Clay and Scott, he passes a young mother pushing a red, white and blue stroller. She eyes Gil with a haughty suspicion pitched to protect her bundled baby whose bare nose and a strip of forehead are all that show. Her stark eyes make Gil feel sheepish, and he is self-conscious about his worn jeans, faded chambray shirt torn under the arm, and scraggly beard. He's in costume. He hums "La Marseillaise" as he passes the suspicious mother.

The Monks speak, "You dress well enough for the Millennium. When we finish, you will be draped in fine cloths for your day of glory. Your rewards will be great."

"But what about the bridge?" he asks.

"First, enter this park. Forget the bridge for now," they say. "That is where you belong."

"But my leap?"

"Put off the leap for now. We need you here. You will meet someone. Stop whining. You cannot follow every thought in your head. Listen to us," they say with a varnish of disdain. "You will be better off than just another corpse."

Cool, green Alta Plaza Park rises from the great steps out of Clay Street and calls.

Gil fills with promise as he walks up the wide Mayan steps leading to the tiered park. He mounts to the first tier of the temple and then to the highest part of the park under a grove of eucalyptus trees. From here he finds a view across the Bay to Oakland. Several Tycoons fake being tourists with cameras. They focus their lenses as Gil stands with arms folded and looks far out over the long sweep of water. Light reflects off diamond windows of white buildings from the emerald leaf of Berkeley Hills. He becomes a monument for the cameras looking out over this great set built specially for the Millennium.

He walks to the silver drinking fountain and tastes its sharp metallic water. From a green bench he gazes out over the city, the Bay and beyond. Peace! The view claims him.

A strange, old-fashioned European professor sits across the small plaza, his white beard is sharp and pointed. A string-tie bow falls over his stiff, white shirt with rounded collar. He wears a pince-nez on a black ribbon around his neck and has a brimless round, bright red hat. It's a strange costume these days. He doesn't notice Gil and reads broadsheets labeled *Gazzetta di Mantova*. A gold glow flows from his eyes.

Now Gil sees a far off light across the Bay that rises dead center over Oakland. The light expands in slow motion and blossoms. The sharp glow strikes the city with a force so astounding that the mere gleam of this knife of light knocks Gil to the ground.

He glances over to the old fellow to see if he's watching. Gil's attention draws the gentleman away from his papers and he smiles. Gil smiles back drawing an echo, a quiet question in his head, "Do you see?"

Gil looks across the Bay again. The light is descending. White flames roar skyward. Gil's head rings as the white-hot embers blind him. He's alarmed. No one in the park has noticed.

Then the old man lifts his head a bit, "Wonderful. Do you see?"

Half of Oakland is subsumed in the light. A veil of smoke rises over the scene. Gil jumps up and points. No one reacts to the hovering light. Gil tries to scream, but his vocal cords are frozen. He can only croak as though trying to shout in a dream. Gil is rendered mute. The light now leaps the Bay and laps the Embarcadero. Still no one looks.

Though he screams near bursting, no sound moves past his lips. Frustration draws the cords of his neck, maddens him. He wants to leap the city streets to jump into the Bay.

Gil turns to the man with golden eyes. He stares back, pleased. And now, of course Gil recognizes him, he is Dante from Giotto's fresco in the Podestà Chapel. Gil tries to say something to him, but Gil has been struck dumb. Dante smiles. As Gil looks toward the Bay again, beyond the roofs of apartment houses, the smoke and flames refract to a dull light. He sits, exhausted.

Dante stands, folds his paper, bows a slight European bow and walks off. At the park's edge he turns and over his shoulder flashes a thought to Gil, "Pay attention. You may see through the window of the gods as I once did." Then he is gone.

Gil is left with Oakland burning in his brain, but he sees only traces of smoke over the city. The voices tell him to go home. He leaves the park still under the spell of revelation . . . but why has he lost the power of speech?

Then Gil spots Kennedy in his Navy dress blues, leaning against a tree, watching. He smokes a vintage Cuban Cohiba that smells like Oakland in flames. He nods "yes" when Gil catches his eye, a look that lets him know that he's on the right track. "See," the voices say, "Kennedy watches you do your job. He approves. He approves very much."

On his way out of the park, back at the corner of Clay and Scott, he sees the young mother with the stroller about to cross. Behind her a low-slung '58 Hudson speeds towards them filled with the villainous boys he saw at Reno's. The mother steps off the curb. Gil watches the car prepare to turn. From fifty feet down the block he throws up his hands and shouts. No sound comes out, but his wave startles the young mother enough for her to pull back as the Hudson cuts across her path and misses the stroller by inches heading toward Gil, who jumps out of the way as it weaves down Clay Street.

On her way, the mother crosses the street and passes Gil without a thank you or even a nod.

Part IV

◆◆◆

Waller Street

♦

I SHOW UP ON THE DOORSTEP without a word.

Claire is there, plump and pretty, holding baby Tamar. She brushes her hair aside with her free arm as she stares, waiting for me to say the first word.

All my friends are waiting for me to say something. It's maddening!

Finally, with no word spoken, she motions me to come inside with silent good humor.

My face is stiff from the fog and cold.

Finally comprehending, Claire pulls me by the collar of my pea coat into the hallway and closes the door with one hand, all the while carrying in her other arm the gawking Tamar, who is less than a year old, and a very smart person. Like me, she cannot speak, but makes herself known with her mind.

In a minute baby Tamar gives me a big smile and sends me the thought to come right in and make myself at home. I feel better right away, so I go into the living room, sink into the faded corduroy couch and put my feet on the coffee table. I had slipped in the park on my way over and so I'm muddy and wet.

Claire follows me inside, shooting a wary look at my shoes, but remains silent.

Don't worry about the feet, Tamar thinks to me. *Thanks*, I think back to her, and stretch out. So, this is where the Elders have directed me to find shelter. In a minute, I jump up and check all the windows, draw the drapes in the living room and turn on the lights. Claire sits there with Tamar, a little uneasy, but without saying a word.

I am determined to hide from the Tycoons and deny them more film of me. They must pay me now. When I sit down to relax, I notice a small cut-glass window high up next to the mantle. This is a likely place for the wily Tycoons to get an angle on me, so I jump up, push a chair in front of the window, take off my coat, stand on the chair, and hang the coat across the curtain rod.

Claire sits and watches. Her wary looks come and go. Baby Tamar, being rocked, whispers the thought to me that now no one is going to find me.

"Safe," I declare returning to the couch, and I stretch my feet out once again, but something is still bothering me. Some unsettling presence, so I get up and investigate all the rooms.

Claire rocks the baby.

The furniture is sparse. The sagging brown couch, an old stuffed green chair, a couple of straight-back kitchen chairs surround the motel coffee table. Several paisley-covered cushions and a Mexican rug are on the hardwood floor. The mantle holds a ceramic totem of six-armed Shiva.

So what if I put my feet up on the table. Physicists say that everything is made from one basic element. It's all the same, floor, table, chairs and mantle. Everything's the same . . . so I can put my feet anywhere I want.

"Do you want something to eat?" Claire asks. "Wayne won't be home until later."

I nod my head "yes," and follow her toward the kitchen. I sit down at a rough pine table in the dining room.

In a minute, Claire, still holding baby Tamar, brings in a bowl of soup and a spoon.

I drink it right from the bowl . . . two gulps.

Then she brings me more soup and some hard brown bread I can gnaw on.

"You can stay in here," she says, and points to a thin mat with several folded blankets in the corner under a window next to the kitchen door.

I get up right away and move the mat to another corner that is away from the window. I sit down to finish the bread and soup, and then I have to get up again and pull the curtains across the window – just in case I see the flash of a lens outside the window. I wonder if these errant spirits from the land of the dead have told the Tycoons where I am. Maybe it's my imagination, but I can't take any chances. After I finish the bread and the soup, I lie down on the mat and pull the blankets up over me. I barely hear Claire and Tamar leave the room before I'm asleep.

I wake in the middle of the night. There's not a sound, inside or out; it is pitch-black now that the curtains are drawn. I stand up and right away bang into the table, shattering the night.

Then I hear a moan in another room . . . I can tell it's Wayne. He's been out late driving a cab or maybe playing at a club. Now, I've wakened him from his tired sleep. I bang into a chair and finally make my way into the living room and lay on the couch to meditate with the six-armed Shiva whose shadowy figure I can make out peering from the mantle.

The parading Brothers return. They frighten me. They are different from the Brothers on the street who send me telepathic messages of how to go about my mission. These Brothers are recruiting me from the other side. They want to claim me in death. I am afraid of them. They don't care about this world. Their concern is to take me up the hill to some sort of everlasting life, leaving the world here to rotate and spin out of control.

So, I see now, there are even divisions among the Brothers. There are factions everywhere I look. No one agrees. Everything is disunity in the name of unity. I must keep my mind on the Brothers who represent Kennedy and his plan to use me to bring peace to the world.

"Stop," I shout, "can't you see that I'm already spoken for. I care about the world here, not the world there. Stop!"

THE HALL LIGHT GOES ON. I see Wayne's rumpled hair as he peers out of the bedroom door.

He yawns and waves at me. "The baby's asleep. You better go back to bed." He smiles and is about to turn out the light when he rubs the sleep from his eyes and moves closer to me. He's in his undershirt and boxer shorts.

"So," he says good-natured, putting a hand on my shoulder, "you been hauntin', eh?" Wayne, between gigs, in order to keep himself righteous, drives a taxi and affects the speech of a white man talking like a hip black jazz man, leaving the g's off the ends of words and such.

He sits down next to me in the half-light from the hall.

I am lying on the couch in the twilight wearing my thick sweater, my boots are still on, and my knees are drawn up to my chest. I think best that way.

I don't want to talk about it but I can't help myself. "These characters followed me back from the land of the dead and are parading around in my head," I hear myself say. "They're interfering with my work."

"Oh, yeah." Wayne nods. "Your work?"

I can tell he doesn't think that I actually have work. I can't decide whether to tell him. Maybe Wayne will understand. No. I don't think he will. Maybe. Maybe he will if I tell him so that he can understand. I could try, but I'm afraid he'll think I'm crazy. These people who used to be my friends, they are limited by their worldly ways. They don't understand. Still, of all of them, the musicians are the most understanding. The trouble is that even though they understand, they just don't care, that's why I can't be one of them. Maybe I can tell Wayne.

I look at Wayne like he is my son. "I am the chosen one," I tell him. "But it's still a secret. Don't tell anyone."

Wayne nods. His eyes widen.

"I've been chosen — against my will. I believe it had something to do with the time I spent in Africa. Something to do with my faith and love and my beliefs. I went to find Kennedy. I went into the land of the dead and found Kennedy, and tried to get him to come back into this world, but he refused. I met death, who I convinced to release Kennedy, but Kennedy himself would not come. He told *me* to return, and that he and the band of Elder Brothers would direct me from the beyond to bring peace to the world. My journey to the land of the dead began the great march to the Millennium in order to set the world right so that the next cycle of peace could begin. My faith to return from the land of the dead has set the cosmos into motion. The Brothers from the stars began to appear to guide me in specific duties to bring about peace. The holy city of San Francisco is to be the center of the new Millennium and from here the waves of peace will wash across the world."

"So, you're gonna' save the world," Wayne says.

"Yes," I nod. "But it's too soon to tell anyone."

"No, no. I won't say anything," he tells me. "You can trust me."

I see a slight smile spread across his lips, not mocking exactly, but amused. I decide I will not let it bother me. I will trust him not to tell anyone even though the Brothers forbid me to talk about my mission.

"You see," I begin again. "I'm going to heal the world. The Brothers are directing me in this. Although," I confess, "some of them don't think I'm up to it."

"Yeah," Wayne says. "This is interesting. How are you gonna' do it?"

"The Brothers are directing me," I say. "The city of San Francisco represents the entire world. Every street and alleyway, every building and corner corresponds to a place in the greater world. When I'm walking down Divisidero Street, I'm really walking down the border between China and Russia. So, the Brothers have instructed me to chant the "OM" chant in order to soothe the people on both sides of the border. Here on Waller Street, we are on the Israel-Egyptian border. I am here now, to bring peace to this area."

"Wow," Wayne says. "That's a plan."

Wayne continues to sit with his arm around my shoulder, not saying a word, but I can tell he's listening carefully.

"Yeah," I say. "But the Brothers don't want the plan to get out until it's already accomplished. So, I'm here, saying my "OMs" and praying. There are other trouble spots for me to visit. I walk a lot down California Street. That's corresponds to the raging war in Vietnam, and around Cambodia and Thailand and all over that area. I spend most of my time walking around that area chanting and praying and bringing the right vibes for peace to descend."

"Yeah, man," Wayne says. "They really need some help to get peaceful."

"Yeah," I say. "So, you see I'm kind of busy these days. I'm sort of like pretending to be out of it, so people will leave me alone while I get this done. Then, of course, I am working for Kennedy and the Brothers. It'll all become quite good soon. I'm almost done. Once the Millennium is declared by the Brothers sometime this year, then it will still be a secret to most, but slowly during the next 50 years peace will be revealed and people will look back and see how this time was the beginning of peace and how every event led to our eventual peaceful world. That's how it's going to work," I say and wink. "That's what the Brothers tell me."

"Man, that's some plan," Wayne says. "So, we're all gonna' see the light pretty soon, huh? I'm glad, 'cause I was getting discouraged, and tired." He winks back.

"Sometimes, I'm afraid, though," I say. "The Brothers scare me. They don't always treat me well. Even though I'm the chosen one, they pretend that I hardly matter. I think sometime, they're going to kill me," I confess.

"They can't touch you." He squeezes my arm hard. "They can't hurt you. They just haunt you man, that's all, and that ain't much." Wayne gets up. "Now I'm goin' back to bed and you should, too. You need your strength for all this peace walkin' and everything. Know what I mean?" He slaps my knee and heads toward the bedroom. This is the same Wayne who baked righteous bread when we all lived together on Steiner Street, and who plays the guitar with an angelic lilt and the accuracy of a machine gun. His attention to my story makes me feel better. I know Wayne means well, but he doesn't always understand.

MY DREAMS ARE SO TORTUROUS that I'm afraid to go to sleep. They aren't like my Ethiopian dream of children leaping that once calmed me to sleep. In addition to this army of parading specters, others too, creep into my sleep and try to drag the ancient mysteries out of me. Often I wake after dreaming of being torn apart, so I try to stay awake for the dark period of the night when my sleep becomes a house of screams. Toward morning, when I drift off, the dreams cloud over so I don't remember them.

This night, after I have talked to Wayne and told him my plan, I have a vivid dream. Once again I'm being tortured. I am poised on the top of a very steep hill with Kennedy and the Elder Brothers. I am naked. They are teaching me to be one of them. Kennedy directs them to bind me with leather straps to a cross of rough boards, with my arms outstretched and my legs crossed and tied so tight they hurt.

The Brothers are in a somber mood. They hold me up and pass me around among them while each one marks me. Brother Bob, tall, with his hair in a pony tail, paints symbols on my chest and others paint my legs in ash. Another Brother in a brown cassock makes a cut that bleeds in my side with his knife. Kennedy shoves a glowing torch into the center of my forehead, so that my head glows with a ruby fire.

After I'm all marked up, they tie me onto the hood of my pale-green '51 Chevy, turning me into a huge hood ornament. They are beating drums and playing instruments, and jumping around before they release the car. Then I am speeding down the hill, screaming in the wind, the fear and fright leaping out of me. All the while, the banshee music is whining in my ears. I plunge downhill, with the wind pushing me, and my screams lashing back on me, the speed hurtling me downward toward a forest of huge trees.

Suddenly, in the heat of my fear, with the trees below coming faster than a train, the cross drops from my back. I am floating free in space among the peaceful stars where everything is far, far away. I drift in space without the burden of a body. I am me and not me. I glide into somersaults and dance pirouettes. I stretch my arms out and fly up and down and all around. I am sure that I am freer than any man has been before. I see the human race in one round light, and I pity those who never knew the glorious freedom of soaring this way.

My pity grows, pulling me down. Before I can resist, the drags of gravity pull on my body. Once again I am hurtling down, down, down, picking up speed, possessed by the earth, pulling me closer, where I catch sight of explosions. Flames and smoke shoot through the dense jungle. By God, the trees are men. Huge warrior eyes suck me down with tremendous speed where my body will be cracked and shattered, speared by the foliage, drained into nothingness by these hooded warrior eyes. The earth is eager to have the life force of my mutilated body to nourish this dark green foliage. I cannot breathe; the speed of air rushing into my lungs chokes me.

At the last second before I crash the dream changes and the muscular arms of Kennedy reach out and grab me. His body is hanging by the legs from a trapeze-bar and I swing back and forth, now secure in his grip several hundred feet above the smoking Asian jungle. I look up into the large, warm smile on his square face that says "now it's not so bad," but my heart is still racing and all I can do is grab onto his eye beams. Kennedy nods to me to look down where I see a huge circus net strung up above the trees. "That net's been there all this time." He's holding me strong while we swing back and forth.

Life seeps back.

Now, we're swinging in a larger arc and picking up speed when he lets go. My heart stops, but right away there is Brother Bob on his trapeze who neatly catches my hands and we swing deep down even closer to the trees, and I can see the net and again I am free, soaring through the heavens. I'm confident and taken care of when Brother Bob lets go and Kennedy is right there to grab me. I am the trapeze artist of my dreams swinging free between Kennedy and Brother Bob.

The next time I look down I see the brown cassock of Kesey, on his own trapeze, swinging low, very low down to the trees and the fire-strewn forest. I see the explosions mirrored in his eyes. He holds a huge jungle machete that he swings past a corner of the net, slicing the supporting rope. First, one corner goes down and then with another pass, and the second corner goes.

I scream, "Stop! Stop! Stop!" But he doesn't look. . . and he doesn't stop. He has a manic smile on his aching fractured face. Past the third corner he slices the thick support rope, and the net disappears into the flaming jungle.

Kennedy looks up at us flying above him with the smirk of the century on his face. He shouts, "This is real, buddy, this is for real."

I'm exasperated, and I'm burning up with fear as Kennedy catches my eye with a noncommittal shrug as though he is looking through me. Letting go, I swing free for a moment, and am caught by Brother Bob. Back and forth we fly. He is pumping hard to enlarge the arc of our swing, then he sends me hurtling toward Kennedy, who allows me to sail past. I am falling, free flight, unhurried falling. I see the flaming jungle. . . feel the heat from the exploding bombs. Warrior faces in the trees laugh while I fall, swallowed by the flame-drenched trees.

I wake up startled in the dark dining room. My heart is beating fast and my mouth is dry. I'm beaten and shredded by the dream. I'm afraid to go back to sleep. I lay in the dark, crouching behind my thoughts, an escaped con on a fugitive journey. Then, the specters parade through the room. Dressed in their robes and tall pointed hats and carrying their banners, they chant the three repetitions as they march, "Om Ah Hum, Om Ah Hum, Om Ah Hum." They sway back and forth through the room melting in and out of the furniture and the walls, encircling me, exhorting me to follow.

"How much?" I shout. "How much do I have to pay before you leave me alone?"

THE LIGHT GOES ON in the hallway outside the bedroom and Wayne walks out, "Hey, man," he says concerned, "you all right?"

I nod in the half-light, shielding my eyes. My mouth won't work to tell him my dream.

Wayne comes over and sits next to me on the pad in his shorts and puts his hand on my shoulder. "Look, man, Claire and I want to help you, if we can, but you gotta tell us what's wrong. Some thing's eaten' you up. You gotta tell someone. Someone real," he adds, making light of the spirits who only laugh as they bend in to listen to my friend.

All I can manage is to shake my head, "I dunno, I dunno," which are all the words I can get out. Somehow, even though I know Wayne wants to help me, I'm afraid he's going to rip me apart. Wayne, who's always been kind and light-hearted with me. I'm so afraid of him and all these marching ghouls, pulling me to them, calling me like they called to Kennedy, "Come to us,'" they chant, "Come to us." Their anger stands the hairs on my arms. I'm filled with fear they are going to rip me apart.

I jump up and go into the bedroom ahead of Wayne and climb into the bed next to slumbering Claire. Wayne crawls in beside me and I'm warm in there between them. Even though I'm afraid to fall into that dream, I doze off, safe for the first time since I can remember. When the morning light breaks through the window, I squirm to the foot of the bed and crawl out and go back into the dining room and lay on the thin pad and stare at the dark curtain.

Baby Tamar is up first calling out that she's hungry, so I go stand next to her crib and send her the thought to be patient. I'm leaning over the crib when Claire still full of sleep in her nightgown comes into the room. For an instant she gives me a strange look, as if to say, *what are you doing leaning over my baby's crib*, but then she comes and efficiently picks up Tamar and goes into the kitchen and starts banging the pots and pans for breakfast.

A little later Wayne comes in and ruffles my hair and smiles and makes me eat some Wheatena. He plays with me, talks to me, and makes fun of me. Wayne's trying, I know. I'd love to be there with him, too, reliving old times, listening to him play the guitar, talking about philosophy and physics, about what is real and what is not, but I'm on a journey he cannot know. I'm out there on the trapeze of my mission, bound to the will of the Elder Brothers, destined to save the people of this world and lead the way into the Millennium. I'm out there now swinging wildly in the wind — flying in the dream — without a net.

After breakfast, Suzanne drops by the house, so casually like she didn't know I'd be there, but Claire called her, I'm sure. She comes into the kitchen where Wayne and I and Claire are sitting in the little nook.

Suzanne smiles with her very patient and beautiful smile, and sits down across from me, and begins to sip her coffee and chat with Claire. I can't understand a word she says. She's going on and on, the way women do when they're familiar with each other and they don't want to pay particular attention to anything that matters. . . . rapid fire, machine gun style. *Where do all the words come from, where do they find them?* If I only had a tenth of the words, I would be able to tell Wayne what is bothering me, and I could be cured, but I can't put my tongue on the words the way these women do, just words, discussing, discussing, discussing, a steady salvo of words.

The whole time, I'm sitting there waiting for one of them to notice me.

What is Suzanne doing here? Is she babysitting me? What of baby Tamar? They're teaching her to talk in this steady torrent of words, while Claire moves about the kitchen cleaning up with one hand and holding Tamar in the other. They are turning baby Tamar into a talking machine.

Finally, when Claire goes into another room with the baby, Suzanne turns her attention to me. She looks full of questions — *all right now young man, it's your time to stand in the shower of my words,* I hear her thinking.

She takes a breath and squints. "Well, Gil, what are you up to?" she asks innocent as a June bug.

I shrug. How can I tell her that it's so hard to get on and I'm sitting here with the Tombstone Blues on Desolation Row? I shrug and move my head and shoulders up and down a little. Then I get the urge to tell her about last night's dream, but it passes before I can find the words. I give her a smile and hunker my head down between my shoulders. I feel guilty and defiant.

"Come on, Gil," she says, betraying a bit of irritation. "You haven't called or visited me for a long time. What are you up to now?"

She's a nurse, or a cop. How can I talk to her? I could be a prisoner of the Viet Cong, or Lyndon Johnson himself. All I can do is stare across the table. She's dressed in dancer's tights, with her long reddish hair tied back and twisted into a pile on top of her head. Her green eyes so open and imploring. *What does she want?* Beautiful Suzanne, who keeps coming after me, reluctant, self conscious, shamefully seeking me out. She wants a martyr's life. She wants to save me, but I can't even tell her what I need saving from.

"Gil, you have to help by telling us what's wrong, or we can't help you."

Why does she think something is wrong? I couldn't tell Wayne last night. I can't tell her. I have to tell somebody, but not even Wayne understands.

"Gil, what's happening to you?" She slams the mug down hard.

I shake my head. I try a smile to charm her, but I can't move the muscles in my face.

She stands up and walks around the table in back of me and puts her arms around my shoulder and bends over and puts her face next to mine. It's endearing. I can hardly resist. I want to give in. *But what does she want?* She wants the dream and I can't give it to her. Ah, lovely Suzanne. How much I wanted to be with her when we first met, but now, I wonder who she is to have taken me home that night and then be with me all this time and now still with her arms around me. *Who is this woman?* I never saw her before. We are strangers.

She kisses me on the neck and nuzzles me with her lovely face, and she pinches me in the arms and tries to josh me into her world.

How can I explain? It's so hard to get on. She's tickling me now and giggling. "Gil, come play with me," her fingers are saying. She has no appreciation of my mission. She does not believe in the Elder

Brothers. *How can I convince her about the Tycoons?* When I point out the cameras following me, she brushes me aside.

"Gil, I love you," she whispers in my ear. "I love you Gil," she repeats over and over, "I love you Gil, I love you."

Somehow her words don't make a dent, because I know that before too long she will leave me and go to her dance classes, and then she has to work at the restaurant, and I never know when I'll see her again. *How can that be love?*

"Come to my place tonight after work," she urges.

I squirm in her arms enough to let her know I'm uncomfortable, and then I twist my body violently and she lets go. All I can do is shake my head and scream, "SUZANNE!" Not a cry for help but a modulated tone of exasperation. With a twist, I add, "Leave me the fuck alone."

Wham! Suzanne's hurt. She withdraws. She moves across the table and picks up her unfinished coffee. Hurt, not defeated, she sits down and tries to reason with me.

And me? I'm powerless to move, though I want to. I want to run out of there and hide behind a curtain. This is worse than running from the Tycoons. This is a job for Superman. So what do I do? I stare across the table until Wayne pads in with baby Tamar in his arms and gives us a sunny look going over to the refrigerator. Leaving the room he is smiling — *only checking he's thinking. Tell her to fuck off*, baby Tamar thinks to me.

Finding no other thought in my mind to express this hassled, anxious feeling rolling around in my stomach, I take baby Tamar's advice, and say very slowly and evenly . . . which is a feat for me, "Fu . . . fuck off."

Suzanne continues to gaze into her coffee cup.

After a moment, though she cannot help herself. "You used to care for me," she lays before me like a wreath at my funeral.

"I still care, but there's more important things to do now." When I first told Suzanne about the Elder Brothers, when I pointed out the Tycoons and explained my mission, she accused me of making things up. Suzanne refused to see the reality of the Millennium. She will not see what's in front of her. It's becoming intolerable. "All you want to do is screw for a baby,!" I say in my frustration.

"Bullshit," she says, bangs the cup on the table, stands up and strides out of the room. I hear the front door slam.

In a little while, Wayne comes in and sits across from me where Suzanne sat. He lights a joint and passes it over to me. We smoke in silence for a few minutes. Finally, he says with a glint of admiration, "You sure got a way with women."

"Yeah," I say, "but she not the kind of woman, who when I go down dyin', is bound to put a blanket on my bed."

I try to forget about Suzanne and get down to the business of the day, which is hiding from the Tycoons. I know that in time the Elder Brothers will contact me and get me away from here. Meanwhile I have to do it myself. Suzanne could help me, but she refuses to see. So, I must go on without her. She will only leave me for her dance classes in the end anyway, and I need someone dependable.

Wayne hands me a cup of coffee, "So, you been hauntin', huh?"

"You might say so," I allow.

"Soundin' kind of weird," he laughs, "I was hearin' ya last night."

"Yeah?"

"Something gettin' after you, man?" he asks jovially.

"The pump don't work cause the vandals took the handle," I say, careful now that he's leading me into a conversation. These dialogues can be dangerous. I know, because they clue-in the outside part of me that's trying to get inside.

"Maybe you ought to talk about what's gittin' your dander up."

"Everybody must get stoned." I say, cautiously.

"You was sayin' some weird things last night, man. Who were you talkin' too?"

Wayne sure is curious. "Some fools up on housing project hill."

"Yeah," he says, "what'd they want from ya'?"

"Sooner or later, one of us must know."

"Yeah. You told me about these people from underground been bothering' you. I heard you tell 'em to leave you alone, but when I come outta' the bedroom, you wuz alone."

"A bowling ball came down the road and knocked me off my feet."

"Yeah?"

"It was a tambourine man, a night visitor, a mister Jones, a Fourth Street banana. Lost in the rain."

"And what did they find out?"

"Nothing'. I'm heatin' up. Positively Fourth Street, man. None of 'em is gonna' get nothing' out of me. That's why I'm here, about you don' know what, do you Mister Jones? We're gonna' take 'em all down to Highway 61 and bust 'em. No thanks until we get 'em out. No heavenly funeral parlor where the man asked me who I was. No thanks till we get 'em out."

"I don't follow you, man," Wayne says.

"Follow me down, man follow me down. You tell me who's lost in the rain? You tell me man, cause I got to know. Who's lost? Who's lost? You tell me who's lost. You don't know, do you Mister Jones? Sooner or later one of us must know."

"I got to go to work soon."

And then bam, the morning is gone.

When Wayne leaves for work I spend the afternoon on the couch, meditating with six-armed Shiva, jumping up from time to time and looking out the windows, checking the closets, and talking to baby Tamar, who is the only sane person in the neighborhood. No sign of the Tycoons. I fall asleep about 4:00 on the couch with my boots on. Baby Tamar is singing in the background.

I wake up with a start to the whirring sound of cameras. I look all around. I check the closets and all the rooms. Claire gives me a strange expression when I walk into in the kitchen and check under the sink. I look out to the back porch and into the courtyard, but no one's there. It's only the sound of baby Tamar cooing. All's clear, but I'm jumpy. I'm afraid the Tycoons are closing in. Any minute they could bust the door open and mow me down with their cameras. They'd catch me exposed and defenseless. Oh, they'd enjoy catching me with my boots off, and my pants down and check my collateral, and press me against the wall and take their cameras and go right into my mind and bleed it of everything, everything I labored for so hard to get there and keep there and they want to drain me for the popcorn crowd.

Even though I try to rest, I must keep jumping up from the couch every 10 minutes to make the rounds to see if they've found me.

Finally, Claire asks, very politely, "Gil what is it you're looking for?"

"Tycoons." I say.

"Raccoons?" she asks.

"Tycoons."

"What are Tycoons?"

I implore Baby Tamar, who smiles at the thought, to go ahead and tell her mother, but she won't understand anyway, so I say, "Tycoons? Tycoons have cameras."

"Oh." She says and goes back to chopping onions. I detect a worried look on Claire's smooth, broad face, a certain wrinkle on her forehead that I haven't seen before.

I'm about to go back to the living room couch, when Claire clears her throat, "Gil," she begins very deliberately, "Maybe you should talk to a therapist or someone?"

"I already talked," I say. "Me and Franco talked to all the doctors up on housing project hill, and they gave us pills."

"Well, what did they say?"

"They just said, 'take these pills and call us in the morning'. So me and Franco called them at 3:00 in the morning. They couldn't tell us a thing, except come back and take more pills. They want to put us on TV now, but I had to scotch it."

"Maybe they want to help you, Gil?"

"Yeah," I say. "They want to kill me."

I walk into the living room and lay on the couch, waiting for the carnival tonight.

After dark Wayne comes home. He looks into the living room where I've been on the couch most of the day . . . with occasional visits to the closets and peeking over windowsills. "Hey, man," he says to me, "wanna smoke a joint?" Then he goes into the kitchen, and says hello to Claire and Tamar. Coming back in the living room he lights a joint and passes it to me.

WILLIAM SIEGEL

"Look," he says reminding me of my father, "I been thinkin'. While you're here with us, there's no need to worry, so you can relax."

"Thanks," I say.

"What I mean, is," Wayne goes on, "there's no need for you to go hauntin' tonight. You know? We both know there's all kinds of unexplained things in this world. Me an' Claire been talkin', and for the baby's sake . . . and us too . . . it's probably best not to be makin' any contact with people from other worlds and such. Get my drift? Cause who knows what's out there ready to leap in when they got a good conductor." He stops right there and waits for me to say something. The silence grows and I'm obliged to say something.

"Yep," I say, "I get the drift". Well, Wayne may not understand what's *really* goin' on, but he knows there's something out there. He's in the stage where he thinks what isn't here, is there. He hasn't discovered yet that everything is really here. He thinks because I'm talking to people who he can't see, I'm talking to people who aren't there. I don't know how to explain it all to him. He has to experience this himself. I know he's not ready to comprehend my mission with the Elders or my growing fear of the Tycoons. "What the fuck," he would say, "If we're all one, what's to be afraid of?"

"What the fuck, what's to be afraid of?" Wayne says in the middle of my thought of him saying, "What the fuck, what's to be afraid of?" This convinces me further I'm able to read thoughts in the same way I communicate with baby Tamar.

Then, it's true. I'm flying higher and higher to some great destiny located deep in the mind of God. Surely, I am directed by the Elder Brothers and driven on by the scourge of the Tycoons who will give me no rest. In an instant, I realize I need the Tycoons the same as they need me, and some bit of rancor falls from my heart, though the fear remains. I wonder if I can tell Wayne about the Elders and the Tycoons. Perhaps, if I open my mind, the great weight will fall from my shoulders and I won't have to do this tremendous job of saving the planet alone — even though the Elders declare I am the one.

"What do you think?" Wayne asks while we hover near the edge of the stratosphere, looking down on the planet?

"There's more going on than we know," I say.

"Guess so, with the haunts you talk to, and all?"

"Even more."

"Yeah? Scary stuff?"

More than you'll ever know, I think, I say, "Nothin' I can't handle."

Wayne gets into it, "Yeah, man, outer-space, billions of planets and strange people, man. Probably lots of civilizations out there, man."

"Yeah," I say.

"The way I figure," Wayne says, putting his feet on the table, "there's gotta be something else out there, 'cause by and large this place sucks. Yeah, there must be beings out there so far advanced they don't even wanna get close to us."

"Some of them are watching." I say.

"I got this feeling that soon they're gonna' come and teach us a few lessons," Wayne goes on. "It don't make sense, you know, if we keep fucking up down here, man, for ten or twenty thousand years, and they're up there watching it all go down, and they don't land and say, 'look you fuck-ups, you're doin' it all wrong, man, this is the way you gotta do it if you wanna do it right.'"

"Yeah," I agree.

"But you, Gil, you're into something' else," Wayne says, changing course. "Spirits creep me, man." He shakes his shoulders to throw them off. "Spirits, man, for some reason scare me more than little men from outer space." We both laugh.

"What if they're big men from outer space?" I ask.

"Yeah," he says, "Twenty feet tall."

"What if they're the same as us? Regular people, and they've already landed and they're living among us. Have been for many years. That's what I think, man."

"Yeah," Wayne says. "But how come there's still war and hunger, man?"

"Cause we gotta do it ourselves," I say logically. "They can only give us guidance."

"Yeah," Wayne says, catching me with a smile and a laugh, "I got a' uncle that's one of those kinda spaceman. Back home, he used to smoke a lot of space. Yeah, I know about those kind, man, no help, only guidance."

I find myself wanting to convince Wayne that the people from the planets are living among us when I realize that I've talked more to Wayne than to anyone for a long while. I put both hands around my neck and press firmly, and that chokes me off. The Elders insist I do not reveal them and may punish me if I talk about them.

"Hey, man, take it easy," Wayne says, "No one's gonna' get you, all you have to do is stop the hauntin'." This strikes Wayne very funny, and he starts to laugh. "Hauntin', man, "hauntin'," he says over and over, "hauntin', man", and laughs and laughs, and I get to laughing too, because 'hauntin'' is such a funny word. If you say it over and over, the meaning disappears and hauntin' is a very funny word. So we laugh and laugh and we're crusin' right along on the laughter when Claire comes in from the bedroom and shushes us.

"The baby's asleep, and you guys are stoned," she says, "just stoned." She walks into the kitchen. Wayne puts his finger to his lips and becomes more subdued, but the giggles bubble up into a game of hold 'em back, and when we can't, the laughter starts, and Claire comes out of the kitchen and says, again, this time with a tint of crossness to her voice, "The baby's asleep".

Well", Wayne says, "Tamar may be asleep but we ain't."

Yeah, I echo, silently.

Yeah, baby Tamar thinks to me. *Well, I ain't asleep neither.*

You're picking' up bad grammar, I think to Tamar. *If you listen to your old man, you'll end up talkin' like a white guy tryin' to talk like a hip black guy, an' you ain't even a guy*, I think to her, *so listen to your mom, and go back to sleep.*

I don't hear another peep out of baby Tamar for the rest of the night.

"Cum'ere an' have a couple hits," Wayne says to Claire holding up half a joint to her.

Claire comes over and sits on the other side of the couch from me and joins us with reluctance. She takes the joint with the scorn of a remedy in which she lacks confidence. She inhales, makes a face, chokes, holds the odious weed out from her, takes another inhale with the same mistrust. Making a castor-oil face and coughing, she hands the joint to Wayne, and finally comes out with a broad smile, her face framed by her long light-brown hair, she blushes. Watching her, I see how beautiful Claire is, how strong she's become with the arrival of baby Tamar.

Suddenly, I'm impelled to tell Wayne and Claire everything.

I stand up, step over the coffee table and walk to the center of the room, where I turn around to face them both. With a flourish of my arm I point to Claire with a fierce look on my face, with my long hair and shaggy beard, and with the Brothers speaking though me, I am the prophet Jeremiah from the movie, "The Ten Commandments," and I proclaim, "I see shinning through you, Claire, the archetype of all women, the pioneer woman, the great-hearted true salvation of the race, the true bearer of compassion and the only reason men have not done even more damage to the world. You are the woman who carries the true force of nature, the woman with the strength to leave the filthy slums of Europe, with the strength to cross this broad country in a prairie schooner, all the while bearing children and cooking, cleaning up after the bloody mess of the men. Here in this time too, you are the pioneer woman, ready to live a full life — even to have joy in life, while all around you there is fire, death and destruction. I am amazed, completely amazed by your strength and your will."

Then I turn toward Wayne, "I'm even more amazed that Wayne takes all this for granted. He has no idea that the world is carried entirely on the bosom of women."

I'm astounded by these words, though I assume the Brothers are talking through me. I raise both arms and continue, "A woman with a child is the strongest force of nature, stronger than the savage firebombs shattering the villages and jungles of Vietnam blowing the woman and children to bits.

"As the Appointed One of the Elders, I will stand in the highest courts of the land with my long hair and beard on the day of punishments, and I will point my staff to all these weak-kneed American male warriors, one by one. These American hoodlums will finally be made to see. You can't get away with slaughtering women, children and innocent farmers. You can't wage a war on the manners and politics of a people just because they're different from you. A higher law will skewer the livers of Johnson and McNamara and all they represent. Even those who support this war in small measure will suffer my sting in the same measure. This is the way.

"The Elder Brothers, those of the Covenant and those Ancient Ones before them, and God himself have declared the way.

"I will dance on the tombstone of these barbarians who have burned, bombed and raped their way into my century. I will dance on their graves and choke their children with flowers of love. I will cut the cancerous warts of war from their souls with the blades of the most Holy. I will impound their flesh in the prisons they have prepared for their enemies until their deeds rot from their souls. They will not get away. There will be revenge upon revenge."

When I stop, Wayne and Claire must believe I am someone other than their guest.

Claire gets a quizzical look on her face.

Wayne can't hold back his great gleaming smile, and claps his hands, "Yeah! We're gonna' put you on a street corner, so you can stop the war single-handed."

"Street corner stuff is not what the Brothers have in mind," I say. Mention of the Brothers rings in my ears, and my clock shuts off. I am silent. I sit back down and stare out the window. No one says a word for a long time.

After awhile, Claire breaks the silence. "I'm bushed," she says." I'm going to bed. It's difficult being an archetype day in and day out. And you're right Gil, it's not easy to clean up after you men all the time either." She walks toward the bedroom and turns a sideways glance to Wayne with a big open flirtation.

"I'll be right there," he says watching Claire close the door.

Right away Wayne pulls out another joint and we smoke it together without a word for the next five or ten minutes. "We got t' do something," he says. "We got to do something." He stands. "I'm gonna' be goin' to bed, man", he says. " I hear your words, man. I hear 'em." Moving into the bedroom, he turns and waves.

Once again I am left alone in the heart of dreaded night. I go into the dining room, where Claire has neatly laid out the blanket on top of my thin mattress. I lay down with my clothes on and try to fall asleep. I toss and turn and pound on the pillow. I realize the Tycoons have managed to get their cameras on me through the side windows, and I get up and peek into the darkness before I pull the curtains even tighter.

Anointed

◆

GIL IS WEARY. He's ragged. He has reached the limit of his body and wits. He's gray and drawn. He's cold all the time. He would lie down in the snow and die, but in San Francisco they have no snow. Just fog. In layers of shirts and sweaters, his head and neck are wrapped in an old plaid scarf. He shivers inside his over-sized thrift-shop tweed top coat. The wide lapels and a torn pocket flap in the wind as he crosses Bush Street. He's cheered only by brand-new cowboy boots he found at a thrift shop, and the familiar chant that rises from the church basement . . .

Om ah hung
Om ah hung
Om shanti om
Ooooooooooom

He no longer tries to out maneuver the Tycoons who continue to chase after him. Two cameras follow him up the stone steps where Franco waits for him by the huge Gothic doors.

"Gil," he calls, "hey, man, great to see you." He ignores Gil's rags. "Yeah, Yeah, man."

Cameras record the reunion.

Gil doesn't trust Franco's eagerness. He suspects this evening is more than a mere reunion. Franco told him only that he wants Gil to meet some friends. Right away Gil figured his old friend was in cahoots with the Elder Brothers.

Gill is weary of the taunts from these old men.

Franco is fit and tan with a full beard. He hugs Gil again, then leads him through the giant doors into the nave of the church where he holds Gil at arms length and looks him over, "Well Gil, you survived," he says. He claps the dreamer on the back with great spirit.

The rolling cameras still make Gil feel self-conscious, while Franco does not even give them a passing glance. Gil is resentful of his old friend who has returned from enjoying an ocean cruise while Gil, dog-weary, has stayed to fight the war in the streets.

Now Franco offers him a folded piece of thick orange cloth. "Take it," Franco says.

"For me?"

"Yeah, man."

Gil unfolds a round orange hat, a kind of skull cap, with silver and gold sequins sewn on among green and yellow embroidery.

Franco slips it on the back of Gil's head, and embraces him again. "Now, you are the Pope. The Pope of Dope. And that ain't all." His thumb and forefinger offer a round white pill, "A little present from Uncle Ho. We may never come back."

"I'm already high. I can't really ride more altitude."

Franco laughs, "The Pope of Dope can't say 'no' to this."

"It's so hard to refuse," Gil says, relenting.

Dusky rays filter through the rose windows and turn the icon of Jesus blood red. Anguished Jesus beseeches Gil to take the pill. Join him in the salvation of the race. Franco places the pill on Gil's tongue, and brings out a pint of Thackeray's Blackberry Brandy. With a nod to the Savior, Gil washes the pill down along with a clot of guilt knowing he already is soaring much too high. As always, he hopes for a level never before achieved, above today's misery and low station.

Pill, exalt me in the white radiance of a greater world.

Do the Brothers have something in store that Franco somehow knows about? Do the Exalted Ones summon him to the church for a reason? He's sure this reunion heralds an extraordinary event. A swell of attention from the Tycoons confirms his belief.

The sweet acid of the brandy barely covers the lemon-ice blanch of the drug behind Gil's eye balls.

Franco smiles and nods and tops a pill with a swig of brandy, too. His eyes widen.

A lens records this sacramental moment.

Then Franco speaks, "Before we go downstairs, I want to tell you something. In fact I've got two things to tell you." He leads Gil by the shoulder into a pew in the empty sanctuary. "First off, I want to apologize for all the ribbing about the Peace Corps and all."

"What?"

"You know, man. All the times I told you that you were a chump to be working for the government and all. Charming all those Ethiopians to buy our toothpaste and deodorants, and all. You remember."

"That's so long ago. Didn't we used to go places together, Franco? Like restaurants and plays and dances?" Gil says and gives Franco an honest blank look.

"You remember, man. I used to rib you about all your do-gooding?"

"Yeah, I remember. Out walking and talking Shakespeare." *Oh, yes, this is Franco, his friend from the old days – oh so long ago.*

"Anyway, man, I apologize. I know you were only trying to do good. Trying to do the best for people that didn't have as much as us. And you were sincere, man, too. That's what I regret the most. You really tried, and I mocked you. So, I'm sorry. Forgive me."

Gil waves forgiveness. *If he thinks I was really trying then, what will he think about me now? Or is he part of the plan? He may even be proof of the plan.*

Franco grips Gil's shoulders to get his attention. "Anyway, really why I brought you here is, I have to tell you what happened out there, man. Because you are the one who put me onto it. I got a new religion, man. I brought you to meet my new friends tonight, since you're the one who led me here."

Gil tries to smile. *What does he mean?*

"Remember that time over in the Panhandle after we dropped acid? And you talking about God. Remember? You told me about how a thousand mics of LSD opened the door of the universe for you. What you said that night kept coming back to me out in the Indian Ocean, and then, I found God, too, man. Found something absolutely huge I can't explain. Only now I understand what you were talking about, Gil."

Dazed, Gil tries to remember as his excitement builds.

"Look," Franco's face draws close in the dusk, "look . . . I saw death out there and I saw beyond it, like the Book says . . . I saw life come to an end, and I saw it begin again . . . I know I'm gettin' ahead of myself, but you gotta listen. There is death out there, and there is life. I saw them both, and I'm here to tell you there can't be one without the other, that's the miracle. That's the miracle."

Franco takes a deep breath, "This wasn't an acid trip; this was for real, man. I finished my watch. Midnight. In the middle of the Indian Ocean. No land in sight, just billions of stars. I went out to the stern deck with a buddy, Marty, who had just finished his shift, too. We went out there, almost every night to smoke a joint and watch the stars. I'm just smokin' dope, man. No more smack. I never used it once out there, man, and I'm clean and going to stay that way. Anyway, Marty was from upstate New York. A sport nut. About 10 years older'n me. Dropped out of graduate school in philosophy. Smart, but all he wanted to talk about was sports. So after our shift, we'd take a few tokes and watch the stars go by. There we were, around the Cape, steaming, steaming toward Thailand.

"This one night, when we get back there, Marty tells me he feels kinda creepy, like something mysterious is goin' on. Actually he has got awful thin. I ask him, 'What can happen in the middle of the Indian Ocean?' He keeps telling me he's got the creeps, and he keeps talkin' about his father and mother and where he grew up and all — not like the Marty who only talks sports or a little philosophy, but hardly ever about himself. Then, after about half an hour, he stands up and tells me he's going inside 'cause he feels so strange. I tell him he's gettin' paranoid.

Just as he stands up, I hear this gigantic whoosh of air and Marty 'whoops' and says he saw a giant bird. But it's dark, and I can't see anything but stars, though I heard this whoosh that sure sounded like some gigantic bird, and Marty tells me he saw something like an over-sized albatross, but I told him, 'We're too far from land for any bird, man.' But, he says how he saw it, and it scared him and maybe it was the dope we smoked."

Franco studies Gil with a keen eye to see if he's following. "Man, I tell you I heard some big whoosh. Anyway, Marty says it's all too strange and he's goin' inside. So I say 'good night,' and watch him turn and take hold of the guide chain along the side and head back to the cabin. Then, I lay down to knock off my joint, when a gigantic swell comes along and lifts the ship up like we was headed for Mars. I actually feel the ship goin' up on this thing . . . outta nowhere . . . this swell and we're goin up and up and up, and I hang on to a rope that's there, hang on for my life, and then we reach the crest of the swell, that awful moment when I know there's no water underneath and we're a little surf board out there in the ocean, and we start falling . . . falling, man, to find the water to support us and I think, man, we've fallen off the edge of the earth, because we fall and fall and fall, and I'm holding on to a rope and a piece of the mooring system, and for no reason I start prayin', and I never prayed since I was a kid, man, and I'm prayin' for God or whoever to just let us hit the water and be back on this planet, when all at once I see a light out in the water about a hundred feet away or so, fairly close as we fall. And then, wham, an answer to my prayer, the ship plunges back into the good old ocean and we bounce, man, no kiddin', we bounce down the side of that swell and the spray shoots up a thousand feet and we bounce like we're going to turn over, man I swear."

And then Franco gulps as if to keep from drowning, then continues, "And then, man, the strangest . . .." He takes Gil's sleeve, "Out in the ocean I see this same glow out of some eerie science fiction movie, and it gets brighter and brighter, and I see its Marty standin' out there on the water, and he's calling to me, motioning with his hand for me to come with him. He's smiling and has a kind of beatific look standing on the water asking why I'm not coming out to meet him. 'Come on, come on,' I hear him call, but I'm frozen and hold onto the rope and that piece of metal like they're my mother, and he's waving for me to come. Then, I hear the siren from the tower, and the intercom speakers blarin', 'MAN OVERBOARD, MAN OVERBOARD,' and the siren's screechin', and 'MAN OVERBOARD, MAN OVERBOARD.' And me, I'm watching Marty, and I'm startin' to get real scared, but I had used all my adrenaline in that fall when the ship was up in space, and I'm real calm watching Marty, even though I'm scared, and they're shoutin', 'MAN OVERBOARD . . . MAN OVERBOARD. I see him right there. I'm amazed. And then before I have another thought, this giant glowing bird, this flaming albatross swoops down and Marty climbs on its back, and the two of them go right up into the sky and I watch their glow get smaller until it joins the stars. And it's just another star."

Gil catches his breath. He's been listening, but now his mind races and wonders how Franco's story fits his own circumstances. He expected Franco to tell how this encounter brought his enlistment by the Brotherhood to present Gil to the world as The Chosen One. Somehow though, Gil did not get this from Franco's story, and therefore is not sure why Franco told him this very outlandish fish tale.

"Course, I never told them at the inquest about seeing' him walk on the water or go off on the back of an albatross or anything . . ., but I can tell you. That's the God's truth of what I saw, man, I swear.

"Something happened that night and I haven't been the same since. I don't know what, but I get visits from Marty's spirit and he tells me to rejoice and live for my fellows.

"Now I'm happy to be alive all the time. Happy to be here with you, happy to be there with them, my friends. It doesn't matter. I have felt this joy ever since I watched old Marty go off on the back of that bird, up in the sky. He showed me there's more to life than meets the eye, more than we have ever been taught, much more.

It's never going be the end, he told me. He charged me with joy. I haven't been the same since.

"Call it religion or whatever you want to call it, but I found something. I started talking to a guy on the ship named Carl, who is a devotee of an Indian guru, Om Banuananda. He told me a lot of strange stuff, gave me a few books to read, and then everything fell into place. I got off the ship in Karachi, and went overland to India, and I went up into the mountains until I found his Guru as he said I would in this little village, and I stayed with Om Banuananda for two months until one day he told me I had to go back to my own country and live what he had taught me, and then I was to return one year later and tell him what I had learned since I left him, and then he would begin the teaching again.

"So, I went back to Karachi and caught a ship. Carl gave me the name of some of his friends here, followers of Om Banuananda, and I called them when I got back, and here I am, man, and you're the one gave me the first clue and I want you to meet my friends downstairs. I know you're gonna like 'em." Franco chokes off his brilliant smile.

Gil waits for more.

When nothing more comes he decides that Franco will tell him the rest after the introductions. As they leave the sanctuary, Gil senses that this miracle story lays the groundwork for Franco and his friends to assist Gil. All is part of the Brotherhood's plan.

Franco leads the way downstairs into a fluorescent-lit hall and toward the chanting. Through frosted glass Gil observes faces of young people of diverse races sitting in a semi-circle on a carpet. Franco cracks the door a bit and they look in on a choir of teens, all in white pants and shirts. Each has a white hat like the orange one Franco gave Gil. All sit cross-legged, boys on one side, girls the other.

To Gil's surprise, older men and women in white sit behind the teens. Along one wall, a long table stands stocked with a punch bowl, paper cups and bowls of food.

Now Gil understands . . . he is to be ushered into the hierarchy of Elder Brothers.

"Come on," Franco pulls at Gil's sleeve, "I want you to meet someone."

"Not yet." Gil resists, fearful to be so close to the Elders.

"No one is going to bite you in there. I thought you would enjoy meetin' my friends and hear their chanting."

"Maybe, but not yet," Gil says. He backs away from Franco. His face flushes with heat. He refuses to feel worthy in the presence of such important people.

The children chant, "Let the Savior come forward. Let the Savior bring us peace. . . . .." First the girls, then the boys repeat the lines.

Gil feels old and hard and unwashed. These open-mouthed children, their bright clean faces so pure in church light and with their round voices, illuminate his shaggy entry. He feels shame at his condition.

Franco takes his arm, "Come on, Gil. It's all right, man, we're not exactly Christian, and we're not exactly Hindu, kind of a meld. It's all right, I promise you. We're going to sing and chant and eat."

Gil longs to go inside, but he's afraid to be recognized, certain the cameras have already broadcast his daily life on TV. But hearty Franco pushes the door open when the chanting ends and waves Gil to follow.

"He has entered, he has come. The Savior of faith has returned," the children chant. First the boys chant, then the girls, then together over and over, over and over.

Still, Gil holds back. They chant about him. *So hard to believe!*

He walks in behind Franco. He must look a fool in this embroidered orange beanie, when everyone else wears white. Franco leads him to a burly, dark man who stands off to the side in a white robe, his hair well past his shoulders. He has a graying beard and steel-gray eyes below an embroidered silver skullcap.

"This is The Om Manu," Franco tells Gil. "Om Manu, this is my very righteous friend Gil. Gil is the new pope." Franco smiles from the Manu to Gil.

Gil keeps his head lowered while The Om Manu grips his hand and shakes it hard.

"Pleased to receive you, here." His deep voice bears a slight foreign accent that Gil recognizes as that of the Elder Brothers. "Very pleased to have your light shine among us." Gil catches the Manu's wink when he turns to Franco. "This is your friend, the special one. A very special one." His burly paw pats Gil's new orange beanie.

Head bent, Gil moves to a group of children's chairs near the back. No one pays much attention or yet recognizes him. He breathes easier in the tiny chair, his knees are bent up and all but covering his face. When he's settled enough to look up, Gil finds The Om Manu seated before the group cross-legged with a set of small hand-drums. Gil's eyes stick to this radiant man.

Now the Manu beats on the drum and sets up a rhythm that bounds through the room. The quick rat-a-tat-tats bring an answer by the boys, "Om Manu Shanti Om" and the girls answer, "Om Manu Shanti Om." The drums and answering chants bloom in Gil's blood. He falls into the cadences themselves. Soon the men seated across from women join in. "Om Manu Shanti Om . . . Om Manu Shanti Om."

Gil, too, forms silent syllables of the chant. The sounds make him warm and soon he grows radiant. Fearing to turn his gaze to the assembled, Gil wraps his scarf around his face until only his eyes shine over the plaid, and so keep from blinding the innocents.

Bathed in the room's rapt holiness, Gil foresees the moment all will turn to him to make some sign. However, the steely-eyed Manu goes on rat-a-tat-tat, and all now sit in silence. Gil gets but a casual glance as he peers over his scarf. Soon, he's comfortable enough to cast his eyes about. Gil sees the men are mostly from the hierarchy of Elders. They've arranged for him to be here among them. *How else would I be here?*

He makes eye contact with a large, bearded man who shows him a faint smile more welcoming than any ever before given him by the Brothers. This face lacks the dark foreboding of Brothers' faces he usually meets trudging the streets. A second bearded man returns Gil's gaze with a half-smile. This smile however has misgiving about it and reminds Gil of his ragged clothing. Instinctively, he reaches up and touches his orange beanie and the Elder smiles back warmly. Gil intuits this means acceptance in spite of his poor look, that the Elders know of his life's unyielding struggle . . . the ordeal of his days march and cleansing of the streets, and of his steps paced to the inch and done with no complaint, as are all his duties toward the salvation of mankind.

Franco takes his place among the elders next to a muscular, bearded man in white pants, shirt and skullcap. Franco in jeans, a plaid shirt and pea coat gives no hint of being self-conscious. This heartens Gil, though he longs for a white robe and to fit in. He smiles to discover the true purpose of his summoning. At the Brothers' direction Franco brought him here for the formal solemnization and to make public the nature of his work and sacrifices. Why else would he be here? The sheer force of this limpid realization lifts him from his child's chair to stand stiff at attention.

Scanning the room, his dope-drenched eyes brimming with light detect a heat shimmer in the walls. Rainbows flash and weave and ornament the bookcases and tables and ceiling. Living patterns in the rug dance. Pearl froth spills from white clothes and his own eyes throb with colors. The room stands bright in the noonday sun of his drugged imagination.

Kingly in sparkling white, the Manu sounds the chant, taps on the drum and the group responds. His eyes glint as the chant begins, Om Manu Shanti Om . . . Om Manu Shanti Om.

Now is the time.

Gil feels transported from where he stands, compelled to glide forward. His eyes meet those of a pale and shy young angel in white sweater and long white skirt. Though all sit with eyes closed, she looks up from the chanting to give Gil an open smile. Her energies fill him with the courage to glide down front and stand by The Om Manu as he beats his drum.

Gil relaxes before this chanting group, Though his scarf still hides his face, a cool breeze kisses his forehead. His eyes fasten on the angel who feeds him her smile. Time hangs in the air. He is still and silent as he looks over the group all with their eyes closed.

Franco is sitting toward the back, bewildered perhaps, in mixed emotions at Gil's triumph.

As bodies sway Gil returns to the girl. Her face and figure form a woman of biblical power whom he knew long ago as Mother Ruth from his unfinished dream in long ago Ethiopia. Ah, the Brotherhood has sent her to help him launch the Millennium. He sends her thoughts, though in the flush of the moment he cannot be sure she returns them.

The walls quiver to the drumbeat with pulsing light. The room's brightness grows and breaks into movement. Shadowy human figures walk out of the light and move through the room. Some stand undisturbed in the middle of people and hope to fathom the goings on.

Curious, Gil watches these half-formed creatures and divines a tie to them from a long time ago. He is tempted to call to them. But the chanting keeps him silent. Then he falls into the chant when the angel gazes at him.

Without a word the large man stops beating his drums. While the chanting goes on, the Manu stands and makes a slight bow toward Gil. He removes both his own skullcap and Gils, one in each hand. After a ritual moment he places Gil's orange cap and on his own head. The chanting grows louder, Om Manu Shanti Om . . . Om Manu Shanti Om. He places his shining silver and white embroidered cap on Gil's head. *This is, of course, a ritual of initiation into the world of the Elders.* Gil manages a deep but reserved low bow, which brings forth a large smile. The Manu sits again at his drums.

Franco's broad smile means, "This is why I brought you here."

Friendly but dim figures move toward Gil in a solemn procession. In robes that sparkle with white and purple lights two headmen carry a pillow each, one with a golden scepter, the other a glittering and bejeweled crown.

As these otherworldly creatures approach, Gil fixes his eyes on the beaming angel. And now cool unearthly hands lift his arms. His hands grasp a scepter. Cradling the cool metal, he senses the delicate pressure on the sacred spot of his head beneath the cap as the leader of these shadow creatures places the crown on his head just as a celestial ermine robe drapes itself over his back. Gil renders a modest bow to these other worldly creatures, denizens of the Elder Brother realms, and, now in full regalia, another less modest bow to the angel.

All the while the Tycoons' cameras preserve for another time the strands of Gil's daily struggles and now his anointing. *Let these grubby Tycoons have a good look.* He stares with scorn at them and hurls his angry thoughts, *"Now you see I am the real thing and no longer fear you. Tonight you learn my true mission. You can do me no further harm."*

How intense the chanting has become! Om Manu Shanti Om ... Om Manu Shanti Om!

With a longing look toward the angel, and a certain righteous air in his stride, Gil allows the shadowy figures to glide him past the chanting men and women as he holds forth his scepter and balances his crown, the ermine robe trailing after. When he reaches Franco, he stops and with his scepter knights his friend with a tap on each shoulder, and tells him, "You have brought me to a good end. And a new beginning."

Gil, flushed and burned in the glory of the moment, turns, bows to the assembled as they chant fervent belief. He bows and points his ghostly scepter all about the room and bows still again, now to these vague shapes and figures who glide about the room.

Franco stands in front of Gil, removes the silver beanie from his head and replaces it with the orange and yellow embroidered one he had given to Gil.

He then hugs Gil and kisses him on both cheeks, and says, "Hey, man, can I crash at your pad for a couple days?"

As they walk out the door together, Gil nods and says with regal simplicity, "My palace is your palace."

Outside the church, he stands in starlight. As trees along Bush Street catch the breeze and bushes shimmer, the scepter fades from his grip, his crown dies in dreams and the robe slips from his shoulders.

Gil blushes from the recognition heaped upon him. He is charged to bursting for his mission. His chest swells. Even though he must face the streets clothed in stealth, he smiles at the golden memory of his anointing. He walks toward Geary, his friend Franco riding shotgun. Buildings and trees greet him. The sky greets him. The Tycoons hunch behind and look weary, cameras in tow, hearts puzzled.

Saving the World

♦

Gil walks to bring the Elder Brother's message of world redemption in the coming order and for his own release from the torture of his mission on San Francisco's streets.

He is taught to spread this message, chanting the chant, by tracing complex paths along the city streets, patterns that mirror geographic segments of the world. Thus, as he walks certain parts of Geary, close to Van Ness, he also straddles the Russo-Chinese border and spreads the message of the Millennium to peoples in those parts. "Om ah Hung. Om ah Hung." Further up Geary, at Fillmore, he crosses over to Eastern Europe, and further still at Divisidero Gil enters Europe itself. "Om, Om, Om ah Hung."

Twilight voices direct him as true as radio voices direct helicopter and bomber pilots who daily strafe and bomb Vietnamese villages. Gil is told to turn left or right, cross the street or round the corner and thus contact various peoples. A simple but weary task, similar to his brothers in Asian war zones who had not found the fortitude to resist the military zeal of the government of Lyndon Baines Johnson and Robert McNamara.

Gil strikes the pavement with his hard heels to wake up the world as he chants the prayer, "Om ah Hung, Om ah Om. Forgive your brothers and the world is saved. Love your brothers and the world is saved. Salvation is at hand. Praised be God." He tries hard not to watch the people who pass. He keeps the chant going and follows what he's told.

He feels himself projected on a screen as a fool and suffers. He puzzles why the Elders chose him for this great purpose. Do they find him afflicted with some freak purity of heart that raises him to higher consciousness? Well, he's tired of suffering and of leading the blind on this forsaken planet. They should know better. He would like to scold these sinners, because they have bad manners and kill and kill and kill, with no thought to the homely, moral upbringing with which each of them were first imbued.

Even now, he watches the Tycoons point their cameras at him from passing cars, from windows along the streets where he walks, from rooftops and sheltered doorways. He's being recorded and one day the world will know that during the Millennium Gilbert Stone did his job, no matter the cost.

Sometimes his faith wavers. Walking down California, toward Van Ness, he is worn out because he hasn't eaten in days. His angry body knows he can't keep this up much longer. His cells grind on empty. His thighs cry to him, joined by calves and feet. "Rest us," they implore him. "Leave off this thriftless vigil, this nightmare." The cells have small dark eyes that pierce him. They brood and plead. They do not jibe with the voices in his head, which show no mercy for those unaware of the dawning of the Millennium.

Gil pushes until his muscles rebel. Something snaps in his head. His legs refuse to move. He finds himself at sidewalk's edge on cool grass as his cells scream with craving. He floats above his body and looks down on his cringing and scrawny remains. He relaxes, then sinks deep into sleep.

Waking, he knows he must get food. The thought of food drives him half upright and sitting. His thighs complain about the terrible exertion they must make to get him up. He promises them food and they roll him onto his haunches. His wonderful feet, always ready, dig into grass for the big stretch of his calves and the creak of his unbending knees. Dew soaks through his ripped jeans. Bone by bone and inch by inch he rises and heads for the Sign of the Fool.

He staggers to a metal signpost and steadies himself. Passersby stare at his leaning figure, turn their heads away and walk on. *Are they going to work, or coming home?* He's not sure of the time. A woman in a hat and long coat stops to look him over. She clutches her purse and asks if he's all right. He sees her pity. He nods, yes, to her question, and does not ask her for help.

He strikes a bargain with his cells and continues to walk. Approaching Fillmore he sees the sign from blocks away — the large tarot card of the Fool that hangs over the door. His destination.

Gil runs the last half block, then standing at the door, he finds the place is closed and locked. He panics. *The place should be open.* It's open all day and evening and now the sun is out and he can't understand. He bangs on the door until Suzanne, who sleeps in the back room, comes out wrapped in a Mexican blanket. She sees him, her sleeping mouth open in a wide scream and lets him in.

"What's wrong with you? It's after midnight. You look like death."

He enters, grateful. She locks the door, turns and walks toward the back without even looking. He follows her, past the counter and dining room tables with stacked chairs into the back room to a long bench built against the back wall and decked out with large pillows. Suzanne uses these pillows for a bed. She gives him one look and throws a pillow to him. He takes another from the bench and lies down not far from her. She turns over and he glimpses her bare body. She casts a look above his head, turns her back to him and nestles into sleep.

His mind races as he watches her breathe, the movement of her bare shoulders. He sways with her breathing, moves his pillows closer to her. Still, inching closer, he cannot help himself. Their pillows touch and he is close enough to hear the evenness of her sleeping breath, close enough to softly touch her shoulder, only he's sure she'll yell, or turn around and push him away.

But he can't stop himself, and even with his voices telling him "no," and his cells crying out, he cannot rest until he has slowly rested his arm on her shoulder. Surprisingly, her back nestles into his front with sleepy movements and murmurs.

He knows how dirty he must smell. He's worn the same clothes for weeks, his beard and hair are matted and dirty. Suzanne overhears these thoughts, for she turns over at once, makes a face and squeezes her nose.

She jumps up, the blanket held around her, and yanks him onto his feet. She leads him into the kitchen, behind the hanging pots and pans near the back door, to the huge sink where the dishes get washed. She grabs the spray nozzle hanging over the double sink, turns on the water and sprays him full blast where he stands on raised wooden floorboards.

Cold water stings him and soaks his rotting clothes. Suzanne stands laughing, the blanket held about her as she sprays him. He shivers in the flood. His cells smile and dance in the icy spray. He sways and prances. Goose bumps ripple up his arms and the hairs on the back of his neck tingle. His legs ache as water runs down his torn jeans. He pulls his clothes off into a soggy heap and stands as naked skin and bones. He rubs spray into his hair and beard as stiff matted bristles break down.

Suzanne hands him the plastic container of dish soap, and he pours a dollop into his hand and oils his body until he covers himself in suds. Suzanne plays the spray on him, and when he's suds-free she says, "Again." He pours more soap over his hair, and suds his beard, shoulders and back, his buttocks and legs and works up another lather. He is white foam. He is running with suds, dripping with water. Again Suzanne sprays him clean.

"Again!" she says, her laughter ringing. Pleasure fills her for the first time he can remember as he endures the frigid water that drains away his weary aches. This time he lathers up slowly in the luxury of the soap and slides his hands all over and touches himself.

Now she turns up the hot water and rinses the last lather from his hair and body. "Turn around," she says.

She throws the blanket over the counter and stands naked with
him, the water turned on herself. She moves close and presses her
raised breasts against him. Her mouth joins his and he hugs her
as she holds the warm shower above them. He puts his hands on
her buttocks and presses her into him and they kiss deeply until
she drops the shower nozzle and holds him close and closer and
they can stand it no longer and she goes to the closet and pulls out
a huge white table cloth and wraps them both and they dry each
other and move out into the room with the pillows and lie there
with the promise of dawn entering the windows. They make love
in the luxury of thick carpeting and deep soft pillows.

Suzanne brings him food. Miso soup, oatmeal, thick pieces of
brown rice bread with tart apple butter. He eats hungrily, but slowly,
chewing and tasting each morsel, as when making love, aware of
food being broken down by his body, entering his blood stream and
bringing life to starving cells now joyful and filling up just on the
mere aroma of food. A miracle of the universe restores him.

Finished and full, he lies on the pillows in the corner satisfied,
although his brain keeps demanding food for his soul. "Only seek,
only seek," he murmurs. His mind does not share his pleasure.
Something has been lost in bodily satisfaction.

Suzanne has dressed him in the chef's spare uniform . . . a loose
white shirt, white pants, white socks, and white shoes. He lies back
on the pillows clean, fed, and nearly content. He dozes under softly gonging pans and dish clatter while Suzanne and the chef and
others ready the Fool for business. Baking bread, sweet and warm,
carries him off.

He dreams of rising out of the depths. Leaving the dark plane,
the earth falls away and gases propel him, breaking the bonds of
gravity and lifting him soaring from the streets to a glistening crystal
city beyond the stars.

The Brothers come for him. Pure music crashes into a rising
chorus. Soaring, the Brothers bring him to their level and come for
his spirit. Rewarded for his service, rocketed up to them. This has
always been his cherished dream.

Gil opens his eyes.

Though he wakes in the same room where he'd fallen asleep, oddly the windows are dark. He slept the entire day. He realizes that the music is coming from the Blessed Angel Baptist Church across the alley. Mighty gospel songs soar on a chorus of huge voices of black men and women and roar out the glory of God.

He is to be taken up. He hears the beeping of extra-terrestrial Morse code messages for him from the Brotherhood. The beeps leap from a station deep in space. These communications usually guide his every movement, only now they take on a tonal variation. The spirit is joyful, not savage and imploring. His job is done. He has achieved the goals of the Brothers. Now they will announce to the world the beginning of the Millennium. Very soon, he will rest and receive his reward.

He is to be taken up as this choir of the Blessed Angels lift him. He lies on the pillows of the Fool as his joy shivers, now that his time has come. Soon his directions will be broadcast and he will translate the beeps. The answer forms within him as the message unscrambles and sets his heart and mind racing. His eyes close in the half-light, as shapes form and a rocket blasts off. He is filled with knowledge. Yes, they have come for him. He follows the rocket's arc into space. Looking closer, he sees his face through a window. How exciting for him to leave this dreary planet and bond with the Brothers and The Way.

The choir rises even higher with "Rock of Ages." Dark, deep tones come from the South, somewhere long ago, when these voices labored over fields of cotton and tobacco, toiled for the white man's family and fortune, sorrowed over abuse and bondage and strained to endure. These are the mighty voices, forged and sculpted by centuries of seeking righteousness — still seeking righteousness — lifting him from the back room of the Sign of the Fool and carrying him to the Brothers.

For all together the Brothers, the choir and he, have come to tell the world the news of the Millennium. But, lo, the world holds back. He must stay no longer with those who will not listen, who see only his unkempt body and turn from his offer of salvation. He must leave those who pass him on the street like a scab, and who go about their business when he's beamed righteousness into their soul, told them time and again to give up their jobs, give up their families and go to the countryside to find God. They do not listen, and he can do no more. He must allow himself to be taken up and dwell with the Brothers.

Confident now more than ever he waits for the rocket. He waits all through the evening, but gets no sign. The Church next door falls silent. The few people who have come into the back room hardly notice him, young couples, laugh and shout between bites. They flaunt the bright clothes of the day, but see no dawn of the Millennium. He sends them thoughts, but these chattering children have no understanding.

Sometimes he cannot comprehend why these people, only a few years younger than himself, do not share his vision of why they've come together here. He is dumbfounded as they turn away from the savage and disgraceful war in Asia. Daily and nightly, the TV sets blaze with the heroic story of our Vietnam War. That's what they call it now. But this war differs little from those of the last Millennium. Year in year out, replacements replace replacements, kill, mutilate, scream their anguish, die.

The dawning of the Millennium brings the message to stop war, but still, they do not listen. How much longer can he carry this message? The Brothers and the Tycoons spend his body. He is left with very few who understand his translations from the Great Brotherhood. He is cursed, not blessed, to carry this message.

Only the crass Tycoons have a notion of the importance of his mission, but they only weigh his ordeal as a chance to make money. Even now, they stand on the roof of the church, behind the steeple, grinding away at the Fool. Do they think he's dead, and at last can hawk their movie?

He waits for the Brothers to carry him up, but no one comes. All the duties they set for him are complete, but now he's the forgotten soul. Once again, the time of promise has come and gone.

He aches with disappointment.

Lovely Suzanne comes to the back room to see if he is still asleep.

For the first time he opens his eyes, really opens them. She holds out a plate, and slowly he sits up. Her eyes adore him so much that he turns from her gaze even as his thoughts cause her to look away. Her auburn hair falls in long strands over a shoulder and hides her face. Her warmth overcomes him. Perhaps she has heard. Perhaps he's found the one other person on the planet tuned to the over-powering magnitude of the times.

Why else would she put up with me?

Streets of Laredo

◆

CLEARLY THE BROTHERS WILL not deliver him up tonight despite the gospel choir and his longing to abandon the planet, so Gil leaves the Sign of the Fool through the back door without a "farewell."

The Tycoons grind on filming with DeMille himself shooting from a new Volkswagen bus.

His panic grows as he nears Garden Street. There has been no word from the Brothers or Kennedy this whole day which he finds ominous. His beehive is abandoned.

The door stands half-open at his house. The bare ceiling bulb burns brightly in the living room. He sees a sailor's duffel bag in a corner half covered by his friend's pea coat. Franco is lying on his back on the mattress. He is very still; a shirtsleeve is rolled above his elbow. His head tilts toward the wall. His eyes are half-open. His lips are parted with spittle. He looks pale in the glare of the bulb.

Gil beams a greeting, "Franco." No movement. Hopeful, Gil directs his thought with force. At last he speaks aloud, "Franco." No response.

A needle gleams from Franco's bare arm.

It strikes Gil that his friend is dead. A syringe lies in a fold of the unmade bed clothes. On the floor there is a scorched spoon, and a pool of white candle wax burnt to the wick on a piece of broken plate.

He kneels, stunned by Franco's white face. Gil shakes his shoulder, but expects nothing from the cold body. He resists an urge to kiss the dead lips, but sits cross-legged on the floor and stares at Franco's corpse.

He asks in silence, *Why didn't you take me with you on the albatross?*

A Brother says, "He tried. He came to share the albatross with you. But we kept you from harm. There is work to do."

He glances out the half-shaded window to see the Tycoons on the mortuary roof across the street. *Could they have something to do with this, just to film his reaction?*

He sees a host of Brothers in white robes with red sashes, who carry swords and knives. They look like those who trooped by Kennedy on his Rock.

"There is no death," they chant and stab Franco with spears of light. He bursts into flame. They become neon demons with gargoyle faces. As their chant echoes, Gil watches the face of his friend harden into a mask.

So Franco is gone and he has no tears for him. Of course Gil thought him gone before, sailing the high seas and delivering Cokes and Mars bars and napalm to our troops in Viet Nam. He's partly glad Franco is gone. Though he loved him and felt grateful for all his friend's worldliness. He depended on Franco too much and that made Gil think he couldn't live by himself. He should be relieved, but he doesn't feel the relief he wants.

What did Franco teach him? He can't remember. He taught him that he should feel guilty because Franco grew up poor. He taught him that because he spent a year in Washington, DC and sailed around the world, that he's always right. He taught him to smoke dope and drop pills and hang out with people who never hated the war the way Gil did; people so cool, who don't care, so non-caring, so cool, so fully packed with shit.

Oh, Franco, if only you knew the way of the Brothers for real. If you could hear the voices I hear, then these cool fakes you hang out with wouldn't cow you. You'd live to set the world free.

Suddenly he jumps up. He's frightened, and wants to flee this body, but he's also fascinated and wants to stare as that bare needled arm cools and stiffens. *Is his spirit still hovering about, looking down? There must be some regret that he made a mistake and paid for it with his young life, one small overdose being one too many. But are there really any mistakes?*

He sees Franco's doting mother and absent father, a cigarette salesman who died at fifty-three of lung cancer. Then savvy Jesuits educated Franco; or so he said, though Gil didn't believe him and thought him devious on his own terms.

Franco would look him straight in the eye, and say, "The Jesuits were tough, you have no idea how tough."

He always borrowed money from Gil, and never mentioned it again. For a whole semester he lived with him without paying more than a month's rent. *Well, he deserved free rides because of his wretched childhood. "Let's go here." "Let's go there," and I buy the tickets and make sure we eat. Me mother, him child, and I hated it and could do nothing about it.*

They once followed Tennessee Williams back to his hotel and Franco kept saying that they had to go up and talk to him to prove that he was only a man, but Gil refused . . . he was too scared so he stayed on the corner while Franco went into the lobby and talked with Williams for awhile, came out and said that this famous playwright was only a man, and he taunted Gil because he hadn't gone with him, and that he was chicken and would never amount to anything. *But here I am saving the world and Franco lies dead with a needle in his arm. Jesuit education and all, dead!*

Gil looks at Franco's prone body. His face is like pale marble, all the pockmarks are gone. So this is the short happy life of Francis MacFranco? *And here you'd just found religion. Now you sail never to return. You came from the Spanish Mountains, and I came from the Peace Corps and we met in Shakespeare – and now you die.*

Sunlight breaks through the window. Franco's face seems even whiter. The veins on his hands disappeared. His childlike arms lie, long and thin, pale in the unforgiving sun.

They would walk together through downtown San Francisco ... Hamlet and Horatio ... and talk about everything, never imagining they might end like this. *I wonder about Franco's widowed mother somewhere in the Midwest. Must I call her? I can't.*

Gil wonders if he will be gone too, before long. Just a word from the Brothers and he will follow in the great parade by the Rock. He knows it will be harder to live in the world without Franco. He knows he could have asked him to help in this great work with the Brotherhood. He needs to find the right direction for the bringing of peace. Now, Franco has it all – solitude and peace, while he must wrestle this great task and no rest.

Gil continues to expect that Franco will wake up, but he never moves, no star to seek! There lies his friend in the flourish of youth, skewered upon the jagged knowledge of his wretched, ignorant life. A bent bough, another rough youth broken in the war, a wisp who never lived long enough to meet his eternal self.

Gil rises and lifts the telephone, but there's no tone. He rips off his thrift-store tweed overcoat, tosses it aside and dons the dead man's pea coat.

He walks backwards out the door, his eyes fixed on Franco. Outside he jumps down the two steps and races up the alley toward Divisadero. The Brothers stay silent, but the clumsy Tycoons led by DeMille hurry down from the mortuary roof to keep up with him.

He stops at a phone kiosk, dials the operator. "Give me the police," he says short of breath, and soon connects to a precinct "There is death on Garden Street," he says to the voice that answers, "at number 4 Garden Street, you will find death."

Coughing and gasping, he hangs up. He starts running like hell again and doesn't stop until he loses himself in the heart of the Tenderloin. He hides in an alley off McAllister to breathe, and ponder his next move. He must get the Brothers to transform him before some mistake has him follow Franco.

Taken Up

◆

GIL WAITS FOR SOME TIME before two uniformed officers walk into the hotel room and find him seated on the bed.

He can tell they know him. Silent, one on either side, they help him up and escort him from room 1129. He intuits these two young men, handsome in their pressed blue uniforms, both with trimmed sideburns and mustaches, have come to finally deliver him to the Elders.

They walk to the elevator down the hallway with its worn, floral carpet. Out of respect, they say nothing. No one speaks as they enter the lobby. Gil keeps his eyes focused on the floor, his demeanor is altogether grave . . . he's become a prisoner of war. Though they let go his arms as they pass through the bright reception area, he is sandwiched between these two officials of the Brotherhood. He suspects they don't know exactly why they've taken him prisoner.

As they pass a wall mirror he spots his bedraggled self in pea coat, long-hair and scraggly beard — the look of a street person of no redeeming value — jeans dirty and torn and boots soaked. He doesn't have socks and he limps because his feet hurt. He had come into the hotel wanting to take a bath or a nice hot shower, but it slipped his mind.

Why did the Elders allow me to get into this ragged shape? He senses betrayal, but whose or why he can't tell.

He's confused as people eye him with fierce stares. The officers, however, treat him with the consideration and the esteem of a hero. They must indeed serve the Elders, not the pigs that bully the legions on the streets when they protest. One eyes him with the same sadness our hero holds for bewildered Vietnamese peasants. The officers will soon know his true identity.

As they walk, he explains to them that he had requested the key for room 1129 and the clerk just gave it to him.

"I had to laugh," he tells them. "Today the Hilton will give a key to any old raggedy-ass hippie if he asks politely. I went up there to bathe, and then a complete stranger walks in, switches on the light, and finds me sitting on his bed. One look and he turns on his heel and walks right out. So I quickly divined that the Brothers would send some emissaries to take me up. Only the Brothers can get me to where I'm going, as you gentlemen know. I can't get there by myself. But then I never bathed, I just sat there in the dark, lost until you came?"

His escorts lead him along thick, red carpeting and past the Hilton's over-sized, comfortable chairs and couches, glass-topped tables and crystal lamps. He walks past the stares of the other hotel guests, and out into midnight. Well, he's never sure of time of day... but he knows something momentous *is* happening, he just doesn't know what. The Tycoons still dog him, no question. Do they know the Elders have agreed to take him up?

His men usher him into the back seat of some official car. He's fearful for the first time. In the dark back seat of this strange car with its worn carpeting and torn black vinyl seats, and a faint smell of stale wine and urine, amid the official atmosphere of guns and badges, he cringes at the mercy of others.

Where are they are taking me? His anxiety rises. His skin itches. He sits, hands in lap and tries to disregard his fears as they head into the Tenderloin. If these fellows come from the Brothers, they should be friendlier. They've barely said two words.

Through the windows he sees a city gone mad as humanoids and animals from *Weird Comics* mix and take over the streets. Giant rats, snakes, lizards and huge insects crawl. Leopards crouch in doorways and wait to pounce. Dinosaurs glare on corners. Gila monsters slither along sidewalks. Though the windows are rolled up, he smells a sewer stench.

This is my ascension? All these killers would wipe me out and send the Millennium down the cracks of the San Andreas Fault. Is this the end of world peace?

Along a tree-lined street he spots Suzanne, so wholesome and innocent, blind to the carnage around her as she carries a bag of groceries. He tries to roll the window down and yell out to warn her, but the window won't budge. He pierces her with eye-beams. She turns an instant, does not see him and goes on. He tries to protect her with his gaze until she's safe on the far side of the shadows.

The officials in the front seat are unmindful of the horror outside, and obey each stop sign and traffic light. He hears no official sirens, only the dull thud of the car being pummeled with stones. The car continues to roll through claws lifted but inches away. He smells fear on all sides.

But he know that *he's* being taken up. He is safe inside a crucible where the Elders forbid that he be harmed. Powerless he watches innocents be dismembered, scenes burned into his brain.

As they turn down Divisidero things change. Here is solace. No reptile dares follow into the velvet safety of this manger, though poverty now crushes and deforms the innocent.

Where are they taking me? To a police station? Not once do the officers in the front turn their heads; neither do they make comment on the horrors they pass through. Even their radio has ground to a gentle ack-ack.

Then, to his relief he sees where they are headed. Behind a huge wrought-iron gate and a grassy courtyard looms a red brick mansion framed by gilt-edged cornices and white Greek columns. There are two buildings, the Royal Hall itself, and a building from which the Elders no doubt administrate.

His confusion fades. These men of the Royal Guard have brought him to the Palace of the Elders. He is to be inducted into the Order of the Elder Brothers and, having accomplished his mission, may now claim his reward. Humility and gratitude flood him as they enter the splendor of the courtyard. They turn into a narrow road and stop before a small gate in front of the second building.

With no words, but with the slightest hint of ceremony, one of his escorts opens his door, and he slides out of the car in delight. As they go into the building through hammered bronze doors, a certain military correctness bubbles through him and he salutes officers at the entrance, though he shuns any show of official welcome.

A long, narrow hallway with royal blue and ivory inlaid mosaic tiles bordered by stripes of gold opens before them. It is a painting's perspective that runs the hall's length. Gil can make out shrouded figures seated near the end of the hall. A slight mist of delicate fragrances hovers in the air.

Despite his preference for no fanfare, three figures in white poise to greet him. A gray-bearded man awaits in a long, white coat of the finest linen and a white silk shirt and white satin tie embossed with ringlets. Two women have white, flapper dresses to their knees, white stockings, their fingers are golden and bejeweled, while a white tiara headdress mounts their golden hair.

Though ready to be received, Gil shies away from any welcoming speech.

However, it becomes clear that this committee has arranged some sort of ceremony and he must await its conclusion. He's so hungry and would prefer to take the first part of his reward in the royal dining room, but it's not every day these people welcome the Messiah of the Millennium and he'd be rude not to let them do what they no doubt have prepared.

The gentleman behind the desk begins. His voice thunders down the hall and bounds off the walls. To Gil's surprise this gentleman starts off with a question, while the woman to his right sits ready to inscribe his answer onto an ivory tablet. Her gaze asks if he is to be ordained her lover. The courtier just asks his name, and after a pause to weigh whether to tell them his real name, his code name, the Elder's name for him or that of the Tycoons, he just nods and lets the clerk choose out of his mind the one he wishes. This he does after a time and the woman by him notes it down.

Next, Gil is asked how he feels. He merely nods, not wishing to go into his personal estate. The dignitary's questioning gaze goes on for some time, then Gil tries for some self-effacing humor and lets the word "hungry" escape his lips. The interlocutor doesn't get the joke however and, with the humor of the streets beyond him, nods to the woman to write something down.

Gil at once nods "yes" to the question, "Do you want to stay here?" He then nods yes to the two officers, who turn to him, a salute in their eyes. He barely brings his right hand to his brow before they march off.

THE BEARDED MAN and his women escort him down a hall toward two huge, white doors floating in mist that magically slide open to an elevator. Many floors up they emerge on an alcove that leads into a huge hall with a floor of yellow and purple tile. Elegant men and women in mint green and white robes walk about in high-toned beige-colored slippers.

Gil's bowels growl and know he has arrived.

Strange music of flutes, harps and horns fills the background. People move about in a slow graceful dance from one side of the hall to the other. This is surely some sort of ball celebrating his arrival. His usual shyness comes on and he hopes not to be called upon for some sort of ceremonial speech. But no one says a word.

One of the woman asks him to follow her to a room where from a whole store of accessories she hands him a mint green robe and pair of the beige slippers . . . thin and delicate as paper, he supposes for dancing.

The woman then introduces his valet, Jim, a large black man in a white uniform whose arms bulge from his loose short-sleeve shirt. A black rose tattoo blossoms on his left forearm. Somewhat familiar to Gil, the man appears to be about forty and seems to know Gil, who can't quite place him. He has an easy manner and gives the hero of the streets a smile and a nod as the dark tattoo somehow prompts an image of Jack on his Rock.

The woman in white gives him a flirtatious look, and then leaves them.

Jim flashes the professional wink Gil has always wanted for his own repertoire. He finds Jim to be the perfect valet for a returning hero of the streets as he leads the way to a shower room appointed in glorious gold tile and with faucets and nozzles of pure silver.

Again, deep sweetness enters Gil's soul, and the warm water of the shower at once cheers him.

Jim stands by, looking in from time to time, and asking if he is all right.

Gil's not sure the valet can read the reply from his mind correctly, because he asks again, out loud. The unwashed hero flashes another "Not yet," and soaps his body again and again, and lets the water rinse and trickle down his legs as he witnesses the soreness of his ordeal drain away until for a third time there is no soap left.

Jim hands him a towel.

When Gil has dried himself, Jim, holding a safety razor, points to a mirror. Gil has to laugh at his unruly beard though he can't move his facial muscles and can only squeeze his eyes like a sweet little boy.

Jim helps him with a blunt children's scissors, and cuts his beard down to stubble.

Gil rubs in shaving cream that Jim has given him, and in the mirror becomes Frosty the Snowman. A smile so longs to form. The face looking back from the mirror doesn't look like him. As he shaves he's surprised to see so young a boy once again living in his face . . . street fierceness faded with his rise in good fortune.

Jim watches intently as Gil shaves with a shaking hand and sometimes, his rose tattoo aglow, he holds the hero's wrist should he need help on his throat. When the reborn boy is done, Jim plucks the razor from his hand. As a most gentle valet, he assists Gil into his robe and slippers. Shaved and clad he stands in splendor before his valet.

"I'm about ready to take you over," Jim says.

"Over where?"

"You'll see. Call it a party."

The lady in white returns.

Our Odysseus feels obliged to let her know that he's not yet up to sex and that he's going to the party to find something to eat. He walks past her with a handsome twinkle.

As she and Jim follow, she says, "I'll show you where your bed is." He turns to her and his look says, "Not yet." He leaves it to Jim to soothe her.

THE BIG BALLROOM SWIRLS in very slow motion and none there look overjoyed. *Are they in the wrong place?* He hears no music, though a sort of hollow drum sound comes from another room, a TV perhaps.

Several women in white and more valets attend the robed guests who circle about. A tall, pasty white boy in a white uniform pushes a cart about, and serves the guests an elixir from a small cup.

Soon Jim greets him with a small cup of his own red liquid. He drinks the shot down though it puckers his mouth and tastes worse than whiskey. *Where's the food set out?* He doesn't see any. He does notice that, except for the people in white, no one talks much. Those in mint green move around in some outlandish dance and speak only telepathically.

His woman in white taps his shoulder and bids him follow her to another room.

He asks her with one word, "Food?"

She points to a wall clock. The big hand points down to six the little hand at ten.

Ah, the appointed hour for food has not yet arrived, and so he follows her into a smaller room filled with people playing all sorts of games and watching TV or joined in dance. Beyond he sees a hall larger than an airplane hanger. Beds fill it, each neatly made and numbered. Beds in rows fill the entire hall. She takes him to number 33, points to the bed and leaves.

In a moment Jim arrives, and smiling, presents him with a thin, green blanket of some super-soft and exotic silk and wool. What a wonder that this great ceremony celebrating his arrival should include a bed for each person. *Will there be orgies throughout the night? With no partitions and no privacy?* So other rooms must hold the orgies.

The woman returns and nods for him to lie down, but he gives her a look. He drops the blanket and returns to the festivities.

In the main room his eye fixes on a very beautiful woman in a green robe with long golden hair who dances and, looking down, glides gracefully alone about the gold tiles. *This is my beloved! My intended!* Though hunger still nags at him, the sight of this woman dims that pain. Gazing, he knows that his ordeal as the Messiah of the Streets has brought him to his reward.

Looking around, he recognizes others who joined him on the streets. Old Pea Coat Boys along with two lower-ranking Elders now have been ushered to their reward. He spies jugglers and clowns from the Psychedelic Circus. To his surprise, he also sees Dylan the Poet, whose songs drove him along and kept him in touch. He sees the Everly Brothers, and a very tall and clumsy . . . but serious . . . man whom he knows at once as Streetwalker Wolfe, the Southerner who taught him so much a long, long time ago. Over in a corner Dante refuses to take part in the dance, but nonetheless waves a two-finger welcome.

According to the plan, he is the last Brother to leave the streets, and so they have waited for him. Now the ceremony will begin to honor them all. More familiar faces greet him. He knows almost everyone, though he's not sure of their names or just where they met. He flashes smiles and greetings. He interprets glances that show he is well-known on the streets.

With the woman — his intended — he remains shy. Though she sends him a thought from time to time, he stands to the side admiring her.

When at last he joins the dance their eyes marry. Hers are a light metal-blue, bordering on gray. They are clear and light . . . perhaps not quick to love or trust . . . but long in devotion as he sees right away. He comes close enough to touch this woman so deeply familiar from a long time past.

The red liquid has lulled his mind. He joins in the dance close to her while a veil clouds his brain. A crust grows over his eyelids and buckle his knees in braces. He dances in the slow rhythms of a dray horse. Doubtless the red liquid means to mix him into the life of the Palace.

Jubilation booms in his bosom. The furrows of his brain find the freedom brought on by the red liquid and he welcomes its veil and slow dance. He's tuning in with the others and now glides about the room. Soon all have recognized the towering stranger with waves and smiles. After his shower and deep shave and now in his grand green robe he has become rather handsome and star-like.

Our golden creature, reclaimed from the streets and his love have now become the axis in the center of the dancing of all those in the mint green robes. Those in white merely attend.

She looks him full in the face. Her eyes flash into his, "I am Désirée," her thought rings, "your intended."

He flashes back, *As I am Gilbert, yours also. This is the honor I've striven for all my life."*

Her hand slips into his as they continue the dance.

Our Lancelot fills with broad energy and swells and glows. All the thousand days and nights he's spent on campgrounds of the Millennium are worth this one moment when Désirée touches her hand to his.

Now, through the virtue of battles won in building the outpost of the Millennium and the peace of mind brought on by the red liquid, he is ready to settle into life in the Palace. He remains speechless and can only flash his energy into Désirée.

They move together in the slow walking ways of the Palace style and know each other on the dance floor until mealtime rings.

HE REMEMBERS THE STRUGGLES, his own dear friend Franco who gave his life, the Elders who trained him for the daring-do, the close calls and the rejection by those who knew no better. Even the Tycoons. He is ready to forgive them all.

THE MEAL, HOWEVER, IS NOT what he would have imagined in the Palace of the Elders.

Steel carts wheeled in carry plates covered with plastic bubbles meant to keep the food hot, that yet are finely designed to resemble smeared, cracked and scratched surfaces. No doubt they are in transition from the streets and will become accustomed later with finer cuisine and china.

He waits in line with Désirée. This is hardly proper treatment for his devotion to the cause and the station he has achieved. He intuits the welcoming ceremony may well be over.

With Désirée, he moves to one of the picnic tables covered with red-and-white checkered oil cloth, and sits by the poet.

"Here I sit so patiently," the poet says, "and wait to see what price I must pay to get out of going through all these things twice."

Gil nods back his appreciation, "Two bits."

Unlidded, the food reveals a feast of bright orange carrots, whipped potatoes and some kind of flesh covered in gravy. Side dishes hold a piece of canned grapefruit swimming in thin juice and a kind of chopped green salad. Not what he'd expect for his feast of triumph, but he is hungry.

Désirée eats slowly and daintily.

Gil cuts and chews and can't remember when last he ate. He doesn't expect the food to taste . . . and it doesn't. His plate emptied and the last drop of grapefruit juice drained from the bowl, he begins to surmise that all might not be not what he thought.

LOOKING ABOUT HE SEES many of his comrades who fought and helped him on the streets and now by some devious force find themselves held captive.

The thunder of this thought hits him with full force.

Our ordeal goes on. Can the Tycoons be behind this? Must I still prove myself? Here gathers the very core of his group, locked up in this Palace to keep the earth in darkness and destroy the Millennium for another age. He's ashamed — taken captive in a child's game of capture the flag.

First, he must be canny, and not show that he knows he's being held prisoner. He must go along with them, pretend he's being celebrated for his bravery and deeds, and that the work of ushering in the Millennium is done. He must stay suspicions without being suspicious. He senses danger and must take care. Get help from someone he trusts. But who?

Can these shallow ceremonies be set up by the Tycoons to jam the wheel of the Millennium? They only want more footage for their benumbed audiences.

Gil is weary. Very weary. He touches Désirée's arm and flashes that he will go to his bed and sleep away the weariness.

She nods her approval.

He crosses the main room passing some TV squawk, and in the great bedroom finds Ward B, bed #33 and lies down.

GIL WAKES IN A START with a sense of dread — his insides are shredded. All he wants to do is get away from these feelings. A lemon bleeds on his eyeballs. He wants to throw up. He sits up, puts his bare feet on the cold floor and wonders where he's been taken. All around him restless sleepers are breathing in dim light. He hears coughing and croaking, and notes a peculiar medicinal smell of ether and burnt limes.

Shaken, he's depressed.

"Stand," his brain commands.

He tightens the strings of his robe, finds his slippers and, like a creaking old man, shuffles through the empty game room. A muffled sound comes from his right. The static shapes of ping pong tables and a dark television set haunt the dim lights. He makes his way into the empty eating room and hears a noise off to the side. He enters a small hallway and stands before a door behind which he hears screams and the sound of a struggle. He's afraid, but he turns the knob and opens the door nevertheless.

Désirée, barely covered in her green robe, is lying on a table and battling a burly man in white. He has one hand over her mouth.

Are they torturing her for secrets?

Another burly man in white stands in front of her with his pants down.

Désirée struggles and kicks. Her eyes beg when she sees Gil, and she cries out.

He can see her private parts underneath her robe while she struggles. He jumps on the man closest to him and lets out a roar from somewhere, and in fury hammers the man.

The one lets her go, and the other attempts to pull up his pants and get Gil off his back.

Désirée leaps off the table.

Gil lets go of the man and takes her arm.

A woman in white appears at the door.

The two burly men stand gawking.

The woman takes Désirée's hand and pulls her out of the room.

Gil follows them to one of the empty picnic tables.

In awhile the woman in white returns bringing them cups of steaming hot chocolate.

THE NEXT DAY Désirée is gone.

Her mother came for her, a lady in white tells him. She left no message.

A WEEK LATER Gil mentions Désirée to Jim.

He can't recall her.

He asks the lady in white if she remembers Désirée.

"No," she shakes her head. She doesn't remember anyone named Désirée. "I would remember a girl with the name Désirée."

In the Palace
of the Legion of Honor

◆

WHEN SUZANNE VISITS, Gil freezes into a fake grin. Of course the tan paper slippers and the green gown hanging just past his knees look comical on him.

"Actually, I like it here," he tells her. "And I'd love to stay, Dearie, but I have other plans. This could be dangerous — the Palace, I mean — and I need help to get out." He feels her faraway loneliness and tries hard for a wink on top of his toothy smile, but he can't close his right eye lid. It feels sticky and doesn't quite work. "I've received permission from the higher-ups." He looks away. "The real higher-ups," he says. "I have important things to do, Suzanne." Instead of a wink he raises a fist.

She doesn't understand . . . just like him, she's a prisoner of the Tycoons.

Susanne sits on the plastic-covered window seat and stares into space above the courtyard, past the brick buildings and the dim, shaded streets of the Castro district.

She is a very serious, sad little girl. Her long auburn hair is no longer lustrous, and her once-straight part is crooked and messy.

Repeatedly Gil tries to get her to smile, but she wants none of it.

Hey, is she working for the Tycoons? Maybe her family of famous fly-boys, who daily bomb and strafe defenseless villages and defoliate forests, hold her hostage. Or might she be in cahoots with Lyndon and baby McNamara. Most likely though, she's just another prisoner of the Tycoons who have gone about capturing the beauties and artistic types on the home front.

Gil feels sad that he cannot convince her to be happy.

Despite his great smile, Gil's eyes drip and burn with fatigue. He knows the foul tasting, red elixir they force him to drink twice a day fogs him over. If he protests, they insist he take it, and once they forced him down and needled it into his ass . . . they tattooed his memory with that needle.

He whispers to Suzanne, "They brought me here on pretexts, and they are keeping me here on pretexts . . . false pretexts." He is not quite able to pronounce the word correctly.

Gil wants her to do more to get him out, but she's just stone. *What does she expect me to do? What can I do?* His tongue is tied by the red liquid.

She follows his every move for clues. Yes, she adores him, but he's a hopeless case.

He's sure seeing him in this outlandish green uniform shames Suzanne. She doesn't understand that he dresses this way to fit in.

It's all he can do just to whisper to her and clue her in, "Get me out of here, and then we'll make a plan!"

HIS ONE REAL ALLY often comes into the ward after dinner wearing his dress whites, and strolls about to see that all is going according to plan. Although Gil is not sure of the plan, it's easy to see by the way the captain talks to the attendants that *he* knows what's up. He gives the others very straightforward instructions, and at once they leave to do some errand or other.

Sometimes the Old Capt'n stops by to say that this soldier's doing a good job, and offers to play ping pong with him, but Gil backs off with a wink and a nod.

When the others aren't watching, the captain flashes him meaningful looks; before long he'll summon Gil to offer him a new assignment. The captain keeps Gil on tap to become the new head of his special corps once he finishes bringing the world to order.

Right now he needs a more dignified uniform. His strings keeps coming undone in the back so that over and over he must stop pacing and tie it.

And these cheesy paper slippers! — a pale imitation of those given when he came for his celebration — keep falling off so that he must skate along the floor.

The attendants in white have real street shoes and scuff up the floor and make it harder for those in green gowns to dance.

Lately he just sits and watches others dance. He's too tired. He'd sleep all day, but that's dangerous because no one guards the sleeping quarters during the day, and an assassin could come and do him in.

Living inside a fog is the only way to veil his brightness and stay safe from the Tycoon assassins. Any moment they could come and do him in.

TV and cracking ping pong paddles echo in the day room. His cohorts shuffle in and out of the room, in and out of their minds. He's the only one here in his right mind . . . it's all he can do to think straight with the assorted candied drugs they feed them.

At times he looks right through people and divines secret information about them from the place where they really exist. Other times he withdraws from their inner life — it gets so scary in there. Some of these scoundrels want to do bad things to each other and to him too. That's why he always stays alert. The guys from his honor guard tend to wander off.

GIL IS SITTING NEXT TO SUZANNE on the plastic, window-seat pad, and looking down on the courtyard in the awkward companionship of the visitor and the visited, as he examines vantage points through which he might escape. "These windows have no bars, but we're on the fourth floor. If we break through the small window on the entrance door, there's only small bars. Why don't you bake me a cake with a hacksaw blade inside? I've seen it done, Suzanne." He tries a wink. "I think we're better off climbing through the window and down the four stories holding onto the bricks with our finger tips."

She gives him a sharp look. "Look Buster, I can walk out of here anytime I want. I'm not breaking out of anywhere, and neither are you . . .." Her tone trails off as she moves her eyes once again to the cloudscape riding the blue wave of sky.

He thinks of his many colleagues from the streets — veterans of wars against the ruling classes. *I have to bust out of here so I can save all these people and lead them back to the battle at hand.*

He repeats to Suzanne for the third or fourth time, "That's Jim, my valet." He waves and Jim, who has just come into the day room, waves back. A black rose tattoo is visible on his arm.

"Your valet? " She fights a smile.

"These are great accommodations. Better than the Hilton." He looks her square in the eye. "But the Palace holds great dangers. It's time for me to leave."

She nods, agreeing.

"I gotta get out before they kill me. They already tried on the streets, but here I'm kept under guard." He covers his face. "There are a lot of good people in here, a lot of famous fighters. Well, famous, but you wouldn't know them, real heroes." He covers his mouth. Is she trustworthy? He's not always sure, because Suzanne can be funny that way, sort of weird and hard to define. He tells her anyway. "No one wants anyone to know they're here. This place is R & R for my soldiers. For me too, but now I'm rested and gotta get a move' on."

He pauses, *Tycoons send impersonators . . . I won't know if she's real until we get back together.* He lowers his voice. "My mission is not fully accomplished. But I'll soon be the old me." He smiles, eyes wide. "When my mission's done we can go live on a farm and have some kids. We'll start a new race." He believes she is grinning. *Did I just invent the wheel?* It looks like a grin.

Suzanne scrunches her nose. "Why not wait awhile? Until things get . . . organized."

344

"Hey, I love to hang out with all my buddies here. But I still have heavy duty out there." He winks, almost. "Lots of work. But I think we can make it out together. I'll tell you, I've already learned a lot from Grace in crafts and I know I could learn more about clay sculptures and painting, lots of helpful stuff, but I just can't spare more time."

THE NEXT AFTERNOON Gil doesn't wait for Suzanne and Busby, but goes to crafts instead. He always enjoyed crafts at summer camp — painting ceramic tiles. Sometimes he'd watercolor the gardens of his mind or make clay ashtrays and paint them red, white and blue, those things he could do by himself and not tussle with others on the ball field or lug a canoe to the water. He liked the simple life of the crafts room at camp.

Now, here in the Palace, he has the chance to be in a crafts room again and, frankly, should Suzanne and Busby spring him he'd really miss crafts.

They usually do crafts after lunch. He tries to be good so he doesn't miss it. Sometimes though, Jim insists that he stick to the TV room or hit his bunk if he refuses to drink the red liquid. So he takes his pills and drinks the red liquid and that way he gets to go to the crafts room.

Grace is the teacher and she has a hand for all the different crafts, and is quite pretty with bleached blond hair.

She treats him kindly and encourages him to finger paint or dig into clay and shape something new.

"Make something that comes from you," she says. "Something you love. Something no one else can make."

So he tries to make something that comes from deep inside.

WHEN GIL RETURNS TO the day room after crafts, something has changed. A lull has claimed the place. Jim sits with his brow propped on his hand. Some other attendants are in tears. Usually the patients sit and the attendants run about doing things, but this day patients seem to pace much more slowly, and their dance nears a standstill . . . there is no waltz.

One clear voice rings through the stillness, and many people — patients, attendants, doctors, nurses — crowd around the television. The voice talks of "a killing," "another man shot," "an important man."

Sorrow drenches the room. Even some of the patients who are beyond sorrow feel it. "Martin Luther King, shot dead," the TV voice explains and goes into details.

Gil tries to remember this man, though he can't quite place him. *I remember speeches. The voice haunts me; the thunderous round tones, the cadences reach out to draw me into his march. I remember we're in the same fight from different spaces. Is it true, this man dead, too?*

SUZANNE WALKS OFF THE elevator with good old Busby. He is smartly dressed and looking employed. His red ponytail has grown longer and his rusty mustache, bushier. Gil frowns on facial hair in his officers, but for old Peace Corps buddy Busby he makes an exception. *Once we always fought. Now he's come to his senses and ready to join the plan.*

"Every thing's already taken care of," Gil calls to them from the window-seat, "we've got us a plan!" He's calm and good-natured, and speaks quite slowly so they understand.

"We're goin' up near Mendocino. We're gonna pick wild strawberries and catch abalone. You can eat the abalone and sell the shells for good money. We got it all planned out, me and Suzanne." He sorta winks at her, then continues. "Her uncle lives up there, and we're gonna have a little house all to ourselves. But we need some help gettin' outta *here* . . . they want to keep me for a long time . . . maybe forever."

He pauses to say more, but feels unsure. He's become a small boy asking to go outside and play when he knows he should be doing his homework. He squirms with lost dignity, but then remembers that for the good of all, he must get out of this place. He lights up and says, "Suzanne's gonna help so we can go away together." He stops. "She might need some help." He's overcome by their sudden

346

closeness and locks onto Busby's shoulder to assure him, "I can make it all right on the outside."

"Maybe you need more rest," Busby says. He is cautious, almost caring.

"Oh, I'm rested." His soldier's smile broadens more than it has in a long time, and he gets serious, "They want to keep me until they get all my secrets." His eyes cloud over. "They're giving me drugs here, bad drugs. I'm living on Thorazine and Stelazine . . . and magazines."

Busby laughs, but Suzanne only fakes a smile.

Busby shakes his head at the idea of springing Gil, which only makes him more enthusiastic.

"I know you're gonna help me, Buzz old boy, you're the only one who can. Come again tomorrow, about the same time. With Suzanne. And bring a chocolate cake with a hacksaw blade inside." Then, he winks. "The Tycoons are after me again. Their scouts watch me all the time."

As they stand he gives them the old "Cave 7 salute" — a two-finger vee straight into the eyes. "Leave no turn unstoned, ha ha."

OUT IN THE HALLWAY Suzanne and Busby talk with a plotter, a young, flashy-haired fellow who claims to be a doctor. Gil stands behind them and peers over their shoulders at this impersonator, he says his name is "Dr. Gold." To Gil he looks like a shipwrecked hippie with his fat mustache and sideburns.

"Schizophrenia," Gold pronounces trippingly on the tongue." *Skiitz-o-frein-ia.* "False schizophrenia," he adds. "It's not really in his blood or in his genes or some chemical in his brain, or, only in his mind."

"Do I hear this diagnosis from a psychiatrist with a license and ten or fifteen years of schooling behind him?" Busby asks, beaming. "I'm only a simple fellow, but if schizophrenia is in the blood and not in the mind, then it's a blood disease, right? However, if it's in the mind, then it's a mind disease. Now, if you're a mind doctor, how can you diagnose a disease of the blood? Follow me? If, on the other hand, you're a blood doctor, then how can you be versed in the mind? So, are we talking about a mind disease or a blood disease? My friend here doesn't believe he's diseased at all. In fact, he believes that he's somebody who he isn't. Perhaps this calls for a whole new diagnosis. I'm sure that with a little help from his friends and weekly one-on-one professional help, he could get along just fine in the world."

No ordinary doctor, but a type the Tycoons might employ as a jailer, Gold stands wise to Busby's ploy and purses his lips, offended. "This is not a philosophical question." He gives Busby a withering look and waves at the room. "Some of these people went too far on drugs and when they come down, they can leave. However, Gilbert and some others are more complex and need long-term professional therapy. Gilbert is a true false schizophrenic. I can't help him any other way than I am doing. Drugs, and we may try electroshock or we may need to keep him here for quite some time."

This confirms the Tycoons' long-term intentions, I'm going nowhere.

"Gil has had too many drugs in his system," Busby says. "Otherwise, he's normal. He needs a rest, that's all. Look, doc, I knew him before. He's practically normal already. I'll take care of him."

Can Busby spring me?

The doctor draws a bead on Busby, as if shooting a rat. "I don't think you have the training or inclination, really. Gilbert needs professional help. Look around." He waves like Moses at the Red Sea, "These people don't want to be here. No one wants to be kept this way. They're here because all they can do, my friend, is walk off their illness." He reaches over and pats Gil on the shoulder, "Your buddy here needs to be with us for some time to find out who he is not, and then maybe he can find out who he really is."

Dr. Gold turns to Suzanne as he walks off, "Some people choose to live life in a very roundabout way."

At that moment, Gil divines that Busby has decided, then and there, to help him out, and in a shock of memory, he recalls Busby in Ethiopia — standing outside at the American Embassy. It was a century ago. Busby/Noonan was disgusted and hurt and hurled a basketball with all his athletic might over the embassy compound wall.

With that, Gil calmly walks over to the ping pong table, grabs the ball in mid-flight between two players, and in imitation of Busby, hurls the plastic ping pong ball at the doctor, who turns briefly to look at who might have done this childish gesture. He spies Gil near the ping pong table.

Suzanne goes into the TV room and sits facing away from the TV with her arms folded. Busby watches. Gil walks back and forth between them in a mock Thorazine shuffle, at times trying to put his hands into absent pockets. This act lulls the Tycoons into thinking he needs their mercy. In the proper clothes he could as well be living back on Steiner Street. He's not crazy.

Gil closely inspects Busby observing Gil's behavior for the effects of the drugs.

Gil sees his friend is more subdued than a few days before. Perhaps he, too, thinks Gil is crazy. Gil must weigh the situation. Will his old friend really help him? *What is the difference between grass or LSD or other herbal medicines? What is the difference really from these grown-up, legal, pharmaceutically prepared drugs? They do the same numbing job on you. If drugs are drugs, we all must be walking in a dream. The whole country shambles along in a drug dream. . . . we just have them reversed is all. These days I may even agree with Gold.*

Gil snaps into the here and now as Suzanne watches. "Thanks for coming, Busby," he says in a perfectly normal tone, and shakes his hand. He then points across to Suzanne who is looking as though she might cry, "Busby's gonna get me out," he tells her.

Suzanne nods, absent in her thoughts, without hearing.

He pats Busby's shoulder, "He's gonna bring me a chocolate cake with a Derringer baked inside."

"This might be hopeless," she murmurs to Busby then gives Gil a limp smile, "Just don't shoot *me*, Buster."

Seeing Busby and Suzanne side by side and so close makes Gil suspect they'd be happier if he stayed in the Palace. *Do I love this long-suffering, somber woman? How has she endured being my lover? Oh, she must be having an affair with Busby.* He has a strong affection for them both and wouldn't mind that too much. It strikes him as funny, in fact. *Maybe that's the way it's supposed to be.*

"Can I sign out, and you be the one responsible?" he asks.

"I'll try," Busby says. "What do you need?"

"Regular clothes. An' a chocolate cake." His wink flutters and fades. "You guys can get me out, I know you can."

Suzanne's eyes glaze over. He breaks her heart.

He wonders why she even comes to see him.

Her forlorn finger presses on his breastbone. "You don't really want to leave here, Gil. And I don't accept you're ready to leave. I agree with Doctor Gold."

"What?" he asks. He claps his hands over his ears. "What?"

Busby's hands sink into his jeans as he looks away.

"I'm tired of your pretenses. You brought yourself right here and checked in. I don't see that we should help you 'escape'. You're out of your mind, Gil."

Because he can hear her every word, he lowers his hands. He wants to come up with some smart remark, winning and clever, but he's speechless. He'd run from her if he could move in these slippers. So he just screws up his face and glares.

She goes on. "I loved you through all of this. Sometimes I even believed you when you talked to people who weren't there. When you thought people were going to shoot you from the rooftops. I can't believe how close I came to believing you altogether. Maybe it's this place that's so sobering, with all these tortured souls creeping around in paper slippers. Maybe I can see now what I couldn't see before.

"You're not ready to get out and go anywhere or do anything just because you take it so casually. But out there you can't even stay in one place long enough to eat a meal, let alone cook one. Then you insult us, treat us like dumb animals. You claim you know how the world should be, but don't even know the name of our Governor. You are so sure that you're so right about this terrible war, but have no clue really how the world should be when all the best minds haven't been able to put it together. You don't even know enough to bathe when you're dirty or eat when you're hungry. You're a crazy fuck, one of these doped-up weirdos who wander around the streets and mutter out loud. You don't make real contact with anyone. You don't help anyone. You don't give anything to anyone, you only moan. You're an old, dying man not yet thirty, and you limp from corner to street corner. You're worse than dead because there's no peace around you. You bring agitation and unrest everywhere you go.

"What about your true friend Franco, who abandoned you in that dirty, filthy apartment and then killed himself with a needle? He claimed to be so smart about Shakespeare and the way the world should live and he knew everything about everything, but was dumb enough to trust street dealers who didn't give a fuck if he needled his life away on a bogus two dollar bag of shit.

"And, you're dead, too.

"Don't you ever ask yourself why people run from you? Can't you see yourself in the mirror? Don't you see your smugness under all that grunge and dirt? Don't you see your total lack of compassion for those who love you? Oh, you have lots of compassion for the Vietnamese whom you never laid eyes on. You have compassion for the oppressed, but you don't care for the people who love you, who try to help you, who welcome you into their lives. No, you step on everyone who reaches out to you. And *me* the most. That's why you're certifiable, Gil, no fucking question. That's why you're nuts and you're going to stay that way even if we did get you out on some pretext of taking care of you. You don't need to be taken care of; you need to look at yourself for awhile. You need to be with your stinking, rotting self and smell where you've been for the past six months; consider what you've actually been doing and what you've been claiming you're doing.

"I've become sane visiting you in these unbearable rooms. Saner than when I followed you around, and over and over put up with your wretched behavior and acting out your crazy schemes. Scrub thyself, from here on. You are hollow and cruel and full of self-hatred. That's what it must be.

"Look what you've done to yourself. This is no 'palace.' There is no "celebration" for your arrival. This is not a place to rest up so you can return to the streets and save the world. This is the loony bin. This is the end of the line. This is where they put the crazy people. You're one step from being locked up for the rest of your life, which is too bad because you're not bad looking and at times you steal my heart blind. But you are getting life in prison because you killed yourself."

She is weeping.

Is she going to go on saying these things to me?

He cringes and walks over to the ping pong table. From there he watches her turn to the sill and drop her face into her arms and shake. Her dancer's legs have grown thin and even her breasts have shrunk. *She believes she's crying for him. I don't have the words to tell her she's crying for herself.*

Ping pong players stop their rat-a-tat-tat to see what's going on. Others in the room have heard Suzanne, even over the TV roar, and rise and stare.

Gil can't see them all clearly, but they are here . . . his comrades from the streets. And three or four bearded Brothers are here. Dylan is here. Tall Streetwalker Wolfe is here. The Everly Brothers are here. Ferryman Jim is here . . . as he now knows. The Tycoons grind away for posterity. Even Jack stands with his hands in his pockets and waits to see what Gil will do.

Suzanne's words have stung him . . . he might even say blistered. His ears buzz as he watches her bent figure continue to shake. *Maybe she'll lose control and they'll keep her here!* He wishes he had a tissue to give her, but he doesn't. She has scared him. She has wiped him flat.

Busby stares off into the distance, but at least he doesn't fully turn away.

She cries on and on.

This world, such a sad place. There's so much to cry about. Maybe Suzanne cries for the whole damn world and these tears will make a difference.

Busby lays his hand on her shoulder. He bends down and his cheek brushes her auburn hair. He pats her and looks over at the good soldier. They have become one against the windows' blaze . . . they've formed a club against him.

Busby looks his way and says, "She's right, you know."

Franco, you should be with me at this hour, Gil's head buzzes. *You should be alive.*

Against the light everyone else and everything, even the miserable fern in the green planter, gets blocked out. His two friends rise in mist and stand before him as fuzzy ghosts. He wipes his eyes, but all is a blur. He stands helpless and friendless, drowning in his own worthlessness, in his shame and guilt unable to lure an insane world to sanity. He finds no respite, no hope of understanding while all think themselves brilliant with enough knowledge and courage to withstand the horrors looming at every turn. He reels in free-fall with no center in an indifferent universe. He's abandoned in this time, in this place.

I LIKE THE CRAFT ROOM in the afternoons when the sun slants through the high window into this dank and dusty basement room.

I work with clay. We even have a kiln caked with dark brown soot to fire our ceramics. The room reminds me of the classroom at the school where I taught, and where I would sit in the sunshine on spring afternoons. Here I look out the window and see the flowers, red and yellow and violet, and beyond those, a brick wall. I see a small piece of the Iron Gate that keeps people out and keeps people in.

Grace works with eight or ten of us. Some work along the plank table in the middle of the room. Some weave lanyards from long strips of red and white plastic. Two people draw with crayons on large tablets of white paper.

Today I sit on a high chair at a small table near the kiln and mold moist clay. I told Grace I wanted to create a sculpture of the Ethiopian village where I once tried to be a teacher. She gave me a very large piece of clay to work with, but I've been having trouble remembering.

Grace comes around and helps me mold the houses and the figures. I find them hard to fashion because my fingers are still stiff and red from my time on the streets. I find her very kind and beautiful ... even with bleached-blond hair. I smell her perfume from under her blue smock. She must like me because she pays attention to me and praises my progress. After each session she always lays a wet cloth over my work so that it won't dry out before my next time. Then we place it carefully on a shelf near the kiln.

I'm happy here with Grace in this room, happier than any other time I can remember. Here I can look out the window and work beside my friends. We rarely talk, because we all have something important that we need to be doing.

THAT NIGHT I CANNOT SLEEP as I lie in Ward B, bed #33, among the acres of people who exhausted themselves on the streets of the Haight.

I find myself longing for the clear boundless sky chasing darkness from my restless mind. I feel myself brimming like the sunshine climbing the Ethiopian mountains in early morning.

I try to remember Sebata, my village in Ethiopia, and the more I remember, the more the Brothers and the Tycoons fade away among the cone-shaped *tukul* huts and the broad shadows under sun-struck acacias. Oh, how the wind sways them, and the twilight arc of sky fades to red and rose gray bringing the floating pinpoints of starlight through the hush of night. How the moonlight washes the countryside in a pale glow.

That night I finally comprehend through the fog that the great leader and orator, Martin Luther King had been shot to death.

That night too, amid the ghosts of Suzanne sobbing, the mourning staff and the groaning, fearful TV, floating past the fading crack of that ping pong ball in the day room, among the coughs and snores of exhausted sleepers, I remember my Ethiopian dream.

After years of trying, I take hold of the barest threads of jumping from a cliff along with Ethiopian children who have promised I can know freedom as they do. I float down as one of them into a green eucalyptus forest broken open by a river, and we land on the river's bank.

Then we are running along a rutted road, my bare feet kicking. We are rushing toward the school. I feel the welling of freedom. As we run on the narrow dusty path leading to the school, we are laughing, shouting at each other, breathless. Flying over the ground we enter the school compound to a host of waiting students.

In a moment I recognize that *I* am the teacher. Powerless, restored and contrary to my will, I set out to become the teacher of my dreams.